THE BRASS RING

A TRIED & TRUE NOVEL

BOOK FIVE

CHARLI RAHE

TRIED AND TRUE PUBLISHING

Cover Art by Miblart
Chapter Art by Etheric Designs

ISBN (Ebook): 978-1-958055-17-5

ISBN (Paperback): 978-1-958055-18-2

ISBN (Hardcover): 978-1-958055-19-9

❀ Created with Vellum

Chapter 41. A taste of what's to come. I'm sorry the characters wouldn't let me make it longer.

And for my children and husband, of course.

Note From The Author

Scarlet's fantastical story follows a woman's journey through her magical heritage in which she encounters several dark scenarios. It is not intended for readers under 18 years of age and includes adult content.

While I'd prefer you to experience it as you go, your mental health matters. Please refer to www.charlirahe.com for a detailed list of possible triggers.

OSTARA
AVES
SUMAR
DAGR
SUNNA
SJOR
MERFOLK
ELDJOT
SOLS
SANDR
WEMIC
THRIMILCI
FAUNELLE
TROLLS
&
FAIRIES
VIDR
CENTAUR
HAUST
RISAR
LODDA
BLAO
ENOX
MABON

TIDINGS
ELIVAGAR
ANGUILLAN
LITR
REGN
ROT
VAR
LYCANS
NATT
BJORN
CRATHODE
VETR
SVELL
GLITRA
MINOTAUR
KALLA
SNJAR
KALDR
DRAGONS
JOTNAR
STRAUMR
MOSSUR
TOWN CENTER
STOKER
TIO
HVALL
VALKYRIES
JARN
LLA

PROLOGUE

"I am sorry we have to leave. This was nice. We will have to do it again when my girls are older," Wren said, bundling up Indigo and Scarlett.

Steel, Slate, and Jett were already in the carriage they'd rented for the trip down to the Valla cottages. Sparrow eyed Wren's supposed brother and the younger son, who looked identical to him. They both looked like Alder. She knew the boys weren't Lark's. He never would have cheated on Sea and while Wren was at Valla U, she been stealthily seeing the Var heir. Then she let her eyes graze the boy they'd adopted.

She could see now why they had chosen him. He was what the son Lark had lost would have looked like.

Lark exited the cottage with Ridge carrying the last of their things and gave Sparrow a kiss on her cheek. He passed her before using air to place the bags on top of the carriage. Sparrow had worried he wouldn't come out of his deep sorrow over Sea; there was a sadness to him that wasn't there before. Whatever doubts Sparrow had about Wren and him truly being a couple evaporated like mist after their weekend together.

Ridge handed Lark another bag as Wren leaned in to hug her goodbye and run her finger over Tawny's cheek.

"She is gorgeous, Ridge. Good luck with this one. Judging by her cries, she will have a mouth to chase off any unwanted suitors." Wren smiled and it looked genuine.

She and Lark were happy.

They skipped the masquerade and vacationed together since things were settling down with their marriage and Wren was no longer pregnant. Lark had nonchalantly hinted that he would like one more for an even half dozen. Wren had blushed furiously behind her goblet, but the eyes she made at Lark told Sparrow she was giving it earnest thought.

It was always supposed to be Lark and Wren and Hawk and Sparrow. With those two together, the world had somehow righted. Sparrow knew Sea and Lark had been wonderful together. A perfect match if there ever was one, but with Wren, he had history. If not Sea, then Wren, Sparrow told herself.

Ridge slid his arm around her hips and Lark jumped off the back of the carriage and pulled his cloak up. As he passed Wren, who was ducking inside, Sparrow caught his flicker of hand movement and Wren's muted yelp as he pinched her backside.

When Wren poked her head from the window to shoot him a feigned glare, he jumped on the step and caught her chin to place a chaste kiss on her lips. He moved to the front to see after the horses. Wren didn't blush when she caught Sparrow watching, and inside, Sparrow was happy for her friend.

"We shall see you at the induction ceremony. We are bringing all of our little monsters so you will know us by the pandemonium," Wren called out as Lark flicked the reins.

Ridge led her and Tawny back inside and out of the cold air. Sparrow was sick of the cold winter. Elivagar was cold, Valla changed with the seasons. They should have vacationed in Thrimilci, where it was always summer.

"They are happy," Ridge said once he shut the cottage door.

"I thought it was a sham, so people would stop sending their daughters to him. You saw how she froze on their wedding day; it was as if she had never kissed him a day in their life. She blushed every single time he pulled her in for a kiss, but not this weekend," Sparrow said, setting Tawny on the blanket with her toys.

"Perhaps they were close friends and it evolved. Look at us. You were cordial, at best, until the month before our wedding. I think I finally won you over by helping you plan." Ridge offered her a wide mouthed smile that Sparrow returned.

It was the sudden death of her parents and then the tragic loss of Sea that had made her hold on to Ridge as if her life depended on it. All she'd wanted to do was run back to Hawk and beg forgiveness. She was the last Dagr and she would not dishonor her mother's name by breaking her marriage contract.

Since they had Tawny, whatever gaps were left in their love had smoothed over by her birth.

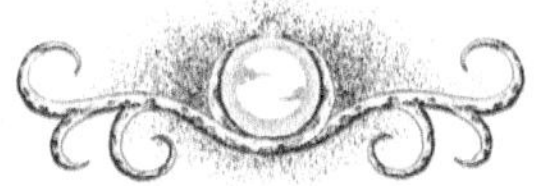

Ridge fixed their packs as Sparrow bundled Tawny for the long ride back to Valla's town heart. Tawny's eyes had changed, and it looked like she would have her father's wide hazel eyes and fair skin, but Sparrow's dark wavy hair.

Ridge locked up the cottage as Sparrow waited at the horse for him to help her up. It had been a quiet, much needed break from his parent's castle, who never seemed to be on good terms. The silence in those stark white and black rooms made Sparrow's very bones feel brittle.

Sparrow handed Ridge Tawny in her bundle of furs. She swung up on her Noriker's back before reaching down for Tawny in her carrier.

Ridge took the reins, and they started out, leaving the cottages in the distance.

"We should try for another," Ridge said out of the blue.

"We will certainly have a lot of catching up to do if we mean to have as many as Lark and Wren. Technically, Steel is her brother, not her son, but he might as well be. Since Pearl had him, she has doted on the boy as if he was her own." Sparrow told him.

"You must be joking," Ridge said, smiling at Sparrow.

"What?"

"Love, Jett and Steel look so much alike if they are not brothers, then I am a Crathode." Ridge shook his head ruefully. "They are Alder's sons, same as those girls of hers. Cygnus told my father Alder wanted to break the marriage contract between him and Delta so he could be free to marry Wren. He let it slip she carried his heir. Normally, my father would not tolerate such rumors tarnishing our family's reputation. However, Wren acted wisely and went into hiding. When she came out, it was on Lark's arm. Everyone who does not know of their situation believes those are Lark's children. Not even my sister knows they are Alder's. If she did, it would not matter that Lark is playing them off as his own. I like Lark. He is a good man."

Sparrow stared, mouth agape, as she processed what he said. "Wren went away for a time. Studying in the States, they said, while Pearl was pregnant with Steel. I know Wren was having an affair with Alder because she is my best friend, but she never told me about Steel or the girls. I knew Jett was his, but..." She trailed off and squinted into the distance at their right.

In the stark snow, she could make out forms moving. They weren't coming towards them, but almost running alongside them.

She pointed. "Ridge, what does that look like to you?" she asked.

Ridge stopped and shaded his eyes, hoping to reduce the glare from the high sun.. His breaths puffed out as he squinted before the horse.

"I am not sure. It or *they* is turning our way. In any case, I am not liking the look of it," Ridge said, picking up pace with the horse.

Sparrow's apprehension grew as they neared. They could move exceptionally fast. There were several *somethings* out there.

"Ridge. They disappeared behind that hill... I am getting a bad feeling. Maybe you should hop on the horse," Sparrow said anxiously.

"Perhaps they have turned," Ridge said distractedly, but got on the horse.

They trotted, careful of the Frozen snow and the ice that slicked some parts of the rolling hills. They were coming over the top of another hill when the group that had been running alongside them was suddenly coming straight for them.

"Crathode!" Sparrow shouted.

They weren't supposed to be on Valla. No tribes were allowed. Panic drove Sparrow to heel the horse into motion, and Ridge held fast around her waist as the horse broke into a gallop.

"This has my father written all over it. If we get separated, do not go to Elivagar. I do not trust my father, and I certainly would never trust my mother. Best to stay away from my sisters, too. We have infested these islands. Go to Lark and Wren in Thrimilci or Hawk. He will keep you safe," he said harshly in her ear.

"Stop talking like that. We are all going to be.... *AH!*"

Her own scream echoed in her ears as the horse reared up, tossing them backwards. Sparrow rolled with Tawny tucked to her chest as the horse fell awkwardly on its side. They had stumbled upon a Crathode camp and the ones chasing them were closing from behind.

Ridge yanked her up by the back of her cloak. She hadn't thought to bring weapons with her and all Ridge had was the quarter staff strapped to his back. She began calling as the Crathode attacked and heard Ridge's staff cracking against their carapaces. Hideous stemmed eyes and spiky teeth from gashes for mouths gnashed at her.

"Run, Sparrow! I will hold them off as long as I can!"

"You need me to guard your back! I will not leave you!" she shouted.

"I need you to *live* with our daughter. Now, *go*! Do not let us all die," Ridge yelled.

The Crathode were hacking apart the dying horse and Tawny was wailing at her chest. Sparrow's panic had set in and her thoughts came in spurts, only to be overwhelmed when she fought against another Crathode.

"For the sake of our daughter and any love you harbor for me. *Go*, Sparrow," Ridge pleaded.

Sparrow used every ounce of her ability to blow the frozen ground apart. She grabbed Ridge's cloak and kissed him as the Crathode collected themselves.

"I did fall in love with you, Ridge," she whispered as debris rained down.

"I know you did." Ridge smiled his boyish, lopsided grin and gave her a hard shove.

She ran.

She ran like a coward for the life of her child and, in doing so, let her husband die. She lifted Tawny from her carrier and glanced over her shoulder one last time.

"Tell father, bye-bye," she whispered, hoping the girl would remember some part of the father who sacrificed himself for her.

Sparrow couldn't believe she had got away. Ridge must have held them off longer than he hoped. Maybe he had gotten away, too. Sparrow tried not to hold too tightly to hope as she ran a zig zagged path to the Tio palace instead of Valla's town heart in case she was followed.

There was a chance the Crathode could have gotten ahead of her if she'd gone north to town, so west was where she ran. The Tio guards knew her well enough, so they didn't stop her when she dragged herself in late at night. She didn't want to speak to anyone, so she went directly to the portal room and hoped the bedraggled woman who ran through the halls and disappeared would be forgotten by morning.

The blue starry light of the Sumar portal room greeted her like an old friend, and she finally broke down into tears. She had no one.

Some of the staff found her and tried to get her to follow them, but she sobbed on her hands and knees until Hawk ran into the room in nothing but his undergarments. He took one look at her weeping on the floor with her daughter tied to her chest before scooping them both off the floor and carried her back to his rooms.

Sparrow nursed Tawny, and Hawk put her to sleep in his bed while he helped Sparrow out of her clothes and ran her a bath. While she bathed, Hawk left to get food for her and to give her privacy. She hadn't uttered a single word, and he had seen to it all.

Wren burst into the bathroom and fell to her knees at the side of the tub. She didn't ask before delving into her.

"You are all right? Where is Ridge? What happened? I checked on Tawny. She is okay."

"Ridge fought the Crathode so we could escape," she said hoarsely. "On our way back from the cottages today. I think he may be dead, Wren." She blinked at tears that blurred her vision. "I cannot take anymore death. I am wrung out." She sobbed.

Wren grabbed a towel and helped Sparrow out of the tub. "You came to the right place. We are going to take care of you and we are going to get to the bottom of this. We will find Ridge and find out why Crathode were in Valla," she said matter of fact.

"Ridge told me to go to Hawk. He does not trust anyone else. Hawk and you and Lark."

Hawk stood in the doorway, running his hand over hair that was silver at the wings already. "You are safe, Sparrow. You and your daughter. Ridge was right. I would never let anything happen to you. You can stay in my room tonight and Lark and I will go in search of him first thing in the morning."

Sparrow noticed Lark for the first time, standing just past Hawk with Flint and Pearl, all in their sleep clothes. "Thank you. I do not deserve your kindness after what I have done, but I appreciate it."

"Sparrow," Hawk said her name with such passion, Sparrow thought her chest was being crushed. "I could never stay upset with you. There is a hot stew on the table. When you are done, it is off to bed. I will stay on the couch, so you are not alone." Hawk offered her a smile, and she nodded, accepting his kindness wholeheartedly.

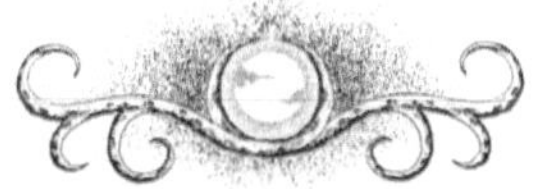

Lark and Hawk entered Wren's wing with grim faces and Sparrow stood with Wren, wrapping her arms around her.

"I am very sorry —" Hawk started and Sparrow burst into sobs.

Wren held her tighter as she cried, and they fell back onto the couch.

"They do not know how the Crathode got onto Valla. There was no sign of Ridge. It was... the Crathode were brutal," Lark finished stiffly.

"They believe you and Tawny are dead too," Hawk continued.

"What? Why?" Sparrow asked, wiping her nose on the back of her hand.

"We believe because they hacked apart your pack, your belongings spilled into the snow. It looks as though you were part of the carnage," Lark informed her. "Ridge was not tortured. The Crathode did not have the patience for it."

"This may be a good thing. Them thinking you are dead for now," Wren said, tapping her finger to her lip. "He said not to trust his family, but his family is everywhere. I think you should leave Tidings. Hawk can help you set up and settle in. He is a tried a true Guardian now and when I finish my Ragnarök challenge..." She trailed off and looked at Lark. "We should discuss this privately first. I am sorry."

Lark smirked at Wren. "I would not mind leaving Tidings for a time. Things have begun to settle and being away from this will be good for all of us. We will go with you, Sparrow."

Sparrow swallowed against the lump in her throat. "Really?"

Wren hadn't taken her eyes off Lark; it was as if she was seeing him as a different person. When she looked back at Sparrow, she saw stars in her eyes.

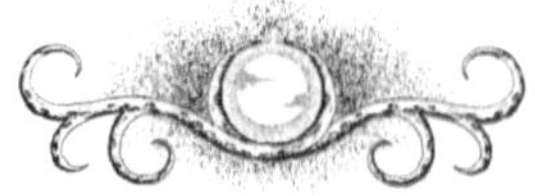

"Good?" Hawk asked, repositioning the bed.

In the States, they were not allowed to use *calling*. Sparrow had to get used to doing everything the myopic way.

"Good," Sparrow agreed and held up the paper plate, saturating with grease from the pizza.

Hawk sat down beside her on the floor and took the plate. His mother had given them all she had in American savings and they'd bought two houses side by side in the city of Chicago. They could be faceless in the crowd if anyone came in search of them.

"Wren and Lark's monsters will like it here," Hawk said, chewing.

"It is a far cry from Tidings. We will see," Sparrow said in a rare moment of clarity.

Normally, she let herself fall deep into self-pity until she became unable to perform basic tasks like showering or walking. Hawk had done everything, including making sure Tawny was well cared for.

"I will be gone for two days, but when I come back, it will be just like old times," Hawk promised. "Wren will do her Ragnarök and in two weeks, Lark and she will be here too."

Sparrow sighed. Nothing would be as it was, no matter what he said to placate her. She felt the change. Crathode in Valla was unprecedented. Someone led them there.

As if she needed more of a reminder that they weren't at home any longer, Sparrow crossed her denim-clad legs and rested her head on Hawk's shoulder.

"Be careful. If they were wrong and Ridge survived, you will bring him?"

"Of course," Hawk said, as if that went without saying.

"I have a bad feeling about this. Without you and Wren... I know you do not want to hear it, but I do not think I could keep going. My heart is too heavy as it is." She murmured.

"Good thing you will never have to live without us then." He turned and pressed a kiss to the top of her head. "I cannot believe how expensive these houses were with expedited closing."

"Greasing the wheels, as they say," Sparrow said listlessly.

"Come. Let us go stare creepily at your beautiful daughter. You did the right thing, Sparrow," Hawk said, getting to his feet. "If I were in Ridge, and in his position, there is not a single thing I would have done differently. Knowing you and Tawny were safe would make my death tolerable. Ridge was always the best one of that lot. The world is lesser without him."

Sparrow blinked up at him and worked her throat. "I am a monster. If I was not sure before, I know for certain now." She dropped her head so her hair shielded her face and set her plate on the floor. "I do not think I could have left you, even if that meant my own death," she croaked.

Hawk sighed and crouched in front of her. "You are wrong. You would have left me and I would have loved you even more for it. If you had carried my son or daughter in your arms and I pleaded for you to save them, you would have let them die with us?"

"I hate you, Hawk Sumar. You should be angry. Instead, you are as understanding as ever. You never even tried to win me back," Sparrow said, raising her eyes to him.

Hawk's mouth quirked. "I have too much respect for you and for Ridge to have tried to disrupt your marriage. I would never be someone's paramour. My father would never forgive me. Besides, the mistake people make when they become betrothed is that they never give their partner a fair chance. I think they would surprise themselves if they tried. Look at Lark and Wren. I doubt either thought they could love another, but they do. Perhaps not quite the same, but it is there. And you... I know you loved Ridge."

Sparrow dropped her eyes. "I am tired."

"Okay. I will go stare at your daughter for you, then."

Hawk left Sparrow along with her dark, unforgiving thoughts and she fell into a deep melancholia.

K *now Thyself*

MOON STRAUMR, Prime of Tidings and Overseer of Valla University for Guardian Mastery, looked at me with his flat obsidian eyes as if I'd lost my mind. The council had gathered at my behest so I could retell what had happened in Karkinos.

Slate had a number of visitors to watch over his unconscious body while I came to Valla U to speak to the council. Tawny, Jett, Gypsum, and Steel were with him since Sparrow was the matriarch of the Dagr line and had to be present at the council as well as Pearl, who was only here because Hawk refused to wear the Sumar patriarch mantle, ever. He hoped to pass it to my cousin, Gypsum, when Pearl retired.

The Prime's seamed ebony skin had a hint of a jowl. Guardians were supposed to age slower, but Moon wore his age like a banner of the misery he suffered since his wife's death two decades ago at the Red King Massacre. I knew this because my empath abilities needed to be muted around the melancholy man or else he'd infect me with his depression. My great uncle Reed spoke in a low tone close to Moon's head as the other seven at the table scratched notes and passed them over the horseshoe-shaped table they sat at. A banner of each of the family's sigil was hung before each carved seat along the table. The dais making the council of nine slightly higher than the people who sat in the pews who watched.

Orion Vetr, Tawny's grandfather, was in the Vetr seat in a scarlet robe trimmed in a white as pure as the freshly fallen snow from his homeland with an auseklis embroidered on its back, it looked like four "M"s with elongated legs that connected with one another like a compass. His hair matched the trim of his robe, his bright blue hooded eyes had lost their bitterness since I'd met him. Tawny had warmed his heart since she found out he was her paternal granddaughter and she was named his heir. He happened to co-funding my five island arenas that I hoped to open in the next few months.

Pearl wore her royal blue sleeveless robe that brushed the floor trimmed in gold and a matching emblazoned sun on the back. Sparrow's robe was sky blue with yellow trim in the same crushed velvet fabric of Pearl's, with a solar cross on the back, a lower-case 'g' inside a circle.

Hawk had cancelled his U.S. History class that he taught to attend the hearing.

"There were Anguillan, Crathode, and Minotaurs in the prison," I reiterated.

Slate had been inside the Guardians' prison that resided on the back of the colossal crab Karkinos. Through the bond we shared, I managed to pinpoint his location. He had been a full barghest when I'd found him in his cell. My husband had never gone full barghest before. He usually appeared as a hybrid, like the other tribes like the Crathode who were half crustacean or the Anguillan who were hybrid eels.

We had been saved from the ocean waters by the Ostara tribe Aves. The bird hybrids had let us stay the night before we brought Slate back, as well as Shale's body. That was two days ago. Slate had been in a coma since we arrived at the Aves. I fed him broth throughout the day, but he was unchanged. I would not lose hope in him again.

Orion frowned at the mention of both Minotaur and Crathode at the prison. Both were from his island of perpetual winter, Elivagar. Cassiopeia Natt had moved back into the Natt palace in Elivagar, leaving her husband Orion in the Vetr palace. Her blonde hair was curled under like an old movie star on the shoulders of her navy robe. It was trimmed in black, a star inside a circle was barely visible on the dark fabric. Her cool blue eyes were set on her daughter, Delta. Cassiopeia was the ambassador to the Crathode.

Delta was my stepmother and ambassador to the Minotaur. The statuesque blonde was as cool as her icy blue eyes in her fair, beautiful face. Delta was all legs and curves with a pouty mouth our half-brother had inherited. Sage was at her side in their pew, tall and wiry, almost too pretty to be a man with blonde hair that was always combed perfectly like a gentleman's.

Since my father died, they'd not deigned us worth their notice unless it was to make our lives difficult. Delta had been tricked into raising my twin sister when she was really the daughter of my mother, Wren. Not until after my mother was murdered by one of the assassin guild members from the Stygian Knights did our father, Alder, claim us and our brother, Jett. Those same Stygians had then killed my father and given me to the Merfolk.

They had told me they were the weapon someone else wielded. I hoped to find the clean-shaven man and find out exactly who contracted him. It was one instance that I felt killing the messenger might be necessary.

Garnet Lodda, new fiancée of Sage Var, sat next to him and Delta. She had been Amber Lodda's cousin. She had always been a bit vapid, which perpetuated the myth of the dumb blonde. We were the same height and the same hourglass figure, though with all the training I'd done since leaving Chicago and coming to Tidings, my body was a weapon and.

Only two members of our father's household had come around to our little trio, my father's brother Jackal and our grandmother. Ruby Geol was reed thin with porcelain skin and dark hair pulled up in a bun like a ballerina. Wide brown eyes peered up beneath winged brows, her orange robe with purple trim hung loose around her slim shoulders, and a triceps on her back. She was the antithesis of her husband.

Cygnus Var was a strapping older man with white-winged dirty blonde hair and powder blue eyes in his stern tan face. Our father looked a great deal like him, but with the hard angles of his mother's face. My grandfather sat in the seat carved with his sigil in the back, the same sigil adorning the back of his emerald green robe trimmed in gold.

Peak Haust gave one of his insincere smiles as he sorted papers. My stomach churned. Slate's uncle had a unique color eyes of an almost lime green, they were light and bright against his deep bronze skin. His black waves were threaded with silver that looked handsome on the tall, powerful man, and he smiled with full lips. The only thing that wasn't perfect on his face was his nose that rounded a bit at the tip.

The barghest shifting was genetic. All the male Hausts were barghest hybrids. While Slate had been imprisoned, I had tried to get all the islands to consent to letting the arenas be built. Peak had refrained from my group meeting, but later asked for a private one.

That was when I found out he was barghest. He drugged me with what the Merfolk called rousen, a philter that overstimulated the pleasure center of your mind, rendering you helpless to anything but pleasure; giving it or getting it.

When I'd come down off it the next morning, I'd confronted Peak. He'd taken me in his barghest form. Something barghest could only do with only one human woman because they mated for life. He'd made me pay for what he deemed insolence, and not even my elemental abilities saved me from his wrath.

"Where did you go after you escaped Karkinos?" he asked with glittering lime green eyes.

"To Ostara, where we waited the night before returning to the Dagr palace, while the others went to Valla," I answered.

'Quick' Silver Regn and his older brother, Brass, sat in the first pew with Indigo. Quick's dazzling smile was nowhere to be seen on his olive face. Black tattoos edged up from under his collar in what hinted at a masterpiece underneath. His dark hair was short with the front long enough to wear stylishly combed, like a modern twist on a gentleman from the roaring twenties. He was powerfully built and the same height as his brother, at a couple inches over six feet. Brass's thick dark hair was worn in a knot at his dark honey nape, with bronze and ebony beads on a few narrow braids.

I hadn't seen either of them since leaving Ostara. They'd visited Slate, and I'd made sure to be far away.

I was a hypocrite. I was in love with Slate, but I loved Brass too. I thought Slate was dead. I'd made plans with Brass. We'd made love the morning before I went to classes and later that night Slate's bond had been activated and everything had changed in a blink.

Again.

When he'd slept with two of the Aves the night before we left Ostara, I couldn't remember a time I'd been more hurt since Slate was tricked by a projected image of me.

No one had tricked Brass. I carried our sons. Our relationship had been complicated from the start and only grew more entangled with each passing day, but I thought my heart had been safe with him.

I had been avoiding his soft amber gaze since I walked in. He and Quick sat shoulder to shoulder. Brass's body was slightly softer than Quick's hundred percent fat free ripped muscles. Quick the lie detector and Brass the mind reader. Their gene pool should have been more highly sought after. I idly wondered if one of our sons would be a mind reader.

Quick was certainly sought after when he flashed that panty dropping smile of his. He was devilishly handsome and had an indefinable quality that you just knew translated into hedonistic nights. My poor sister sat with her body leaning away from him in the pew.

Indigo might become the one that got away from Quick.

Everyone needed their heart broken once. They couldn't appreciate when times were good otherwise. He was getting a heaping helping of hurt. When Quick had been dying after being caught in Karkinos's claw, Indigo had professed her love for him and had never been sweeter. Then they had another blow up the morning we left the Aves. I didn't know all the details.

Her powder blue eyes were focused on me. Her tan skin was the same shade as mine and Jett's. Straight corn silk hair framed her oval face and fell to her waist. She was classically beautiful and would be until the day she died, one of those irritating people who would age with grace. Indigo smiled at me with her pretty, pink pout and it raised the beauty mark just below her right eye.

"Where your husband is still in a coma?" Peak asked.

"Yes," I answered.

Brass, Quick, and Indigo knew about what Peak had done to me when I went to his castle for his meeting. He'd wanted me to come for another "meeting" the day we were with the Aves. I'd told his son, Sterling, to let him know I wouldn't make it.

I was frightened of Peak. He was powerful in *calling* and powerful as a barghest. I was two months pregnant with Brass's twins and terrified he'd hurt them if I denied him again. After losing mine and Slate's pregnancy the night my father was murdered. I would do anything to protect them, even debase myself.

That everyone thought they were Slate's children may have been the only thing that saved my sons when Peak assaulted me.

"I trust you are offering my nephew the utmost care?" Peak asked, as he scanned his papers before him.

"Yes, of course." I answered.

Willow Natt was Peak's wife; Delta and Tawny's biological father's sister. Her creamy skin was as fair as her younger sister's, with the same curves in a shorter stature. Willow had a mass of black chin length curls and violet eyes that she had passed to her son Sterling. He wasn't at the hearing, but his evil twin sisters were Novaculite and Quartzite. Where one was blonde, the other was brunette, they were both short and Quartz had an ample bosom, but Nova had more attitude with wide hazel eyes eerily similar to Tawny's now that I thought about it.

Ash Straumr sat with his fiancée, Quartz; my ex-fiancée. I wouldn't look at the caramel skinned nephew of the Prime. He'd no doubt sneer with his sensual mouth below those celadon green eyes. He was always so damn cocky.

I'd tarnished his reputation and while he thought he loved me; he also hated me. His chestnut hair was freshly cropped above his straight dark brows that lifted when I'd mentioned Slate's coma.

Reed Tio sighed. "Scarlett, darling. I do not know how you get yourself into these situations."

My great uncle and patriarch of the Tios had a soft spot for me and my family. Pearl's brother had the same coppery hair she did and olive skin, but with big dark eyes, unlike Pearl's emerald cat eyes. He wore his hair in a pompadour like my uncle Hawk, with a trimmed mustache. He and his wife Fern Rot had a gaggle of red-headed children who were all provosts at Valla U.

"Trust me. I'd much rather spend time with a healthy husband and popping out his babies," I said with a sheepish smile that elicited a laugh from the people gathered, despite the severity of the situation.

"That is what we would rather you do as well," Peak replied, and bile rose in my throat.

"We will send Guardians into the portal to Karkinos. If for no other reason, you deserve a Mjolnir for the rescue of Slate Dagr," Moon Straumr said, and I detected his doubt.

Mjolnir's were the highest award you could give a Guardian. I had one for defeating a swarm of Jorogumo that attacked in the desert lands in Thrimilci.

"Thank you, but I would not have survived if it weren't for the help of my friends and sister. Brass and Silver Regn as well as Indigo Tio. Our friend Shale died during the rescue, saving Silver's life. If anyone deserves the Mjolnir, it's Shale Sandr. I believe her mother would be here to accept it on her behalf."

I couldn't honor Shale's death any more and I heard a sniffle from the pews. I turned to see Asp Sandr with her brother, Boa Sunna. Both were provosts at Valla U. Their family resemblance to Shale, with their up tilted dark eyes and pin straight raven hair, was unmistakable.

Moon gestured for her to approach the horseshoe desk where I stood before it. Asp wiped her eyes with a red kerchief.

"We are deeply sorry for your loss, Asp. Please accept our condolences and the Mjolnir in her name," Moon said in all sincerity. "If Brass and Silver Regn would please approach with Indigo Tio as well. I believe you should all be awarded the Guardians' highest honor for courage and loyalty."

I was dwarfed by the two men that stood at either side of me as Moon came around with Reed to pin the little gold inverted hammers to our chests. Reed's dark eyes met mine with a conspiratorial smile and he held out his hand. It was a gesture I recognized as asking permission to delve with his *calling*. I nodded with a small smile as Reed put a hand on my stomach and heat washed through me.

Reed sighed dreamily. "Your mother must be clapping her hands in the heavens, ready to meet these two." He eyeballed Brass and Quick. "Better friends would not have permitted the pregnant wife of a friend, as well as cousin, to join in a dangerous rescue mission."

It was a tangled web. Brass's mother was Slate's father's twin, but I hadn't known that until Slate revealed his true parentage *after* we were married.

Brass cleared his throat. "With all due respect, Second, no one *tells* Scarlett what she can and cannot do." If it bothered him, they did not know the boys were his, he didn't show it.

Reed laughed and Moon must have heard his comment, because he chuckled as well. My eyes bulged. Had I ever heard the Prime laugh before?

"Right you are, son. I beg your pardon. We Guardians are a powerful breed; whatever our gender." Reed chuckled as he walked away, showing us his gold robe with silver metallic trim. The starburst sigil shimmered on the back.

When Reed and Moon sat back down and Moon straightened, his black robe trimmed in both silver and gold and emblazoned with the three interlocking triangles on the black. I met Sparrow's dark, heavy eyes as she swiped a tear from her olive cheek and pushed her long, dark tresses away.

She never recovered from my mother's death. Hawk was my mother's twin and Sparrow's best friend; closer than sisters.

"Please take this warning under advisement, Mrs. Tio," Moon stated. "In light of your past tragedies. Put your feet up and be thankful you have been given a second chance at love and motherhood."

His candor, though heavy on patriarchy, threw me for a loop, especially in front of at least a hundred Guardians that sat in the pews behind me. No small amount of guilt and apprehension shot through me like a lightning storm that crackled its bolts through my heart.

Slate or Brass.

Wife or mother?

"I will. Thank you." I replied in the same proper tone I'd used during the hearing.

"We shall update you on our findings when we receive word," Reed added.

I turned around and walked down the tiled path that split the pews. When I glanced out of the corner of my eye, I spotted Canis whom I hadn't seen since my father's funeral. He was at Slate's presumptive funeral, but I hadn't really spoken to anyone that day besides when I declared myself Slate's wife.

Canis was barrel chested with a shock of spiky short white hair; his blue eyes were hooded in his round tan face. He had a grip like a vise which I knew from personal experience because I'd told him I knew he was having an affair with Cassiopeia Natt. Not very smart of me.

My father's uncle was not a good man. Cygnus, his twin brother older by minutes, had inherited the Var castle, while Canis had never married and was ambassador to the Anguillan. An otherwise coveted position, though I doubted Canis thought of it that way. It was yet another reason for him to hate me since I revealed his tribe had rogues.

I thought back to what the Aves sachem told me about the nine stone pieces I needed to collect. Supposedly, they were for a great works that no one knew details about, or even a rough idea of what it was for, but that it would save our world. Unless I didn't, then we were all in the same sinking boat. Corvus, the crow hybrid had told me one of the Var's had taken it from the Anguillan. Was that Canis? It had Sage written all over it, but would he treat with the tribes? I imagined my half-brother would think it was beneath him.

I wore three stone pieces around my neck on a silver chain. I resisted the urge to touch the stones and patted my Yggdrasil necklace instead. Every tyro inducted into Valla U received one. I wore a silver torque on my wrist for passing the first challenge of the Wild Hunt. In a few months, I'd have my second challenge. The Ragnarök, then I'd receive my golden torque and be proven tried-and-true.

Indigo was thrown out of Valla U for slapping Ash, but even she was permitted to compete in the Ragnarök. Valla U had a zero-tolerance policy for fighting unless it was during battle training run by the three Straumr brothers; Crag, River, and Fox.

Crag was my uncle Jackal's longtime lover and as polar opposite as one could get. While Crag was ebony skinned like his father, Jackal was tall and tan and blonde. Crag was bald with a sharp chiseled face and a powerful build while Jackal was wiry with a sharp wit and tended to use an inordinate amount of sarcasm. Crag was stern with dark eyes, and

Jackal was always smiling impishly as he taught Languages at Valla U. There was an eight-year difference between the two men, that wasn't an issue now, four years after they first got together. I loved my uncle Jackal.

Fox sat next to Nova Natt, his wife. Good natured with sky-blue eyes and the caramel skin of a Straumr, he had tight dark curls that contrasted with those bright eyes making them pop. He was a flirtatious, attractive man.

Amethyst and Cherry were in the pews beside Hawk. My brother's wives were also lovers. Cherry was due around the same time as I was, and like me, you couldn't tell we were pregnant. She looked like a pin up version of Snow White with long black hair and cobalt eyes on a fair face. Her real name was Cerise Kaldr, but no one ever called her that except her father. Amethyst Geol was Moon Straumr's only daughter whose mother had died when the Red King rogues of the Crathode tribe attacked during an induction ceremony twenty-odd years ago. Everyone knew he'd only reopened the university so she could become a Guardian. Moon could deny his daughter nothing.

She was mocha skinned like her brother River, with long dark hair. They both had dark eyes, but hers were wide and deep with all the knowledge her father had bestowed upon her. She had the slight figure of a Geol even after having Gigi, the only child in the marriage. River, in contrast, had a wife and several children already; the only Straumr brother to have kids.

Hawk rose swiping a hand over his silver pompadour. "Well done, Scarlett. Do you want to head straight home?" he asked.

My uncle had the body of a dancer, short for a Guardian at five foot ten, but all Tio men were average height. Gypsum had grown taller than his father over the last two years and now stood at a height with his uncle Steel at six feet, who also happened to be his brother-in-law. Tawny was a Vetr, not a Sumar, but Hawk was her father even though Sparrow's first husband sired her.

"Yes," I said, suppressing a sigh. "I had Tawny bring my books home so I can study while I watch over Slate."

I'd ran away to Chicago for almost seven months when I thought I couldn't have Slate's children. I hadn't known at the time that my body would repair the extensive damage that the Merfolk's fluids had done to me. I'd missed all that time, thinking I didn't want to be a Guardian. I'd come back for Brass, only to realize once Slate was captured that and that he needed me more and maybe I needed him, too.

"We have him taken care of, Scar. You can go out to dinner or something. Go for a walk, get some fresh air?"

Two years ago, Hawk, Sparrow, Tawny, Gypsum, and my mother had come from Chicago with me. I had no idea I had all this family or that I could *call* to the elements. Indigo and I were the first elementals in hundreds of years and I was stronger in *calling* than anyone else I knew. We were Guardians; hand-picked by the Mother to protect beings who couldn't protect themselves against the modern world.

I'd felt tense ever sense we brought Slate back, and he still hadn't woken up. The idea that I could still lose him was too much to bear, but I dared not voice my concerns out loud. Instead, I'd kept my demeanor cool and imperious. No one could get close that way. They couldn't know how afraid I really was.

I felt a hand on my shoulder and I knew who it was before I turned around. Since he claimed me, there was an unwanted attraction to him. He'd branded me. I'd been branded in a claiming by Slate as well, but the connection to my husband was deeper. I smoothed my expression and faced Peak Haust whose hand still sat on my shoulder.

"Please send my nephew my best wishes. This weekend you will have to come to dinner and let someone else watch him for a time. Standing guard over an infirm man could be tiresome," he said, and I heard the threat.

I plastered a smile on my face. "How considerate of you. I'm sure my husband will come around soon."

"Saturday, then. Good day to you, sweet Scarlett. Hawk." Peak inclined his head and moved past us.

My whole body shivered involuntarily, and I was face to face with Brass. His eyes were like molten lava. I turned from him without a word to face Hawk again.

"Let's go home. This wore me out. I like caring for him myself," I said and Hawk's dark intelligent eyes twinkled, understanding my deeper meaning.

"What was that about?" Hawk asked as we walked down the path between pews.

"Peak, *uh*, Councilor Haust has taken an interest in Slate," I lied. I never outright lied.

Indigo looped her arm in mind and bent her head to mine, her lotion combined with her natural scent making her smell of honey and freesia. "The Regn brothers are hot on your heels with very intent looking handsome faces," she whispered.

I hoped I hid the thrill I felt well when I rolled my eyes. "I have nothing to say to Brass. I'll hear out Quick though. What happened with you two? One minute you love him, he next you run at the sight of him. Are you even training?"

I was the delegate to the Grand Mistress who ran the Shadow Breakers. I'd arranged for Indigo to train with the Regn brothers so she wouldn't fall behind. Slate and Brass were two of four captains in the assassins guild. I'd made Brass captain myself and found his team for him. While Slate was out of commission, Quick ran the team. Cordillera and her boy toy Chafer were actively looking for team members for my arenas.

I'd almost forgotten. The Regn brothers were supposed to be running the arenas for me. If it was arena business, I had to speak to Brass.

Indigo's cheeks heated. "I'm not, but I'll pick it up again soon. I've moved back into the Sumar palace and we had Shale's funeral yesterday. I've been busy."

We walked somberly down the steps until we reached the floor the portal room at Valla U resided on. It was a long room with a wall of arched, intricately carved wood doors with sconces between each one fastened to the yellowed stone of which the entire university was comprised. Two huge tapestries hung at either end of the room, one of Mother Earth and the other was the Yggdrasil of the University's sigil. Along the wall were vine carved doors that would lead you to any other door in Tidings, all you had to do was think about where you wanted to go.

"Indi!" A male's voice rang out in the room and we stopped.

It was Sterling Haust, Slate's cousin and son of Peak. He was also the heir to the Haust's and future ruler of Mabon, the island of perpetual fall. Indigo's cheeks heated. She was right, Quick and Brass were right behind us and stood between Sterling and where he'd paused.

"I'll meet you there," I told Hawk who nodded and was engulfed in the bright white flare of the portal door.

Sterling was boyishly handsome with intentionally mussed up chocolate brown hair and wide cheek bones. His violet eyes that seemed to ignite at the sight of Indigo. They drew you in, barghest eyes. He was a couple inches shorter than Quick and built like Hawk; lean and toned with broad shoulders.

"Actually, Scarlett I need to speak to you, too," Sterling said in a low rasping voice.

He skirted Brass and Quick and we walked towards the tapestry of Mother Earth. Worry etched Sterling's tan face as he smiled apologetically at me. I gave Indi a side glance, and she averted her eyes.

"You told him!" I shouted.

I reined in my temper. She must have thought she was helping. I waited for her to explain.

"Scarlett, I am sorry. I had no idea my father was capable of something so abhorrent."

I felt vulnerable. I hardly knew Sterling, and he knew his father had forcibly taken me to his bed.

"Yes, well, thank you. You'll have to excuse me if I seem crass, but your father just informed me that he wants me over for dinner again Saturday when I know exactly what is on the menu." My scalp prickled with the flush that came to my entire body.

Sterling's own cheeks heated. "I can try to arrange it so my mother will be home. I could let you know Friday if I succeeded. That is what I came to warn you about, that my mother was to see Delta for a visit."

CHAPTER 2

INDIGO

Apprehension stewed my insides. Would Silver rub it in Sterling's face that I said I loved him? I hadn't spoken to Sterling since the night we left to save Slate. We'd been making love shortly before Scarlett had blown into my old room at Valla U like a lunatic. Then Silver had said he'd been down the hall with another girl and heard the commotion so he'd broken into the bedroom, too.

Sterling's hand reached up to cup my face despite the Guardians going in and out of the portal doors. He was never so careless, but then, he had nothing to lose if they ousted our affair. I turned my face away from his hand and he leveled his eyes at me.

"What is wrong, Indi? Are you okay? I cannot believe you broke into Karkinos. What were you thinking?"

I gave him a dry look. "I was thinking my sister's husband was unlawfully imprisoned, and I had to save him. What would you have me do? Besides, I waited in the boat while Shale, Brass, Silver, and Scarlett went in. You could have helped us, but you didn't."

Sterling looked as if I'd struck him. "Has he started officially courting you?"

I looked in the direction he shot daggers and saw Silver leaning against the yellow stone wall. Brass must have followed Scarlett; she would not be happy. Silver gave us a mocking smile and a little wave. That arrogant ass.

"Absolutely not."

"What is he doing then?" Sterling accused.

"I have no idea. He's Quick, who knows why he is the way he is."

"Indigo, are you coming back to the palace?" Pearl's cultured voice came from behind me and I turned towards her.

Her emerald cat eyes flickered to the doorway, and I followed them. My grandmother was an empath like Scarlett. I wondered what rage she must be feeling from Diamond Natt who was hovering half in, half out of the doorway to the portal room.

Ash's younger sister was Sterling's betrothed. She had his light green eyes and caramel skin. Her hair fell in thick chestnut waves over her shoulders with an hourglass figure. Diamond chewed on her full pink lips as her eyes kept flickering to where I stood too close to Sterling. She was having an affair with Gypsum, but no one could blame her. Sterling knew and hadn't cared as long as she kept it quiet. Tidings was strange like that.

Because Sterling's mother hated mine, we could never be together. The same went for Gypsum's father, my uncle, Hawk, and Dahlia Natt after what happened with Scarlett and Ash. Scarlett had slept with Slate and gotten pregnant. She'd lost that baby. Ash had dumped Scarlett because at the time, she couldn't conceive again. That was what Moon had referred to in the hearing.

I'd been with Sterling for the better half of a decade. He was my first, I loved him still, and we'd promised each other that no matter who we wound up betrothed to that we would find a way to be together. It had worked out with Sterling seeing Diamond, but I'd been alone until last Yuletide when Scarlett officially introduced me to Silver.

Everyone knew 'Quick' Silver Regn; notorious womanizer and more handsome than anyone had a right to be. I was hurting because Diamond started at Valla U this year and had come to the annual masquerade on Sterling's arm. We'd sat kitty corner to them as they joked and laughed that night. When Silver had asked me to dance I was so grateful. I'd taken him back to my room and surrendered myself to him.

Well, as much as I could. I had rules.

The Gods only knew why he kept coming back. A glutton for punishment he'd admitted to me. Problem was, I kept letting him back in.

I'd told Sterling immediately, and we'd had a tiff. He got over it when I told him it wouldn't change us, but he just didn't like that it was Silver. The feeling was mutual. Silver couldn't stand that I still saw Sterling. I used harsh words to keep Silver at bay and it usually worked until he'd almost died.

By the Mother, I'd said so much that day. I wasn't myself.

Mortality had hung over my head like a guillotine and I'd flailed for life support. My hands had landed on Silver. I told him I loved him and that he could do with me what he wished. It wouldn't have been so bad if I hadn't spoken to Sterling about possibly entertaining suitors for a husband the night before and Sterling had told Silver I meant him. Sterling wasn't a stupid man, he'd done it to push Silver away, but it was no easy task to push the persistent Silver Regn away.

He never stopped until he got what he wanted, and for now, I struck his fancy.

"Your betrothed is watching you," I hissed and took a step back. "Yes. I'll be right there," I told Pearl, and she nodded to Sterling.

"I see that," Sterling said in a cool flat tone.

I turned around and Silver was now speaking to Diamond and Garnet. Good. Garnet could take him off my hands even though she was engaged to Sage. Silver had slept with Garnet as well as at least half the girls at Valla U.

"Gods, I'm going to go while he's distracted. Sterling."

Sterling's violet eyes twinkled at me and I knew he wanted to kiss me.

"Don't fail Scarlett this weekend," I said coolly and his smile fell.

I walked through the nearest portal ignoring Silver's shouts.

CHAPTER 3
SLATE

I flexed my heightened sense out. It smelled like Thrimilci, but this was not the Sumar palace. The smell of spiced apples and vanilla clung to the white sheets in the obscenely stark white bed I awoke on.

Where was my bed? Black leather and furs.

It was a woman's room.

I pressed a hand to my head, when was the last time I had a headache? By the Mother, I needed to be healed. One of these doors had to lead to the bathroom so I could take a piss and wash my mouth out.

What the fuck did I drink last night?

The last thing I remembered was Jett and Steel coming to Valla with me to meet up with Brass and Quick. Wren was coming with her daughter. Jett was trying to play it cool, but he had waited his whole life to meet his mother and sister.

Scarlett.

The girl from my mother's prophecy. She was supposed to fall in love with me and then kill me. I hadn't made up my mind if I would put her out of her inevitable misery yet. It would be easy to arrange an accident to befall her. Sooner rather than later or else Wren and Jett would be heart broken. There was the matter of the twin daughter that was missing. A number a possible candidates came to mind, but it was Scarlett that lived in my dreams.

Jett's uncle Hawk, his wife Sparrow and cousins were coming too. Gypsum and Tawny. Pearl kept pictures of them all and Wren sent Jett photographs of her and Scarlett. The harbinger of my doom looked sinfully innocent and sweet. A callow girl.

I liked my women older and experienced, ones who were no longer fertile so I would not risk them growing a barghest bairn in their wombs. They used me and I returned the favor. Cordillera understood this. Take and take. No one gave. I didn't have the luxury of letting some fool girl fall in love. I was a dead man walking. Now that this Scarlett was coming, my days were numbered.

I would not kill her. For Pearl, Jett and Steel, I could not do that to them. I wanted to. Call it self-preservation. An accident may be permissible.

There was Wren. The only mother I had known before Pearl took over my care. I would not want to kill her daughter after she cared so lovingly for me when she had no need to. Curse my prophet's memory.

The bathroom, finally.

I frowned at the aquamarine and bright pink. Where the *fuck* was I? I relieved myself and walked to the mirror and started.

Who the fuck kicked my ass? I ran my finger over the silver scar that ran from my hairline over my left eye to stop halfway down my cheek. I started checking my body for other marks and found small silver scars all over. *Fuck.*

Wait until I saw Jett. He had to be a part of this. First, a toothbrush. More pink. I did not fuck women who wore *pink*. Red and black. Those were the women I bedded and never in *my* bed. You could not get rid of them then.

I picked up the black brush and gazed at my reflection as I scrubbed with the refreshing taste of mint in my mouth. Better. Anything was better than the acrid taste I'd had.

My grey eyes widened at my reflection and I grabbed one of the fetishes in my hair. Where was my jade barghest? What the fuck was a love rune doing in my gods' be damned hair? Freya's burly boar. Jett was going to pay for that one.

I let it drop and spat into the sink and shut off the tap.

A shower. That would help refresh my memory.

Two low tiled walls, behind the walls was a huge shower. Water sprayed from every direction, there was even a waterfall of sorts at the entrance that fell across the low wall so no one could see you if you were showering past it. Now this was like home. We had the same showers at the palace.

Was I in one of the rooms on the upper floors?

The last thing I remembered was Quick teasing Jett about how he would take his sister to bed as soon as she met him. Jett had laughed, but his face turned an alarming shade of red. How the tables had turned. Jett had been part of their group. Steel, Quick, Jett and I out of the town picking up women, starting fights and drinking until dawn.

I had met with Lera at headquarters and then... it was blank. I could not remember anything past leaving Lera's bedroom the night before the masquerade. I ran my hand over my face and went to look for some clothes so I could get the fuck out of this nightmare.

Back in the room with the big white bed was a closet. I chanced that if the woman whose place this was had a husband, I might be able to borrow clothes. He would not miss it. If I was there, he should be more concerned about what his wife was up to, not his missing pants.

The clothing looked oddly familiar, but I dismissed it as I grabbed a black linen sleeveless 'V' neck and a pair of black pants that happened to be my size. Luck. I would not be borrowing another man's under-garments.

With my heightened hearing, I heard someone enter a room near what had to be the front door. Two people. A man and a woman arguing. Gods, I did not want to have to hide. At six foot six and about eighteen stones, hiding was no easy task. Did I want to fight the poor bastard whose wife I likely fucked? It was not *his* fault.

Discontent housewives were my specialty.

I knew that voice. I stepped out into the ludicrously white bedroom and listened.

"I don't have anything to say to you."

"Doesn't it make it easier?"

"You sleeping with the Aves, *two* Aves is supposed to make my life easier? Gods, Brass. I *heard* you. We'd made love the day before! I chose you to safeguard my heart. I knew you were special from the moment I met you. Forget it. Go about your life."

Brass and a woman? He hurt a woman? I did not believe it. He never would. Was this her house? Shit. I did not fuck some girl Brass was seeing. Never. When did he see an Aves? *Two* Aves? That was not the Brass I knew. Aves had been recluses for almost two decades. None of it was making sense and my head ached, making it difficult to think.

"I did not know that. I am sorry." Brass paused. "Are you... okay?"

"No. I feel like... like I lost one of my closest friends. I wanted... I wish... Couldn't you have waited just a few days? I... I miss you. Your company and solid presence tethering me to my sanity. If anything should happen... *Gods*, I can't even say it. Do you regret getting me pregnant? Be honest."

Her words rocked me. Brass had knocked someone up! He must be in heaven. What was he doing sleeping around?

Had I fallen into an alternate universe?

"No. Not for an instant. I am their father and I will raise them with you. You are right. I shouldn't have done it. Seeing you two together again. I knew my time with you was up. Forgive me. I don't know what I was thinking. It was incredibly stupid and short sighted. Hurting you... the mother of my children by being with other women. I don't recognize myself."

Brass was speaking with an odd dialect as if he'd spent time outside of Tidings when I knew he never had. Could I be wrong? Was that a different man? I was not sure of anything at that point.

"I'm so sorry." Her voice hitched as if she was going to cry.

Kiss her, you idiot.

"Don't. We can't... I have to go take care of him." Her voice was thick.

Did she mean me? Just how did she plan on caring for me?

"I know. Me too, love. Forgive me. Please. I haven't slept thinking of how deeply I've wronged you. You weren't wrong. Your heart is safe with me. I'll prove it. I'll..."

It *was* Brass. I was not mistaken. He was talking to this woman in his head. Brass cursed.

"What's wrong?" She sounded nervous.

"Go. He's awake."

She gasped.

Brass exhaled noisily. "I will come back tomorrow and keep the others away."

"No, Brass. You have to go. I don't want you listening. Promise me you will go far away," she pleaded.

I could hear the smile in his voice. "You and I, success through sacrifice. You deserve happiness, Scarlett."

Scarlett!

Brass kissed her, I could hear her breaths quicken as she struggled and then relented with the rasp of his stubble against her jaw. Jett would not be okay with Brass knocking up his sister. Shit! What day was it?

"*You* make me happy," she whispered, but he'd already left.

Heeled footsteps approached with the slide of slinking fabric Thrimilci women wore over the ground. She entered the bedroom and stared at the bed as if I would magically appear there.

My breath caught.

That was not the same girl from the photographs. *That* was a grown woman. She wore a white dress with a slit in the chiffon fabric to her tan toned thigh. The top of the halter was sheer with a strip of fabric that covered her breasts in a way that more than hinted at the lush curves underneath.

The way she held herself was that of a woman who knew what she was about, in and out of the bedroom.

I only saw her profile, but that caramel-colored hair was unmistakable. She'd pinned in up so loose waves fell from a low twist. Two narrow braids fell over her slim shoulder. My beads! She wore my silver Celtic etched beads and an ivory starburst, a pearl, and two of Brass's beads a bronze and an ebony. Oddly, two feathers hung from the tips of the braids; a peacock feather and a white one. Who she could have gotten those from was anyone's guess, but with all the Aves talk, they were a safe bet.

Her face turned, and she spotted me lurking in the closet like a burglar. She didn't scream as I thought she would. Her pictures did not do her justice. She had a narrow chin that led to full sinfully luscious lips. Almond eyes the color of turquoise shown from long lashes above high cheekbones. Her nose was straight with a small lift to the end in a purely feminine way. She brushed pink painted nails past her forehead to push a loose strand from her face.

She took a step towards me and I froze. I never froze. It pissed me off. I glowered at her. Did she have some talent that made my mind go numb?

"You heard?" she asked.

Her voice had a gravelly tone and my cock got hard at the sound of it. "I did." My voice came out rougher than I had intended and her high cheekbones reddened in a flattering way. It made me wonder if other parts of her had changed color too.

I looked over her long dress in a purposefully intimidating way. I could see her skin prickle from there, the shadows of her hard peaks shown through the white dress. My cock pressed against the pants I'd hastily put on. The shirt was useless in my hand.

She slowly reached behind her neck and I could see her breasts heave beneath the sheer fabric. The dress slid to the floor, and the beast rattled its cage. I watched her eyes dilate.

She was a rousen trained khoraz! Only rousen trained khoraz pupils did that. I would know. I used to be addicted to rousen myself.

Callow my ass!

Gods, that body. Tight and soft at the same time. She had not been wearing undergarments. Everything on her was neatly trimmed and manicured.

She stepped out of the dress without taking her eyes off mine. *Fuck.* She was coming towards me. Jett... Brass... I hoped they would forgive me.

"I'm sorry," she whispered when she stood before me with wet parted lips.

Her skintight over her breasts and I wanted to cup that backside I'd seen in her silhouette. Fuck it.

She gasped as I grabbed her in my rough hands and pressed her against my hips. She felt *fucking* fantastic. Supple round cheeks, but firm. Her stomach was defined, not hard like Lera's but not soft like Lynx's. She was not afraid of a little hard work.

Oh, how I was going to make her work.

While I started to run down the things I was going to do to her in my mind, she ran her fingertip over that scar on my face. I stiffened. It did not turn her off though. She seemed to be even more excited by it. Poor Jett. He would have his hands full with this one in an entirely different way than I did then.

She lowered herself to her knees as she slipped through my hands. I shut my eyes as she unbuttoned my pants.

Was I some prepubescent boy? Was I going to blow my load, and she had not done anything yet? I gritted my teeth as she pulled me into her wet warm mouth.

Fuck. It was not going to last long.

She sucked and swirled her tongue running along the length of me which was no small feat. She took all of me deep in her throat and my hands fisted in her hair holding her in place.

Not yet. My breaths were already ragged and my heart was beating so loudly I couldn't hear hers. Was she enjoying it or was she just doing her job?

Rousen trained khorazes didn't come cheap. I wondered how long I had her for. I started to pull the pins from her hair and it tumbled over her back to her waist. I gripped it tightly as I fucked her mouth.

She let me. So pliable.

She smelled like spiced apples and vanilla. It was her place. I moaned as I came into her mouth, pouring into the back of her throat, her tongue licking at the base of my shaft. She was damn good. I told her so.

"Your mouth," I said roughly, and she pulled back gently. "That was —"

She placed her pink polished finger over my lips silencing me and the beast rattled its cage. She kicked off her heels and took my hand, leading me over to the bed. I followed her unable to take my eyes off her tight round ass. Frigga's sweet grass, Brass was an idiot.

I had formed a theory about her.

She would let me do whatever I wanted, and I planned to test that theory. As she bent to climb into the bed, I pressed her spine down as I grabbed her hips and she clutched the white sheets in her fists as she submitted to me.

Oh yes. It was going to be a good night. I would take her this way and then push between those cheeks. When I was done, she'd never forget me. I'd take her every way a man could take a woman *twice* and every man after me she would find wanting.

Mother fuck.

That was... if her skill set was impacted her cost, someone had spent a fortune cheering me up. Maybe I would pay back whomever got her for me. She was worth it. I had never paid for a woman before, but... it was different. Perhaps she'd done it as a favor because we were technically family.

I wiped both my hands over my face.

What had I done?

I took her into the showers and she had fallen on all fours. She raised that delectable ass in the air.

The beast had rattled in his cage like never before and I flattened against the wall to keep from shifting. Then she said those magic words.

"Claim me."

I could not stop it. It was out of my control. I had shifted and taken her. Gods, and how she howled when she came. Her muscles clenched around me like a fist. I thought I would wear her out and sneak away. We had been at it all day and half the night.

By all rights she should have passed out long ago. Still, she fucked and she came and she took as much as she gave and I had fallen asleep too.

I never passed out.

I was a barghest shifter. I could only mate with a woman once in that form and she had taken it. She had not even blinked when I shifted into the seven-foot-tall beast with fangs and claws and horns. That was when I smelled the other barghest, just below the surface of her skin. She had been branded, and I had grown in enraged.

How dare some other barghest brand what was *mine!*

It did not dawn on me how absurd that thought was until now. It was light out again in the white bedroom and I had spent the night. I never spent the night. I had broken so many rules.

She slept now on her back. Her breasts rising in falling with perfect pink peaks. I had tasted every inch of her — sugary sweet. She had overwhelmed my senses. When she rode me, she had smiled and laughed with her head thrown back. I had never been more turned on. I lost track of how many times I had brought her to climax or her for me.

If I thought about it, I could remember. I was a prophet and I could remember every single detail I had ever seen. My mother passed it down to me before she died. That was why the gap in my memories had left me confused. It should not be impossible.

The white sheet was tossed over her hips and I could not help it. Now that she was asleep I could check. I caught the scent of her pregnancy; I had only felt a slight bit of guilt about it at first and then I had claimed her.

The alarming urge to kill Brass so she would carry my bairn jarred me.

I gave myself a mental shake. That was the barghest's thoughts not mine. I would never father children. I would not leave an unmarried woman with children and I would never marry. *This* woman's presence signified the beginning of the end of my life.

Shit, but it had been worth it.

Looking at her the beast stirred. I wondered how much it would cost to keep her for another day, or for the weekend. I wasn't as confident as I should've been that I could convince her to stay of her own volition.

She was young, younger than I was. What day was it? Should we be in classes? Had she dropped out of Valla U to work a brothel? Pearl would not have allowed it.

Fuck. I will have to tell Jett I fucked his sister.

He must know she is a khoraz. A barghest khoraz at that. I did not stand a chance against her.

My thoughts tumbled. Could they have sent her to kill me *now*? Was she working for the Stygian Knights? Too much temptation to pass up? It was no secret I liked a good romp, and she had been better than good; she was... incomparable.

Gods, I would be spoiled for the rest of my life. Perhaps she and I could work out an arrangement?

Yes. She had enjoyed herself as much as I did. She would work with me. I was willing to bet she booked up fast. Her time would be expensive. Why did that infuriate me?

I pulled the sheet from her hips exposing her tan, toned, naked body to the morning sunlight. Freya's burly boar! She had a Shadow Breaker tracker on her hip. The inguz tattoo held a small Celtic compass inside it, only another Shadow Breaker would recognize it. It had the blood of another Breaker mixed into its design. Who was she *really*?

I *called* her short seax from its sheath. It's black handle carved into the goddess Freya and etched in gold, its black hand stitched scabbard had gold embossed wings and gold buckles. It was a very good blade. By the way her body was muscled, she knew how to use it. I shoved it under her pillow and climbed on top of her, pushing her thighs apart to fit my hips.

Her full lips pursed, and she purred.

That was all it took and my cock responded. The beast purred back in my chest and she smiled. *Gods.* That fucking smile might be how she planned to kill me.

"Sex for breakfast. Delicious." She purred in her gravelly voice and I changed my mind about interrogating her.

No. Now I wanted her to stay. I could question her later. Sated... with that smile. Torture by pleasure sounded appealing.

My fingers slipped between her legs and I moaned.

She was ready. She was always ready. I tried not to be flattered by it because she was just good at her job... but *fuck*. I slid my finger into my mouth and she tilted her hips up to me as she slid her hands over my ass digging her nails in firmly and I gritted my teeth.

She liked it rough when she liked it rough, but she liked it slow and deep too. Almost spiritual. She drove me crazy in the worst possible way.

I gave myself a mental shake. She was the khoraz, not me. Well, we both were.

I pushed into her velvet folds, slick and hot and she moaned parting those lips I could not help but slide my tongue into. The woman sucked on it and I moaned. She knew what men liked. She hit every spot when she was supposed to, made all the right moves and kept surprising me with her talents.

I withdrew. I needed her to stay, or I would stay. Wherever we were. I did not care anymore. I wanted to fuck her as the barghest again and again and again.

Gods be damned. She really *was* going to kill me. I did not see it coming. When she touched me, I felt alive. Electricity pulsed through my veins when our skin made contact.

A man could get addicted.

"What time do we have until?" I asked roughly as I felt her pulse with me deep inside her.

She liked my voice.

"Hm? As long as you want," she breathed.

Oh, I bet.

"How long were you told to stay or you stay as long as we are together? Do you know who purchased you?"

I barely got the sentence out. I hoped it made sense because I could not focus on anything but being inside her.

"Purchased?" She asked her turquoise eyes fluttering open.

She was playing coy. It pissed me off. Gods be damned Guardians and their games.

"Yes, *purchased*. What time did the madam tell you to return to the brothel? Do you have other clients today?"

I had stopped moving and her eyes were wide as she blinked at me. She put her hands against my chest as she scanned my eyes.

"Slate. What are you talking about? Brothel? That's not funny," she said, trying to grimace, but it looked like a pout with those lips.

"Enough games. I am asking if you are booked. I want you to stay another night. I am not accustomed to paying for the pleasures of khorazes, but you are —"

She slapped me. Hard. My head jerked as she shoved me off her and I grabbed the seax under the pillow and slammed her back on the bed. She yelped when I held the knife to her throat, pricking the skin so a bead of blood welled down the blade. It was wickedly sharp. She gaped at me.

"If this is some kind of payback for being with Brass, it's not funny. You're going to hurt me," she said, jutting out her jaw like Jett did.

"You can fuck who you want, *khoraz*. Did someone send you? Tell me and I shall release you unharmed if you go quietly," I said to her.

Curse my cock. Her naked underneath me would not let it go down.

I would have to interrogate her before we could continue. I had no choice with her possible plot in motion. She was not volunteering information, so I would have to force her to talk.

Her brow creased. "Have you completely lost it? It's me, Scarlett. Your *wife*. You spent the last month wrongfully imprisoned in Karkinos. Shale *died* rescuing you."

I slapped her hard enough, so she knew not to lie again and she cried out.

Shale was not dead. I saw her yesterday with Ama.

What the fuck was she saying!

She turned back to me and I pressed the seax back at her throat. Her gaze was hard and cold and I wanted to plunge into her again.

"Never ever strike me unless we're sparring and hope your blades are sharper than mine because I'm going to make you pay dearly for that."

I felt cowed and I hated it. The haughty bitch had made me feel regretful.

I should not have hit her.

"Do not lie again. I will not harm you. Tell me who sent you," I growled.

She nocked up her chin so she could look down her nose at me. "No one. This is the Dagr palace. I had the wing redone for us." She shifted and slowly held up her wedding ring.

My mother's emerald ring. I growled and pressed the blade into her throat.

"How did you get that?"

"You gave it to me when you asked me to share your life," she said through gritted teeth.

"Bullshit."

"You're Slate Dagr. My mother adopted you and my grandmother Pearl raised you. We married after my father's funeral at the Var castle. You're wearing his wedding band. If you do not take that blade from my throat I'll be forced to fight you. I don't want to jeopardize my children,

Slate. Don't make me do it," she said, sounding truly loathe to have to hurt me as if she could.

I looked at my ring finger and sure enough. A wedding band. I blinked at its stone finish. She knew I was a Dagr. Problem was, the Dagr palace was abandoned. What she said was impossible.

She was clever as well as drop dead gorgeous. While I was distracted, she started on fire. Her whole body.

She was a fire elemental! Churning fire burned in the shape of her body and her hair writhed around her face. Her turquoise eyes had turned into hot coals. More importantly, she had burned my cock.

I flew off her, dropping the knife and clutching myself with gritted teeth. "Fucking bitch!"

She got to her feet, and the flames died. She touched her hand to her throat, and they came away bloody. She was regal, standing there naked, looking down at me.

"Are you finished? If you don't want to be with me anymore, that's fine. Calling me a bitch and a khoraz? You have never ever spoken to me like that. I'll be damned if I tolerate it now. You have no idea what I went through to get you back." Her face tightened, and I noticed she was trembling.

I lunged hitting her around the middle and she screamed.

"The babies, Slate!"

I didn't give a shit about her babies. I pinned her arms above her head and growled at her throat. I should kill her now. Tear out her throat and let her sweet, hot blood pour down my gullet. The beast would love that or would've if she hadn't tricked me into claiming her. Her pulse raced in the artery in her neck and my tongue slid out to lick along it.

"Whom do you work for? This is the last time I will ask nicely, if I have to ask again, you will force my hand. I do not want to hurt you, but you should not know I am a Dagr. You should not know I am a barghest, but I will take blame for that." I said in my softest most dangerous tone.

She sniffed. "How *big* of you. I suppose I forced you to shift?"

"You are a fucking barghest khoraz. I smell the brands on you. One barghest was not enough? I admit you have the stamina. I had believed them all extinct but me. Your employer must have trained you exceptionally well to ensnare barghests and bring them out of hiding," I growled.

Blood welled over the blade and she sneered.

I heard the crash of a door being thrown open and I thought, this was it. She was supposed to distract me until her back up came to kill me.

I grabbed her by her hair and lifted her to her feet to use her as a shield if they *called* first and questioned later. Strangely, she grabbed a sheet with her and wrapped it around her body with one hand while grabbing my fist with the other. I pulled her to her tip toes and pushed her forward, blade at her throat.

Brass, Quick, Jett, and Steel burst into the bedroom and I heard female voices. My brothers-in-arms gaped, appalled at us and I narrowed my eyes. Steel turned and hurried to the women coming into the wing.

"We'll take care of it. Better if you don't see this," he said in a calming tone.

"Scarlett was screaming. *I* take care of Scarlett, not you." A saucy woman argued.

"Tawny, by the Mother, trust me. Don't let anyone else in here. I'm serious. Can you handle that?" Steel asked sternly and was greeted by speculative silence. She must have nodded because Steel charged back into the room.

"What the fuck are you doing?" Jett asked, wide eyed staring at the khoraz.

"Who let her in here? She knows about the barghest, she knows about my heritage. She is a crazy khoraz. If this was supposed to be a joke, I do not find it amusing."

Eyes bulged, and I started to doubt myself. The khoraz sniffled, and I realized she was crying.

"Gods, she is good." I gave her a shake and all the men lifted their hands as if to take her from me.

"He thinks I'm a spy. He doesn't know who I am." I heard the dejection in her wavering voice.

I yanked her tight and Jett winced. "I know exactly who you are. A fucking khoraz sent by the Stygian Knights to distract me. You are good at your job. Damn good. *Salvation comes from the shamed daughter's babe.*

Temptation takes shape, her love lights the flame. The son of the beast is finally claimed. In his blood, destiny takes aim."

She gasped. It was the prophecy my mother had when I was born.

Their faces seemed to redden and darken. What was going on? Brass's jaw was clenched as he took a step towards us.

"Let her go. Everything she said was true. You've been through much as of late, and I can tell you do not have all the facts. We'll sit down and fill you in on the gaps." Brass beckoned me forth and to give him the girl.

Never let it be said I was stubborn.

I shoved her, and she collided into Brass's arms and burst into sobs. I *called* my pants from where she'd pulled them off by the closet and sat on the bed to yank them on. They were all staring.

Brass was healing her and she clung to him like a child. She had gotten to them all. Putty in her hands.

I grunted. "If she is my wife as she claims, why is she fucking you? Why is she carrying your fucking sons?"

Brass stiffened. He had never looked at me like that. Was he going to attack me? I shook my head trying to clear it and only succeeded in making my headache worse.

"She *is* your wife. It is a long story," Brass said.

Jett's fists clenched and unclenched as he looked at me. Steel had his hand on Jett's shoulder keeping him in place and I arched my scared brow at him.

"There is no way that is your sister. I read those letters from our mother with you. *That* girl was innocent and sweet, too sweet. This one does not have an innocent bone in her body, though she is very sweet."

I meant to diffuse the palpable tension. She could not be who she said she was, how could they not see it? Instead, Quick let out a low whistle as the other men looked ready to kill me.

All over a woman. If one that encompassed every man's fantasy wrapped in the guise of a goddess.

"Freya's burly boar. I hope you do not get your memory back," Quick said rubbing a hand over his mouth. "You are not going to believe this, but everything he says... he thinks it is true. Sorry, Scarlett."

The woman they kept calling Scarlett, but was not her, pushed from Brass to look at me. I would not shy away from a woman no matter how powerful she was. I rose to my feet to tower over her with her fierce little expression on that tear-streaked beautiful face like a siren luring men to their deaths. I asked her.

"Can you sing?"

She gave me that same superior look. "Why? Do you know many khoraz *bitches* with exceptional singing abilities? Does that make me a spy as well?"

How she made the bed sheet look like a queenly robe, I would never know. I chuckled at her joke and her nostrils flared.

"I thought you might be a siren here to lure me to my death. I knew who you were the moment I saw you. Death personified in this goddess of temptation. Perhaps I will call you Siren since you have my friends here fooled, if I slit your throat as I intended, likely they will not forgive me."

"Torch," she said coolly.

"Excuse me?"

"You call me Torch. As in the blues singers. As in, your light in the darkness. As in, when you are lost, I lead the way and give you hope. You carry a torch for me." She sucked in a ragged breath.

I stared at her a moment longer before I burst into laughter. Her lips popped open and she looked distraught.

"That is quite the load of bullshit. I would never say such things to a woman, let alone one like *you*."

"Like me?" she asked, shaking off Brass's hand.

I stepped closer so she had to crane her neck back. "A barghest fucking khoraz," I whispered and her eyes went wide. "One who fucks my friends."

I expected her to try to hit me, but she stepped back so Brass caught her. He helped her in the direction of the bathroom and I sat back down on the bed scooting to the headboard and crossed my ankles as I folded my arms behind my head.

"Give it to me straight. Who paid for that crazy bitch, because you should get half your money back at least for this absurdity. On second thought, she was worth it. Still, file a complaint with her madam."

"My sister is not a fucking khoraz, you smug bastard!" Veins popped on Jett's neck as his face turned a splotchy red shade.

Jett had cracked.

FOUR

I hated vomit. I had vomited enough for two lifetimes. I hated pregnancy.

I could hear Slate bad-mouthing me to Jett, Steel, and Quick and it was shattering my heart into a million pieces. Slate had called me a bitch. He thought I was a khoraz. He'd smelled Peak on me and hadn't even cared. Even though he thought I was a spy, he still wanted me to stay another day so he could keep fiddlesticking me.

He'd offered to *pay* me for sex.

Somehow, it was worse than what Peak had done, worse than the Merfolk. I'd slept with Slate thinking he was my husband and he loved me, but I had no idea who that monstrous man was in there.

He'd never told me about his prophecy before.

Brass rubbed my back until he left to get me some clothes and came back with a glass of water and a fresh dress.

"Thanks," I said numbly, and I wiped the blood off my throat before I dropped my sheet and started to pull on a blush pink chiffon dress with off the shoulder sleeves and a sweetheart neckline.

"This is my favorite," I said, running my fingers through my hair.

"That is why I chose it. It is my favorite too," Brass said, holding his chin between his thumb and index finger.

He'd made no point of looking away as I changed and I didn't care. He'd kissed me before I'd gone to Slate yesterday afternoon. We were looking less like a love triangle today and more like an obtuse angle.

"I thought I said not to stay nearby," I told him as I turned around.

Brass shrugged. "So you did. I felt something off yesterday and thought you would be able to tell after a while. I was wrong."

"We didn't do much talking as he would be quick to inform you."

"Do not listen to him. He does not know what he is saying." Brass switched gears just like that and he was pulling me back into his arms.

"This is worse than if he had died," I whispered.

"Do not say that, we will set him straight," Brass reassured me.

I drew back. "I want to know what he thinks is going on. Beside you know, that I'm a whore and a bitch and a barghest fiddlesticker – which was wonderful to hear from him."

Brass put his arm around my shoulders as he led me back into the bedroom. "We are going to fix this. If not, I will hold him down and you can beat him. He deserves it after trying to kill you."

I sighed.

Jett saw me and pulled me away from Brass and held me tight. "That bastard."

"I'm fine, Jett. Hurt, because my husband thinks I'm a *whore*, but my body is fine."

"I call it like I see it and how I *fuck* it," Slate said with a smug grin of his full lips.

I let my lips curl. "Fine. I'm a whore. What else do you have, Dagr?"

I beckoned him with my fingers urging him on and *called* over the bench from my vanity to sit across from where he sat on the bed.

"If you are not a rousen trained khoraz, then I am a Crathode," Slate said bitingly, and I laughed.

"I suppose I *am* rousen trained. By Dion're, Non're, and Larn'ra... then you. What else?" I asked, crossing my legs and straightening my skirts.

"You admit it."

"I was taken by the Merfolk and given rousen for three nights against my will. I was trained, I suppose, while I was there. You helped wean me off when I was rescued," I answered. "I'm your khoraz and none other," I conceded with a tight swallow.

Slate's bronze brow drew down. That silver scar threw me. He smelled like my husband with his crisp fallen leaves, spicy cloves, and musky scent; all Slate. He had a new collection of scars over his tall, broad muscled, bronze body. I'd wrapped my fingers in his long wavy midnight mane, let the silver beads slip through my knuckles and over my thighs. His predatory gaze, intensely carnal, and primitive was his. Silver flashing eyes and soft grey now that he was calmer. The way his body had moved with mine was the same, it's countless hard ridges of muscle. I would know the feel of the roped muscles that formed the 'V' at his hips and the firm round fanny pack of his even if I was deaf, blind, and mute.

He was my Slate, but not.

The way he looked at me had a hardness to it. He didn't trust me. Worse. He didn't even *like* me. There was no love, other than for what my body could do for him, in his gaze.

"Truth," Quick confirmed.

Slate's face was chiseled, the hard planes of his cheeks could've been carved from marble with a nose so masculine and symmetrical the most talented artist would have cried in shame as they tried to duplicate it. I'd made sure he was well groomed so his strong jaw was clean shaven. The only way you could tell he'd even been through something was the scar. It helped me. My Slate but injured. He hadn't meant those things. He couldn't have.

"Quit looking at me like that, girl or else we will have to ask these fine fellows to leave. I would not mind another day or two in you. I have already asked how much."

Slate's mocking smile made me irate. Thank the Gods I had never known the extent of his cache holeness.

Steel's grip tightened on Jett's shoulder and Quick slowly shook his head as Brass's hands curled into fists.

"Any affection my gaze holds for you is not for the man you *are*, but for the man you *were*. I want my husband back," I said frostily and Slate laugh was deep and rich making my toes want to curl.

"Affection? You want to —"

"Stop," I snapped. "You obviously have no respect for me. I can hardly blame you since... I thought I was giving myself to my husband. Not... a knuckle dragging barbarian, so enough. Whatever you think of me, I'm Jett's sister and Steel's niece. Brass...and Quick are my friends and they deserve a little respect. You are pissing them off the way you're speaking to me. Does that not tell you something?"

"It does. You have gotten to them. You are under their skin, and have brainwashed Brass. Really, I am surprised in you, brother. Not that I can blame you, I could not think either when she —"

"It's not cute or funny!" My facade crumbled as I shouted at him.

Quick took a step forward to come next to Slate where he laid on our big white bed. He put his hand to his head and delved.

"He is healthy. Just an asshole," Quick said, giving Slate a puckish smile.

Brass left my side and walked over as Quick shoved Slate's legs over and sat. Brass delved.

"There is a mental block. Not erased, suppressed. That is a rare talent. They had probably done it so he would have nothing to fight for." Brass turned to me. "They essentially erased his memory of you. What is the last thing you remember?"

Slate's eyes slid to me. "Fucking Cordillera the night before the masquerade."

My blood boiled.

"Well, that explains it. You are your old self again. Pre-Scarlett. I do not think she ever saw this side of you," Quick said, leaning back on his palms.

Slate gave him a wry grin with those full lips. "How did I manage that?"

"You had to be *nice*. You met her at the masquerade, when you were not supposed to meet her until the morning after at Pearl's," Quick said.

I interrupted, "You cornered me in the bathroom. Forced me to kiss you under the mistletoe and then snuck into my bedroom that night."

"So why did I keep seeing you after I got what I wanted?" Slate asked with that gods be damned arrogant smile.

Jett moved to put his hands on my shoulders and I felt him *call* to check on the twins. "She didn't want you, you bastard. She started dating Ash Straumr."

Slate chuckled. "Of course she did. Look at her, conceited and self-important. What an *advantageous* match for Ash Straumr. Why did I get stuck with her?"

I snorted. "You chased me for a year before I relented. I never slept with you until *after* you proposed to me."

Slate ran his index finger down his jaw. "Why were you so easy this time then?"

Indignation fueled my fire, and I felt my eyes flare. "I thought you were my husband! I am not a whore!" I shouted, balling my hands into fists.

I wanted to punch him in his stupid, smug face.

"How many? Can you even remember?"

"Men?" I asked incredulous, he gave a nod and gestured for me to continue.

"Four," I answered curtly.

"Hundred?" he asked and Quick chuckled and then coughed to mask it.

I should have asked the others to leave, but if he attacked me again, I would need them to talk him down.

"Four human men," I said through gritted teeth.

Slate arched a scarred brow. "How many Merfolk?"

"No —" Brass interrupted.

"I don't know. Just three, I think. They heavily drugged me," I said, taking a fortifying breath.

"How many barghests?" he asked with a sly smile.

It was the question he was getting at. "Two," I whispered and Jett's hands stilled on my shoulders.

Slate leaned back and gestured towards me. "I told you. A barghest khoraz. I did not even know women like her existed. I thought we were extinct. I have been with over a hundred women and only this one has been with two barghests. If that should not make me suspicious, I do not know what would. The first one must have trained her how to seduce me and sent her to kill or distract me."

I spluttered gripping the bench edge. "A hundred!"

Slate smiled smugly at me and a little part of me died as I sank back against the chair.

"A hundred," I muttered. "That was before you went to Valla U where you added at least half of the first years and the second years…"

My heart sunk into a pitch-black abyss. I was another notch on this man's belt as I always feared. It wasn't the first time I was glad I'd given myself to Brass first.

A hundred?

"Scar, who is the other barghest? Is that number four? I thought you'd only been with these two and Chris," Jett asked, coming around the bench.

Jett was as big as Slate. Our father was tall and broad too. Jett's eyes were just like mine and Steel's, big turquoise almonds against our tan skin. Jett's mouth was full like our father's, so was Steel's. Those two could have passed for twins. Jett's dark blonde hair was cropped close to his scalp and his face was chiseled like our father's had been with a square jaw, but his lips and prettily lashed eyes softened his otherwise features. Steel's face wasn't as severe and he was a half foot shorter than Slate and Jett. My mother's younger brother could have passed for her son.

Quick and Brass's posture had changed and Slate noticed it and became intrigued. Steel had come around to sit on the edge of the bed beside Quick. I did not think they would want to sit on it if they'd known what we'd been doing in it.

I nodded, meeting his level gaze with one of my own.

"When? He couldn't have been from Chicago if he was barghest," Jett said pointedly.

Quick and Brass were staring at me wanting to help. To offer some sort of explanation that would stop the truth from coming out.

If Slate already thought I was a whore, then I supposed it wouldn't matter. If Jett found out I'd been assaulted, he'd leave that instant and kill Peak. In the end, my love for my brother and the other men who would feel obligated to avenge my honor won out.

I lifted my chin. "While Slate was captured, Brass and I weren't seeing one another until… I was with Peak."

I straightened the skirts of my dress again and crossed my legs placing my clasped hands in my lap. Bile rose in my throat.

"*Wow*. Thank you for letting me wed this one, brothers," Slate said, crossing his arms over his chest, but something flickered in his eyes.

Was he jealous? The notion was ridiculous after how he'd been speaking to me.

"It's over. It does not matter," Brass said, leaning against the wall.

"Does not matter? Scar, you're not going to see him again, right?" Jett asked, squatting in front of me. "For the Mother's sake! Brass, you have every right to be pissed off at her. She's carrying your sons! Does he know he's been coming to Valla U calling you *sweet* Scarlett for all of Tidings to find out?"

"What I do in the bedroom is not your concern, Jett," I tried to scold.

"You are very good. The best. You managed to get two barghests to shift and claim you," Slate said plainly and I glowered.

"I did not trick you. It's not my fault you can't control yourself. Frankly, if it was that easy, I'm surprised you didn't claim Lera," I snapped and Jett and Quick sucked in breaths and looked away.

I hit a sore spot I didn't know existed.

Slate swung his legs off the side of the bed and rose. I folded my arms over my chest hoping he felt like a peasant in my queenly court of judgement.

"If Lera let me fuck her six ways from Sunday and asked me to claim her, I would have. She has too much respect for herself for that. Unlike you," he growled.

I scoffed though he'd cut something crucial inside me. "I'm all or nothing. I give myself or I don't. I don't put restrictions on the love I give and I expect the same in return. That is why I'm *so* good. Part of it might be skill, but I pour myself into my actions. If I love you, you feel it. When I love or make love, it's with all of me and my lovers feel that. They feel special. What I feel with you, is used and dirty. I did the first time and I do now. It's a wonder any woman ever returns to your bed. Never *ever* have I been happier to have Brass be the first man I'd lain with. If you had just left me alone *we'd* be happily married! I never would have gone back to Ash, I never would have been taken by the Merfolk, my father, Ama, Shale and countless others might still be alive, and I would only have made love to one *single* man, as I'd intended! I gave up everything for you!" I slapped my hand over my mouth. "I didn't mean that," I breathed, disgusted with my finger pointing.

Slate's head whipped to Brass who was furiously rubbing his lips together. I rose and walked to the closet.

I shouldn't have said that. He was hurting me and I had wanted to hurt him back. I was the bigger person. I always had been and I let myself lose control. I didn't mean any of it. I was angry... no excuse my mind conjured justified my vicious words.

I stepped into a pair of nude wedges and grabbed the small bag I had put my weapons in as well as a few changes of clothes and my boots. I exited the closet and found them all sitting in silence.

"Scar, where are you going?" Steel asked, getting to his feet.

"I'm not running. I promise. I need to punch something." I turned to Slate. "Until we work this out, I would appreciate it if you do not bed other women. If you can contain yourself for a day or so that should be enough. If you want to leave our marriage bed, that is fine too, but you will not be allowed to return if you do. I will not be married to a philanderer. I promise to do the same. If after they fill in the gaps of your memory and you still don't remember or you have no wish to be with me. You are free to go. No strings attached. I had your things moved here so you will have to pack yourself a bag when you leave." My eyes flitted to Brass and back to Slate. "I've sacrificed enough for you for ten lifetimes."

"I will not be staying. The staff will move my belongings back to the Sumar palace. I will not be party to this farce." Slate said with a look that felt like the fatal blow that would end my life. "Please feel free to continue fucking my friends."

I started to leave the bedroom but paused without looking to them. "So be it. This business with Peak... please don't tell anyone. I'm not proud of it."

CHAPTER 5
JETT

"You stupid bastard," Jett growled at Slate.

Steel wiped a hand over his face and Quick's face had darkened.

"Did you know about Peak?" Jett asked Brass and he nodded.

Jett sat on the bench Scarlett had been in and held his head in his hands. "I don't believe it. She doesn't... She can't. She's incapable of it. She fell in love with that bastard." He pointed to Slate. "Chris moved in with her and proposed and-"

Brass looked at Jett dryly and Slate grunted. "I am curious. Why would you sleep with my wife? If she is who she claims to be."

Brass pursed his lips. When Slate said it like that it sounded pretty damn bad.

"I fell in love with her, too. She has that effect."

Slate let out an exhale. "She has blinded you all. You especially, with her face, and that body. I place no blame. She has a vulnerability that makes you want to —"

Slate cut off and glowered as if we forced the words into his mouth. One night.

That's all it took for Scarlett to ensnare Slate who thought he hadn't met her before. Jett shook his head with a laugh.

"Not an appropriate time for a laugh, Jett," Steel said.

"This is just too ludicrous. She didn't sleep with Peak for that arena, did she?" Jett regretted his words the moment he'd said them.

"She is your cursed sister. If anyone knows how prudish she can be, it is you. She would never be with a man for a payment. *Now* to protect someone she loves... she would do anything," Quick said with a sigh.

"By the Mother, you are not in love with her too, are you?" Slate asked.

Quick glared at him. "I admire her and you are a Gods' cursed fool for speaking to her that way. Entertaining though it was, she will not forget. There is at least a score of men who are lined up waiting for you to screw this up so they can steal her away from you. Ash Straumr never gave up on her. We cannot go anywhere with her without drawing her admirers."

"I am first in that line," Brass said, facing Slate. "Hurt her, abuse her, do anything, but right by her and I will take her away. I have always cleaned up your messes where she is concerned. You and I made a bargain. You get to marry her. I was allowed to be close to her and when your prophecy came true and you passed, I would take care of her and raise your children as my own. You and I swore blood oaths. You married her with a blood oath so I can never be her sworn husband in Tidings, but I can outside of Tidings. If you break her heart, I will take her back to where she lived in Chicago and, so help me Slate, I will marry her in their way and you will never reach her again. She has my children in her, but she feels too Gods be damned guilty about leaving you to let me near her. You have no idea how I have to tip toe around afraid she'll push me away. My *sons*. You know how hard it has been for me to find women who does not constantly think about other men. I would kill for the devotion she shows you. I should kill you for how you treated her with my sons growing inside her," he ground out.

Jett stared in shocked silence. Slate regarded Brass with a steely gaze.

"You can have her with my blessing. Any fool can see how much you care for her, despite —"

"Not another word. Do not even think to ask her about the Merfolk again. I will not listen to it. I don't do it yet because she needs closure with you. That, or for you to love her the way she deserves to be," Brass answered.

"She fucked my uncle," Slate said.

Jett cocked a brow. Was that jealousy? Barghests couldn't possibly be the sharing kind. By the Mother, what had Scarlett been thinking?

"And you were with a hundred and fifty women. Was it necessary for you to tell her? She has never met *this* man. From the moment you met her, you had tried to get her to come around. It was amusing at first and then we realized you actually cared for her. Be *that* man." Brass said.

"What about you, Quick?" Slate asked.

"Scarlett and I have not always seen eye to eye, but a better, more loyal woman as beautiful as she would be hard to find for you. Do not think I am rooting for you. She has my nephews growing in her and my brother has been smitten since they met."

Slate smiled roguishly at him. "You have all changed. Soon you will quote poetry, Quick. What girl have you entangled with to —"

As if summoned, Indigo and Tawny burst into the room. Tawny's wide hazel eyes zeroed in on Slate. Her fair heart-shaped face flushed; her wide full mouth pinched into a little rosebud.

"You!" She stabbed a finger at Slate and tossed her long dark waves as she stormed over to him.

A couple inches over five feet, the little spitfire was even to Slate's eyes from where he sat on the bed. She slapped him as hard as she could and his head barely moved. Steel was already grabbing her around the middle pulling her away.

"Tawny, right?" Slate asked, flexing his jaw. He looked to Indigo who was staring daggers at him. "What is Indigo Var doing here? Is her group not the upper crust of greater families? Or has she come over to our band of miscreants?" Slate leered.

Indigo gasped and looked at Quick.

Slate looked at Quick and held his stomach as he laughed. "I do not believe it! Her blood is a little too rich for the likes of us."

Indigo looked affronted, and she moved to sit next to Quick where Steel had just leapt from. She put her hand on his thigh possessively and gave Slate an impressive glare.

"I am Indigo *Tio*, not Var. Jett is my brother, Scarlett is my twin and *you* are an ass," she said with that same regal manner Scarlett had adopted since becoming Cordillera's delegate.

"And my future wife," Quick added and Indigo's smugness faltered.

"Lover," Indigo amended and Quick wrapped his arm around her slender shoulders.

Jett rolled his eyes. "Sometime lover, sometime worst enemy. You two are —"

"Droll," Brass murmured.

"And who does that one belong to?" Slate asked, watching Tawny and Steel attempt to glare one another into submission.

"Tawny and Steel are married. I married Cherry and Amethyst. I had a daughter last spring and Cherry is pregnant again, due next spring same as Scarlett and Brass's sons. Quick and my little sister Indigo are off and on since last Yuletide. You married Scarlett last December. Wren and Alder Var are dead. Killed by the Stygian Knights. Alder was our father. That was the night Scarlett was delivered to the Merfolk, to the Merfolk prince Non're. She'd turned him down, and he had a vendetta against her. He kept her drugged on rousen until she managed to activate your bond and you led us to her after Sear're confirmed she was there," Jett spouted out as if a blunt rendition had made it easier to speak. It didn't. It simply waited until he inhaled to punch him in the guts.

"She bonded me! Was I drugged?" Slate admonished.

Quick started laughing hysterically and even Jett smiled. Brass's eyes softened.

"You had me bring Dhole to her room while she was unconscious and had her bonded," Brass told him and Slate gaped.

"Where is it?" Slate asked and Brass pointed to his chin.

Slate exhaled roughly. "So, I would have to kiss her to deactivate it. That sounds like something I would do if she was resisting me."

Brass held up his ring finger to display the tiwaz rune. "I bonded her as well."

"You bonded my mate!" Slate roared.

You could hear a pin drop.

"And hand-fasted her. In her defense, she did not know that was what we were doing." It was Brass's turn to look smug. "You should not have sworn the blood oath. That was not part of the agreement." Brass rubbed his lips together. "Slate, you took a second wife who was pregnant with your child. She was killed by Nirrin the night you were captured. Amber Lodda."

"I do not know who that is," Slate growled. "I do not know how to grieve for a wife and child I knew nothing about."

"You did not like her," Quick said as if that offered some explanation.

"Did I develop a taste for rich little girls?" Slate asked rhetorically and Tawny sniffed.

"You stalked Scarlett. Breaking into her room at night, *begging* her not to marry Ash. She left us all so you could have children with that twit! All the stupid things she did, for you! What did you say to her, you Neanderthal? Why was she crying?" Tawny accused.

Slate looked like he could use some air.

"Girls. Could you give us some time? Please. Go to the Sumar palace and tell Pearl and Sparrow he's awake and get lunch ready. We'll fill him in and bring him over. Tell the girls to dress Gigi up for her uncle Slate," Jett said, giving them his best grin and Indigo rolled her eyes as she smiled.

Quick grabbed her hand as she rose from the bed. "I will go with you."

She snatched her hand back. "We don't actually have to make lunch. You're not needed there," she hissed.

Quick got to his feet and looked down his nose at her, Indigo licked her lips. "I am coming with, or without your consent, Dove. Things are going to change."

Indigo's eyes scanned his. "Well, come if you're coming. We'll talk about it there." She spun so her blonde locks smacked him in the face, but Quick looked as if she'd just professed her undying love to him.

The poor sap.

Indigo, Quick, and Tawny left and Gypsum entered. He'd turn twenty this coming year and at Yuletide, he'd be inducted into Valla U. The first step to being proven tried and true and becoming a Guardian for Mother Nature. We were the ones who kept balance across the world. We had Guardians everywhere who tended for the Mother. Her most devout Guardians were chosen to become wights who would live on as sentient beings of nature to look over their own lands. Wren and

Alder were one wight; two souls bound in an oak tree in Mabon. They had no memory of their past life, only their love for one another.

Gypsum was as tall as Steel with the same lean, swimmer's build. Scarlett called him chief for his dark features and long black hair that he now wore copper beads threaded through like Slate's. The kid was a killer with the ladies. He wasn't taking Ama and Shale's deaths well; he'd been lover to them both.

The kid flashed Slate a dimpled smile that made girls go all gooey and clasped his forearm. Slate had only seen Gypsum in pictures, as far as he was concerned. The truth was, Slate had taken Gypsum under his wing like a little brother and Gypsum worshipped the ground he walked on.

"Judging from the girls' reactions. Things aren't so good, huh?" Gyps sat in Quick's spot on the bed.

"Amnesia of a sort. Some Guardian has a talent for mental blocks and erased Scarlett and all the time since she arrived in Tidings from his mind," Steel said.

Gypsum's dark eyes rounded. "You don't remember me then? Or Scarlett or Amber?" Gypsum started to run down the list of things Slate didn't remember.

It was a long list and then he came to Shale and Ama.

"Shale and Ama. They're dead. Shale died rescuing you and Ama died in the Wemic village saving the pups. Jorogumo attacked with the Stygians when they captured you." Gypsum said in a thick low voice.

"Scarlett mentioned it," Slate said in a rumble. "She was not lying?"

Slate knew better, but he needed to hear it again. Jett could understand that. He'd lost almost two years' worth of memories in which he had found the woman he loved, lost her, and won her back. As far as he was concerned, he was still a tomcat on the prowl living a half-life, not taking anything seriously and they were telling him that everything he knew was wrong.

"She was not lying," Jett said in a soft tone. "Slate, I don't know why, but-"

Tree-gold jumped onto the bed and Slate stared at the twenty-five-pound white long-haired cat with green too-intelligent eyes. The thing was a monster.

"We have a fucking skogkatt?" Slate lifted his eyes to them, but Tree sauntered over to Brass who reached down and lifted the fatty up to scratch her head.

"She chooses Brass. When Brass lived in Chicago with Scarlett, Tree fell in love with him," Gypsum said with a dimpled smile.

"Gypsum is a zoolinguist," Steel said, sounding exasperated. "If you see him speaking with squirrels, he's not crazy. It only looks that way when he starts laughing when a dog walks past."

Gypsum gave a rueful grin. "Dogs tell the best jokes."

"The cat does not even like me," Slate growled.

"Can't blame her," Brass said.

"Let's give you a tour of your wing of the Dagr palace," Jett said, needing to get out of the bedroom that smelled like sex and Scarlett.

The bedroom was dominated by the oversized white bed. A modern down comforter laid across it and billowing sheer white panels that were swathed around the bed in a canopy. Piles of pillows ran along the white upholstered headboard. The walls were a pale green with a white chaise and a long-distressed dresser which had our mother's pictures in glass frames as well as intimate pictures of Slate and Scarlett kissing. Light pink peonies sat in vases to either side of the bed at the nightstands.

Slate picked up a picture of him and Scarlett in an intimate embrace which they were both smiling as they kissed on a white bed. From the photo, you could tell they either just had sex or this was the foreplay. Brass skipped the bedroom photo display and walked into the dining room.

The bathroom was attached to the bedroom and similar to the one at the Sumar palace. Dozens of shower heads were built right into the tiffany blue tiles, the waterfall separated the shower from the rest of the bathroom was activated by an energy plate when you used *calling*. Two white ornate mirrors hung above the ivory sinks in front of the huge ivory clawed foot tub that would fit both Slate and Scar easily. Bright pink floral accents decorated the bathroom giving it a feminine touch.

They'd save the two doors in the hall for last. The dining room had enough room for a circular table that sat six; the same white oak wood as the coffee table. The chairs were upholstered in the same dusky blue as the living room with a white hutch. One of their mother's paintings hung on the wall across from the collection Moroccan lanterns that hung in whites and blues above the round pedestal table.

White marbled tiles spanned the floor of the light dusky blue front room, a soft beige couch and oversized chair occupied the front room throw pillows in varying shades of creams scattered across them. The sheer curtains blowing across the floor from the open arched doors that led to the covered walkway before the cloister. A rectangular light wood table sat before it on a modern white and beige rug.

"Did she do all this?" Slate asked, leaning on the frame of the arched doors to look out at the cloister that rested at the center of the Romanesque styled Dagr palace.

"You did first. Scarlett was pregnant before and she accepted your proposal, but you nearly slept with Mirage who came to you as Scarlett to hurt her. The bond was active and Scarlett felt it all. She decided to go back to Ash, that was when Alder was murdered," Steel said, sitting on the beige couch.

"When she left you after finding out you needed to continue the Dagr line, you trashed the wing you'd designed for you both. She replicated it here. Come on. There's another room." Jett led Slate alone back to the hall. "This one's a bathroom." He pointed to the door on the right and then opened the left door.

It was a nursery. Sea foam green walls and two off-white crib and dresser complete with changing table. An off-white plush chair sat in the corner piled with stuffed animals next to a short bookcase filled with bright colored titles. A wood carved rocking horse sat to the side, a picture of Wren and Scarlett was framed of them picnicking at the lake.

Above the first crib was one of the paintings their mother had sold right before they moved. Sparrow had tracked a bunch down, that one was her favorite. It was the tree of life with deep curling roots, a blazing golden sun shone down on a cat and a deer dancing next to a pond a mermaid leaned from. A second painting was above the next crib. Slate walked over to it and ran his hand over the dark character. It was a whimsical painting of a merman sitting astride a Centaur with the solar cross of the Dagr sigil in the sky and a lion hybrid with a black beast.

"Scarlett painted it for your hand-fasted wife."

"If I did not care for her, why would I marry her?" Slate asked, not taking his eyes off the painting.

"Amber? She looks like Scarlett. We all thought you started seeing her because Scarlett turned you down. When Scarlett left you after you were married, you wouldn't see other women. Scarlett set it up through Indigo so Amber would be around when you went out. She came home with you one night and she proposed to you. You accepted and were hand-fasted. You did the ribbon ceremony and everything. Scarlett didn't know what getting the bond on the vein of love meant," Jett told Slate.

Slate moved Alder's band and saw the love rune tattooed there. "Who painted this? Did she?" Slate asked.

"She did."

Slate smiled. "This is my form as a barghest. The lion is Keen, I recognize the Centaur as the clan leader Cordillera uses as an informant, Lewt. That Merfolk is Sear're. Did she paint the other as well?"

"No. You had Sparrow find something suitable for a nursery from my mother's collection. This one is Scar's favorite. Slate, I haven't always supported your relationship with her, but give it a chance. I'd hate for you to get your memories back and have done something stupid," Jett said, pushing the rocking chair with his leather boot.

"Why erase her from my mind?" Slate asked, turning towards Jett.

Jett ran his hand over his close-cropped head. "Your guess is as good as mine, but if you're twisting my arm, I'd say it has something to do with having a Dagr heir and your prophecy. There's more. Come on. Brass can tell you what the Faunelle said."

Slate and Jett went back into the living room where a warm breeze blew in from the opened slatted doors along the covered pathway. Slate sat on the beige couch next to Brass and ran his palms over his lap.

"The Faunelle?"

Brass gave him a cool look. "You owe her an apology."

Slate narrowed silver eyes at Brass. "Done. I will not playhouse with her. Now tell me everything that happened."

"She is the key; you both are to a prophecy within the tribes. You are a beast they name the Grar Dyr. She is supposed to be the mother of your son, the daughter of spring and summer. You need to find nine pieces of a works we know nothing about — including where it is or what it is. She has three pieces so far. She can't do it alone. Lera said she would send out Breakers to look for this works."

"Lera knows the girl?" Slate asked in disbelief.

Brass gave him a wry smile. "She's second in command at head-quarters, answerable only to Lera. Chafer and Lera are an item now."

"I do not want to break any of these nice things. I am going to head-quarters," Slate growled and walked towards the bedroom.

Brass and Jett met eyes. "Are you going to do as she asked?"

"Which part?" Slate called out.

"Any of it." Jett wanted to throttle him.

"Stay here? Not fuck other women? All that?" Slate rumbled.

"Yes, *all that*," Brass said in a measured tone.

Slate came back into the living room buckling his wrist blades on. "These are nice. Mine?"

"Scarlett got them for you after you were inducted into Valla U," Gypsum said.

"Of course she did. She knows me well, apparently." Slate looked around. "Except for this place. This is all her." His expression grew serious as he sank back in the sofa chair. "It is strange to think Guardians know about my heritage. Do they think she is my wife?"

"Sparrow tried to have a funeral for you and Scarlett absorbed the pyre with her elemental powers and announced that you two were married, and that you were alive. Those arenas she is set to build were to find you," Jett explained.

"How so?"

"She needed access to each of the islands and since her and Lera are so chummy she thought it would be a good front for the Shadow Breakers and give them security duty. She also... cares about Brass and Quick so she's placing them in charge of them."

Slate's eyes slid to Brass. "I cannot stay with the girl who kills me. Any woman who loves me is a fool." Slate shook his head. "It is better that we go our separate ways. The girl loves you."

Brass returned his stare. "She feels responsible for *you*. How can I compare to her husband, the man who weened her off rousen, and her first love? We struck a new bargain. Just before we left to the Wemic."

Brass rubbed his fingers along his forehead looking to the other men in the room. Jett knew the new bargain.

"Of course, now it doesn't work because Amber has passed." Brass leaned forward. "I'll take her anyway I can get her. You may not understand that now, but you will. If you help me get her to say her blood vows to me, I will help you so after she has my sons, she will have yours."

Steel looked to Jett wide eyed. It was a terrible plan.

Slate got to his feet. "I am hungry. We can go for lunch at Pearl's and see if Quick won his woman back. She does not seem to like him much."

SIX

That was exactly what I needed.

Chafer was one of the few people who would still spar with me since I was pregnant. He was careful enough to aim his hits around my stomach, but he never took it too easy on me. We sat side by side on the otherwise empty floor of the combat ring. I was missing Ama and Shale so badly my eyes would randomly blur with tears before I could rein back in my emotions.

Ama would have something positive to say about the situation like we got a chance to start new with no heartache. Shale would remind her in a dry tone that *I* still retained my memories, so it was twice as bad. Ama would thumb her nose behind Shale's back and get me to smile despite myself. Idly, I hoped Gypsum was okay.

The Crash Course had weapon racks and several combat rings. The left half had the Guillotine with all its razor-sharp blades. Tall trees stood in the center of the room looking like a small woods dividing the room. A simulated earthquake, with falling boulders was next, a lava pit with floating rocks on its surface after that, and wooden rafts that bobbed over crashing waves was its finale.

Stone stands wrapped around the arena that looked down on the course. A wrought-iron balustrade lined the ledge of the stands that kept people from falling in. The left half had two-way mirrors that hid Cordillera's suite as well as the patrons' rooms.

Chafer had sharp features undoubtedly as sharp as those long seaxes. Large brown almond eyes beneath thick slanted brows had a mischievous gleam that matched his wicked grin. There was not an ounce of fat to be found on Chafer's lean muscled body. He was average height, by Guardian standards, but stood a half foot taller than me. He was one of the most unpleasant people I'd ever met and I was proud to call him my friend.

"I wish I could have a beer." I sighed, wiping sweat off my brow with the back of my hand.

I leaned back on my palms and Chafer gave me a side glance. He held up his hand to offer healing, and I nodded. He placed his calloused hand directly on my stomach and I arched an eyebrow at him.

"You're not getting sentimental on me are you? Did you miss me, Chafer?" I teased.

The warmth of his healing ran through my veins. "I would never miss you." He said with glittering dark eyes. "What are you going to do about the councilor, delegate? You cannot let him get away with it. Eventually, he will corner you again. It is only a matter of time. Now that Slate is awake, he will find out."

His hand was still on me. I hadn't thought of much else since leaving the Dagr palace. Well, that, and the fact that Slate had been inside me when he held my own seax to my throat, that he called me a bitch and a whore after he tried to pay me for sex.

Yup, that pretty much summed it up.

"I want him dead for what he did, but does hurting me warrant death? I know his son, and he's not a bad guy. I wouldn't want to take his father away from him no matter how terrible a person he is."

Chafer snorted. "Motherhood is making you soft. It will be simple. I will mind blast him, then you will have the satisfaction of killing him while he is stunned."

I'd told Chafer that the babies were Brass's. I knew he'd tell

Cordillera. I didn't have the stomach to tell her I carried her nephew's sons while trying to make amends with Slate.

"Slate is here," I said, feeling his knot of emotions become more prominent in my mind.

Someone had slapped or punched him. Blood had activated the EH rune that bonded us. I wondered if he knew he had it, because it didn't seem he knew it was active. Chafer was careful not to activate mine. Gods, Slate had slapped me. Not hard, but it made me want to cry. I couldn't put my finger on why exactly, we'd sparred before and he'd sliced me with blades. Why would a little slap that didn't even leave a mark bother me so much? If he did it again, I would seduce him and wait until he was inside me before going full elemental and incinerating his man parts.

"Is he with Lera?" Chafer asked with an edge to his tone.

I quirked my brow. "He *is* happy. If he gets too happy, we'll mind blast them, then set them on fire."

"Done." We shook hands.

Chafer was one of the few men I had grown close to that was not attracted to me in the slightest. He was all Lera's, incredibly loyal and incredibly in love with a woman as old as Peak.

Lera was a bit of a cougar. I'd gone in search of Chafer to warn him about Slate's memory loss after I told them he was awake. He and I would suffer the most if Lera and Slate rekindled their relationship.

I had told him once we'd reached the lowest floor of headquarters where the Crash Course was so Lera wouldn't know about my concern. We had agreed to take it as it comes. I wasn't sure a more awkward conversation had been had. Though, while Slate had been talking about what we'd done together last night, that had been very embarrassing.

"He's coming closer."

Chafer gave me his patented wicked grin. "My, my you are *nervous*."

"Shut up, Chafer. My husband thought I was a prostitute, if you'd seen how he looked at me like he didn't even know me, because he didn't... Imagine if Lera woke up one day and had no idea who you were, but had slept with you anyway and then claimed you were a whoring spy? My dignity hasn't recovered from this morning."

He was getting closer, probably in the prep room, and it took all of my effort not to fidget. Chafer's hand slid from my stomach just as

Cordillera and Slate strode into the Crash Course. He could pick up my scent, so I schooled my emotions to stay calm.

He towered over the petite Grand Mistress. She had on crimson lipstick that matched her nails, as she always did. She brushed her chin length waves from her olive cheek and her dark eyes twinkled as she arched a meticulously manicured dark brow at us. She wore black pants and a fire engine red shirt that hugged her curves. She had a firm body to go with those curves even at her age. She'd been the one to wean Slate off rousen when he was fourteen when she trained him, Jett, and Steel. They'd been on and off until I came along.

My heart lurched as they stopped before us. Chafer was the poster child for cool arrogance and I attempted to mimic him. Slate peered down at me from his long thick lashes with silver eyes. Slate looked like he wore mascara. Any woman would kill to have those lashes. They were a much-needed softness to the hard planes of his face. The scar that sliced over his eye didn't help soften him one bit.

"Get into a cat fight?" Chafer prodded.

"Very big cat," Slate rumbled.

His voice sent a thrill through me with its deep bass that made me think the barghest must have another piece of anatomy that made it vibrate in his chest that way.

"I have been filling Slate in on our goings ons since his memory faltered." Cordillera smiled at Slate, but his eyes were on me. "It seems the last thing he remembers was being in my bed before the masquerade."

"I remember seeing the two of you together that night," I said coolly, and she laughed in a sexy feminine way.

"Yes, you did. He did not know you made Brass a captain."

"He deserves it," I said suddenly feeling like I was under the spotlight.

Chafer leaned his shoulder inconspicuously against mine offering me unspoken support.

"I bet you thought so," Slate answered with glinting silver piercing me.

Lera placed her hand on Slate's bicep and Chafer's muscles flexed. "Slate was asking me how I dealt with the news of your marriage. I told him I offered to join you, but he was the one who turned me down. We have been revisiting that option."

Chafer leaned forward and flashed a killer smile and not the sexy kind. I nudged him.

"I think that's a fantastic idea. I wouldn't want to leave Chafer out though. What do you think, Chafer?" I asked, putting my hand high on his thigh.

He didn't miss a beat. "Why wait?"

Chafer moved lithely as he rolled himself over me, pressing my back to the floor and unbuckled my belt one handed, before I could blink and pulled it through the rungs to hold it over my head and drop it to the floor. I started laughing as he gave me a puckish grin and lowered his head as if he was going to kiss me.

"Chafer," Lera hissed.

"Scarlett?"

I gasped, shoving Chafer off me roughly and scrambling to my feet. My cheeks pinked as Brass came through the prep room doors with Quick and Indigo.

"That wasn't what it looked like," I spluttered.

Brass's brow was drew down over his amber eyes. "Really? It looked like Chafer removed your belt and was going to kiss you."

"He wasn't. We were just playing," I said as he crossed his arms in front of me.

"Playing?" Brass said, pursing his plump defined lips.

I ran my hand through my hair smoothing it down. "I'm sorry."

"Don't apologize to me. Your husband was watching you," Brass said coolly, but I was the glitter in his molten pools.

"Oh," I blurted and glanced at Slate who had turned to watch my interaction with Brass.

Lera was standing off to the side speaking in a low tone to a smug-looking Chafer.

...I'm not going to say sorry to him because it would be a lie. I'm not sorry he saw it. Lera and he were talking about a threesome. Never...

"Do not let me interrupt. I only came to train," Slate rumbled, moving to stand next to Brass and me.

Indigo and Quick stood back watching our triangle waiting for the flame to cause us to erupt. "And to flirt with, Lera," I added.

Slate gave a slight shrug of his shoulders. "Perhaps. Do you still spar even though you has lost one of your pregnancies already? Seems a needless risk."

I bristled. "My husband…" I trailed off.

I was going to say he would understand my dedication, but that was a lie. Slate would want me in a padded room with round-the-clock care. If I'd let him, he would've carried me everywhere.

"You were saying?" Slate purred if he were the kind of man who purred.

"I do still spar, but I'm careful. After the Ragnarök, I don't plan on sparring anymore and scaling back on my training until my sons are born. I promised Lera one more competition next month."

"No," Slate and Brass said in unison and Quick let out a low whistle.

I crossed my arms. "Luckily, *you* don't even like me and *you* are not my husband. Besides, I'm inviting the great families who held the deeds so they can see what they're getting involved with. I'm not asking. This is what I'm doing."

I looked from Slate to Brass. To my surprise it was Slate who spoke.

"Come. We need to have a private conversation." Slate lifted his hand to grab my elbow, and I stepped back.

"Not a chance. I will see you tonight if you decide to stay at the Dagr palace, but this is my training time."

"Don't be stubborn," Brass scolded, and I widened my eyes at him.

… Whose side are you on?…

"Both."

"This does not bode well for my marriage bed," Slate rumbled with a hint of amusement and something else that looked like genuine irritation.

Through the bond, I *felt* his bone deep lust. Good to know some things didn't change. There was also this underlying jealousy, at Chafer or at Brass I wasn't sure. The most curious emotion I felt was a rage. It was simmering now, but it was a bomb ready to go off at the slightest provocation.

"Whatever you have to say you can say in front of Brass. I don't have any secrets from him," I said haughtily and Brass sighed.

"Frigga's sweet grass, Scarlett. you are not doing yourself any favors," Brass said, sounding exasperated.

"I don't need favors from him," I spat and realized what I was missing. "Brass, go on. You don't have to mediate. I'm sorry." I started to reach up to his cheek and caught myself.

I bit my lip as I looked at Brass. His amber eyes softened.

"Me too," he said before he turned around and ushered Indigo and Quick out.

She looked over her shoulder at me and I nodded. While I'd been preoccupied, Lera and Chafer had left. I was alone with Slate and I was abruptly wishing I had more clothes on. Like a hoodie I could shove my hands into.

His powerful body sank to the floor, and he stretched his long legs in front of him and crossed at the ankles before resting his palms behind him as Chafer and I had been doing a moment ago.

I couldn't face him. I sat down next to him and crossed my legs with my hands in my lap.

"I am used to two types of women. Those who are afraid of me and those who want to fuck me. There is a third kind, but they are a combination of the two."

"I hope this is going somewhere," I mumbled.

"If it had not been from men I trust and count reliable, I would not have believed all the things they said you have done. It is remarkable," Slate rumbled.

I looked at him out of the corner of my eye and he offered me a smile only slightly less mocking than his previous ones. "You were speaking to our family and Brass. Not reliable sources of information when it comes to me. They are somewhat biased."

"Yes. You and Brass. Why bother to try to convince me of this life when you have found happiness with him?"

His question startled me. I turned my head to face him.

"I love Brass. You should know that before we go any further. If you hadn't come back...I had already discussed moving him into the Dagr palace after Yuletide." I swallowed and pressed my palm to my stomach. "I would've spent the rest of my life with him."

"I hope *this* is going somewhere," he rumbled.

I felt the urge to smile at him and suppressed it. "If I feel that way about him and am willing to give it all up... it should tell you how I felt about my husband. I never should have left him when I thought I was barren. *You.* When he was captured — *you* were captured — I was having doubts. Tika thought we were supposed to get married, so they let us hold a ceremony with Tika and Keen. It was our fake wedding night... the night they took you. I wandered the desert for days until I reached the Faunelle with Indi. When I couldn't find his body, I hoped he was still alive — *you* were alive."

I dropped my head to look at my hands.

"I swore off Brass until..." I sucked in a deep breath. "Anyway, I don't think if there's a chance it might work I could walk away from him a second time."

"From me," he corrected in a low deep tone.

It made me whip my head to him. I scanned his eyes.

"I wanted you to be him so badly I didn't stop to notice you didn't even know me."

Hope was a dangerous thing.

Slate glanced away and pulled his full bottom lip along his teeth. "I apologize for my behavior this morning."

"All of it?" I asked, perplexed at the one-eighty in attitude. "I know Jett is charming, but I doubt his wiles work on you after all this time."

Slate's head turned to me and he came very close to giving me a real smile. My heart fluttered moronically in my chest.

"All of it. There is one thing I need from you before we can lay this matter to rest." His expression serious and that simmer of anger boiled to a fury.

"Depends, but I'm flexible," I said carefully and his mouth quirked as the lust flared in his emotions.

"I know," he said, and I threw my walls back up.

The Crash Course wasn't running. There was no whirlpool swirling, or lava boiling and hissing, the earthquakes didn't exist. I could smell Slate from where I sat; an intoxicating blend of spice, and fall, and sex. He must not have showered before he came.

Gods, he smelled good.

"You should work on that."

"What?" I asked, being dragged out of my revelry.

"When you are aroused, your pupils dilate. It is the mark of a rousen trained khoraz. Mine do as well, but the silver from the barghest masks it," he said simply, and I blushed.

Damn the man.

"What is your one thing?" I asked irritably.

"If my uncle seeks out your company, let me know. I will handle it. My father and he were brothers. It puts you in danger. The Natts do not take well to paramours," Slate said it so bluntly I stammered.

"I am no one's paramour!" I blinked rapidly and started to shove to my feet, but Slate's hand snapped out and he tugged me sideways.

He would always be faster than me. At least now I knew it was because he wasn't entirely human. I stumbled, and he caught me as he rolled so my back hit the floor and his body was flush against mine. I couldn't help but swallow as I tried to moisten my parched throat. *Calling* water would stroke his ego more than I was willing to do.

His eyes settled on my lips as I spoke and not licking them became the bane of my existence. "Your promise. I see now why I called you Torch. It suits you."

My nickname on his lips made my blood rush and the beat of my heart thunder in my ears. I never thought I'd hear him say it again. It was how Slate told me he loved me. His hope. When we made love, he'd ask to hear my torch song. The sultry singers who sang of love lost. How he meant it was different.

I laughed nervously as my chest expanded against his. "You can't possibly know what that nickname means to me. I didn't think I'd ever hear you say it again."

Slate brought his hand to my cheek as he scanned my eyes. I felt another tear roll over the side of my face. I was entranced by his gaze. *This* was how he used to look at me, tender. Just for me.

"Do you need this promise so you can walk away from me?" I said, furrowing my brow.

Slate's hand rested on my cheek and his expression was smooth. "If nothing else, I claimed you. I cannot claim another. My uncle claiming you as well was tactless on his part. I will not share you with another barghest."

"I didn't know he was barghest," I whispered. "I can't make any promises, you understand?"

His eyes hardened to gunmetal and what little hope I had that this conversation would end well died. "So be it," he growled, rolling off of me leaving me bereft. "I was right about you," he said, getting to his feet. "Stay away from me, girl. Your puerile affections and wild imagination of what we shared is not needed, nor wanted."

Silver and predatory. Slate's eyes diced the remnants of my heart into pulp. I didn't bother telling him about the bond. It's ice-cold emotions that knotted in my mind hurt so much worse than his words because I felt no love there.

I pushed open the metal double doors and into the modern prep room with black metal cubbies and gray marble tiles skein with white and black marble benches. I turned where three massage tables were set up and showers were off to the side. A screen that alerted the Breakers of their price and room number for patrons rested blank against the wall.

A hot shower is just what I needed. Scalding.

He was not my husband. I had to remember that. I wouldn't let this shell of a man ruin the memories I had with my Slate. Gods, what I would've done to erase how I abandoned him! Now it was erased, but with it, all of our happy memories. Never would I have wanted that.

CHAPTER 7
INDIGO

With Scarlett and Slate having a private discussion in the Crash Course, Brass and Silver decided to go to the hot studio so we could stretch. We walked up the stone steps to the floor above the Crash Course, my hands gripping the polished wood railing on the wrought-iron balustrade. The smell of cool metal and leather saturated Shadow Breaker headquarters.

The hot studio reached a hundred and five degrees as we faced the wall-to-wall mirror of the long room. Headquarters had high ceilings that gave it an industrial feel offset by Lera's love for rich red and purple textures and opulence. Brass had turned the heat on when we reached the room and begun to strip down. We did the twenty-six postures in as little clothes as possible.

Ama and Shale's deaths had never been more evident to me. They would have been there with us, joking and laughing, but there was just us three. Silver would step down as captain of Slate's team now that he was back but would replace Brass as Slate's second in command. Slate's team had dwindled down to seven from the ten he'd previously had.

Normally, seeing Silver's barely covered tattooed body would have given me butterflies. Today was not one of those days and it was far from normal. Slate had lost his memories of Scarlett and had not taken Ama and Shale's deaths well, so Brass had told them. Then there was the small matter of Peak. The roiling storm cloud that would send its bolts of voltage shooting into their lives whenever the topic was even briefly skimmed.

Brass said Scarlett lied about it. She said she'd taken him as a lover. The things she did to protect those she loved...

An hour and a half later, I followed Silver and Brass to the prep room showers where Slate was dressing without Scarlett. He lifted his head as we approached and I kept my eyes averted from my sister's husband who had about as much modesty as Silver did, which was none.

Guardians were bred and born into a lifestyle of training and power. You'd be hard pressed to find an overweight person in all of Tidings and there wasn't a man under five foot nine, and that was considered short by Guardian standards. Brass, Slate, and Silver were neither overweight nor short. The glimpse I caught of Slate's body made me wonder how Scarlett could cuddle up to it.

Hard packed bronze muscle covered every inch of him to sculpted perfection. Scars now riddled his skin where there was none before. Brass was broad with the illusion of softness since a dusting of dark hair covered his dark honey skin, but he was far from it. Silver was on the opposite end of the spectrum. Tightly muscled and just as broad, he took great care of his manicured body. Black jagged Celtic tattoos covered Silver's left side from his collar to his ankle where not a spare hair was to be found.

As we'd walked into the prep room, Brass had held open the metal doors for me and our fingers had brushed. That was all it took for me to absorb his powers. Brass got into the shower beside Slate and Silver between Brass and me. I pulled out the frosted partition and Silver gave me an approving look before I removed my towel and turned on the water.

...She is all yours. I want nothing to do with her. I doubt the children are even yours. Likely my uncle's...

"So help me..." Brass murmured.

...She is a khoraz, brother. Good for one thing. I do not want to hurt her any more than she has already endured. If you want to risk it, go ahead...

"How big of you," Brass mumbled dryly.

...I did not ask for this....

Brass didn't reply, but with Scar's talent of empathy, I could *feel* his anger.

Silver poked his head around the partition and gave me a once over. I scowled. He took his index finger and flicked my lower lip.

"What is with the sourpuss? Does it irritate you too when they do that?" Silver asked, running a hand over his handsome olive face.

"Not as much as you leering at me while I shower. Get back on your own side, Silver," I hissed.

He gave me a mocking smile and purposely let gold-flecked chocolate eyes rake over me.

"If you are about to tell me you can turn my frown upside down, I'll kick you where it counts."

Brass and Slate chuckled and my cheeks heated. Curse Slate's heightened hearing and Brass's mind reading!

Silver stepped around the partition forcing me against the black marble and I held out a hand as I crossed under the spray.

"The next time I sleep with you, Silver Regn, will be in a place you have never had another woman. Is this shower that place?" I asked dryly, knowing well it wasn't.

Silver sucked on his teeth and looked away.

"That you need time to think about where you can take me right now should be enough of an answer for you of how eager I am to be your bed-sport conquest." I grabbed my towel and wrapped it around myself storming to the cool black metal cubbies.

I dressed and walked upstairs to the rumpus room before the guys could come out of the showers. I walked over the walnut floors to get a water from the polished bar. Pinball machines rang out through the dark purple room. Low hanging lamps from the ceiling creating spots of bright light between darkness in the loft like room. The sound of pool balls cracked against one another. There was a bar complete with bottles with tender, and stools. Scarlett said the rumpus room used to be half empty all of the time, but since she recruited another dozen people, the room was hardly ever empty.

I thanked the bartender, who was also a Shadow Breaker that went by the nickname Cory. He had the great misfortune of being named Albacore. Scarlett called him Cocktails; he owned a bar with his sister in Valla. Scarlett recruited him for Brass's team and since then he'd been tending bar here whenever he wasn't running his own bar or training. Shadow Breakers followed me with interest from the two pool tables and four couches that were placed around the large room. Maybe they thought I'd be replacing one of the empty positions in Slate's team.

I could hear Scarlett's worried thoughts coming from Cordillera's office. The arched wooden door was exactly across from the hall that led from headquarters. I took my water as I knocked on the door and waited for the filigree knob to turn. Chafer opened the door and took a step back to let me in.

The office held a couch and two wing backed sofa chairs that faced an ornate deep cherry wood desk and matching chair upholstered in a dark red. Cordillera sat behind the desk and raised her eyes to me briefly before continuing her discussion with Scarlett, who gave me a small smile.

"We were discussing my last competition. I think we should compete against one another. It would be your first time and since you completed the Crash Course last week, you could do it with me. If you want, of course," Scarlett said in her gravelly voice.

A thrill shot through me. I was nervous about winning and being bid on by a patron. I'd have to go into one of the three rooms above the arena which Scarlett affectionately called Vegas because the Breakers said what happened there, stayed there. It was her loathing of patrons but love of the Crash Course that inspired her arenas.

"I think that would be fun," I told them, sitting in the high-backed chair beside Scarlett.

I watched Chafer sit down so close to Scarlett on the couch his thigh was flush with hers. What was that about? Lera tapped her lower lip with a red nailed finger as she watched Chafer slide his arm around the back of the couch. Scarlett seemed vaguely aware of him, but her mind was preoccupied.

Slate didn't love her.

A rap on the door announced Silver, Brass, and Slate. Brass gave Chafer and Scarlett a frosty look, but she didn't catch it as Slate moved to lean against the wall in the spot Chafer usually stood in. What game was this? Silver's backside pushed my arm off the side as he sat atop it and wrapped his arm behind me.

"Scarlett and Indigo are competing as the headliners for next month's competition," Chafer said.

"Not a chance," Silver said.

I elbowed him hard in the thigh. "Get over yourself, Regn. You don't tell me what to do."

He looked down his nose at me with that expression of his which meant he was not budging. Good. This fight would push him away because I wasn't budging either.

"Indigo..." he said in his low most serious tone.

I rolled my eyes.

"Nephew... I did not think you were the jealous type," Cordillera said with a smirk.

How Scarlett got along with her, I didn't know. She was manipulative and ruthless. Her and Chafer made a good team.

"I am *not* jealous. She cannot handle a patron," Silver said and I shoved him as hard as I could off the armrest making him flail for the wall.

"I do not expect to win, but I can handle a man, Silver, or a woman."

Silver's handsome face contorted as if he tasted something bitter. I had been helping Shale pack up Ama's things when she invited me to stay the night. That was two days before she died and far too fresh in my memories.

"As entertaining as this public tete a tete is, there are larger matters at hand," Slate rumbled.

Scarlett's emotions spiked at the sound of his voice, but she kept her expression cool and regal. I would have to take notes.

Chafer crossed his leg so his ankle rested on his knee next to Scarlett. She finally noticed what he was doing and I *felt* her emotions lean towards thankful. Then Chafer leaned towards her and dipped his finger into her cleavage. Slate pushed off the wall, eyes flashing, and Brass clenched his jaw. Perhaps Slate's claiming of her was deeper than he had anticipated. Lera's dark eyes narrowed as Chafer pulled the long silver chain she kept the three stone pieces of the work on. Scarlett had frozen not sure what Chafer was doing but trusting him not to be a lech. He held them up in front of her eyes before letting them slide back between her breasts.

"The works. Lera and I have discussed it and we think the arenas will serve your purposes there as well," Chafer said.

"Are those the pieces?" Slate asked, crossing the room to stand in front of Scarlett.

...Too preoccupied to see the three pieces of stone hanging from my necklace. I'm surprised he remembered my face...

Scarlett's aggravated thought stunned me and I looked across at the wall. Brass would hear those thoughts too. She lifted the chain from her shirt and Slate caught the swinging stones in his palm and rubbed a thumb across them.

...I wondered what kept slapping across my knuckles...

My cheeks heated. Gods, Brass heard these things all day every day. I would lose the ability in two days. There was no limit to how many talents I could absorb, but they always faded in a few days.

"Stone pieces from the work that I need to find to help the Mother. She's ill, or so the wight told us. You were there too. You're a part of it. It's a piece of your prophecy. There are nine pieces we need to find, I have three. Someone in the Var family took the Anguillan's and I plan to get the fourth soon now that you're safe." Scarlett pulled the stones from his hand and tucked them back into her shirt.

"Our idea is the same when we had planned to search for Slate. Now, we will look for the works and my informants will query about the rest of the pieces." Cordillera said.

Slate hadn't moved and Scarlett finally looked up to meet his eyes.

...I will get a closer look at those stones the next time she is feeling lonely...

Brass's dark honey cheeks reddened.

...If he thinks I'll let him into my bed without his memories he is out of his mind...

Slate moved to sit on the edge of Lera's desk facing them. Chafer's irritation spiked. That was his spot.

"We'll need to include Jett in our plans. I feel like my whole family may be involved somehow. I know Indigo is. Call it a hunch. I don't think my mother was supposed to have twins. Someone said something to me recently that makes me think it could have been either of us," Scarlett said and my mouth popped open.

...And keep Brass far away so at least one of us will be safe for our children...

"You mean the Faunelle?" I asked.

She looked to me and nodded. "They asked if I carried the Grar Dyr's son. Since Slate's bond was broken, there was a chance he was dead. They weren't convinced he was. Then I thought of Sterling Haust. He's a male descendant, so I thought maybe..." she trailed off.

My cheeks heated. "It's not impossible. Sterling hasn't claimed me. I didn't even know he could until..."

Crap.

"Until his father claimed Scarlett," Slate finished.

"He said something to me that makes me think... He said barghests never lose fertility like the rest of the Guardians do."

Scarlett spoke as if she was taking a particularly hard test and couldn't remember the answers. I didn't think she realized what she just revealed. Slate jumped off the desk and clenched his fists. Brass had turned to her, eyes molten.

"He plans for you to have his barghest sons," Slate gritted in his deep voice.

"He knows what my babies mean to me. He won't take them." Her arms wrapped protectively over her stomach.

... if he wants me under his thumb, he'll let me keep them...

"Since you will not promise to stop seeing him, you must enjoy my uncle's wiles," Slate said harshly.

He was the only one in the room who didn't know the truth. Scarlett's face darkened and I could tell by the twitch of her eye that she was going to say something brash. I wanted to stop her, but it was like watching two trains collide. She wanted to hurt him the way she was so obviously hurting.

"How right you are. One Haust is much like another. I could hardly tell the difference between the two of you, now that you mention it," she spat, eyes burning like coals in her lovely face.

Her hair lifted from her face and started to writhe like coiled snakes as she stood on the brink of shifting in anger. Slate watched her with his jaw clenched in disgust. How that look must have seared her heart.

"He —" Brass began softly and Scarlett lost it.

She shot to her feet and gave Brass an expression so filled with hurt and betrayal I felt tears prick my own eyes.

"*Brass*," she whispered in such a tone that encompassed the accusation and desperation she couldn't utter.

Brass got to his feet rubbing his lips together. "They should not think less of you in any way, love. Letting them believe a lie —"

"It is not your secret to tell!" she cried out. "Isn't that what you always say?"

It had been a hard day for Scarlett and she did not get more than a nap in this morning after being with Slate all night. Slate who didn't love her and had woken her up with a blade to the throat.

It was too much.

She slapped him. Not nearly as hard as she could have. Brass wrapped his arms around her, pinning her leaden limbs to his body and her fingers clutched at him. He kissed her cheek and his eyes flew up to take us in who sat in stunned silence at their intimate moment.

...take me away...

Brass didn't say a word. I *called,* opening the door for him and he scooped her up, cradling her like a child.

...my thanks...

The door shut behind them and Silver blew out a breath. "It would be easier to rip her heart directly out instead of playing these games with her."

Lera and Slate shared a look. "Our mistake," Lera said amiably. "I cannot appreciate the shock she must be going through. At least you know Brass will cheer her up."

Like I said, manipulative.

This time she was working for Scarlett. Slate had to notice how when she was upset, she turned to Brass. It had always been that way, but now Scarlett's relationship with him had changed. Slate was still staring at the door, but he put on weary expression.

"Lera, not you too. What was he saying?" Slate queried.

...If he forced her, I will kill him...

I pursed my lips. That was an enlightening thought.

"Why exert the effort? It's not like you owe her anything. She just saved your life, but whatever. Not a big deal, right? She was the only one who refused to accept that you were dead when everyone else told her to let you go. If she hadn't found you, had that bond with you, you'd still be in the bowels of that prison. I never thought I would miss the old you, but *this* is the man I always thought you were."

"Easy, Dove. Two years of his life have been taken from his memories. They both have a right to be upset," Silver said in a soothing tone.

"He's free to leave. She's put it all on the line. All we're asking is that he try to remember and not be a complete ass in the process. Is that too much to ask? You want answers? Ask your wife. Don't make her friends betray her. Brass never should have opened his mouth." I got to my feet.

"I will walk you home," Silver said and Slate grunted.

I sucked in a deep breath and let the retorts wither in my throat. I opened my palm and Silver stood and slid his hand into mine. I almost laughed at his self-satisfied smile.

...I thought of a place...

CHAPTER 8

JETT

Wow. A more awkward dinner had never been had.

Scarlett didn't show. Indigo said she was with Brass and Slate had come alone. Quick had come with Indigo and he was wearing Jett's clothes. That meant he had been there awhile. That meant, he had changed there and was naked at some point with Indi.

The Sumar palace was home. The Moroccan palace was a sprawling testament to their ancient line. It was done in royal blue, white, and gold mosaics. The colors of the Sumar sigil.

They always ate in the informal dining room. Its high domed ceiling had curved white beams trimmed in gold. It started out dark blue at the walls and faded to white at the peak of the dome with distant birds painted in the segments between the beams. The walls were predominantly white but with smaller subtler mosaic patterns in teals and blues. A terra cotta pot sat against the north wall, a vine of blue morning glories covered the wall from when Pearl had demonstrated *calling* for the first time to Scarlett, Tawny, and Gyps.

In the center of the room was a rectangular table that sat sixteen made of a light-colored wood with delicately carved and painted in golds and silvers. The chairs were the same type of wood and upholstered in heavy gold and silver embroidery on white fabric. Lanterns hung from the walls in copper, blues, and gold in with intricately shaped metalwork framing the glass.

Everyone was there except for Scarlett. Sparrow and Hawk hadn't seen Slate yet. Even though Slate didn't know them other than what we'd told him and through Wren's letters, he tolerated their affection well and even hugged Sparrow back. She was his aunt. Hawk's best friend had been Slate's father. The web of connections between their families was an entangled mess.

Cherry and Amethyst had brought Geol, Gigi for short, down to meet her uncle Slate and had held her with an amused look. She melted the coldest hearts with her big powder blue eyes. She had dark hair and mocha skin like her mother, but those were Alder's eyes and Indi's, and Scarlett's full mouth.

It was like old times when Scarlett was dating Ash. She had spent all her time at the Straumr palace and they avoided the obvious fact that she was missing. Slate took her absence well. Too well for Jett's taste. Pearl looked as if Slate's return signified a change in luck. Whenever Jett hugged his glamorous grandmother, her floral musk took him back to simpler times. Slate looked more relaxed now than he had all day.

When they had licked the halibut and chimichurri from their plates. Pearl had retired sensing their need to talk. Sparrow and Hawk had asked Slate if he had intended to come home. Home being the Dagr palace. Jett held his breath. Slate said they he planned to move back into the Sumar palace.

Indigo took the napkin from her lap and placed it beside the gold charger. She looked ravishing in a blue chiffon halter dress that matched her eyes. Her corn silk hair was pinned up on the side by a glittering silver comb. No more braids from the illustrious Quick.

"Since we were both there when this story was told, we're going to call it a night." Indigo looked to Quick to confirm, but all she saw there was a bold smile.

Her lips quirked, but she didn't smile as they left the room.

Slate asked one of the staffers to bring in a few carafes of wine.

"Plan on drinking away the rest of your memories?" Jett asked amusedly when he drank deep and refilled his goblet.

Slate's silver eyes met his over the rim, and he put down the goblet after another swig. "After today's illuminating information, a drink is a given. What I truly wish for is a few glasses of whiskey and a willing wench on my knee for some laughs."

The girls seemed to bristle like cats as if he'd just stomped on their tails. Tawny's face reddened and Slate chuckled as he took another swig. Old Slate was back. The one Scar, Tawny, and Gyps had never met.

Jett sucked his teeth. He was stumped on how to broach this disaster. Would Slate fall in love with Scarlett again? Therein laid the real problem.

That was when Slate started to tell them about the pieces Scarlett was keeping and the work they were supposed to find. He told them about Lera's plan to have her Breakers search for it over the islands in the guise of arena work. It was a sound plan. They had nowhere else to start and going from tribe to tribe asking if they had stone pieces would draw attention to them. If there was someone else searching for these pieces and they had more information than Jett and the others, it could make them collect the pieces sooner.

Everything hinted that it would be very bad.

"What does Scarlett plan to do to get the pieces?" Tawny asked, furrowing her fair brow at Slate.

Slate sliced his head to the left. "She has a lead on one. She left with Brass before she could tell us where."

Silence. Slate didn't seem to care that his wife could be laying with her lover as they spoke. She wouldn't, but with Brass... Scarlett had a weakness for him. If she was vulnerable and sought him for comfort... there were many ways she could be comforted. Normally, Brass was just about as honorable a guy as there was, but his weakness was Scarlett. He had done quite a few things out of character when it concerned her.

"I have no intention of claiming her as my wife," Slate rumbled into his goblet.

It felt as though someone had died. Slate picked up a carafe in his fist and stood.

"I have much time to make up for if anyone wishes to join me. I shall be with Lynx," Slate said, prowling from the room.

Jett was speechless. Lynx was a khoraz, a Minotaur khoraz, who could frequently be found at the local brothel, but never charged Slate since she was sweet on him. Old Slate indeed.

He wasn't coming.

I shouldn't have let my emotions get the best of me. Brass had carried me out of Lera's office like a baby. He'd carried me all the way home using Lera's secret portal door. We'd fallen asleep and when I woke up, I was tucked to his body as we used to sleep together. It had taken all my will power to push away and wake him. I was starting to wonder if it would be worth it.

I couldn't give up on Slate though. He didn't give up on me when I'd been on rousen. Brass had called me love. I'd temporarily forgotten everything and let him hold me.

Did Slate think we slept together? We didn't. He did kiss me, but it was a sweet chaste kiss when he went through the Dagr portal door. I had needed that reassuring affection.

I'd showered to get Brass's scent off me and one of the staff had changed our sheets while I went out into the cloister. I'd put a lattice up in the cloister and planted a snippet of the blue morning glory vine that grew in Pearl's dining room. It reminded me of my mother and our first day in Tidings. When Slate was unconscious, I'd come out there to be alone and cry.

I'd slowly been growing the vine which needed to be tended with how hot it was during the day in Thrimilci. I sat on the stone bench in my champagne satin robe covering the pale pink nightie that Slate liked. Don't ask why I wore it. I had no intention of sleeping with him, but I wanted him to want me.

I'd cried some and then gone back inside leaving the slatted arch doors open. It was my favorite feature of our wing. I climbed into my empty bed and Tree padded up the bed to sleep curled by my stomach. I liked to believe she wasn't just offering comfort to me, but the babies as well.

Tomorrow was another day.

Lombard bands lined the grey stone monolithic columns that wrapped around the covered walkway that I ate breakfast with Sparrow and Hawk in.

I poured orange juice from the pitcher into my glass and sat back.

I loved the covered walkway, the cloister.

He didn't come. Slate never showed. I'd woken up feeling achy which could have meant only one thing. Slate slept with someone last night and because our bond was active, I felt it in my sleep and had been too exhausted to wake fully. I'd told him if he left our bed he couldn't return. I'd drawn the line, and he crossed it like he said he would. It was over.

"Your chef makes the best pancakes. Sure beats IHOP," I said, stabbing my fork into another pile of chocolate chip pancakes.

Sparrow smiled and looked to Hawk. He should have been at the university by now to start getting for his class. "He told us he was going to sleep at the Sumar palace last night. He needs a little time."

"He doesn't remember me. He woke up, and we told him he was married to a woman he didn't even know. It's better he leaves now than give me false hope," I said candidly.

Hawk looked uncomfortable with my reasoning. "Slate may not be the same man, but he was raised the same way. He'll do the right thing by you."

I smiled at my uncle Hawk, the man who was my only male role model in my life. It was funny, Steel had grown up on a completely different country and managed to be so much like his older brother. Even funnier that Tawny married a man exactly the same as her adopted father.

"I don't want him to do the right thing. I want him to *want* to be with me."

"He'll come around," Sparrow said, placing her hand over mine on the wrought-iron table.

"I should get to class."

"I'll go with you," Hawk said, getting to his feet.

Groin vaulted ceilings with Corinthian grey stone columns and marbled tiles spanned the Romanesque halls. We walked in silence to the portal room. Recessed lighting made it look like a cathedral as it lit the sculptures of the Dagr matriarchs along the walls like saintly beauties. Sparrow was having a statue commissioned. Slate would get one, too. The first Dagr patriarch ever.

I sucked in a sharp breath making Hawk stop to delve into me for fear for the babies.

Storm and Wind the Guardian version of Romeo and Juliet. Storm Natt became obsessed with science and *calling*. He claimed to have devised a way to keep nature in balance forever with one of his *projects*. They created a divide between Wind Natt and Storm Dagr. There is no record of what this project that came between them did, but Wind Natt believed it would give Natt ultimate power. Even though she loved Natt, she came against him believing such power was not meant for Guardians. A war raged between the Guardians, the only one ever. Dagr confronted Natt after his side fell.

Dagr went to him and sacrificed herself to stop Natt. Storm destroyed the project, but the energy we knew as Mother Nature was heartbroken. She came to Natt revealing her displeasure. Mother took away the elemental powers of the Guardians and separated the lands with the hope that with more space and less power, they would never war again. The Natt line had only been women since. They created the council, named Guardians to separate tribes, and have worked together as a people much better than those in our history. It was the only time the energy Mother Nature was said to be seen by a Guardian. The project was presumed to have sunk into the ocean when the land was divided and had never been found, although many have gone searching for it. Some never returned.

What if the work I was looking for was actually the project? It would narrow down the search around the islands to the coasts. The Merfolk had a piece, that would make four of the nine I needed and since I had a bone to pick with the Merfolk, they had better lend a few hands to search the coasts.

"Sorry. The babies are fine. I just thought of something."

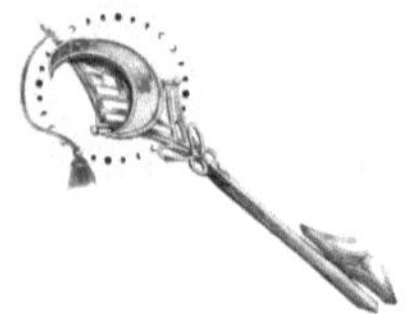

Hawk walked with me down the sweeping stone steps of Valla University to the hall of classes. All the classes were on the second floor of the sprawling castle except for battle training and Nurture and Focus taught by Boa Sunna, Shale's uncle which was taught in the conservatory.

I wore a black caftan dress with a 'V' neck and a sheer overlay on the skirt with gold trim and a wide yellow belt. First years wore red belts, the young men wore all black jerkins with thinner belts. Tyros were split into four groups. I was in the Embala course, the other second years were ask course.

Tyros milled about as I said goodbye to Hawk. "Scar, keep your chin up. You found him. Now he needs to find himself."

"That's very deep," I joked and Hawked kissed my forehead like he used to do when I was little.

"He's a smart young man, his father's son. You've never failed once you put your mind to something. Don't let your pride get in the way."

My throat had closed up on me so I nodded.

"Love you, Scarlett," Hawk said, walking down the hall to his classroom.

I was dreading Dahlia Natt's class. Ash's mother hated me. While Ash and I were together, he had his father, Basil Straumr, who was the record keeper and claviger of Guardian history, put us in the same course. Sage, Quick, and Tawny were also in the Embala course. Hunter Snjar, Amber's brother and the blonde ultra-fit lackey of Ash and Sage was also in my course.

The rounded room was lit by artfully crafted pewter sconces in the yellowed stone walls that were lined by columns that reached the high ceilings. There were tiers of stone steps with mismatched pillows resting side by side. Before the seats, an inverted 'L' shaped wooden desk pulled from behind the back of the tier in front of us.

Quick and Tawny already sat in the third row and smiled when I walked into the room. I bit down on my bottom lip avoiding Ash, Sage, and Hunter who sat on the opposite end on the room. I slid in next to Quick and he leered.

"How did last night go? You and your husband make up?" Quick teased.

"He never came home," I said flatly.

Tawny gasped. Quick's smile fell.

"Shit."

I shrugged. "Better now than...What the fiddlestick is he doing in here?"

Quick awkwardly raised his hand and Tawny elbowed him hard in the ribs so he grunted.

"He cannot sit with us," Tawny hissed.

"Fiddlesticking sugarfoot. Maybe he doesn't remember this isn't his course," I whispered.

Slate drew the eye. The silver scar gave him a sinister look. More villain than hero. His winter storm eyes swept over us as Dahlia handed him back the paper. She pursed her lips as she followed Slate's towering, muscled body to where we sat. If I started crying now because my husband left me in front of Ash and Sage, I really would run away to Chicago again.

Slate slid in next to me in the aisle seat and pulled up his desk. Tawny was leaning forward so far to give him the stink eye I thought she would fall over her desk.

"Hey, captain. What are you doing in here? You are in the other course," Quick said, speaking over my head.

"Reed pulled me out of the other course and informed me of my new schedule," Slate rumbled and I felt his eyes on the side of my face.

"Where did you sleep last night?" Tawny snapped.

"I do not believe that is any of your business," Slate rumbled. "Was my wife worried I had found another woman claiming to be my pregnant wife?"

I turned away from him. "I think the works that the Aves and Faunelle mentioned is the project Storm Natt created. I'm going to tell Lera to search the coasts. Non're offered me a stone piece before. I didn't know what it was at the time, but he owes me. After I get this arena stuff settled, do you think Steel will escort me to them?"

"No way, Scarlett." Quick shook his head. "The Merfolk king has a thing for you. You walk in that place; you are not walking back out. They will put you back in that pleasure palace. By the Mother, if Non're knows you're there..." Quick shook his head.

"Barghests and a Merfolk king *and* prince," Slate rumbled. "Are you a rare cock collector?"

My stomach burned. "Non're won't give it to anyone, but me. If Steel won't help me, I'll go myself."

"Steel will take you. He won't like it. Jett will like it even less. Worry about Jett. Jett and Brass. Brass won't let you go, Scar," Tawny said pointedly.

"I can take you. I always enjoy myself with the Merfolk" Slate added though I knew that wasn't true. He was purposely antagonizing me.

"If I become desperate enough, I'll keep you in mind," I said haughtily as Dahlia started her lesson.

She powered up a laptop on her desk with her projector. The internet was only available at Valla University. There was a whole room dedicated to technology there. Slate leaned in close so his lips were pressed against my ear.

"Did you make up that slap to Brass last night?" he whispered and my skin prickled.

"I don't know how you ended up in this course, but it was a mistake I mean to rectify," I whispered almost inaudibly.

"Do you have plans tonight? Are you going to let Brass stay in your bed again?"

The inside of my ears burned. "We fell asleep by accident. I had the sheets changed so his scent wouldn't be on them."

"I noticed when I went there this morning and caught his scent despite your efforts."

"Surprised you care," I whispered as Dahlia clicked to the next slide. "I am going to check out the arena site tomorrow in Thrimilci."

"Alone?"

I turned back to him and I leaned close, my cheek brushed his as I pressed lips to his ear. The fire that never extinguished that was the rousen was stoked as his scent changed. My nostrils flared.

"Alone time with me is a pleasure earned, but I promise it is worth the wait."

I'd lost my mind.

Slate slowly turned his face so his lips were detrimentally close to mine. His nose brushed mine.

"The night before is very vividly imprinted in my mind," he purred.

"Before or after you —"

He pressed a finger to my lips. "You did not tell me you slept with the Merfolk King."

"I said Dion're. You were too busy with accusations to pay attention."

Slate's eyes scanned mine. "Dion're would not bed just any woman. Who else? You said Non're?"

"And Larn'ra."

"The princess too?"

"I heard you have history with her. Lucky us."

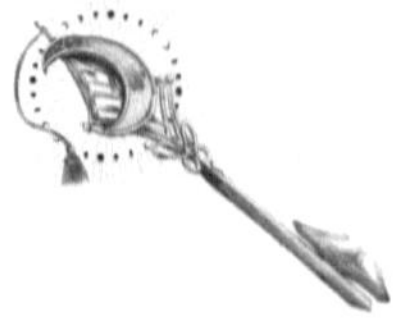

We sat the rest of class in silence. When the class was over, bells like the ringing of church bells that marked the hour. Slate walked down the steps and actually waited for us by Dahlia's desk.

"For public appearance's sake," he said, regarding me with cool grey eyes.

Tawny and Quick were right behind us. I froze when Ash, Sage, and Hunter formed a human barricade which Dahlia slipped past to leave the seven of us alone in the room together.

Ash's celadon hadn't gleamed in such a way since he and Slate fought on Jett's birthday. He'd slapped me that night. Peak said Slate had then killed Jonquil in retaliation. I couldn't ask Slate now if it was true.

"Good morning," I said in a sickly sweet voice.

"Dagr —" Ash started.

I could tell by his sneer; it was not going to be nice. "Did you know they adjusted his schedule just so we can be together? That must have come from high up. Reed, or maybe your uncle, Moon. I guess since I have a second chance at being a mother, the Prime and his Second have decided to grant me a few concessions."

I put on a good show as I slid my arm around Slate's waist and patted my hand on his abs. *Gods*, they were rock hard.

Ash and Sage seemed to be thinking twice about whatever they planned on saying. Hunter's blue hawk-like eyes narrowed. He wasn't very tall, but he was all sinew and muscle. His eyes zeroed in on Slate. I pulled my arm from around him and stepped in front of him flaring into an inferno. Flames licked up my skin, my hair writhed around my face. The hot coals for eyes burned in my sockets.

"Touch him and I won't think twice about reducing you into a pile of oily ash," I said in a disembodied voice.

Hunter jerked. Slate could have taken care of Hunter if he'd followed through with that sucker punch, but he couldn't even remember why Hunter would want to punch him.

"You scammed my sister and she wound up dead," Hunter said, jabbing a finger.

"Her death is not his fault and you know it. No one is more upset than he is to lose his child," I spat, looking to Sage whose pouty lips quirked.

"This is not over," Hunter threatened.

"Touch him on Valla U property and I will use any influence we have to get you thrown out. Just like you did Indigo." My fire fizzled, and I was a twenty-year-old woman again.

I stood like a sentry until they walked away and let out a breath that made my shoulders slump as I let my arms drop from Slate. Tawny stepped to my side.

"How did you know that's why they changed his schedule?" she asked.

"I didn't. It was a wild guess, but after Moon and Reed's reaction at the hearing I figured they had a soft spot for my situation," I told her as Dahlia walked in and her pinched face grimaced at me like a grubby little troll that had shown up at her doorstep.

I turned around to roll my eyes at the others and caught Slate's unreadable look. I blushed and looked away.

"It didn't seem right that he'd hit you for something you didn't even remember doing," I murmured.

"You are possessive," Slate rumbled.

"I protect my own." My hand went unwittingly to my stomach and Slate rested his hand at the small of my back leading me from the classroom.

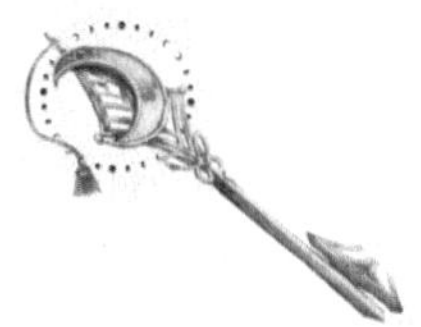

"Reed winked at me. That's enough of a hint as to who switched Slate's course." I sighed at the dining hall long table.

The dining hall at Valla U had long polished wood tables and benches along each side separated into four sections. At the front of the hall sat Moon and all the provosts before a huge fireplace. The stages of the moon were painted across the ceiling and food sat on platters in a home style buffet before us.

I heaped sliced fruit, creamy potatoes and roasted honey ham onto my plate. The hum of conversation was a relief from the whispers and sidelong glances. It'd been this way for a while with no end in sight.

"Jeez, Scar. Pregnant much?" Jett teased.

Cherry gave him an elbow to the ribs for me and he chuckled before giving her a kiss. When we'd seen Jett in the halls and walked to lunch, he hadn't acted any differently towards me in spite of finding out the about Peak.

"Bite me, Jett. I'm eating for three," I said with my cheeks burning.

"She does have a robust appetite for one so fit. I have a good guess as to how you stay in shape," Slate rumbled and my spoon stopped just before my lips.

"Don't watch me eat," I scolded and Slate smirked biting off a piece of ham from his fork.

We had gotten into a sort of groove while we went to classes. Slate was comfortable walking beside me as if he'd been doing it for two years instead of only today. Now, his shoulder was pressed up against my back. He was keeping in constant contact with me and I tried not to like it.

"Don't worry about it Scar, you still can't tell yet," Cherry said with a sweet smile from her red stained lips.

"What are you planning for your big twenty-first birthday? Now that things are back to normal, you can actually do something," Tawny said.

"When is your birthday?" Slate asked.

"The end of the month. I was thinking about going to Chicago and making sure the movers got everything. I want my laptop too. I think Indi is planning on hiding out for a few weeks when Sterling gets married." I pursed my lips to the side.

"What?" Quick started from beside me.

"I don't know. Sorry, Quick. You're more than welcome to go with her if she wants. It's not big, but —"

"Where did you sleep last night?" Jett abruptly asked Slate and my stomach flip-flopped.

"Huh?" I asked my eyes widening. I knew he was with a woman, but I assumed he went back home. "Hawk and Sparrow said you stayed at the Sumar palace."

His brow arched as he looked down at me. "I stayed with a woman. A grown woman named Lynx."

I put my fork down, having lost my appetite. I'd seen Slate with the buxom brunette occasionally.

"I'm well acquainted with Lynx the khoraz," I mumbled, "I didn't think about what would happen if the mental block hadn't been lifted by my birthday. I'm not feeling so well. Excuse me."

I pushed up from the table and waved my hands at the others so they wouldn't follow. I walked down the marble tiles to the exit with my stomach dangerously tossing. When I crossed through the high wood double doors, bile burned in my throat. I turned the corner into the hall and ran smack dab into a wall of a man.

"Scarlett. What a pleasant surprise," Peak said with a flash of teeth.

I put my fingers over my mouth as the urge to vomit spiked.

"Allow me, sweet Scarlett." Peak's bronze hand slid smoothly over my stomach and the acid settled.

The heat kept warming me and I knew he was checking on the twins. The scent of him ignited the part of me that was branded by him. Vetiver and fall. His lust was deep and having me alone in the hall only a few feet away from the tyros where anyone would see us didn't seem to matter to him.

"Are you coming to dinner tomorrow night, sweet Scarlett?" Peak took his other hand and trailed his fingers through my hair.

I wanted to pull away, my first instinct to knee him in the groin, but with his hand threatening my babies, I was helpless. "I'm going to visit the arena site in Thrimilci tomorrow."

"A late dinner then," Peak said.

I ran my teeth over my bottom lip and looked away. He saw the reluctance in my eyes and grabbed my wrist. My feet skidded over the floor as he dragged me around the corner. There was an alcove door that he dragged me against.

Fear. The taste of fear in my mouth was like battery acid on my tongue.

"Scarlett. Scarlett. Scarlett. I thought we had an understanding." Peak's body blocked out the incandescent light from the hall.

"Anyone could walk past," I whispered, and he smiled.

It creased his cheeks making my brow quirk. It was too much like Slate's. He leaned forward and cupped my chin tilting my face up.

"If not tomorrow, then today." Peak breathed and his big hand turned the doorknob behind me.

The room was dark and smelled like old stone and shame. Peak cast a shadow over me as he dressed. He'd shifted into his barghest form to reclaim me. In his barghest form, I couldn't say no. I could literally say the words, but I had been set to squirming like I'd done for Slate's barghest form. The knowledge was horrific.

I leadenly buckled on my wide yellow belt and began to smooth my hair.

"My nephew is awake then? It is safe to assume he knows about us?" Peak's lime eyes caught the smallest light and reflected it back at me.

"He does. He doesn't remember me though, so he only cares that you claimed me in your barghest form," I said in a flat tone.

Peak walked over to where I'd slid off the abandoned provost's desk and lifted my chin. I resisted the urge to spit in his face or pull away. In his human form, I was only attracted to him. It was a bitter pill.

"No matter, sweet Scarlett. I will take care of you. Today went much better, yes? Almost as if you had something to prove," Peak said with a lascivious smile. It made my blood curdle thickly in my veins as if my body wanted to lay down and die.

A number of retorts came to mind, but I had no desire to be beaten as well as abused. "It was better," I replied.

"Being my paramour comes with certain privileges, Scarlett. If you are looking for an out from your marriage. I can be of service. I have already raised one barghest son, I have well-trained servants who can help us raise my grand nephews."

Peak's strange affection vexed me. Why not take what he wanted and leave? He deluded himself into thinking there was something between us.

"He's my husband and for better or worse, I'll stand by him. I'll keep your generous offer in mind, Peak."

I could do this. The shame was tolerable knowing I had someone at home who loved me, but since I had no one, I felt nothing.

Peak kissed me deeply, and I played his game well. "Wait a few moments before leaving, sweet Scarlett. Take this. It is yours."

Peak left after pressing something cool and small into my palm. I counted to one hundred before opening the door. In my palm was the jade canine fetish I'd taken from Slate. It was actually barghest. It had been torn from my hair during my fight with Peak. I swallowed hard as I threaded it into one of the two narrow braids I wore and stepped into the hall.

We'd been in the empty classroom for an hour or so. I'd missed my class after lunch; Arithmetic with Magnolia a red headed Rot twin.

I walked to the battle grounds instead where today it would take up two periods since Hawk's American History class was redundant for Tawny and me.

The prep room was at the back of the university on the ground floor. The preparation room smelled of the polished wood that made up the beautiful walnut cubbies. I quickly changed and stowed my clothes in one, then strapped on my belt of daggers, my short seax to my thigh, and stuck two blades into my boots. I sat on the chocolate brown padded leather bench that ran the length of each aisle as I buckled on my gold lace and black leather wrist blades. Slate had given them to me, they were the feminine companions to his own.

I hung my head in my hands as I tried to collect myself staring down at the black supple boots Hawk had gifted me after my induction into Valla U. I could do it. It was just sex. People had sex with people they didn't even like sometimes. He wouldn't hurt me again if I did what he asked.

I cursed my feeble attempts to bolster my spirits and kicked the cubby door before leaving.

I walked out through the doors that led to the sprawling grounds. You expected gladiators to come racing out at us on the battle grounds. A track spanned the tiered stone seating like at home, but an enormous globe of a dome capped the room. Also like ours, there was a section for weights, and archery. The combat ring did not have pads, and you usually needed healing after class.

"Where have you been?" Tawny hissed, holding her unstrung bow.

She was in head to toe black, the training uniform so you wouldn't see blood. I was flushed from the rush and I stammered. My fluster grew worse when I saw who was striding down the battle grounds towards us.

An irritated expression marred my brother's tan chiseled face and even Quick was looking at me reprovingly, Slate was just along because he was invited. I sensed his frustrated curiosity through the bond.

No love, but lust. It was always there.

I pulled my hair up into a ponytail and hoped the flush to my cheeks would die down in the five seconds it would take to reach me.

"Where were you? We thought the worst. Haven't you learned by now to leave a message as to where you're going? Freya's burly boar, Scar!" Jett was furious with me and I dropped my eyes.

Quick sucked in a sharp breath and I felt Slate's alarming rage burn in my mind. I blinked not knowing where it was coming from.

"Scar, is that —" Tawny broke off, her eyes had skipped to my neck.

I slapped a hand to my throat. My whole-body heated, and I took a step back as I scrambled for an explanation.

"My brother?" Quick asked, looking perplexed.

"No! Of course not," I said, trying not to wring my hands.

"Truth."

Jett pinched the bridge of his nose and gestured with one hand. "Scar. If not Brass and Chris... there's no way you slept with this jackass." Jett pointed to a stone-faced Slate. "Then..."

"Drop it. We do not keep track of everyone *you* have slept with. Could not, if we tried." Quick tried to laugh, but it sounded forced.

Realization dawned on Jett and he looked impossibly disappointed. "Oh, Scar."

I would not cry.

"Who?" Tawny asked irritably.

"Really? I am very glad your bed did not entice me last night." Slate smirked like a man who was proven right in the face of adversity. "Khoraz to the core."

"Shut your mouth, Slate. You have *no* idea what you are talking about," Quick's growl shocked me.

"It's fine, Quick," I whispered. "Peak."

Tawny gasped. "Fiddlestick! Scar, no."

Slate chuckled. Jett dry washed his face. Quick was getting angrier by the second, I had never seen this side of him.

"Neither of you have room to judge. Slate, you sleep with my aunt who is the same age as Patriarch Haust. As have you, Jett."

I placed my hand on Quick's back and he turned around to face me. "Thanks, I don't care, Quick."

"Scarlett Tio. You are not having an affair with a married man who is your husband's uncle while you are pregnant! Who *are* you?" Tawny cried. "You can't even make something like this up!"

"Keep your voice down!" I hissed. "Someone heal this crap off me." Quick's hand was on me before I finished my thought. "Butt out of my private life. I have an *estranged* husband."

"He came here? Like, for a *nooner*?" Tawny asked, appalled.

I wanted to scream in order to end it now, instead I said what they were afraid to hear. "Yes! Peak comes here just for me. Apparently, I can hold on to all sorts of men I don't want but not the ones I do!"

"We get the idea, girl. Fox is looking for you," Slate interjected in a stern tone.

I blinked several times at him until Quick put his hand on my shoulder and started to lead me away. I was out of it and let him guide me to the caramel skinned battle trainer with baby blue eyes. The youngest Straumr brother of the three who trained here.

"Why lie, Scarlett?" Quick whispered.

"Because, if Jett finds out the truth, he'll get himself killed or imprisoned. An opportunity will present itself. Until then, I just need some time."

Quick stopped and hugged me. "Now that he has had you, he will not stop."

I bit my lip not wanting to bury my face in his chest. "Don't be nice to me, Silver. I don't think I can stand kindness right now."

"Come. You are more skilled at battle than any of these other tyro women and most of the men. They will forgive your absence." Quick led me back past the others.

"Where are you going?" Tawny asked.

"Playing hooky. Want to come?" Quick dazzled her with a panty dropping smile.

Tawny bit down on her lower lip. "Yeah."

CHAPTER 10
SLATE

She had been teasing me all day with her scent. A constant sphere of her warm spiced apple scent mixed with vanilla wafted from her all day as we went to classes. It filled my lungs while we sat during lessons. Her skin was silky, soft and I could not stop touching it.

She was fierce and strong. An elemental. I should have guessed from the scent of fire on her skin. The woman had defended me from the greater family brats. No one had done that since I was fourteen and first shifted into my barghest hybrid form.

As far as my memories were concerned, two nights ago I went to sleep in my black leather bed in the Sumar palace after hours of Cordillera's red room. The next morning, I had a wife. My secrets had all been revealed.

I believed her. I believed them all. That did not make things easier.

My uncle's scent was all over her and she stank of lies. Not the kind where she denied what she did, but the kind where she lied and hurt herself. She did not lay with him willingly, shame and guilt hung heavy in an acrid scent around her. I would kill him on principle. Peak should have known better. Barghests did not share.

Now I had to pack my own things and bring them back to the Sumar palace because Pearl refused to have the staff help. She must have spoken to Sparrow and Hawk as well since their staff also refused to move my clothing back.

I entered our wing — *her* wing. It was late. She should have been sleeping. I would get my clothes and go. The obscenely white bed laid empty. Was she with Brass or Peak?

She came out in a blush pink satin nightie with cream lace. Her caramel hair fell to her elbows, and she acknowledged me with a lift of her green-blue eyes and then went into the bathroom. That was it. She did not say a word to me. Fury rose as the beast roared inside me.

The light from the bathroom cast shadows of her nipples. I watched those ripe, heavy breasts rise and fall with her every breath. The satin fluttered with her racing pulse. *Her* with her soft supple curves, her taut abs, and long lean legs. On top of which, she was clever and proud. I was merely acknowledging facts, not admiring her.

I wanted to bend her over the sink and feel her from the inside.

Bright almond eyes met mine in the mirror. Her pupils dilated and her nostrils flared. By the Mother. She could not mask her arousal. It was constant. Confined in the small room the air sizzled with our chemistry. When she had smiled, my cock got hard. She was not smiling now. I had forgotten what I was doing there and why I had followed her into the bathroom.

"Come for your things?" she asked as she turned off the faucet.

Her neckline dipped as she leaned and I caught myself leaning to peer down her night dress like an adolescent boy. "I have."

She arched a brow a shade or two darker than her caramel waves. "Do you need help?" she asked, obviously wondering why I was in the bathroom staring at her.

"No," I said curtly and walked to the closet.

At least the staff had brought the boxes I had asked for. I began loading my clothing into the boxes knowing once brought to my rooms, the staff would put them away for me so there was no need to take care. Boots, belts, weapons, it was all there.

Her scent proceeded her as she entered the closet and began to help in a more orderly fashion. When she reached, the satin lifted to reveal the firm curve of her backside. She did not appear to have panties on, or if she did, they were quite small. Her hair hovered by the curve of her spine, swinging as her movements became a rhythm.

"Thank you." It was the least I could say.

"It's no problem. Sparrow and Hawk informed me the staff would not be helping you move out. It's silly really, you are a grown man. You can do as you wish. If I'm not giving you a hard time, why should they? Did Pearl forbid the staff from helping too?" she asked in a genial tone.

"She did," I rumbled, noticing my mother's emerald ring remained on her slender finger with a pink polished nail.

I dug in my pocket remembering where I had placed my own ring and slapped it to the top of the drawers. She froze and stared at the ring. I turned away, fearing she would start crying, but she did not. She would not show weakness to me again if she could help it.

"Keep it. You may not want it now, but once it meant a great deal to you. It still means something to me and I would never give it to another man," she said and picked up a pair of boots off the floor and packed them securely among my things.

"I have no use for it. It stays here."

"Then I will give it to one of my sons," she said in a rush without faltering in her rhythm. "Are you going to ask for your mother's ring back?" she asked with a flick of her eyes to me.

"No. I never thought any woman would wear it."

"An heirloom for my future daughter as well then, my thanks," she said stiffly and pulled off the ring to reveal her tiwaz tattoo that she shared with Brass.

She slid the rings around her necklace so it joined the stone pieces on its chain and rubbed her finger absently with her thumb. "I think you have some things in the bathroom," she said, her voice growing thick.

She rushed off and her scent wafted to me with the salty hint of tears to come. She would not cry in front of me. With my heightened hearing I could hear her sniffles and deep fortifying breaths from behind the closed bathroom door. It opened, and she came back dry eyed with my toiletries in her hands and began packing them into boots.

"I think that's it," she announced, running her palms over her stomach.

I closed the last of the boxes and took in the room. That was everything.

"Do you need help? Give me a moment, I'll put on my robe."

She came back with a champagne half robe that did not cover much more and a pair of comfortable looking cream slippers that hid her bare feet. "All right."

She *called* four boxes in the air in front of her as I carried two and *called* another three. We walked down the halls together in silence. The slapping of the soles of her slippers on the marble were the only noise so late at night.

We reached the cathedral like portal room and she gestured for me to go first.

I was embraced by the bright white light and came out on the other side in the Sumar palace. She was right behind me and bathed in the faux blue star light.

"I'll just set them here if you don't mind," she said, lowering the boxes against the wall.

"My thanks," I said to her, feeling inexplicably guilty.

Her hands went to her stomach which had not begun to swell as yet. Jett had mentioned it was because she was so sick with worry for the past couple of months that she had lost weight instead of gained.

"Slate?" she called, stopping me in my tracks.

I turned to face her and set down the boxes I held. She walked forward, her hips had this way of swaying in a sultry manner even when standing still. She looked up to me, hands clasped. Her thumb rubbed against the tendon of her palm as she spoke.

She gave me a nervous smile, but it was like a punch to the gut for all its radiance. "If your stupid prophecy doesn't happen for another five years say, just know I'd really like to have some kind of relationship with you. Even if it's just as a friend," she said and flashed another nervous smile.

I wanted to invite her up to my room. A real bedroom with black leather and furs made for a man. She would look fantastic naked in my bed. I must have installed a mirror on my ceiling to better see her move, because one now resided where there was not one before. I had no memory of any woman being in that bed, but Jett had informed me that Amber and Scarlett had both stayed with me in my room.

She scanned my eyes for an answer. "I shall consider it," I said more brusquely than I had intended and she nodded.

"Good night, then," she said and her pulse suddenly jumped as if she was afraid.

"Something wrong?" I could not help but ask it.

Her breasts rose and fell heavily as she tossed her waves from her face. "No. It's been a while since I've slept totally alone."

"You are a pretty girl; I doubt you will stay alone for long." I suppressed a wince at my condescending tone.

Her face darkened, and she walked back through the portal without another word.

I kicked myself. Pretty? *Pretty* was the best I could come up with? She had been so insulted she had run off.

I bent down to pick up the boxes when the white light blazed again and she was back in the room. I stared at her as she charged purposefully towards me.

"I forgot something," she said with determination in her eyes.

She stepped up to me and stood on her tiptoes as she grabbed my hair at my chest giving it a hard yank. My head bowed down to her mouth with a willingness that frightened me. Her lush full lips scorched mine as electricity crackled around us. She withdrew and sucked in a breath.

"It must have activated sometime yesterday. I felt you when you had sex with Lynx. Thanks for that," she said without a hint of emotion and before I could stop her, she was gone again.

I stared at the door for a time debating if I should go back and apologize. Had I known the bond was active... I had no wish to hurt the girl more than I was already doing by leaving.

Irritation stewed, and I climbed off the bed.

Two gods' blasted hours since she walked out.

I knew she'd known Lynx. Lynx was surprised to see me when I came to her rooms. She had informed me that I denied her and told her I was faithful to my mate. Lynx knew I had claimed the girl and was irrationally jealous. The Minotaur khoraz had wanted me to claim her ever since Lera brought her to help take care of my urges while in barghest form. I could not mate with another woman, but there were other things to do aside from mating.

Lynx had not stayed sore for long. She had hoped I would come back to her. I always did, she said pointedly. I had been her lover as long as I had been Lera's with longer gaps between our trysts.

She had tried to buy my time through Lera. That was how she had met the girl. I had no idea the girl and Lera had grown so close that she was leading clandestine meetings with clients. Lera never liked any woman, but she grudgingly liked the girl.

Lynx had tried to ask questions about her, to ridicule the girl's appearance out of jealousy. There was nothing to poke fun of, the girl was flawless. In any case, it was not something I could abide, no matter our situation. Lynx had stopped once she saw she was only succeeding in irritating me.

I shook my head as I strode the covered pathway and looked both ways. She was not in the ludicrously white bed. Had she gone to Brass?

I padded barefoot into the cloister. I had been impulsive. I could not sleep remembering the way she had cried in the bathroom and how she had felt me with Lynx last night. I had the terrible suspicion that my uncle was threatening her into sleeping with him and here I was leaving her after she saved my life.

Curse my guilt and Quick's self-righteousness. It was he more than any other that made me feel like a scoundrel. The way he defended her made me believe all of her insane tale.

I heard the rhythmic sound of a woman sleeping as I walked across the well-kept grass. There was a stone bench she was laid across. A lattice with a vine of blue morning glories that looked similar to what Pearl had in her dining room wound around the lattice.

Her hands were folded under her cheek, her hair hung over the side of the bench, her legs curled up to her stomach. Her long lashes fanned across her high cheek bones and her too-full lips were pursed in a pout. So soft, those lips.

I carefully scooped her off the bench and she shifted in my arms to nuzzle my chest and wrapped her arms around my neck.

"I love you, Slate. Forever and always. Yours, mine, the world's. For all time," she murmured.

I froze. By the Mother, she was beautiful.

I brought her inside and laid her on the bed before crawling in beside her. She rolled onto her side and I pulled her against me. I delved. Her sons were healthy. How easily I could pretend they were mine.

This was not half bad.

"I hope you were not in town dressed like that."

I caught Pearl's musky floral scent the moment I opened my door but dismissed it. It had been years since she entered my rooms. Six or seven if I was not mistaken.

"No."

"Then at the Dagr palace?" she probed, and I hit the energy plate *calling* a sliver of lightning into the room to charge it.

Pearl sat in a grey satin robe over her long draped sleeved nightdress on my black tufted leather couch. I entered further into the room and sat on the opposite couch.

"To check on the girl," I said, keeping it brief hoping she would drop the subject.

She had no intention to. Her presence should have warned me enough.

She sighed gustily and ran long elegant fingers into coppery waves that were coifed even at the ungodly hour. I had barely roused with enough time to make my escape. I did not want to give the girl false hope.

"Darling, I try to stay out of your lives only offering my advice when it is sought, but I fear you are making a very grand mistake."

She held up her hand when I started to speak and I blinked at her.

When had she felt the need to discipline me in any manner? I was dumbfounded.

"You are my grandson and she is my granddaughter. I love you both dearly and I have sat back hoping for the best. Your actions trickle into each of us, your family. You are fated. Fighting only makes it harder. Hundreds of twists and turns have led to this path you are on together and we have each lost many dear ones. Do not be so quick to dismiss the possibility of happiness with her. I have never seen you happier than when you were together. I would not want you to lose your only chance at having a full life."

"If we were so happy, why does she carry Brass's son?" I asked, feeling a flare of irritation that the others had already decided whose side they had chosen.

"She was frightened of you. You were an unknown, and it reminded her too much of her mother's situation, darling. If you had been a little less... persistent, she would not have entertained Brass, I believe." Her smile deepened. "I do not think you know another way. She was raised differently and Brass has the right amount of finesse for her to feel safe. I do not need to illuminate for you how out of control she feels with you."

With that she stood, fabric sweeping the floor as she bent down to stroke the top of my head and place a kiss to it.

"I had always hoped Lark and Wren would live long full lives with many children, but I was wrong. You and Scarlett were the ones destined to be together."

She left me alone with the hurricane of information I had been given in the last forty-eight hours.

ELEVEN

I changed into snug khaki pants that I tucked into a pair of suede beige boots and a white ribbed tank top with a loose white scarf to cover my head just in case we were traversing a long distance to the arena site. I didn't remember falling asleep last night, and I had no idea how I got into my bed.

Once I was dressed and armed, I closed up the wing and started for breakfast. Hawk and Sparrow were eating already at the wrought-iron table. They lifted their heads to me and I saw the moment they realized I was alone again. Sparrow's smile was a bit weaker and Hawk glanced away as I sat. It was sufficiently awkward when I told them he was all moved out, but I planned on switching with him once things settled down since it was, after all, his palace.

It became clear once I came to the Sumar palace and caught the tail end of breakfast, that Pearl had planned on me and Slate going alone. I stood beside her with the faces of my family looking over to me and plastered a false smile on my face.

"Fresh air will do me good. I've been cooped up in my room for so long, I could use a little trek," I insisted.

Pearl's emerald eyes slid to Slate. She was not budging.

"Slate should go with you since he is the reason you were by his side for all those days caring for him, darling," Pearl said.

I avoided looking at him. "I'd prefer to keep this within the realm of those directly involved in the arenas. I'll have one of the Shadow Breakers come with me for protection," I urged.

"Brass?" Pearl asked amiably and poured herself tea shooing away one of the staff with a flick of her long-nailed hand.

"More than likely."

Pearl nodded. "Very well. Brass does have a fondness for you and so handsome. He knows how to treat a young woman." I leaned down to kiss her cheek and took the maps she had readied for me as well as the packs.

"Why so much?" I asked. "Is it far?"

"There are three places for you to decide on. It would be best if you spent the night rather than try to return in the dark, darling." Pearl said and sipped her tea.

My cheeks heated. "My thanks," I said, holding up the rolled-up map and nodded.

Jett laughed when he thought I was out of earshot. "Subtle, grandmother."

"Darling, I am sure I have no idea to what you allude to," Pearl said with a smile in her voice.

I heard Slate grunt in response.

Thrimilci's town center was at the bottom of a cliff side. The white palace covered the entire top, several pointed domes and turrets in metallic blue and golds glittering in the sunlight. Its arched hundreds of windowless windows were sculpted into the face of the palace. Two rivers that flowed around and behind the palace that led to the water fall behind it. Royal blue roofed white pueblos lined the cliff side to the palace gates. The cliff ran at the same level as the rivers and then fell off the side where the waterfall was.

The portal door behind me, was less of a door, and more of a fifteen-foot gate. It had a high mosaic arch, done in whites and blues, spiraling ironwork below it radiating from a blazing sun and below that an iron patch work door.

A white shimmering road of tightly compacted bits of stone had shops with blue signs and gold lettering. Big glass storefront windows and white Doric columns lined the stores. Brass and I walked the road that ran parallel with the river Mani in silence.

Women walked in their flowing light fabrics while men had sleeveless linen 'V' necks. Few people making longer journeys were dressed as we were and with just as many weapons. Brass had agreed to join me, but I sensed his reluctance not wanting to get in the middle of things.

The people didn't give him wide berth as they did Slate with all his scars. Guardians didn't have scars. We didn't get sick and thank the gods we didn't get STIs because they were all so hedonistic. Beautiful, strong, and hale. Most Guardians stayed in Tidings, but many would leave for higher education in the States of anywhere they wished once they were proven tried-and-true.

As we walked along the road, we froze before a familiar pair of people. Brass muttered a curse and the pretty blonde pinked when she saw us. Katydid and Solder, strolled down the street arm in arm with a belly that would put her at least six months along.

"Katydid. Solder!" I exclaimed with a broad smile and embraced them both.

The shop owner of the Armored Armoire was a few inches taller than I was, but heavily muscled which was only spoiled by how beautiful he was. Too beautiful for a man really with big, luscious lips that rivaled my own and glittering blue eyes that held a hint of mischief. Katydid was the twin sister to Cricket, who made up one of the three parts of the salon that were renowned for their talents. She had been on and off between Brass and Solder for years.

"Scarlett!" Solder exclaimed.

He gave Brass a nod as did Katydid who waved with a quick waggle of her hand and placed her hands over her stomach reflexively as we spoke. "Congratulations."

Solder had a small scar in his brow, one of the few Guardians I'd ever seen with a scar. He smiled and it warmed you deliciously from the inside out.

"My thanks. I hear we are to congratulate you too. That bastard finally wore you down?" Solder said, laughing.

Part of me thought I should start to tell people of the true paternity of our sons and our estrangement since Slate was already whoring around Tidings, but I couldn't bring myself to do it. After I had risked and sacrificed, it was much too much like admitting failure.

"Thank you. We've run into some hiccups, but I'll iron those out soon enough," I told them as people bustled by.

Katydid giggled and Solder smile deepened. "Hiccups you say? We would not know anything about those," he said with a wink.

"We eloped. I should not have been able to conceive. We are very blessed," Katydid said, blowing her blunt cut bangs away from her eyes to gaze at Solder adoringly and I let my eyes flit to Brass.

Once again, he didn't claim our sons. My heart sunk to the shimmering stones.

"We should be off. Katydid, if you and the girls are looking to expand your business, I would love for you three to help me in readying the competitors for my arenas once they're built."

Her blue eyes grew to saucers with excitement. "Cricket has been looking for another business opportunity. We have taken on two more girls that are training, but they will be ready in a few months. That will work out splendidly for us."

"Excellent. When I visit my site in Valla, I'll bring by a contract for you all to look over. Solder, the competitors need fine armor to wear..." I told him and Solder ran his hand carefully over hair styled the same way as Quick's, but a chocolate brown instead of Quick's espresso.

"I never say no to business. With our little one on the way, any extra money is a help," he said, patting her tummy gently, and I thought I would swoon at his care for her.

"Then when I get back, I'll have my people send something over.

Enjoy your day," I told them, as I started walking before Brass could join me.

"I didn't know that was a thing."

His amber gaze lay straight ahead as we walked. "Has been for some time. I am happy for them. Annoyed, but happy."

He gave me a sheepish smile, and I turned away. We were keeping up with the facade that our sons were Slate's for their own well-being, but I was starting to think it may be best for my less than stellar reputation. The problem was, I wanted people to know they were Brass's. I wasn't ashamed of my children, only of myself.

With the hot Thrimilci sun overhead it smelled like warmed clay and sunshine. Brass's fingers laced through mine and I reluctantly sought comfort from him. Idly, he rubbed the tiwaz tattoo before he worked up the nerve to asked me what had taken the form of a pink elephant floating above us and rudely didn't offer any shade from the perpetual summer sun.

"Your lack of ring and husband leads me to —"

"He moved out. It's over. He doesn't remember me and has no desire to be with me other than in the bedroom." I pulled my chain out with the rings on it. "Reduced to heirlooms." I sighed.

Brass slid his hand from mine to wrap his arm around my shoulders. "Give it time."

"He slept with Lynx. I felt it through our bond. It's over, Brass. I just haven't come to terms with it yet. I suppose that's what needs time. He's alive. That's enough for me. I can look myself in the mirror again."

There were three sites to visit. Judging from the three meals and rolls, Pearl intended this to be a bonding experience for Slate and me. Now I was sharing it with Brass. I was trying very hard not to seem starved for affection.

We reached the third site at dusk and I walked around what Pearl had someone outline with orange tagged stakes. "What do you think?" I asked, noting how close it was to the River Mani.

Brass looked around; the sky turned purple in his background. The light of the stars began to peek through. Palm trees were scattered along this part of the river, coconuts that had fallen free sat on the ground.

"It is a good location," he said, walking over to me.

He began to unpack and snapped out the rolls. My lips quirked.

"It's only a two-hour walk back."

"If we are to make him jealous. It is better that we spend the night away together," Brass said in his smooth deep voice.

"Games. I hate games. Why would he care?" I said bitterly as I planted, grew, then chopped down a tree for firewood. It was good to have *calling*.

Brass tossed me a pear which I plucked from the air as the fire crackled and I sat back on one of the rolls he'd placed together. I wouldn't have to sleep alone tonight.

I bit into the pear.

He sat down next to me stretching his legs out in front of him. He took out one of his many daggers and I watched him as he pricked his thumb. A bead of his blood welled to his pad and he took my hand wiping the blood over my tiwaz and repeating the action on himself. His emotions bloomed in my mind and even though he had this nervous flutter to him, I found it reassuring.

I sighed as I leaned back to mirror his posture.

"I'm not your fail-safe," he said out of the blue.

"I know. I didn't ask you to come with so I could seduce you despite how it may look. I asked you because I'm sick of putting on a fake smile and a brave face. I don't want to give in to my weaknesses either. I miss my mom and Alder. I miss Slate. I miss everyone we've lost. I keep wondering when things will settle down and we can live wonderfully boring lives like the rest of the world. No imminent danger or life-threatening situations.... I'm not the right person for this saving the world business."

I folded up the wax paper that held the meat and breads and put it into the pack. I laid back on the roll and folded my hands over my stomach to look at the stars. Brass did the same and turned towards me. I shifted my face to look at him and gave him a small smile.

"He came to you again," Brass said in a low, knowing tone.

I glanced away. "It's not something I want to discuss now or ever. It is what it is." I told him shifting, so I gave him my back.

Brass's strong arm banded around my stomach as he pulled us together. I almost whimpered at his kindness. I was pathetically vulnerable. I hated that Peak was the last one to have touched me in an intimate way, but I wouldn't use Brass as a palate cleanser to rid myself of Peak's bad taste.

Cinnamon and morning dew on a field of wildflowers. I knew he tasted like cinnamon too. His hand settled on my stomach as he tucked me to his body in a way that we had slept together for many nights.

"I am sorry, love," Brass whispered. "I know if you were not carrying our sons you would never let him force himself on you. You would die first."

"You don't have to apologize. I would do anything to protect them, Brass. Are you... ashamed that I'm the one carrying your children? I understand why you would be. If you and I were only ever friends and you trusted me to have your children, I would have, as your friend."

Brass rolled me onto my back and looked down at me, his brows creased. "Scarlett. Don't be ridiculous. I didn't tell Solder and Katydid because I do not want to risk your well-being. I thought that was what we agreed? Once Peak was taken care of, we'll tell everyone the truth? I will shout it from the top of Valla U if you let me."

I stared into those soft inviting amber eyes. My vulnerability was spilling over. I would take advantage of his kindness and kiss him. That would just be the *first* thing I did. I *called* putting him to sleep before my wanton ways got the best of me.

I'm walking through carnage. I feel her, I hear her, my mother's standing in a white dress arms held out, her face distorted. She tells me I can fix this. I try not to look at the bodies, the battleground alongside Valla University. Not everyone is dead. Frozen faces stare up at angry faces on the castle, I can't even tell if the faces are human. They all look like monsters to me. The wind is whipping at me, I look up at the sky, even the sky is angry. Black clouds, lightening without rain. She's all around me, "You are night".

I stand in the middle of a circle, people around the edges, Slate lies bleeding on the ground. Light and gushing wind blasts from my body, my hair, my hands, shoot up. My mouth opens in a silent scream.

"Slate!" I screamed as I woke up trembling.

I had to find him. He was still alive. He had to be. I couldn't breathe. I clutched my heart; it pounded in my chest so hard it hurt. Arms banded around me and I screamed again.

"*Shh.* Scarlett. Easy. A nightmare, that is all," Brass soothed.

I let him hold me as I collected myself. I'd been having that dream for as long as I could remember and it grew more vivid the more I found out about it.

"He's safe. We rescued him," Brass reassured me and I nodded in acknowledgement.

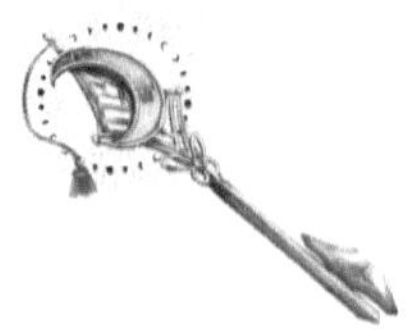

We made it back for breakfast and Brass sat next to me at Pearl's table across from Slate. Everyone had looked at us with too much interest and I had wanted to growl at them to get away. My hormones were raging and the only thing that kept me from snapping at people was Brass's calming presence through the bond.

"The third site was excellent. Indigo can get in touch with the contractor so we can break ground by the end of the week. I'll have to get in touch with Orion to make sure those portals of his are coming along. An arena so far away would be no good to anyone without a portal. Brass thought it was good, too."

"Why Brass?" Slate interrupted.

Fury raged and Brass found my knee under the table giving it a reassuring pat.

"Brass is going to run the arenas for me with Quick's help. There will be someone to run each team who will be tied to each arena, but overall —"

"Why Brass?" Slate asked and someone cleared their throat.

My cheeks stung. "Because the Regn brothers aren't connected to any one greater family more than another. They're smart and charming. We'll need someone like that to run things for me because I'll have two newborns to care for in six to seven months. I want the arenas open before I have the twins. This January if I can push it."

"Thank you," Quick said with a dazzling smile.

"You're very welcome," I said, returning his smile.

"*Gods*, Scar don't make his head any bigger, his neck isn't thick enough to hold it as is," Indi murmured so only Quick and I could hear her from where she sat between us.

"I should get going," Brass said, getting to his feet.

I was the saddest version of myself as I scrambled to my feet and placed my napkin on the table. "So soon?" I cursed myself internally for my public outburst.

Brass gave me a warm smile, and I bit my lip looking away from those knowing eyes. Brass offered his hand, and I took it lacing my fingers through it without a second thought.

He said his goodbyes and led me out to the portal room. Brass slid his hand along my jaw and into my hair. I would not nuzzle.

I did sigh as Brass lifted my chin and I gazed through my lashes at him.

"Oh, love," he whispered.

Our bond had been deactivated by our hand holding, but I understood what he was saying. He didn't want me to only go to him because Slate rejected me.

Bright white light lit the room as a snowy-haired man entered the portal room making me pull away from Brass. "Mrs. Tio. Just who I was looking for," Orion said.

He always wore his sleeveless councilor robe, and he actually quirked his lips up in a sort of smile.

I returned his smile with my megawatt grin. "Orion, how are you? We secured sites for two of the five islands now. The pressure is on. I hope to break ground in both places by next week's end. How are the portals coming along?" I asked.

"They are done. That is why I am here. I promised you one to each site and one to Chicago." Orion gave me a wink and I drew my brow down with a smile.

"I'll be staying here now but thank you. That's fantastic news."

I looked to Brass hoping he would agree, but he was watching Orion like he was some shifty eyed character out of a cartoon. I nudged him with my hip and he smiled with an edge that made my brow quirk.

"You will want to visit again, I am sure. You need only drive it across the country and deposit somewhere safe so you may enter and exit through it and directly to your apartment there. Tawny tells me you plan a trip soon, seems the perfect time," Orion said.

"I planned on going for my birthday. Driving is just as good as flying."

"It is settled then. Whenever you plan to go to Chicago, we will have the gate prepped to transport and you can visit the site while you are in Elivagar. Your husband is invited too, of course."

I didn't waver. "We'd like that though he doesn't have any interest in the arenas. I'll come with Tawny. Harvest break then, the week after next?"

Orion nodded. "Wonderful. Now, I must go see my granddaughter."

I eyed Brass who had watched Orion leave. "You're being weird."

"He is hiding something." Brass's defined lips pressed together.

"How very cynical of you. Do you want to train with me? Maybe we could go next weekend to Ostara if I get in touch with Ruby Geol. It would be wonderful if we could have them all started by my birthday."

Training snapped him out of his thoughts. "Light training. You should be taking it easier these days."

I gave him an indulgent smile and looped my arm through his as we walked towards the Sumar training conservatory.

CHAPTER 12

INDIGO

"I like doing it in your room. You have only had me here," Silver purred, kicking the door closed with his heel.

I was reversing through the sitting room as he sauntered forward. He even *walked* like he'd blow your mind in bed. How was that possible?

"I thought we were going to train? I have to get in touch with the contractors so I can give them the site locations. Scarlett wants to break ground —"

"I heard her. It can wait. It can all wait. I cannot." Silver flashed me a smile that seemed to be directly connected to my loins.

I licked my lips and his chocolate eyes glittered; he knew he had me. "Sometimes I regret ever having invited you back to my room."

He slapped his palm over his heart but didn't falter. "Ouch. Truth, Dove." He feigned heartache, and I wanted to kick him in the shin.

Silver moved in a way that bespoke the cause for his nickname and caught me around the waist as I yelped with what I was sure was a lunatic grin.

"We're not making it to the bed are we?" I asked in between Silver's hot kisses pulling the hem of his shirt from his pants.

"Why use a bed when we have this perfectly good chaise here?

Seems a waste not to utilize it," Silver purred, letting me tug his shirt over his head.

My index finger found his tattoos and I traced its lines as he found the zipper of my dress. "Pearl's plan didn't work. Unless her plan was to rub it in Scar's face that she's not with Brass. She's heart broken, not like when he's screwed up. This was worse. This was intentional. She's flailing."

Silver pulled back and looked down at me. "Really? *This* is what you choose to talk about during our foreplay? Babies and philandering? Gods, Dove. You are lucky it takes much more than that to turn me off." Silver growled as he lowered his face to mine again sending me into a ridiculous fit of giggles.

"I'm serious. I'm worried about her. I think Scar is vulnerable and Slate can't remember how much he loves her. It's a terrible mix. Maybe we should invite them out on a picnic? Like they did for us?" I asked as I lifted my hips so Silver could finish disrobing me.

Silver lifted his wry gaze to me. "That was a very good day, was it not? We can. It is the least we can do since that was the first time you let us be seen outside together. Slate hides what he feels, but she is under his skin. Notice how silent he was at breakfast? Likely because Brass kept making moon eyes at her when she was not looking."

I slipped my bare toe into the cuff of his boots and pushed them off before removing his pants. "Brass does not make moon eyes. They love each other. They thought he was with Amber; he *was* with her. They made plans. It's hard for all that to go away just because he is back in the picture," I defended.

Silver pulled back again and narrowed his eyes at me. "Sounds like you speak from personal experience, Dove. Am I Brass or Slate in this scenario?"

"I don't make plans with anyone past the night. You know that. I don't think anyone is wrong, not Scar, Slate, or Brass. The heart wants what it wants." I slid my hand to his close-cropped nape and rubbed my palms across the stubble.

Silver shut his eyes and made a contented sound. "I know that. Perhaps we *should* make a few plans."

My hand stilled. "Silver..." I warned.

That topic of conversation always led to a fight, and we'd had two days of lovemaking and smiles. No need to spoil it with talk of not seeing Sterling again or Silver's latest ridiculousness, marriage.

"All Guardians get married at our age. Brass is a freak of nature with his mind reading that is why he has not settled down, but otherwise, we are entering our prime. I know you want kids. We have four to five years left for that at most." Silver said raising himself onto his hands.

I took a deep breath before my anger could wash over me. "Ask me again in two years."

"Two years, Indigo!" Silver's ego was bruised.

I laced my fingers behind his neck and he pulled me up as his shifted onto his knees. "In two years we'll still be younger than Brass is now. If neither of us is married, we can marry one another," I promised.

Silver's gold-flecked eyes searched mine. No one should be so good looking. Silver drew the dagger from his boot and sliced his palm before handing it over pommel first.

"Promise me," Silver said, daring me to go back on my word.

"I have a few conditions. You can't have any bastards and I can decide how big or nonexistent I want the ceremony," I said, feeling a lunatic like exhilaration.

"Done. Give me your palm Indigo Tio, you are not weaseling your way out of this one."

I gave him my palm, and he kissed it before he slid the blade across, its bite didn't sting. My adrenaline was making me feel loopy. Silver clasped my hand to his.

"*By the name gifted by my ancestors, I give my word. May I never stain it. From my blood, I vow with the voice of my forbearers. On my honor, and the honor of my descendants, I hereby swear to keep it.*"

We said the blood oath in unison. Provided he didn't impregnate some hapless girl and neither of us were already married, two years from today we would be married even if we lived on the other side of the planet from one another.

What did I just agree to? I should have added more stipulations. It was a bad idea.

"No, you do not," Silver growled as he healed my palm. "Drop that look from your lovely face, Dove."

I did the same for him and he took it looking victorious kneeling between my bare legs.

"Now I am going to make love to my betrothed," Silver said with that cursed smile.

Butterflies fluttered in my stomach. "I didn't get permission to be betrothed from my matriarch or patriarch," I said numbly.

Silver kissed me and I sighed. He was a fabulous kisser — unparalleled. Sterling was going to be furious with me.

"Hush now, my betrothed," Silver said, making his way down my body.

"You're not really going to start calling me that, are you?" I asked dryly.

I gasped as he made his way south of my navel, my fingers curls into the jacquard cushion. "I am. We are. Promised to be married in two years. If there is a better word for what that means, I suppose I could call you my fiancée," Silver teased smugly as his tongue met my most sensitive flesh.

Freya's burly boar! He was right! What had I done?

CHAPTER 13
JETT

If Slate managed to retrieve his memories, he would regret what he'd done for the rest of his days. Funny thing was, Slate's fists had clenched when Brass had held her hand. They had spent the night together, though any idiot could see Brass was holding back and they hadn't been intimate.

Well, not slept together.

Brass and Scarlett had the intimacy level of an old married couple, words weren't always needed because they could feel one another. On second thought, there had likely been a lot of intimacy in a way she didn't have with anyone else.

It had been a good plan. Pearl thought a night away from them all, no pressure, and they could reconnect. Not so much. There was always the trip to Chicago if they could convince Slate to go. Scarlett always had fun when she was there. She could show him her old life, totally Guardian free and maybe then they'd bond. Attraction wasn't the issue unless you counted it against them. They danced around this palpable heat in the room while they were together. It'd always been there, but now it was a tension, not the good kind.

Orion Vetr swept into the room; his scarlet robe slid to an inch above the floor. He came in and gave the girls kisses and inclined his head to the men before taking the seat at the foot of the table. Pearl's emerald eyes watched him, still wary after all this time of working together. Indigo and Quick had left shortly after Brass and Scar had, Jett only needed one guess to know what those two were up to.

"I just informed Scarlett that the portals are ready. She shall be bringing the one that leads to Chicago for us," Orion said, his hooded blue eyes on Pearl.

Pearl was quite the catch, in her youth Canis and Orion had wanted to marry her, but she chose Flint Sumar who died at the Red King massacre. She was a catch even now, a female Tio that ran the Sumar house until Gypsum came of age since Hawk wanted nothing to do with it. Technically, Gypsum was already the patriarch, but they'd kept that under wraps so they wouldn't overwhelm the kid.

All that greater family business could be daunting. Jett should know. Whenever Cygnus died, Jett would be the patriarch to the Var house. Amethyst was giving him lessons since she was a Geol and a Straumr, both greater families. It was all very dull. It was a lot of work governing an island. It was better being the second son, like Steel. He would stay as an ambassador to the Thrimilci tribes unless Tawny who was now an Elivagar heir wanted him to be her arm candy. Jett doubted Tawny would do that, she was fiercely independent and would want Steel to do what made him happy.

"That's wonderful!" Tawny beamed.

She was quite the beauty when she wasn't in a fury, though Jett had to admit her fierce little glare could be sexy. Women like Tawny were rare. Steel met her, and she was swept away. It was mutual. She never looked at another man after that even when they were on the outs. There had been the time Jett turned Divine Beauty on her and she'd pulled him under the table in the middle of the great hall at Valla U. Her soft porcelain thighs had straddled his waist caught in his spell as she rubbed her lush chest...

It'd been hard to look at her the same way since.

"Indigo will be happy. I think she plans on taking an extended vacation once she's proven tried-and-true," Jett said, leaving out that it would coincidentally coincide with Sterling's wedding to Diamond.

Orion nodded as if he thought as much. "I could not help, but notice her lack of wedding ring, and yours for that matter." Slate's hand paused with his goblet to his lips. "And that she was with that lesser family young man. Has she taken a paramour?"

Jett coughed. The Regn family would love hearing one of their eligible sons had become a paramour for a greater family girl. It was a good thing Quick had gone already. Talk of paramours was not usually done in front of spouses without a reason. That reason being to humiliate them.

Pearl normally would have come to Slate's defense, but Jett was getting the distinct feeling she did not approve of Slate's behavior in the least. "Brass Regn is an honorable young man Scarlett has chosen to be the commissioner for her arenas. They work very closely together."

Orion grunted in amusement and Pearl smiled at him. Some silent communication passed between them.

"I remember. He spent a great deal of time in my castle with her last month. That is how those things happen. A common interest, late night meetings, you find yourself having more in common with those you work with rather than the one who awaits you at home. Since you are here," Orion said to Slate, "I take it she does not have anyone waiting. Just as well since when I entered the portal room, the young man looked ready to profess his love. They left together. Out of respect for you I am sure, so you would not have to bear witness to their affections."

Slate's face went as stony as a cliff face.

"He has a mental block," Steel said simply and Orion nodded.

"I may be able to help if you are interested. I have many connections and finding someone adept at mind manipulations may be difficult, but not impossible," Orion told them.

"Orion, that would be marvelous. Thank you. He will think about it," Pearl said politely, since one look at Slate would tell you he had no interest in being near Orion now or ever.

Orion left, and they went to train after breakfast with all the girls. It was a conservatory the size of the stadium. All types of plants and trees lined the gravel track. It was divided into several sections, an obstacle course, a weightlifting area, an area that held all different kinds of weapons with mats, and a section for archery.

Their theory was, what you practice in, was what you were most comfortable fighting in. They wore lightweight sleeveless tops and black fitted pants; each had a set of soft black leather boots to wear specifically for training.

Tawny and the girls jogged around the track as the men went into the weight section. Jett started his Bluetooth speaker with songs he'd downloaded in Valla U's technology lab. They could tease him all they want; they liked having some background music while they trained.

Slate was lifting more than ever, his scar looked angry against his reddened skin as he worked. Steel and Gypsum shared a look and Jett walked over to spot Slate. Not that really needed spotting when they could *call*, but maybe he needed to vent.

Jett stood at Slate's head as he lifted with flashing gunmetal eyes. "Do not think I missed those barbs sent my way. Talking about a wife's paramour to her husband. She is free to fuck whom she wishes." The weights settled with the clank of metal and he sat up. "She was right when she said I had slept my way through the girls at Valla U. I have forgotten them all. I spoke to one briefly and she was insulted I forgot her." Slate wiped a hand over his face and used a hand towel to dry his hands.

"You're not sleeping with the girls at the university again, are you? Give her a little respect and don't do it in front of her face," Jett said in an even tone although what he really wanted to do was *call* up that barbell and whack him over the head with it.

"I could not if I wanted to. There is no way to tell who I have already been with until they slap me for having forgotten," Slate rumbled.

Satisfaction coursed through Jett. *Good.*

"All the old rules are back in place? No sleep overs? No one in your own bed? None of the staff?" Jett asked as Slate moved to another machine.

"Tried-and-true Guardians; they have served me well in the past," Slate confirmed.

Jett walked away having heard enough.

Swimming was always a great cool down workout. Guardians didn't need chemicals like other pools needed. Their *calling* kept the waters clear. The pool was huge, the walls were the royal blue that matched the rest of the Sumar palace with gold patterned trim. The ceiling was done in gold landscapes, exposed gold rafters spanned it. Plaster statues lined the pool, as well as globe lamp posts, already lit, thank goodness. The pool itself was tiled in royal blue with gold blazing suns.

Slate walked out from the prep room first in his swim shorts, Jett wasn't paying attention and slammed into his back.

"By the Mother, Slate," Jett said and caught what had frozen Slate in his tracks.

Scarlett. Her eyes shut on the far side of the pool with Brass. She had one hand fisted in his hair and the other at the end of a line of claw marks down his back while they kissed in such an intimate way, Jett had to check to make sure Brass had his shorts on.

Brass cursed and her eyes opened. Her claws retracted, but the mark her passions left were still on his back. Jett nudged Slate with his shoulder and he shook himself out of it as he started forward and jumped into the pool.

Scarlett's lips were swollen from their kisses and Brass's cheeks red with embarrassment as they swam over. They had been dressed. An intense make-out session, that was all. Tawny laughed when she saw how guilty they both looked and the rest filed out of the prep room surprised to see Brass and Scarlett. They hadn't seen them together, but their squirrelly looks were unmistakable.

Cherry was always quick on the uptake when it came to these things and since Slate was on everyone's shit list, it was the perfect opportunity to rub it in a bit.

"What are you two looking so guilty about?" Cherry teased.

Scarlett licked her lips and blushed. "Doing a little training."

Brass smiled at her unknown innuendo and raked a hand through his hair to push it from his face. Jett looked at Slate out of the corner of his eye.

"See. I said you would not remain alone for long, girl," Slate rumbled.

Scarlett bristled, as did the other girls. Brass saw the thunderhead that was Scar's beautiful face and he swam over to her to block her line of sight of Slate.

"I need to report to Lera. Would you walk me out, love?"

Scarlett's anger melted as she raised her eyes to Brass's. "Yeah," she said as she started towards the tiled steps.

Brass's hand rested on the small of her back as she ascended the steps and she twisted water from her hair. Cherry groaned.

"Hurry and put a towel on, Scar. You're making me look bad. How do you have two and I have one, but you can't even tell you're pregnant yet," Cherry pouted.

Scarlett looked down to her stomach that had a slight swell to it and smiled at Cherry.

Slate snorted.

"I think it is bigger than when I last saw you undressed," Slate rumbled.

Scarlett's smile slid from her face and was replaced by hurt. Slate hadn't anticipated that. Slate straightened from where he had been floating on his back and took a step forward.

Brass was grabbing towels for them and returned to her to place his palm flat to her belly and smile just before he bent down to place two kisses to either side of her practically flat stomach.

Scarlett's slender fingers slid over his damp hair and Brass straightened to put an arm around her shoulders. "Looks perfect to me."

Jett thought he would have to swim to the edge in case Scarlet swooned so she wouldn't drown. Her eyes darted to Slate as she let Brass lead her away.

Gypsum splashed Slate who wiped the water from his face. "By the Mother, how can someone so clever be this stupid?"

"Watch yourself," Slate growled.

"Go after her, you idiot," Amethyst said, astonishing Jett so much that he guffawed.

"Why would I do that?"

"So you don't have to watch your best friend making a life with your wife. So this is the last time you walk in on your wife wanting another man instead of you," Jett offered dryly.

Slate practically roared the way he growled and slapped the pool's surface. He looked towards the doors.

"She will always be the mother of his bairn."

"It's not the first time something like this happened. People work out understandings. They were close before. Brass didn't have any prospects. If he'd asked, since his fertility will wane this year, she would have said yes," Steel confirmed. "Slate, I don't think you would have been able to stop her no matter how angry it made you."

"She should show more respect to our family's home. We both have to be here." Slate had found his excuse.

He climbed out of the pool and prowled after them.

Steel sighed. "I forgot how much he hated the idea of marriage and children."

"We saw how he brooded for months after she left. He loves her, he just doesn't remember it. We have to remind him," Gypsum said as if it was that simple.

CHAPTER

FOURTEEN

It wasn't fair of me to throw myself at Brass. Brass loved me and I had used him to make myself feel better. I did feel better. Brass never left anything half done, and he had so thoroughly kissed me in the pool sex was not required... but desired. *He* forbade it.

I thought that was what he'd hinted at when he wanted to leave the pool, but once we got into the prep room, he changed and kissed me again before leaving.

"He cares. He needs time. I won't let him hurt you," Brass promised, pressing his forehead to mine.

Too late. I was hurting, and the wound felt like an ulcer on my heart.

"It's not your place to balance him out," I said, furrowing my brow.

He gave me another kiss. A chaste one this time and I pouted. Brass's lips parted into a warm smile and kissed me again.

"I do believe you are attempting to use me for my body, Scarlett," he said in amusement.

"Attempting, but not succeeding. I don't know a woman alive that would blame me. It is a fine body." I flirted. Brass arched a brow, and I groaned. "Okay, go... Brass?" I called as he walked away.

He turned around, tall and powerful. None of the hardness Slate harbored, and all the warmth a woman needed. He cut a striking figure, and I selfishly coveted him knowing I was married. I bit my lip.

His lips curled. "I know, love. Me too."

Brass walked away not needing me to remind him that though I did most definitely want to sleep with him, I also loved him very much. What he did when Slate had poked fun of my belly had made me doubt everything I'd ever had with Slate.

I sunk down to the bench in front of my cubby and hung my head. My hormones were wildly out of control. My lust was indiscriminate, my appetite bottomless, and my feelings hurt at the smallest slight. I started to cry. A good cry would be cathartic and I could have a clean start for the rest of the day.

My crying was rudely interrupted by an electric hand that pressed to my back. "Brass did not hurt you, did he?" Slate asked in a near growl that made me scoff.

"Don't be ridiculous. Brass would never hurt me," I said bitterly as I swiped tears from my face.

Drops of water glistened down his muscular shoulders, collecting along the ridge where his chest met his collarbone. Hard, dark pink nipples accented his sculpted chest, the trickle of water trailed down the crease between his pecs and led south to tight hard abs. The corded 'V' that angled along the silky black happy trail and under his swim shorts made my mouth go dry.

He bent down, his powerful bronze thighs flexing as he lowered himself down to the bench next to me so his shoulder brushed me. "I suppose not."

I unbraided the jade canine fetish from my hair and held it out. "It's yours. I'll take the other one."

The jade love rune. Slate got up, and I listened as he retrieved it from his cubby, then walked back. I opened my hand without looking and he pressed it to my palm before taking the canine fetish. I opened my cubby and placed it on the nearest shelf before shutting it again.

"What is wrong, girl?" he rumbled, taking his seat next to me again, this time his thigh rubbed against mine and I threw my guards up.

I sniffed a laugh. "Nothing. All my loved ones are safe for the first time in a long time. My body is doing something I didn't think I was capable of doing any longer, and it brings me an incredible feeling of fulfillment."

"Then why are you crying?"

I tilted my head to him and arched my brow giving him a dry smile. That scar did nothing to diminish his handsome face. It added character, and I loved a beautiful man with a little character. His snowstorm grey eyes looked genuinely curious to know my answer.

How could I tell him that I wanted a family complete with a loving husband and father and that it was impossible for me because that meant having two different men? How did I explain how my heart felt torn in half and I felt like I was losing my mind, trying not to lose Brass and fix things with Slate? The words wouldn't rise to my tongue which lay dead in my too dry mouth.

My hand rose of its own volition to his strong jaw and his brow quirked in surprise at my tender gesture. I couldn't help looking deep into his eyes wondering if he was in there somewhere acknowledging my touch. That the feel of me might rip some memory free that would set it all straight.

"How strange it is for you to look at me without the love I'd taken for granted in your eyes," I whispered and glanced away letting my hand fall. "Sorry," I whispered.

I slid to the edge of the bench and started to pull my things out of my cubby. He hadn't moved or spoken since I drenched him in my self-pity. I ignored him as I threw my towel over the bench and turned away to remove my top and pull my dress down over my head.

His hand gripped my elbow and spun me around. Frowning at his hand, I was blindsided when Slate crushed his mouth over mine. I was a powder keg, and he'd thrown a match. He sprouted a hundred hands and was everywhere at once, knocking us into the cubby.

The cool cubby door stuck to my hot skin as he kissed me frantically, I couldn't breathe. I winced as he roughly palmed my sensitive breasts under my fringed sea foam bikini top. He didn't stop. His emotions were in turmoil and I couldn't get a read on him other than the lust that devoured everything in its path.

My hands were tangled in his wet waves as I kissed him back

caught in his undertow. I hardly had time to gasp before he lifted me off my feet, his hips started to grind into me. We should not have be doing it. It was not what I wanted. I clung onto him, pinned to the cubbies by his body. His full lips imprinting everywhere they touched until my nails bit into his skin. He pulled back, and I saw his eyes flash. Two sets of fangs elongated from his perfect white teeth. His barghest teeth.

I *called*. A thin razor of air sliced against the swell of my breast that began to trickle blood over its soft curve. Slate inhaled sharply with flaring nostrils. Full lips latched to my breast greedily as he lapped up my blood. The force of his suction made me groan.

The prep room door swung and Cherry's laugh carried to us. I gasped, pushing off his chest. Moving a mountain would have been easier. Slate pulled his mouth from my chest and swallowed my mouth as he moaned with a deep vibration that shook through his chest. I felt his muscles tense as the voices grew closer.

Panic burst in me and I shoved at Slate as hard as I could. His eyes widened as he stumbled back and the bench tripped him. He was still holding me when he went over making me land on top of him.

A hiss like a cat escaped my lips as I shoved off him and pulled my discarded dress off the floor to yank it over my head. I was drying my hair barefoot with when Tawny and Steel walked past the aisle. Slate had managed to slide onto the bench with his shorts unable to hide him, he sat at an odd angle to mask it as Tawny shot me a questioning glance. I shrugged.

Once I heard someone else drying their hair with their *calling* and my waves were fairly dry, I spun on Slate. I imagined his expression mirrored my own. We blamed each other for the loss of control, but he blamed me for knocking his head against the cubbies. We were both irate. He rose when I turned and towered over me.

"This never happened," I spat.

Slate grunted derisively. "You will not catch me telling a soul."

"Then we're agreed, you never should have done that." I whirled to my cubby, dropping my wet suit to the floor. I grabbed my panties and pulled them on, then dropped my shoes so I could step into them.

"What *I* did? You with your dilating khoraz pupils, your bouquet of sex and arousal, stroking my face and speaking of love. You practically begged for it," He growled, turning me around a scant inch from my face.

I gaped at him. "Are you kidding me? I was trying to be *friendly* by opening up! I was getting dressed! You accosted me!"

Our chests heaved as we glared at one another. Heat rolled off him in waves permeating my skin.

"You are doing it again," he growled, locking in on my eyes.

My fists were on my hips as I glared up at him. "So are *you*," I grit out.

Slate slammed me back into the cubby, his tongue claimed my mouth. He pinned my hands above my head as he moved and I moaned against him. I used my *calling* to shove him around and kicked off the bench with a barefoot as we spun. Slate caught me under my backside as if we'd choreographed it. We slammed back into the cubbies. His responding animalistic growl made my insides squirm.

He squeezed firmly with no regard for my backside and spun us around again. Only I had dropped my shoes there and we were off balanced. He released me as his hands shot out to catch our fall. I grunted as the small of my back hit the bench.

Slate's hands had caught against the opposite cubby, his body over mine, but my back was bent over the side so my head was at the floor. Luckily, his body pinned me to the bench so my head hadn't whacked on the marble.

Slate's silver eyes glittered roguishly, "This is an interesting prospect," he purred if he was the kind of man who purred.

I narrowed my eyes. "Help me up. I hit my back."

As if it wasn't obvious with his enormous body on top of me. How could his massive weight falling on me at such an odd angle not hurt me?

He braced his weight on one hand and gripped me around the waist so his hips wouldn't release me from the bench and pushed off lifting us both. I winced as pain shot through my back. He caught my expression.

"Sit," he ordered, and I did.

It was then that I noticed Gyps staring at us with a bewildered expression. He must have been walking past to his cubby. No explanation came to mind. Jett appeared and punched Gypsum in the shoulder and he visibly shook himself before walking away.

Fantastic. We'd made a spectacle of ourselves.

Slate started to unzip the back of my dress and I leaned forward so he could check to see if it was only a scrape. "Most women wear a bra." He rumbled running his finger next to my tender flesh.

"Most women's breasts don't feel like over-inflated balloons with pins waiting to pop them at the slightest touch," I retorted.

Slate chuckled.

The bastard chuckled.

"I happen to know that they feel much better than that. From the outside anyway. It is only bruised," Slate notified me as he zipped my dress back up.

"Well, you definitely got more than your fair share of rough gropes in," I muttered. "Could you heal it? I really don't need any more random aches and pains."

Slate hesitated, and I scowled up at him. "For the gods sakes, Slate. They don't know who is *calling*. Unless you're telling me you're afraid of a couple of unborn babies. You know what? Forget it. I'm sorry I asked."

Slate clamped a hand on my shoulder when I started to rise. "Not any bairn; Brass's bairn in my wife's belly. It is no wonder why I have chosen to forget it.

I pinched my lips together to prevent something horrible from escaping.

He was sitting next to me again, so close, his damp hair slid over my shoulder as he pressed his palm to my belly. The warmth of his *calling* was combined with the thrum of energy I always felt from him.

I couldn't stop myself from ogling him as he delved. My chest swelled with joy when his full lips quirked. He'd felt them. The impulse to kiss him while his guard was down so potent I started to lean into his cheek. He flinched away and rubbed his cheek on his shoulder. His hand was gone.

"Your lashes touched me," he accused.

I struggled with a smile. "I believe the word you're looking for is *tickled*."

He gave me a sidelong glance, and I had to break his gaze for fear of laughing. "I do not get *tickled*, girl."

I ran my fingers through my hair and stood. I took out the fetishes and my sheath. I threaded the beads and fetishes into my hair and pushed up the lemon-yellow chiffon skirts to buckle on my short seax to my thigh. Slate rose to his feet when I let the dress fall to the floor. He stood, blocking my way and I raised my brows at him.

"Did you bed Brass last night?" Slate asked.

I smiled, and he nocked up his jaw. "I haven't slept with Brass since before we rescued you. I have slept *next* to him and we occasionally kiss. He won't take it any farther until he decides what is going on between us."

"I told him it was over," Slate rumbled.

"As did I. He doesn't want to be another obstacle."

I started to step into my nude wedges and blindly groped for the cubby to balance myself. Slate caught my hand and held it. Momentarily, I stared at our clasped hands. The last time I held his hand like that was the night of our wedding at the Wemic village. Of course, at that time, the ring he'd given me after my mother's death was on my finger.

I pulled away and rubbed my hands together to rid myself of the feel of his rough calloused palm from mine.

"You kiss Brass and have an affair with my uncle. Is that because Brass refuses you?"

Peak was like my nightmare. While it was happening, it was the worst thing that I could ever imagine, but when it was over, I pushed it from my mind and never gave it another thought. It's how I survived through it.

"Brass doesn't refuse, if I really wanted to, we would."

"You do not want to?"

I sighed. "It's complicated. I shouldn't."

Slate was still in his swim shorts and so much of his flawless skin was exposed. It was distracting.

"Why my uncle?"

"Why so many questions?" I snapped, coming to the end of my rapidly fraying rope.

"Tell me you take pleasure from Peak and I will never ask again." Slate rumbled, his silver eyes flitting between mine.

I started to turn away, and he grabbed my chin.

"Look me in the eye when you say it."

"It's no longer your responsibility," I said softly.

"Responsibility to do what, girl?" Slate asked in a low dangerous tone.

Sugarfoot. I hadn't meant to say that.

"*I'm* not your responsibility."

"Say it."

I pinched my lips together and glared at him. "Don't make me say it."

"That you do or do not?" Slate asked dryly. I shook my head and Slate sucked in a breath. "How long? Does Brass know?"

"Brass, Quick, Chafer, Lera, Indigo… they all know. I don't want anyone else knowing."

"What does he hold over you, girl?" Slate's fingers on my chin had grown tense and were pinching my face.

"You're hurting me," I whispered, and he released my face.

I rubbed my chin and looked away.

"Nothing," I lied.

Slate scoffed. "Do not lie to me. How do you think I knew you did not want him? Your scent changes when you lie."

I slumped down to the bench and stared at the cubby. "What's the point?"

"I need to know. As a barghest, you belong to me. He knew that. What he did was backhanded. He should have challenged me for you."

"So, this has nothing to do with me? You should have claimed Lera."

Slate growled and he was on me flattening me to the bench with gritted teeth. "Lera would not let me."

My chin wobbled. "I was the default? Wonderful."

Slate's face softened a fraction. "I claimed you because I could not resist you. I could resist Lera, so she remained unclaimed. It *is* about you. Tell me the truth. The whole truth."

"I can't," I pleaded.

His eyes flickered to my lips. His weight on me made me want to wrap my legs around him again.

"You are doing it again," he growled.

"*You* are," I said maturely.

"Answer me. I want the truth, Scarlett," Slate growled.

My name. He said my name. Such a silly thing should be common-place, but even before he was this jerk he rarely used my name.

"Stop doing that," I said, resisting the need to squirm.

His brow quirked and the corner of his mouth tugged as if it wanted to pull into a smile. "Doing what?"

"You know very well what you are doing. May I remind you that I can very easily burn through those very tiny shorts in a blink," I said imperiously.

"Ah, but you will not. You did not *finish* and I can scent how bad you want to. Besides, you have already burned me there once," Slate said with a curl of his lips.

"I am sure Lynx healed you so you could help *her* finish, so I should do you the favor of burning you again so you have an excuse to return."

Slate could sense my change and leapt from me before I could burn him as I shifted. He stood back watching me as I started down the aisle.

"I'd prefer we keep this to ourselves," I said, facing away from him.

"Whatever you want," Slate growled in frustration.

I narrowed my eyes and turned my head back to him. "You can't handle what I want, that is why I must find it elsewhere."

As I returned to my wing, a royal blue clad messenger from the Sumar palace found me and handed me a message from Valla. Reed and Moon wanted me to come to view the land for the arena. I groaned. It'd been such a long day already; I had no desire to play diplomat. I had used all of my diplomacy to not kill my estranged husband and there was no doubt in my mind that Ash would be there.

It was fall in Valla, the only island with seasons, which meant Mabon styled clothing would be in fashion. I hurried to my closet and started to change into a corset with a petticoat with a bustle. I chose an amethyst Basque with three -quarter sleeves that flattered my hour-glass figure splendidly. I paired it with a pleated skirt of heavy taffeta ruffled with velvet.

While I pinned my hair in a loose chignon, Gypsum came into the bathroom without knocking. "Hey, Scar. Is everything okay?"

My adorable cousin even had dimples when he frowned. His hair was plaited like Slate's with copper beads threaded through a dozen braids. He wore a grey sleeveless 'V' neck with two jade toggle buttons on the side tucked into black pants. He was the epitome of Thrimilci men's fashion. His golden belt buckle was the blazing sun of the Sumar's and his black leather boots had two small golden suns at the buckles in greater family fashion.

"Sure. Why?" I asked, tucking in the last pin and beginning to sweat profusely in all the layers.

"Slate was even more of a dick after you left than before. I didn't think it was possible." Gypsum shook his head ruefully with a small smile.

"He's not the same person. We are our choices and there are hundreds of choices this Slate never made to make him my Slate. Try not to hold it against him. It's not his fault." I wished I could believe my own words; they were very convincing.

"Did you..."

"Chief! If you're asking what I think you're asking, I'm going to grab a bar of soap and wash your mouth out. Do you want to come to Valla with me? I have a meeting about the arenas and could use some company. Hawk probably has a jerkin you could throw over your shirt."

He followed me as I left the bathroom and headed into the bedroom to find a pair of earrings. "Yeah, yeah, I'll come," he said dismissively and went on, "It's just...what if you *did*. Like... regularly... maybe he needs to remember what it's like to be loved by you."

"Love is a feeling triggered by several actions not one action we do very little thinking during. I didn't fall in love with him because I was sleeping with him and I doubt that's why he fell for me. It was more likely because I *didn't* and he was forced to get to know me. That ship has sailed with this version of him," I said dryly and Gypsum laughed.

"Why would he be so angry then? I thought he'd be happier since he'd been staring at you all the time, asking if anyone else was coming to meals and such."

"No clue. Maybe one of his lovers turned him down."

Gypsum's smile had a devilish gleam that promised juicy gossip. "Diamond said Slate spoke with one of the girls he'd been with before you guys got together and he didn't remember her. It's going around that he's slept with so many he can't get them straight so the girls are mad at won't speak to him. Diamond said that even if they weren't mad, that they wouldn't touch him because they're afraid *you'll* touch them as an elemental and there wouldn't be ashes to have at their funeral."

"Why don't you go get that jerkin?" I asked, jiggling the emerald-cut diamond earrings in my palm as we walked to the living room.

"Sure thing," he said and trotted off.

I frowned at his retreating back. People were already discovering that he'd lost his memory and that he couldn't recall who he had been with. There was a straight line in that thought process that would bring people to him not remembering me and him being back on the market. How could he be married if he didn't even remember it?

The Straumr palace was done in the height of Gothic architecture with elegant rose windows, pointed archways, and ribbed vaulted ceilings. Deep purples, reds, blues, and greens colored the elaborately ornate castle.

I'd worn purple intentionally, it was one of the colors of the Straumr sigil; the white crescent moon lit on a darker full moon on a purple field. Ash always loved me in purples, I hoped that applied to all Straumr's men. Reed would be there as well, as long as I acted like myself, he'd help me.

Gypsum had borrowed a silver jerkin with a high collar and black striped long sleeves. He looked exactly what I imagined he would when he grew up, but then, he had, hadn't he? He'd always be a fifteen-year-old scoundrel to me, but he was a man. The patriarch of the Sumars made for dazzling arm candy as we were led to a waiting room by the Straumr servants.

"Remember the last time we were here together?" Gypsum whispered with a smirk.

I did. Ash showed me how to *call* that day, and then showed me how to use it on a man. I had caught Gypsum and Diamond together that day for the first time.

We sat in the green embossed velvet chairs of the parlor. Rich mahogany wood winged the chairs and pedestal table, while a low fire burned in the burgundy marble fireplace. A tiered tray displayed a variety of powdered pastries and Gyps picked one up and began to eat as he looked about the room.

The door opened, and we got to our feet. Moon, Reed, and Ash entered the room. Quartz, Dahlia, and a man with skin the color of creamy coffee swept into the room he had obsidian eyes like his brother, with a tightly manicured goatee. Basil Straumr was the aloof younger brother of Moon Straumr, and Ash's father. He was also the official record keeper of Guardian history. Before the door shut, Diamond Natt slipped in and the room seemed to go off kilter with the surge of emotions from both Diamond and Gypsum.

Frigga's sweet grass! It had to be obvious to everyone they were smitten.

I bobbed my head to them. "Thank you for taking the time to show me the land."

The group greeted us and since we were in company, I even gave Ash a kiss on the cheek as suitable for our previously close relationship. There weren't enough seats for us all so Dahlia led the way from the parlor and Gypsum gave me his arm as we followed her through the halls. I had guessed right on the appropriate attire.

"I was under the impression your husband would be joining us," Moon said from alongside Reed who walked before us.

"He was otherwise detained. Slate will be sorry he missed it. I brought my cousin Gypsum Sumar. He'll be inducted into Valla University this Yuletide,"

Curse Slate.

I had no wish to include him in my arenas. Moon had no reason to assume he would be involved unless it was a sexist conclusion, which it very well might have been.

Gypsum made polite conversation with the ebony skinned man until Dahlia and Basil held open the massive double doors that led to the front of the castle. They closed the doors after us, leaving Gypsum and I with Ash, Quartz, Reed, Moon, and Diamond. From the look Dahlia's pinched face shot Diamond, she was going off script.

Reed was slightly shorter than Gypsum. Hawk bore a striking resemblance to him, Flint Sumar and Reed had been very good friends, and Hawk took after them though Reed's coppery brown hair bore none of Hawk's premature silver. Reed spoke with one of the servants and smiled at Gypsum and me.

"I hope you have taken the time to learn how to ride," he said, giving me a wink of his dark eye.

Gypsum flashed a dimpled smile.

"I have. I wish I had known; I would have brought my horse."

"You have a horse?" I asked in wonderment.

I did not have a horse, nor did I know the first thing about them. My skirt was not made for riding either. I started to grumble internally as the first of the majestic creatures were brought out and Ash helped Quartz and then Diamond onto their mounts. They sat in sidesaddles which made my stomach drop.

There was no way I wouldn't make a fool of myself on the ride. The urge to ask how far of a walk it was burned on my tongue until Ash gave me a knowing smile.

What a cache hole.

The beat of hooves announced three more horses and a rider I was not expecting. Slate sat astride a refined looking chestnut colored horse, much more delicate than I would've thought a big man like him would have rode. He swung off the beast in a graceful way that belied his size.

I would have thought it an extraordinary coincidence, except he wore a black jerkin with gold solar cross buttons down the front, metallic gold thread striped the long sleeves. His lips curled triumphantly when he saw my open-mouthed astonishment. Curse the gods for putting the man on my path through life.

Gypsum caught the reins and laughed. He patted a chestnut stallion with white legs in a familiar way. "Sleipnir, my horse," he told me.

Reed and Moon chuckled the way of old men recognizing their own acts in a young man. Slate greeted our party before crossing to me. The stable master had brought out the last three horses and looked relieved we had brought our own.

"Wife," Slate said with glittering grey eyes before we pressed a kiss to my cheek.

"What are you doing here?" I hissed in a whisper as he walked me to an elegant looking white horse.

"Bringing you your ride. Safanad. She is yours. The stable master at the palace said I had been training her for you."

She was lovely. Large eyes looked out at me from a wedge-shaped head. She had a distinctive concave body shape and a beautifully arched neck. Her tail was carried high as I ran my palm over her flank. There was a sidesaddle.

"Safanad isn't a Celtic nor Nordic name," I said, trying not to sound too awed.

"It means *The Pure*, she is an Arabian purebred. She will follow my stallion who is lead," Slate rumbled at my side and feigned checking the saddle to speak to me in low whispers.

"Why are you here?" I hissed, looking at his black maned beast who looked as arrogant as he was, I decided.

"Al-Fadee. *The Redeemer*, I have a sense of humor it would appear," he said with a wry smile as he followed my gaze.

"If you mean because you named my mare, The Pure, I'll punch you right here in front of everyone," I grit out and Slate laughed.

It caught me so off guard that I forgot we were pretending to be a loving couple and gaped at his glorious cheek creasing smile. The one he saved for me. He caught my enraptured gaze and brushed his lips to mine before I could pull back. I decided it suited our temporary needs and decided not to punch him after all. I reconsidered as he picked me up at the waist like a child and placed me in the saddle.

I tensed unwittingly, and he patted my leg as he handed me the reins. "Relax. She will take good care of you. Let her lead, you only need to stay atop her. I know how well you can ride; it should not be that difficult for you."

My cheeks flamed as he smirked and walked to his mount.

Ash and Quartz led the group and Diamond fell back to ride along Gypsum. Reed and Moon moved up alongside Slate with me on the far end. Slate was right, I just had to relax, and she followed Al-Fadee wherever he went.

The men discussed weapons, fighting styles, and eventually came to

Tidings politics. Reed carried most of the conversation until Ash fell back and leaned to my horse to urge her next to his. We cantered ahead, and he released the reins knowing full well how inexperienced I was.

"I am surprised he came. From all the whispers, I deduced you no longer shared a marriage bed," Ash said in a low tone.

"You should know better than to listen to rumors, Ash," I said as Quartz fell back to walk alongside Diamond and Gypsum.

All the rumors I'd heard about him had been true. Gypsum turned around and spotted Ash and I together and raised his dark brows. I sliced my head to the right, and he gave a slight nod. I didn't need rescuing just yet.

Behind the Straumr palace was a small dirt path that into the woods. The trees were well into their seasonal change in burnished golds and scarlet reds. Sunburnt leaves crunched under the horses hooves as we alternated between a trot and a walk.

"Are you cold?" Without asking, Ash leaned and pressed his hand to mine.

I wasn't wearing a cloak, but I didn't get cold any longer. My elemental power didn't allow it. I felt him *call* and stiffened. Safanad felt my change and tossed her white mane. Ash leaned back into his saddle.

"I don't get cold anymore. Not since I became an elemental," I said flatly, he had no right to touch me.

"Your sons are doing well. I thought perhaps you had lost them since you are not showing. Are you not in your second trimester?" Ash asked, and he turned his light green-eyed gaze on me.

What was his game? He was almost being friendly, and it unnerved me.

"Yes. Stress I suppose. I don't eat enough and not training makes me feel useless. I'll be better once the Ragnarök is through. I didn't know you cared. The last time we spoke for more than a few harsh words was almost a year ago," I said, lifting my eyes to his.

"You are a fertile Tio again. For the success of the greater families you need to remain so," he said as he cantered forward.

I narrowed my eyes at his back. Ash was always up to something. Slate filled his empty spot leaving Reed and Moon back, but not for long since Gypsum fell back to ride alongside Reed.

"That one wants to bed you. You did not when you were betrothed?"

Slate asked.

"No. I already told you, four men. You know their names. Ash wasn't one of them," I said curtly.

We rode in silence for a time before he spoke up again. "They tell me you only bedded me after I proposed. When was this?"

I gave him a dry look. "I didn't trust you with so much of me until you proved to me you were interested and not just for my body. Then one night with you in your big black leather bed after you showed me a wing you designed for us to start our life together ...*BAM* ... I was pregnant. It was the night of the Wild Hunt. Congrats. Your swimmers must have GPS. We lost the baby and I was rendered barren. I didn't sleep with you again until after you saved me from the Merfolk."

"GPS?" he asked with the most interest he'd shown in me while dressed.

"Global Positioning System," I said with a sigh.

"I would like to remember what you were like that first time," he said in a tone best reserved for bedrooms.

"Knock that off. You think I don't get your suggestive remarks, but I do," I snapped. "How did you know where I'd be? And that I would need a horse?"

"The messenger came to the Sumar palace first. I sent it along to the Dagr palace. Gypsum and I ran into one another and I asked him to stall you so I had time to ready the mounts. I can see why I liked him," Slate said with a mocking lip curl.

I would have to speak to Gypsum about loyalty when this was over. He kept me in the dark so I wouldn't make sure Slate couldn't come. I *had* been relieved to see him, and that irked to no end.

"Why did you come, then?" I asked, facing straight ahead where the road opened up to a clearing.

"You needed a husband. Guardians are easily unnerved by the unconventional. A single young woman endeavoring to make a name for herself is not only disregarded, but eventually shunned. I owe you for rescuing me. Without our bond, I might never have been found."

He was right. Outside of Tidings, a twenty-year-old girl proposing something this huge would have been little better than a joke.

"Thanks," I said and grew brave as I brought Safanad to a trot into the clearing.

CHAPTER 15
SLATE

She held her own with Moon Straumr as the Prime and his Second gave her a run-down of the land. She smiled often, her high cheekbones rounding as her lusciously full lips curled.

I had her today.

For a moment, she was vulnerable and I had exploited it. It was an enlightening experience. As much as I wanted her, she could not say no to me. Her mouth said no, but she contradicted herself with her body.

That body.

Seeing Brass's hands on it had awakened thoughts best not felt with friends. The beast had nearly torn free from its cage.

I could scent the lust on the Straumr boy. With the other two so infatuated, their mounts veered into one another from their leaning. Blasted girl was trouble for my cousin. All Straumr's were trouble, even the ones I did not mind.

Her escort.

That was what I had been reduced to. She was wearing so much clothing. If I could try to get her into bed tonight, it would take ages to remove it all unless she would let me tear it from her. That was an option. She knew what the beast liked. She had let her blood flow free knowing it would lap it up.

He needed her.

Their business was done and Moon invited them to sup at his palace. You did not say no to the Prime. Unless you were his Second, Reed Tio declined as did Quartzite Natt. Gods, I hoped she was not one of the girls I had forgotten.

I picked up the girl by her waist again, she was too light, and placed her back in Safanad's saddle. She scowled and quickly masked it with a loving smile for the others to witness. I feigned checking the stirrups and slid my hand under her many skirts; petticoat, but no drawers. No nylons either from the way her skin prickled as the pads of my fingers rounded the inside of her thigh. She jolted but did not make any sign of what I was doing other than the reddening of her cheeks.

I found it difficult not to smirk at her as I removed my hand and mounted Al-Fadee. I had cared deeply for her to have trained her mount in my precious spare time. The stable master had been insistent it was her mare that I had trained personally, he said it was a wedding present. That I had bought the mare myself during Yuletide and had been training it in secret. I added it to the tally of uncharacteristic actions I had done when it concerned her.

The Straumr informal dining room had a long mahogany table with golden candelabras and a multitiered chandelier that lit the wood paneled room. The marble fireplace was lit when we entered to join the others for dinner, our booted footsteps were muffled by the maroon fringed carpet.

The Straumr brothers rose as we entered. Moon Straumr, Prime and Overseer of Valla University, sat at the head of the table, with River on his right, and Crag on his left. Basil sat at the foot of the table with

Dahlia on his right and Ash on his left. River's wife and kids sat beside him. Fox and Novaculite, Quartz's sister sat next to Crag.

Diamond took the seat beside Ash and Gypsum filled the empty seat next to her. We were the last to arrive. Several empty seats separated Gypsum from Fox as did Dahlia from the youngest of River's brood. I sat across from Diamond with her beside me. She had received kisses from both Crag and Fox as she made her way through the room. Basil smiled warmly at her as if he had forgotten she had gotten pregnant while his son was betrothed to her.

She could have kept the entire affair a secret.

A six-course meal was served. Oysters followed by cream of barley, then a poached salmon. She was looking like she wished to loosen her corset which gave the already impressive swell an added boost. I *called,* knowing my way around women's undergarments, and loosened the lacing. Instead of an appreciative smile, she shot daggers my way. It had the same effect regardless on my want for her.

A sauté of chicken was then served followed by roast duckling with an apple sauce. As dessert, a lemon meringue parfait was served. Watching her eat was an unexpected bonus for coming to her rescue. Her tongue swirled in an improper way she was oblivious to after she scooped the last raspberry from the bottom of the glass. I needed to adjust, but it was not the appropriate time for it. Neither was it appropriate for her to be licking that spoon in such a provocative way.

I was not the only one who noticed. Fox and Ash were doing a poor job of hiding their interest in her mouth. What was wrong with the girl? Was she doing it deliberately? Or was she blind to her wiles?

Moon rose and asked if we would join him in the drawing room. He pinpointed exactly whom he wanted. Ash, Crag, myself, and the girl. Gypsum contented himself to go to the parlor with the others.

The doors slid into the walls to reveal a richly decorated room in reds and greens. From the high vaulted ceiling hung an ornate golden chandelier larger than the sofas that adorned the room. Moon gestured to the sofas before the marble fireplace and she took a seat across from where Crag and Ash sat. Moon produced a wooden cigar box.

Cigars were contraband in Tidings, but to turn one down from the Prime would be a worse crime. I accepted gladly, rolling it between my thumb and forefinger, not too soft or hard. It smelled woodsy as Moon cut the tip. I *called*, lighting the cigar and rolled it again to be sure it was evenly lit. Her expression of astonishment was deeply satisfying.

The Straumr boy was looking satisfied as well, which boded ill for me and the girl.

"First things first. Mrs. Tio. Your deed." Moon handed her the rolled-up parchment and she smiled as she took it.

Freya's burly boar.

I cursed the Mother for allowing such a woman to possess a smile that could bring any man to his knees. Even the old Prime's scent sparked at it. The beast growled. To placate it, I snaked my hand along the back of the couch behind her. She sipped a tea one of the servants brought in and held the saucer in her lap.

"On to new business. Scarlett, would you mind speaking to me in private?" Moon asked and I sensed her wariness.

She looked to me as she did at times. At one point, my opinion mattered greatly to her and the habit had not been broken. With my *calling*, I gave her shoulder a reassuring squeeze. Her mouth quirked and then her face darkened as if I tricked her into feeling comfort from me.

"I don't keep secrets from my husband. You may speak candidly in front of him," she said in a regal tone she armored herself with.

Moon's dark, seamed face glanced over me and nodded as he took a seat across from the fireplace. "Then I shall be frank. You are at the end of your first trimester, yes?"

Her pulse quickened. "Yes."

"A Dagr? You shall have your heir?" Moons continued.

She looked to me pleadingly. I had caught a rumor or two that the bairn were mine. Our family believed they were Brass's. She made no claim that they were mine. I finally understood why they let the rumors go. What Peak held over her. My first instinct as the beast was to force her into a miscarriage to replace the bairn with my own. Peak would not do that to my bairn but would have no qualms about doing it to a lesser family son's.

"If all goes well." She glanced away and sipped from the delicate glass.

Crag's dark face was stern, it usually was, but a tightness around his eyes displayed his disapproval of the new topic of conversation. Moon's eyes were darker than his skin and bloodshot as his intense gaze settled on her. She held it admirably as he addressed her. Not just any young woman would meet the Prime of the Guardians eyes as levelly as she did.

He nodded as if she confirmed something for him. "You are an elemental. The like of which has not been seen for hundreds of years. Your offspring are likely to inherit the trait as well."

I saw where this was going and nocked my chin up to meet the Straumr boy's glittering eyes.

"You could have another five pregnancies after this one. It is our duty to strengthen our bloodlines. An elemental will be born to the Tio and Dagr lines. What I need is one in my own line. There is much we could offer you, as well as any other families you may choose to help."

The girl placed her teacup on the saucer and ever so carefully leaned forward to place it on the table. She sat back and lifted her chin. Her hair was pinned up so her long neck was elegantly displayed.

"For clarity's sake. What you're asking me to do is lay with a man from your line and give you the child or children born from that union? What if it's a girl, or if the elemental power doesn't take root?" she asked in such a measured tone I almost missed the clenching of her fist hidden in the folds of her skirt.

Moon nodded. "We would accept a girl as well. She would be raised by our family with no ties to the Tio or Dagr families. Our men are all married, so the children would be raised by them and their wives as their own. You would have no responsibility for them. I have it on good authority that a child coming from an elemental woman would inherit her powers."

"Are you only making this offer to me or are you making it to Indigo as well?" she asked, letting her eyes shift to Crag and Ash.

Ash smiled at her and she focused back on Moon, even her scent bristled at the Straumr boy's smirk.

"Indigo is a water elemental. We would prefer fire, but she is unmarried. If she approves, we would not turn her down," Moon informed her.

The girl lost her temper. "As Guardians, water nourishes the land. It is essential for growth and our way of life. Fire does nothing but raze and destroy." She caught herself and took a fortifying breath. "Fire is very powerful. I do not expect my husband to take well to me laying with any other men, even for such a noble purpose."

She glanced to me and I gave her a nod. If I opened my mouth, I might shift. The cigar sat burning between my fingers. Moving a muscle might unleash the barghest. To ask a married woman if his nephew could bed her in front of her husband, no matter the reason took a special kind of audacity.

Moon gave her a rueful smile and looked to Crag. His turn. Crag leaned forward with great reluctance.

"We wish no offense, Mrs. Tio. Patriarch Dagr. It has come to our attention that you have taken a lesser family man as your paramour and that you are having an affair with a member of a greater family of substantial influence."

She visibly stiffened, her expression cool and tight as she listened.

The Straumr boy's lips curled into a mocking smile. "Not to mention that our informants tell us you no longer share a marriage bed and your husband has been seen frequenting the khoraz brothel in Thrimilci on more than one occasion."

Victory shown in the gleam of his eyes. She could not stop herself from whirling around to face me. An expression of betrayal on the deepest level marred her beautiful face. The Straumr boy stank of triumph.

What she would say next would be detrimental. Her skin had an unearthly glow of fire beneath the surface.

"Had I known that whom I laid with was such a popular topic, I would have chosen more interesting men. The lesser family man you speak of is no paramour. He is a close family friend as well as a brother-in-arms to my husband. To say otherwise is a grave insult to his person. If you hear such rumors again, I hope you will put a stop to them." She stopped for a breath. "As for the other, affair is not the word I would use, but it is not a lie."

"We mean no insult," Crag said again, and she raised her hand for silence.

Crag Straumr was her battle trainer and older than her father would have, but her bearing was queenly and his mouth shut tight at her gesture.

"What my husband does in his private time, is not my concern. I have two healthy sons coming into this world and we both have our own ways to relax at the end of the day. His secrets are his to keep and I do not appreciate them being revealed to me when I have no desire to know them. What his actions have to do with my fertility or willingness to bear your grandnephews is beyond me." She leaned forward and picked up her teacup. She drank to dampen her throat. "Now. For starters, if say, you chose to name this year's theme minerals, Opal Geol has a certain ring to it. I may be able to offer my time and energy to you, provided I chose which families in what order starting with the lesser family Regn. I'm assuming it would be Ash from your family line?" she asked.

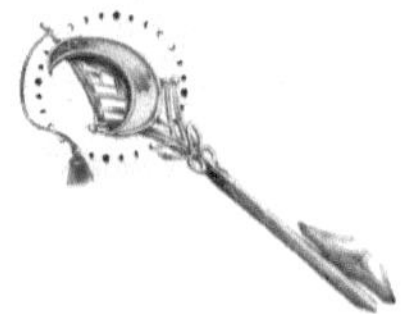

Gypsum met us at the portal room at the Straumr palace. The Straumrs had the horses brought back to the Sumar palace through Valla's town heart, the way I had brought them. She had negotiated a list of demands and had told them she would consider bedding Ash Straumr after the bairn were born.

I had not said a word. She was not really my wife. I had left our marriage bed and gone instead to the khoraz brothel as they said. It mattered not to them that Lynx lived there and did not charge me. We were friends of a sort.

She had not asked a single request for herself except for the theme for the following year; birds. She didn't say it, but she wanted my bairn. She brought up the names Lark and Wren.

Damn the confounding girl.

It was as much for me as it was for her. I had been struck speechless. I would need an heir; she was my wife. Brass's absurd bargain was not as ludicrous as I had initially thought. She made no promises, but the writing was on the wall. She had no reason not to agree. She even argued that if she wanted more children with me, that she could choose to skip an ovulation for her own uses.

Any prospect of bedding her dissipated with the news of my extra curriculars. She stoically marched to the portal room and Gypsum saw her expression. He knew better than to try to reason with her. The kid smelled like sex. He had bedded the Natt girl.

With my heightened hearing I knew no staff was about. "We should speak. Are you coming to Pearl's or —"

"Thank you for coming and bringing the horses. If you were my Slate, I would tell you she was a beautiful mare and a wonderful gift. Good night, Slate. Gypsum, your company was appreciated — truly." She stepped into the portal door.

White light flashed, and I cursed. Gypsum let out a noisy groan.

"You were supposed to make up with her, not piss her off even worse."

"I did not speak a word after we left dinner," I ground out.

"Maybe *that* was the problem? She's always fighting for everyone else. No one fights for her. She won't let them. You were the only one who didn't listen to her and did what you thought was best, regardless. She hated you and loved you for it. You know why Brass knows what happened with your uncle, but she won't tell you? Because *you* were the one who would do something about it. Brass was the one who comforted her, but he wasn't the one who acted. You knew what was best for her even when she didn't." He wiped a hand over his face in a manner like Jett.

"You know what happened with my uncle?" I asked in a growl.

"No one knows I know. Don't expect me to tell you either. Fix this. Fix all of it. You're happy with her. She makes all the years of knowing you'll die young worth it." His face creased as he stressed the words.

I scoffed. "You have been reading too many romance novels, boy."

"You told me that, or rather, I overheard you say it to her. It wasn't perfect, but it was real. Fix it already. Life is short. Your life in particular."

The kid walked through the portal leaving me alone with the beast.

CHAPTER
SIXTEEN

Training, classes, eating. That's what I did for days. Sleeping was a thing of the past as I thought about having sex with Ash every night and not in an anticipatory fashion. It would be after I had my sons and hopefully after I provided Slate with an heir. It seemed the prophecy demanded it and I had no idea how much time I had left.

Classes were starting to get back into a groove despite having Slate there. I sat next to Tawny who sat by Quick with Slate on the end. In the halls, I looped my arm through Tawny's and walked ahead of the two men.

He was seeing a khoraz.

After all the cruel things he said to me. What difference did it make anymore who I slept with? Ash, Peak, just bodies. I wouldn't be with Brass. Not if it meant tarnishing his reputation.

I went to headquarters to tell him what they guessed at and he hadn't cared. Of course he didn't. I loved him even more for it. He also didn't seem surprised Slate was visiting the khoraz brothel.

My emotions had been in tumult ever since. I resigned myself to staying away from all men.

We were all set to break ground in two days on Mabon, Valla, and Thrimilci. I had received two letters by messenger at lunch. Ruby had time to show me a site in Ostara after classes, and she wanted me to bring Jett and Indigo.

"Jett what are you doing tonight? Ruby invited us to go visit her in Ostara and check out the arena site. Are you down?" I asked him, stacking the letters under my plate and piled it with my own little Cornish game hen.

"Yeah, sounds good. Indi too?" Jett asked, breaking off a drumstick.

"Yup. I'm kind of excited. You think she might want to get to know us?" I asked, waggling my eyebrows at my brother as I made a mental note to send a messenger to Indigo after lunch.

He waggled back, a lopsided grin on his chiseled features. Jett was gorgeous. My first instinct was to distrust him when I'd met him because anyone as good looking as he was had to be a liar. Jett wasn't, he was just blessed... and arrogant as all hel.

"I think she does. Who wouldn't want to know us?" Jett jutted out his jaw as he chewed.

Tawny frowned. "Is Brass not coming? What happened with you two? Last weekend I thought you were getting back together and now you have seen him once this week."

Quick sat next to me, Slate was on his other side. It was the only way I could sit with my family and not have to look at him. "We're... friends. No. I... I have no idea. Just as we've always been. I see him all the time and he is always very attentive about *them*. But I'm married," I said, unable to stop my sigh.

"So you're single?" Tawny asked with a smile. "Single for your much anticipated twenty-first birthday?" She waggled her thick brows at me and I smiled.

"I'm not single and I don't want to get dressed up and parade myself around to be ogled. We can do something in Chicago or in our rooms. I'll ask Indi."

"I have got Indigo; you have your own fun," Quick said with a dazzling smile that made me shake my head.

"Break my sister's heart and I'll fry you, Quick," I said and Jett chuckled.

"Glad you said it and not me."

"Did your sister tell you she is working to get this year's theme to be minerals?" Slate rumbled from Quick's other side.

Cherry gasped excitedly and Jett smiled skeptically as he looked at me. "How are you managing that?"

A number of retorts came to mind. Honesty was the best policy; Jett wouldn't believe it, anyway.

"I'm contemplating having Ash's child. In return, I get a number of very generous offers. This year's names and next year's are included in the deal. You're welcome." I smiled sweetly at Jett who laughed then looked to Quick.

Quick was ashen. Jett was no longer smiling.

"Why?" Tawny breathed, her fair face pulling down in sorrow.

"It turns out that the Straumrs want an elemental in the family. I'm just an old-fashioned surrogate." I said returning to my meal forcing bite after bite down my throat.

"Did they mention Indigo?" Quick growled.

"They'd prefer fire to water. Poor Indi," I said facetiously.

"She would not do it, anyway. I would not let her," Quick said and my heart warmed for Indigo.

I could *feel* what Quick felt, and it was wonderful. I grabbed Quick's face and planted a kiss on his cheek. His eyes widened in shock and I giggled.

"You're a good man, Silver Regn."

"Hormones," Jett said teasingly then sobered. "You can't do it, Scar. You couldn't look yourself in the mirror if you laid with that smug bastard. That's what he wanted from you all along and now he gets it because his uncle is Prime."

I shook my head laughing. "You guys don't get it. They know every-thing. They called me out on Brass and the affair I had. I think they believed that Brass wasn't my paramour, I hoped I was convincing. But I can't be seen with him again. I won't let my reputation and marriage ruin him even if he doesn't care. He can still find a wife and have.... legitimate kids. I won't take that from him. Face facts, there's no one waiting for me. The best I can hope for is a steady, low-key paramour." I sighed. "No one from a greater or lesser family. I'm going to do what they asked. It's two or three nights a month until I'm pregnant then I can do whatever I want for nine months. I choose what other families —"

"Others too! Freya's burly boar! No way, Scar," Jett cursed.

I held up my hands to quiet him so I could finish. "Straumr, Dagr, and Haust from the greater families. Snjar and Sunna from the lesser. Three more men. That's not a lot."

They were gaping at me. They didn't get it. I didn't care as long as they weren't asking invasive questions about which Haust when it was obvious. Peak would want to impregnate me and pretend it was Sterling's. I could consider my friendship with Diamond over.

"Look. Having slept with eight men in my life is not completely outrageous," I defended.

"Nine if you find this hypothetical nameless paramour," Tawny said.

I shook my head. "Eight. Ash, a Haust, Hunter, and Boa's son. The fifth would be the paramour."

"You mean because you will have Slate's child," Quick said pointedly, and I nodded averting my eyes.

"It's stupid not to. Unless he has someone else to have his heir picked out," I told him with my eyes firmly on my plate.

"She plotted it out with Moon," Slate told them.

"Mind your own business. No one cares to hear what you have to say. You lost your right to an opinion with your memories," I snapped and realized I looked like I was shouting at the bones of my Cornish hen.

"I will not be the only one with opinions you do not want to hear if you whore yourself out to the families," Slate retorted.

I could tell that I was on my own on this one. That everyone, but Cherry, believed what he said was true.

"I don't see how sleeping with a few men would make it any worse when my own husband calls me a whore while he himself visits brothels. At least I'll be getting something in return for my efforts. When all I have now is regret. Excuse me," I said stiffly as I stood from the bench.

"Scar! Don't go," Jett called after me, but I didn't want to hear it.

Ash saw me coming and got to his feet to walk out with me. I saw him glance back to where my family sat and I rolled my eyes.

Out in the hall, I stopped and faced him down. "I didn't agree to anything yet. If you were smart, you would get on my good side so I'd be inclined to make it less than clinical."

Ash was gorgeous, it was too bad he was such a conceited cocky bastard and not in the way Quick was. Ash had a mean streak, and he believed himself better than everyone else. He'd also do anything to get ahead, and that's what our betrothal had been about.

"I could not help but notice your argument with your estranged husband. Sleeping with khorazes in a brothel should be beneath even him. I am sorry to be the one to have revealed it to you." Ash's eyes glittered.

I scoffed. "No, you're not. What do you want, Ash?" I asked, sounding bored.

He stepped closer. "Stop seeing Patriarch Haust, Scarlett. I can see to your needs."

"I don't mean to insult you. I really don't, but I'm not the one pursuing Peak. I don't need any lovers, Ash. I'm done with love period. It's for suckers and children. I'm a grown woman with two children to raise, probably alone. Good day, Ash." I turned around to find Quick and Jett standing in the doorway to the hall.

"Truth," Quick muttered and went back into the hall.

My brother's towering form gave me an apologetic smile. I stood in his shadow and thought about telling him it wasn't true. It was though. I was done with trying to fall in love. I left my brother with Ash in the entranceway.

CHAPTER 17
INDIGO

A sprawling view of the waters beyond Ostara stretched from the window. You could almost imagine Mabon on the other side of the waters. We followed a staff member in a silken pale green dress to a large sitting area. Light blue couches with white wood carved backs were scattered around the coffee tables where tea waited. The artistically painted ceiling of the sitting room was rounded with arched windows at the top of the pastel green walls, trimmed in carved gold.

The Vars used the room for semi-formal entertaining. It told me a lot about what Ruby expected of the meeting. What was supposed to be only be myself, Jett, and Scarlett ended up being quite the party. The girls came with bringing Gigi who crawled around the floor refusing to sit in Amethyst's lap.

We were early and Ruby was running late. Sage and Garnet's engagement party was at the end of the week and a lot of planning was being done. I nearly choked on my tea when Garnet and Sage joined Ruby as they swept into the room.

The Var castle itself had a sleek white glass appearance was climbing spires and unparalleled beauty. The inside was a mix of French revolution and baroque architecture. Lots of gold elaborate trim and pastels.

Ruby wore an indigo caftan dress with a wide white belt. Her dark hair was pulled back into a high bun, she seemed to glide into the room with her ballerina like frame and wide dark eyes that took us all in. We all rose, and I gave my grandmother a smile. I was the only one who had grown up with her.

"Indi, how I have missed you. We never see you anymore," Ruby said in her soft cultured voice.

Sage gave me a look of disdain. As if we hadn't been raised together as brother and sister for nineteen years. Garnet's eyes were on me and I wanted to strangle her. She was a lesser family heir now that Amber had been murdered.

"I've missed you too."

"I worry about my Indi; you never wanted any suitors. I thought perhaps you had gone the way of Sapphos, but I hear you are being courted by a Regn," Ruby queried.

Jett chuckled. Sapphos, from the island Lesbos. Did all families have a way of making you feel like a child no matter how old you were?

"Indigo is very much into men, Matriarch Geol," Cherry said with a suggestive grin.

"Have you told any outside of the Sumar and Regn?" Sage asked in a honeyed voice.

Sterling.

"Yes," I replied, simply not wanting an argument to start.

"And where is the first patriarch of the Dagr line?" Ruby said, turning to Scarlett.

Scarlett embraced Ruby before she had a chance to offer her a polite nod. Ruby looked astonished, but quickly recovered.

"Unfortunately, he has been detained, but he sends his well wishes," she lied.

"My other granddaughter. We should have been properly introduced ages ago. Congratulations on the children and your marriage. Will you being throwing a reception now that you are together again?" Ruby asked.

Scarlett shook her head. "I'm not big into weddings and the like. We could do a larger Ausa Vatni to celebrate both the children and our marriage next year," Scarlett said with a straight face.

She beamed at Ruby who relaxed. It was hard not to fall in love with Scarlett as many a poor man discovered. She was warm and funny while being strong and ambitious. When she let you into her inner circle, you felt like you'd won some great prize. She once told me Brass had made her feel that way. They were too much alike. That must have been why she chose Slate, her opposite. Dark and dangerous, he loomed behind her daring anyone to upset her. Or at least he used to. Now, they never said a kind word to one another.

Ruby turned lastly to Jett and the girls. Amethyst came forward with Gigi in her arms and kissed Ruby's cheeks with a smile.

"Aunt. You look much better," Amethyst said and Scarlett's eyes bulged.

Scarlett didn't know how closely related we were to Amethyst. Her mother was Ruby's sister. Idly, I wondered what she would think if she knew Slate and Brass's grandmother had been Ruby's first cousin. Lark and Robin's mother had been a Geol. The greater families did what they needed to keep the lines strong.

Jett came forward next and Ruby substantially brightened.

"Oh Jett, so handsome and with such lovely wives," Ruby acclaimed.

"Ruby. I get my good looks from my parents and theirs from their parents." Jett gave her an inappropriate wink, making Ruby laugh.

Jett held his arm out to Cherry, who came forward with her hands over her stomach. "Ruby, I wanted you to be the first we told with my sisters."

"Cerise carries a Var!" Jett announced.

Scarlett clapped her hands in delight and we gave hugs all around, Gigi started clapping with them. A boy! Lucky, Jett. Ruby always did favor Sage over me. Now she favored Jett over Sage and I could see how much he enjoyed that revelation.

"Garnet also carries a Var. How wonderful. All my grandchildren... Indi when do you plan on having your first?" Ruby asked with all sincerity.

Freya's burly boar! I wondered if Garnet's son was really Silver's. When Slate was with Amber, the cousins had shared Silver and Slate.

"Whenever I marry I suppose," I said weakly.

Ruby smiled and nodded. "Best to get all of that out of your system before you settle into motherhood. You are having twin boys are you not, Scarlett?"

"Yes," she noted.

"That must make Slate very happy," Ruby said.

"Exceedingly so," Scarlett lied through her white teeth.

Garnet pursed her lips with a smile. I could spit.

"Shall we get down to business?" Scarlett interjected, and they all took their seats.

One thing Ostara had that the other islands didn't often use was carriages. It had less to do with distances and more to do with our uppity Var family wanting privacy. I recognized the road we took to the arena site as did Scarlett. It was where the Aves had dropped us off with Slate and Shale's bodies. Amethyst and Cherry had gone home with Gigi, but we had still needed two carriages to make the journey along the crushed glittering stone road.

I sat with Garnet and Scarlett, which left Ruby to travel with Jett and Sage. They were playing nice to curry favor with Ruby so they were safe for now. Scarlett held one hand to her stomach as we jostled about. Garnet glared across the carriage at us, but we deigned not to notice her.

"I wish Brass had come so he could charm her into the arenas." Scarlett sighed.

We hit a root in the road making the entire carriage bounce.

Scarlett winced and touched her hands to her breasts. "Frigga's sweet grass, these things are so sore. I think I'm going to have to buy new bras I can hear my old ones crying out for mercy."

I laughed as the carriages came to a stop and Garnet hopped out to reach Sage and Ruby before us.

A floral citrus scent permeated the air and I looped my arm through Scarlett's as Ruby began to show us the site. It was a lovely little patch overlooking the water. Orion's portal gate would work wonderfully for it. He'd only made seven he'd said but was going to make one for the Natt's and the unoccupied old Geol palace. It took a great deal of *calling* to make a portal and the fees must have been astronomical. Orion was only doing it because of Tawny. He was not the kind of man who did things out of kindness.

"Does Sterling know his favorite paramour is being courted?" Sage appeared at my side.

As children he was always picking on me, but I still loved him. We didn't know we were half-siblings then, they thought I was adopted and low born. That was why no one ever came courting, not because I didn't want them to.

"I've been talking about marriage to Sterling for the last month. He knows where Silver and I stand. He'll be getting married himself in less than two months. This was bound to happen sometime," I said flatly.

You couldn't let Sage know he could get a rise out of you.

"Silver is such a good choice, sister. I imagine when you come home to one another at night, you could talk about your married lover and he can try to remember whatever woman he spent that day with," Sage said in a bored tone.

His pouty pink lips spread in a scornful smirk. Scarlett stiffened at my side, but I held tightly to her hand.

"It didn't have to be like this, Sage. It still doesn't. Scarlett and Jett are good, forgiving people and aren't responsible for Wren and Alder's actions. You can be a part of the new family we've —"

"And be a part of your merry band of misfits? The khoraz, the orphan, the polygamist, the whore, and the changeling? Never. You have made your choice; you live with it." Sage turned on his heel and headed back on foot.

"Ignore him. Alder should have eased Jett into his position instead of uprooting Sage the way he did. He is bitter and angry," I told Scarlett.

"He should be more specific when he mentions a whore," she mumbled.

Ruby, and Jett were smiling as they brought over a rolled-up paper. The deed to the land. Four down, one to go. Elivagar was next.

EIGHTEEN

I practically skipped up the stone Shadow Breaker headquarters' steps. I couldn't wait to tell Brass we had the Ostara lands. They were the ones we were most concerned about, but Ruby had come through.

The upper levels housed the Shadow Breaker bedrooms. Though the Regn had a manor in Ostara, Quick and Brass lived at HQ. I hurried down the hall lined with doors to Brass's and gave the wood a quick knock before opening the door.

"Brass? We have the deed for Ostara! You should have —"

There was no dramatic gasp. I stopped short just inside the short hall. His room had just the essentials. We'd made love in that bed. I'd given myself to a man, *this* man, just outside the hidden entrance. Now he was disentangling himself from a coffee skinned vixen with exotic honey eyes and glossy black ringlets. Her head hung over his looking annoyed at my intrusion.

I stared stupidly. I didn't think I was breathing. Maybe it was a second, maybe it was a minute. It felt like a good ten minutes that I stood there unspeaking as Brass lifted her from his hips and stood as she lounged on the couch behind him wearing sheer taupe undergarments.

Whatever was going on, it was just getting good.

I knew he would move on. I told him I wouldn't marry him; I was trying to get back together with Slate, sort of. I just never imagined a world where I would be pregnant with one man's children and married to another and be in love with both. What does one *do* in such positions?

Brass's dreamy amber eyes were unusually round as he smoothed his loose dark hair away from his face and approached me. His rumpled shirt was still on the floor. I couldn't take my eyes of the gorgeous slender woman I had recruited to his team and was preparing to make love to him. Was this the first time or had it been going on for a while? Brass would spare my feelings and never tell me.

The girl, Rosasite was her name, kicked a slender bare foot of the end of the couch in irritation. She was fox faced and sultry. I felt... I felt....

Numb.

Brass's delectable lips were moving, but the sound lost its way to my ears. I took a step back and forced a smile.

"Whoops. So sorry, Rosasite. Brass. I should have waited until you answered. Just came to say we got lands in Ostara. Goodnight." I reversed to the door and felt Brass coming after me.

As soon as I set foot over the threshold, I bolted. Rosasite couldn't see me and I didn't care if Brass saw me running. He called my name twice in an eager, hushed shout but I was gone.

CHAPTER 19
JETT

Jett knew he was a bed hog, so imagine his dismay that Cherry had taken to hoarding up the valuable space in the bed. *His* bed.

Gigi had recently began sleeping through the night so they could start sleeping at home during the week if they chose. It gave Amethyst the bed to herself after having Gigi attached to her all day.

Frigga's sweet grass, Cherry was using him as a body pillow, he could hardly breathe!

They had all gone to Pearl's for dinner and to celebrate the fourth deed Scarlett had procured. Her love life might be in shambles, but his baby sis could really talk when she needed to. No doubt whatever deal she'd worked out with Moon would end up with her on top, possibly literal sense.

Freya's burly boar, how could she even think about touching Hunter or Ash? Jett still had a hard time believing she had been with Peak. Though, if she was missing Slate, he was an older version of him.

Much older.

He tossed and turned in bed and tried to fall back to sleep. Slate and

Quick were fast asleep. One of the rare nights Quick wasn't with Indigo at the Sumar palace and Slate wasn't out only the Gods knew where. They'd stopped joining his ventures in protest because of Scar.

Light burst through the room as the door swung open with a man's curse. Jett shielded his eyes as he looked to see if Cyan Tio, the unfortunate fourth roommate, was just drunk or if there was a problem.

Only it wasn't his red-headed cousin once removed, it was Brass. Slate and Quick both stared at him groggily as he looked around the room. He cursed again.

He shut his eyes and flexed his fingers. "She's not here. She's not at HQ. She's not at the Dagr palace or the Sumar. I don't know where else she'd go."

"Frigga's sweet grass, Brass. Play crazy somewhere else it is too late to be having melt downs," Quick said, shooing his older brother away.

Brass sucked in a deep breath and that was when Jett realized he looked unusually disheveled. He sat up in bed and pulled on the linen night pants he wore earlier from off the floor.

"I thought if I was with someone else, it would alleviate the guilt she has for leaving me so she could figure out what she truly wants," Brass said, running his hands through his loose hair and pulling a strap out of his pocket to knot it at his nape.

Jett dry washed his face. "Scarlett saw you with this someone else?"

"Yes," Brass said in a gust of breath and came to sit down at the foot of Slate's bed. "I had not told her that I was going to yet. Things... escalated tonight."

Quick chuckled and Jett shot him a glare.

"So she saw you with another woman. According to them, she has seen me with other women and she married me," Slate said noncommittally.

Brass shook his head. "No, I don't think she will forgive me as she has forgiven you. I swore I would never hurt her. She trusted me."

"She did not set you both on fire. That is a good sign," Quick offered.

"Did she say anything?" Cherry sat up in bed.

Jett hadn't even known she was awake. Her big, blue eyes looked distressed even in the dark.

Brass nodded. "She acted as though everything was fine. She said sorry and told us goodnight."

"Does not sound like she was angry to me," Slate rumbled and laid back down.

Brass shook his head. "Her mind was blank. Totally blank. No pain, no fear, happiness, nothing. Not like she was hiding her thoughts, like she wasn't having any. I told Ro I had —"

Quick clicked his tongue in mock disapproval. "Rosasite? Sleeping with your team, Captain? Naughty boy."

Jett clenched his teeth. Cherry's fair hand brushed his elbow to get his attention.

"If she's not at home, not here, not at the Dagr or Sumar palaces, where would she go?"

"Sleep on it. She hasn't activated any bonds has she?" Jett looked at Slate and Brass who both shook their heads. "Then maybe she'll be back in the morning and just needed to blow off some steam."

"Go back to your girl. How old is that one, that *Rosasite*?" Slate teased.

"Nineteen," Brass said, glancing away and going to the door. "She does not act it."

"Right. That is what all the lecherous old men say," Quick chided and Slate chuckled.

"We will send a messenger when she shows up tomorrow. Rest easy, brother," Slate said as his chuckling tapered off and he laid back down.

Cherry rested her chin on Jett's shoulder. He wondered if it burned her since he was stewing inside.

"Tawny or Indigo will know. She doesn't do anything without at least one of them having the details. Get some sleep, babe. I bet it's nothing."

Nothing sat like bricks in his gut as Brass left the men's second year wing.

Jett hurried down the yellow stoned hall of Valla University after his first class to meet Quick. He could already see him shaking his head as he approached.

"Neither of them. They did not show up to class." Quick shrugged his shoulders.

Slate came up behind them. "I could activate my bond so she knows we are looking for her," He offered and Jett scoffed.

"Quick, you should let Brass know she's gone. Slate, if I thought for one minute that you could go an extended period without bedding Lynx, I'd say do it. But if you make her feel what you do at that brothel, I will kill you with my bare hands," Jett threatened.

Slate arched a brow dryly before using air to slice open his pointer finger and rub on the EH rune he shared with Scarlett. "I can go several days without a woman. It is that I choose not to."

"By the Mother! Why am I surrounded by bastards!" Jett ground out as Cherry led him to his next class.

Jett raised his brows in question as Quick and Slate sauntered down the aisle between tables to where they sat at the long bench.

Slate's lips were pressed into a firm line, his silver scar vivid against his deeply tanned skin. Quick's brows kept drawing together no matter how he tried to smooth them.

Cherry pursed her pouty red mouth. "I take it they are still missing?"

"She has my nephews. She would not run back to Chicago would she?" Quick rubbed the bridge of his nose. "Brass is going to beat himself up about this."

Slate focused on his meal, glowering at it as he ate. "She has not responded to the bond."

Quick scoffed. "Would you in her position?"

Jett got to his feet unable to stand any more of their cavalier attitude about his missing sister. "I'm going to the technology room. If she went to Chicago, perhaps she will respond to an email."

"We will join you," Slate said, getting to his feet and Jett gave him a side-long glance.

He didn't notice Brass walking amongst the tyros that filed into the great hall, but the younger women did as several turned to watch him stride across the polished floors.

Scarlett had changed him, less controlled, not as easy going. On the opposite side of that coin, he was willing to push for what he wanted. He didn't look like he'd slept all night.

"No word," he said, exhaling heavily through his nostrils.

"We're heading to the technology room. I'm going to send an email."

Jett led their group from the great hall simmering with irritation. He already knew what Scar would do. She'd slowly been doing it as it was. She'd shut them out as much as she could to protect herself. She'd be back, Tawny wouldn't leave Steel for all the gold in Scrooge's vault.

TWENTY

Not everyone was as good as Slate was at walling off their emotions, but I'd had a good teacher. I couldn't stand another second in Tidings. I had to get away. So when I fled to Elivagar and found Tawny and Steel at Orion's castle, and he suggested we take the portal gate. I jumped all over it.

Tawny kissed Steel goodbye and Orion brought us to the ordinary U-Haul he had waiting with the portal door enclosed.

It took us five days to get to Chicago from Bristol, Rhode Island where the other portal gate was. There was one more portal in the States, but way over in Idaho. Not sure why Idaho, but someone said it was because there was a fancy golf course there that a previous Prime liked.

We stayed the first night in Newport, Rhode Island and spent the day at the beaches there exploring all the little shops. Since we were driving right through NYC, it seemed crazy not to spend a day in the Big Apple. We shopped on Fifth Avenue with the accounts I still had open with my U.S. currency going to waste. We indulged in a sundae so big at Serendipity 3 that it spoiled our lunch, and then we went to Times Square and asked a random passerby to snap a picture of us together on my cellphone.

That was the day Slate's emotions bloomed in my mind, frustrated and worried. I tried not to be too smug.

While we drove through Pennsylvania, we stopped at Hershey Park and rode the rollercoasters and made a detour to drive through Gettysburg where we bought a CD narrating the battle. We made a pit stop in Ohio to visit the Rock and Roll Hall of Fame to take a picture with the Beatles exhibit. Finally, we stopped in Alexandria, IN to see the world's biggest ball of paint in a friendly older gentleman's shed.

It was late when I got off I-90W and drove to Labough Woods. Slate's emotions were now an angry knot that occasionally flared to remind me he was still there. We set the portal door in the forest preserve by our old houses in the middle of the night so no one would see two girls in their early twenties with a floating twining of tree limbs that formed a portal door. Orion assured us that only people who had *calling* in their blood could activate the portal, so we only needed to put it somewhere accessible by car. We laughed as we set it up knowing thousands of people would see it and never think more of it than a couple of cool looking trees.

I brought Tawny back to my old apartment; the rent was paid until February. I was beyond ecstatic that I had thought enough ahead to have automatic payments on all of my bills. My blacktop challenger was parked out on the street. I had picked it up before we returned the moving truck that carried the portal gate.

I introduced her to the show Chris and, and I had watched, Game of Thrones, and we ordered deep dish from Giordano's. We picked up pints of ice cream and once we finished settled in for the night, we watched chick flicks.

Rom-coms up the wazoo until I was streaming tears and my stomach hurt from all the pizza and ice cream. Tawny leaned against me as we watched the cliché movies and then we readied for sleep. She crawled into my extravagant bed that would have been plain in Tidings, but in Chicago it was outrageous with its tree trunk pillars and leather padded clam shell headboard. Everything else in the apartment was toned down; beige sectional couch, simple entertainment center, my television wasn't fancy either.

The morning of the sixth day of our escape, we went to the DMV and renewed her driver's license which made her do a happy dance now that she was twenty-one and she had driven to Jewel-Osco to grab a bottle of wine just because she could.

"Come work out with me. I've been pigging out and I feel like a blob," I said as we made our way home.

Tawny scoffed. She looked fantastic in skinny jeans and a loose sweatshirt we'd picked up in NYC we cleverly called fancy sweats since it had a studded bib that somehow made it fifty bucks. Her long dark hair was piled loosely on top of her head as she scoffed.

"I don't like working out in Tidings, why on earth would I do it on vacation?"

I gave her my most innocent smile as I leaned my head on her shoulder and batted my eyes. "Because I can't drown my sorrows and you love me."

She sniffed and gave me smirk. "That smile may work on your men, but it has no power over me."

I smiled at her Labyrinth reference. "Thanks for coming with me, Tawns."

"Thanks for a much-needed vacay. Orion has been shoving governing Elivagar down my throat like I'm going to take over any day now. He's perfectly healthy." She shook her head. "I like it though. I think I'm going to enjoy running the island even if I have to deal with my grandmother." She frowned, thinking of Cassiopeia Natt.

"I don't know what I'm going to do. I don't want to go back, but I have the arenas and I really want to be a Guardian." I sighed.

"So you're in love with them both, sit back and let them show you who wants you more. Why do you think *you* have to do something while neither of them are putting any work into trying to win you to them?"

A laugh burst from me. "Honestly, Tawny that... I have no idea why I didn't think of that. Why am I losing my mind trying to keep them both when no one tries to keep *me*?"

"That's what I'm saying. Okay, I'll go to your stupid gym. Gives us more shopping time anyway because I don't have any gym shoes here."

She waggled her thick arched brows, and I settled back into my black leather seat, feeling infinitely better.

Working out was cathartic. I tied my hair up in a ponytail and put my earbuds in as I used the elliptical after doing some lightweight training. Tawny was beside me, but much less enthusiastic. I was so deep in my own mind I almost fell when someone tapped me on the elbow.

"Chris! You scared the sugarfoot out of me," I said, wiping my face with a towel.

I pulled the ear plugs out and hopped off the elliptical. Chris immediately embraced me. I'd seen him only three times since we'd broken up. He was as handsome as ever. Almost as tall as Slate, a college football player with a perfect tan body and baby blue eyes that would've shut down the Crayola factory if they'd tried to recreate it. They were just that dreamy.

"How's it going, shug? Damn, you look good."

Shug, short for sugar lips. Our compromise because sugar lips implied far too much. He held me out at arm's length and I blushed. I was glistening with sweat with no makeup on. The bright purple halter I wore to work out in covered up the baby pouch.

"Thanks. You always look good. How are things with the blonde from the cruise?" I asked, squirting water into my mouth from my water bottle.

"She's still around. How about Brass?" Chris asked politely.

"We're still friends," I told him, smiling.

Chris looked to Tawny who gave him a small wave, and he waved back flashing her a killer smile of perfect white teeth. Last time we spoke, he was still modeling.

"How's school?" I asked as he ran a hand over his stylish chestnut hair.

He was wearing a grey men's tank top and a pair of navy basketball shorts. Chris was still taking great care of his body.

"Good. Good. You know, doing the football thing. I'm only here because I was visiting my family for the weekend. That's too bad about Brass. He's a cool guy."

"Yeah. We still see one another often." Chris raised his brows. "No, not like that." I laughed nervously as his dark brows lowered.

"Yeah, you're not that type of girl," Chris said, giving me a nudge.

Was he flirting with me? If he was, it felt too good.

I shrugged, playing with my water bottle top. "I dunno about that."

Chris's eyes glittered as he looked down at me and he ran his teeth along his full lower lip and I glanced away knowing my pupils would likely be dilating.

"Scarlett, we should go grab lunch," Tawny said, appearing at my side.

"Chris, have you eaten?" I asked, not taking my eyes from Chris and walked along with him.

Chris joined us in the cafe across the street and told us things were going well with the Barbie blonde. I confessed to being pregnant and told him how Brass and I were currently taking a break if that's what one would call it.

Closure. When we went our separate ways, guilt I'd felt about our break-up lifted. He was happy, and he was happy for me because I could have children and he knew how important that was to me. We decided to keep in touch. He had been such an important part of my life, I loathed to cut ties completely.

It was our last night away. We bought steaks and smothered them in onions, mushrooms, and sprinkled the tops with blue cheese and bacon with garlic red potatoes and asparagus. We ate and reminisced about high school and I realized that this was what my life would have been if I'd never gone to Tidings.

Tawny and I had planned on getting an apartment together after we graduated college and then our parents had told us we were moving. The night made me feel like everything else had been a bad dream.

I had a single glass of wine and we moved to the living room to watch The Exorcist, The Ring, and then Army of Darkness so I could sleep played while we carved pumpkins we picked out at the grocery store. Tawny said it was fixed. I should have had to do it left-handed. She made a cat while mine looked like the magical coach from Cinderella.

After our week of road tripping and normalcy, I realized I didn't want to give up my apartment. It was a refuge of sorts especially since I took down all the framed pictures of Brass and I. Indigo had mentioned escaping to it after she was proven tried and true.

"I'll be right back," I told Tawny and went into my dining room where I kept my check book in the built-in drawers.

She nodded engrossed as the movie continued.

My landlords had a mailbox in the laundry room where we could place our rent checks. I walked down to the basement and wrote my check for six months. I would have to remember to add funds to my checking account when I got home.

Wherever home was these days. I would have to move out of the Dagr palace soon.

I heard Tawny's voice when I closed the back door and stepped into the kitchen.

"She's not running! Why do you even care? We're celebrating her birthday; we'll be back tomorrow don't get your panties in a twist," she snapped.

I knit my brows as I walked into the living room to find Tawny yelling at my open laptop.

Her eyes met mine, and she stood and whispered. "I was trolling the web when the video call came up, I didn't mean to hit it." She mouthed *sorry,* and I waved at her dismissively.

I came around to where she plopped back down and looked into the screen. Jett, Brass, Quick, and Slate huddled around the screen with Indigo. I was already in my pajamas, a pink racer back that said *Angel*

Love and a pair of horizontally striped knit pants. I smoothed my sloppy bun as I plastered a smile on my face.

They couldn't read my mind, couldn't catch my scent, couldn't tell if I lied. It was oddly freeing.

"This is a surprise. It's... what time is it there?" I asked, pulling my legs up on the couch.

"Six," Tawny said and gestured to the time stamp on my laptop screen.

"What are you all doing at Valla U so early? Happy Birthday, by the way Indigo!" I said flashing my brightest smile and Jett groaned.

"Right back at you. When are you coming back? I am probably spending tomorrow with Silver, but maybe we could do dinner?" Indigo asked.

She was positively glowing. Whatever Quick was doing, I hoped he never stopped. Tawny and I shared a look.

"I'm going to get my new license in the morning cause I'm twenty-one." I waggled my brows at her. "Then, I guess we could come back." I shrugged and beamed another smile at the screen. "What's up? Why the call, just wanted to know when we'd be back? Everything all right at home? How's the most beautiful niece on the planet?"

Jett sucked on his teeth as Quick chuckled, sounding relieved. Slate stared at the screen dubiously, I couldn't look at Brass without seeing the ebony-haired vixen.

Jett sighed. "Gigi is good. Everything's all right. What about you? You two ditched classes last Friday."

I wrinkled my brow. "Yeah, we're good." I scoffed. "That still doesn't explain why all of you are video calling us. Didn't Steel tell you we were here?" I asked.

"He did," she said with a warm smile. "How are the boys, Scar?" Indigo asked.

"Good. As always. I ran into Chris at the gym —"

"She made me work out on vacation." Tawny made a face beside me and I rolled my eyes with a smile.

"How is he?" Indi asked with genuine interest.

"Good. We went to lunch, and I told him about my sons. He's happy."

"Chris the Myopic?" Slate asked, his voice dropping.

"Yes."

"I *bet* he was happy for you," Quick said, pursing his lips.

I rolled my eyes again. "It wasn't like that. We were friends long before we started dating."

"As *we* were?" Brass finally spoke, and I had to remind myself he couldn't read my thoughts.

I was glad the flickering tv cast shadows over my face so they couldn't see how my face flushed. "*Are.* I hope." I offered a brilliant smile that hurt my cheeks from how hard I had to fake it.

They all turned to look at Brass except Slate who narrowed his eyes at me. Brass stared into the screen as if he was either trying to read my mind or send emotions out to me. After a protracted silence his lips tensed.

"Friends," he exhaled.

"If there isn't anything else, could someone let Steel know I'll be home tomorrow around lunch?" Tawny interjected.

"Will do," Indigo said perkily.

"I'll have to take a raincheck on dinner. I've been wing man all week and miss my husband." Tawny gave Indigo a devious grin and Indi and I groaned.

Talking about our uncle's love life was not something we ever wanted to do.

"Why did you not respond to my bond?" Slate suddenly asked as my finger hovered over the touch pad.

Tawny gaped at me. She had no idea.

I shrugged. "Was I being summoned? I thought perhaps one of your lovers was a little too aggressive or you'd been slapped. My apologies, Slate."

"Are you *on* something?" Jett blurted, and I found my laugh ready.

"Don't I wish. Nope. We've just had a really great week. See you guys tomorrow," I said, waving and clicking the end button before they could ask another question.

Tawny leaned back and blew air from her mouth. "Well played. You were cool, but friendly. Now we'll go back and make them insanely jealous so they're climbing over one another to get back with you like they used to."

I fell back and slid so my head was on her shoulder. "What if they're relieved? What if neither want me back?"

"Then they didn't deserve you in the first place."

The walk to the portal door we placed in the woods made me feel like I'd just been convicted to be executed — dead woman walking. Tawny was practically bouncing on the balls of her feet to get back to Steel. She woke up extra early, and we waited outside the DMV before it was open so we were in and out in five minutes with my new ID that informed the world that I was officially twenty-one.

I changed into a borrowed Elivagar styled dress made of ivy embossed rose fabric. The cut of the neckline plunged in an ivory trim that also circled the hem of its bell-shaped skirts. I wasn't used to the multiple layers of petticoats and corset I wore to make my waist ultra-tiny while the skirts were twice as wide as my shoulders. Hers was similar in burgundy and gold with black embossed roses.

It dawned on me I hadn't gotten Indigo a birthday gift and I kicked myself for having been to a week of foreign places, to her at least, only to come back with something from Tidings. Tawny suggested we head to Ostara so I could get her something from the land she was raised in even if I would break out into a sweat in the heavy dresses the instant I set foot on the island.

Every land had its own beauty. Its own peak of the season the island embodied. Ostara was always in bloom. The phrase "pretty as a picture" applied to my father's home island. I walked down the path into Ostara's town heart. Men and women in pastel satins, charmeuse, and gorgeous sheer fabrics crunched over the glittering white gravel roads. The occasional carriage of a wealthy family passed by rustling the heavily trimmed skirts of the women's caftans.

"What would she like?" Tawny asked as we walked arm in arm past the white lace carved trim cottages.

Bells tinkled above the quaint doors with each customer. Flowers with colors I had no name for were planted in the carved boxes in front of shops and in the beautifully tended gardens in between cottages.

"I thought I would get her another carved fetish for her hair. Maybe a teardrop for Regn," I said conspiratorially and shared a giggle with Tawny.

A sign hung above a shop that promised rare gifts and had the look of a place that wouldn't be cheap. Tawny gestured to it as a small gilt navy carriage pulled by two black Akhal-Teke stallions stopped in front. We watched curiously at who would exit ornate carriage.

The navy clad footman opened the door and Tawny grabbed my wrist as the man descended. "By the Mother," she whispered.

I made a noise of agreement in my throat. The man had a powerful bearing. I felt like I should know him but had never seen him before that day. His glossy dark hair was peppered with silver and combed to the side of a strong-featured olive face. From his profile, I could tell his nose was straight, but not pointed above dark pink lips with a bold cupid's bow. A muscle leapt in his anvil jaw as his head swung our way and my breath caught.

His deep brown dreamy eyes glittered as he turned his head our way. Tawny and I stared like a couple of imbeciles.

"Are you ladies entering?" he asked and Tawny let out a low scoff of disbelief that a man so handsome could have such a seductively smooth voice.

"Yes," I said, jarring out of my stupor, and pried Tawny's frozen hand from my wrist.

He held the door open, so we had to walk right past him to leave. Well over six feet, his bronze satin short sleeved jerkin displayed well-muscled arms for his age which I placed at around fifty.

He smelled divine. A rich musk with an understated floral scent. I inhaled deep as I passed him and offered my thanks. His eyes had an intensity to them that made me want to squirm when he focused on me.

The inside of the shop was much larger than the outside hinted at. Modern recessed lighting lit aisle after aisle of case full of baubles. It was the perfect example of Tidings, where the old world met the new. The entire store glittered.

A woman with champagne curls down to her waist sauntered over to us. She would have been a supermodel outside of Tidings, she was tall and lean with a provocative smile.

"My name is Firefly; how may I be of service?" she asked with a plummy accent.

Her dark eyes swept past us to the distinguished man who was still standing just behind us. I wouldn't look at us either with him there to ogle.

"We're looking for gifts for my sister. Something personal, like a teardrop carving," I offered.

Firefly nodded tearing her eyes free from the fox behind us as another woman sashayed over to help him. We followed Firefly down the many aisles until we reached the exact gift I wanted to give her.

"That one."

I knew right away the teardrop Indigo pendant that hung from a silver chain would be the ideal gift for my reluctant sister.

"It's Azurite," said Firefly as she picked up the lariat necklace.

"She'll love it." I smiled and started to hum Treasure by Bruno Mars.

Tawny pouted as Firefly went to gift wrap my item. "You suck. Get her a blade or something and let me give her the necklace."

"You're jealous I saw it first," I teased, and she nudged me with her hip.

"Perhaps you may find this suitable."

Butterflies took flight in my belly as the man from the carriage held up a thin indigo cloak made of taffeta and lined with sable fur. The kicker was that its clasp was two tear drops. I ran my hand over it and smiled.

"If you don't get it, I will."

"Not a chance," Tawny said, and the man handed her the cloak.

We watched her walk away, me trying to avoid looking directly at an eclipse and him trying to get a better look at a woman far too young for him. "Thank you for that." I said looking anywhere, but at him.

"My pleasure. I did not mean to eavesdrop, but you caught my eye on the road and I have been finding it hard to concentrate on little else."

I melted like ice cream in July.

Sure, the man had sexual predator written all over him, but he wasn't a man I had seen with Brass or Slate. He seemed to have one goal in mind, and I was currently unattached.

I turned towards him and tried not to let myself get intimidated by his lordly bearing. The full force of those deep-set dreamy eyes nearly knocked me back a step. For a moment, I simply stared.

"Hi, I'm Ilisha and this is Scat, year of the fish. Thanks for all your help..."

Tawny paused for him to insert his name looping her arm through mine and I gaped at her. I had no idea why I needed a new name. Our names were well known, but what did that matter?

"Are you ladies ready to complete your purchase?" Firefly interrupted.

I *felt* irritation. The fine lines pinched around the supermodel's lips.

She was jealous. I wanted roll my eyes, but instead I settled for giving the older gentleman a smile and following Firefly back to the front where I opened my coin purse and gave the girl a single golden daymark with the runic compass molded on it. Tawny placed three silver crescents on the granite counter. They were imprinted with a crescent moon.

Rich musk with floral accents wafted to me before he used his *calling* to open the door. Tawny nudged me with her elbow as we descended the steps.

"He is absolutely dreamy. Why didn't you talk to him?" she asked in a whisper.

"Why did you lie about our names?"

She shot me a dry look. "That's what you do when you have a one-night stand with a beautiful stranger."

I chuckled because she must've been joking. Her dry expression remained.

"Tawny, no," I told her, hearing the door shut to the shop with the soft jingle of its bell.

"Pardon my boldness, would you ladies like a ride to your next destination?"

His footman hopped to the shimmering ground and took the thin box from his hand and hurried to the side of the carriage. The footman opened the door to reveal a plush navy interior and gold damask lined ceiling.

"We'll take you up on that offer," Tawny said, leading me directly to the carriage.

My eyes widened as I tried to dig in my heels. Hadn't she ever heard the phrase 'don't talk to strangers'? Now she wanted to get into a carriage with one? A handsome one who could probably beat us into submission, either with his powerful form or with his seductive voice. Either or.

I climbed into the carriage after Tawny. As I reached for the footman's hand, another took its place and I felt like a bottle of pop that had been shaken up. Fine dark hair climbed dusted the back of his hand. I expected it to be soft and smooth especially since his nails were impeccably manicured, but his palm was tough. I knew those callouses well. The older man used blades.

He inhaled deeply as if fortifying himself and kept hold of my hand as he followed in behind me. Only when the footman shut the door did he finally, and reluctantly I might add, release his hold. It was even more opulent than I had suspected and with his *calling*, he cooled the small space. Our knees were only a few inches apart as we sat across from one another. His eyes never left my face, my eyes never met his.

The crunch of the gravel and stamping of horses' hooves should have been louder, but I suspected the tiny carriage was finely crafted.

"Did you find what you came for?" Tawny asked, dousing the simmering tension in the confined space.

"And then some," he said, letting his gaze linger on me before smiling at Tawny. "For your sister, you said?"

"Her twin sister. It's her birthday, too," Tawny offered, beaming her most flirtatious smile at him.

His gaze returned to me. "And yet I see no gift for yourself."

"We returned from a week-long vacation today. It was gift enough for me." I answered, watching the tug on his lips at my voice.

"She speaks. You and your husband?" he asked, looking down at my bared tiwaz rune.

I self-consciously covered it. "My cousin," I answered curtly.

Who was he presuming to take two young women he just met for a ride and asking such personal questions? He shouldn't be giving me such steamy looks with such suggestive remarks.

"No husband then?" he asked, continuing to nose around in business that wasn't his.

"We're both married. I am happily, but Scat here hasn't lived in the same quarters as her husband since last February."

I turned to stare at Tawny and gave her a look that said, *shut your big fat trap!*

"So I suppose you do not have plans to celebrate your day of birth then?" He continued ignoring the glower I gave Tawny.

"She doesn't."

"I do. I have dinner with my sister planned." I would not sound petulant.

He placed his fingers over his superbly shaped lips and tapped his forefinger, I suspected to hide a smirk. "I have two tickets to *Cymbeline* tonight. My companion cancelled last minute and I planned to go alone. Have you seen *Cymbeline*, Scat?"

For a brief moment, I wondered who he's speaking too. "No. I've seen three stage plays in my life, that is not one of them." I started and realized I was perilously close to agreeing to go with him.

"Let me guess. *Romeo and Juliet, Macbeth,* and —"

"*Romeo and Juliet,* but the other two were musicals, actually. I doubt you've heard of them."

I glanced back out the window as my cheeks heated. I wouldn't be telling him I saw *The Lion King* and *Hairspray*.

"I may meet you at your home or at the portal. Your choice. It is here in Ostara at eight. Is that enough time?" he asked.

The carriage came to a halt and Tawny nudged me. "She'll be here at a quarter till. Thank you for the lift."

I would've been sent sprawling if the footman hadn't had a hand ready to balance me the way Tawny pushed me out the door. I didn't wait a heartbeat before rounding on her.

"Are you out of your mind? As if I don't have enough virile men in my life trying to get in my figurative pants."

"Thank me later. You need a date. A real date. Where you get dressed up and a man treats you like a queen. I'm not saying make him your second husband. I'm saying, live a little. He's charming, handsome, interested..."

"Is that the criterion these days?" I sighed.

He was extremely good-looking. Naturally, I counted that against him.

"He'd better not expect anything from me. It's just a play and then home."

Tawny giggled and led me through the portal.

CHAPTER 21

INDIGO

Strong fingers intertwined with mine at my stomach as I shifted in bed. It took me more than a moment to remember where I was, but since I never spent the night with Sterling, there was only one other guess. Silver. His sandalwood, patchouli, and cedar scent stuck to my skin.

I had repeatedly tried to chase him away. I should have known the man was too hardheaded to give up that easily on something he really wants. I had no idea what he saw in me, but as long as he kept coming around and kissing me with those lips, I would let him.

"Do you think they're back yet?" I asked with eyes still shut.

The warmth of the morning's sun was coming through the bedroom window. Scarlett was slowly placing a wall around herself, brick by brick. She'd shot Brass down, nicely of course. If what Silver said was true, I didn't blame her. Then she'd boxed out Slate as well. I didn't understand that move, but maybe she was sick of all the rumors. I went in search of a distraction. If Silver Regn wasn't the planet's biggest distraction, then I didn't know what was.

"A few more hours." Silver's voice was thick with sleep, its low timbre sent a thrill through me and I arched my hips against his front.

Silver's palm went flat to my stomach, and he made a contented noise in his throat. "Be careful, Dove. I am getting used to waking up next to you."

Silver elicited the most asinine feelings from me. I cursed him several times a day and now was no different as I felt a fluttering in my stomach.

"When we're married, you'll get sick of me," I cooed.

Did I mention he also coerced the most witless words from my mouth?

"Freya's burly boar."

Silver slid his hand from mine and up over my hip, pushing my green silk nightdress up to my waist. He could curse all he wanted as long as I got him first thing in the morning. If there was a better way to wake up, I didn't know of it. Silver had introduced me to sleep overs and love making until we passed out.

With Sterling it was always on stolen time. Stolen kisses, a few stolen hours. When we'd use sleep overs as an excuse to stay the night at one another's houses, his sisters or Sage, we would always sneak into one of the empty rooms to be together. We could never sleep though, a quick nap at most. Nothing at all like what I did with Silver.

I wasn't being smart with him. I didn't have my tea with me and we weren't using any other protection. If I didn't know any better, I'd say he was making procuring contraception deliberately difficult.

Mind muddled. The coil sprung and my body gripped around Silver.

I sucked in a noisy breath squeezing his fingers at my hips. "*Ooh.*"

Silver didn't snicker. I couldn't help the way my mouth formed a perfect 'O' when he gave me pleasure. Dove. He was such an ass. Speaking of... I gripped his firm backside as he flexed with a moan. *Gods*, I was going to get excited all over again. It was a vicious cycle.

Silver pushed the hair away from my neck and began to press his notorious kisses along it. I smiled moronically but didn't move so I could relish in the feel of him inside me.

"Say it," Silver purred.

"I love you, Silver Regn."

"I, you, Dove."

My whole body liquified against him. A rapid rap of knocks sounded as an older man opened the bedroom door and walked in with two women wearing navy-colored caftans. I froze and Silver pulled the blankets over me as he shifted away.

"Good morning, grandfather. We can discuss things at breakfast. I have a guest over," Silver said, standing naked beside the bed to pull on a pair of pants that laid on the floor.

The two women were sharing scandalous glances of Silver, leaving no doubt in my mind that it was not the first time they'd seen Silver naked. Lots of men and women slept with their over eager staff.

His grandfather grunted in doubt completely oblivious to me. I saw the resemblance right away. The Regn patriarch looked just like Brass, but with Silver's short hair and olive complexion. He had aged better than any man had a right to. That he had looked even better in his youth seemed an impossibility.

Tired of the provocative looks from the women and the disregard of the patriarch, I got out of the bed not caring that all I wore was the thin green silk. The older gentleman spun towards me with speed belying his age. He had a deep chocolate gaze that raked me. He wore a bronze satin jerkin with tear drop shaped brass buckles. Those eyes held a hint of mirth that he never lost.

"You brought a woman *home*?"

The older man's intense gaze made my skin prickle which didn't do me any favors in my thin garment, but I would not fidget. Scarlett always managed to make any article she was wearing look regal; I could do the same. I crossed the room in my bare feet, the nightdress ending just past my backside.

"Indigo Tio, pleasure to meet you," I said, extending my hand.

He took it in a big rough hand and shook it but didn't release it as he gave me another once over. "Spinel Regn, please call me Spinel."

"Spinel," I repeated with a smile.

Silver was at my side and took me back a step forcing his grandfather to release my hand. He wrapped his arm around my shoulders possessively as he addressed his grandfather.

"My future wife," Silver announced without a hint of jest.

I wasn't sure who was more surprised. Possibly the girl dusting a vase who knocked it over at his announcement. I cursed the Gods for setting this man in my path.

Spinel smiled, and I found where Brass and Silver got that dazzling smile from.

"Did you not get your betrothed a ring?" he asked, looking to my naked finger.

"I have not asked her patriarch just yet," Silver said, shifting.

The girl seemed to be crying as she picked up pieces of the shattered vase. As if Silver needed any more reason to be conceited. Out of frustration, I *called* the pieces into a small vortex and sent them into a small trash pail. The girl yelped, and I tried not to let my irritation show.

"A *powerful* greater family woman and you did not ask her patriarch first? You are not betrothed, Silver. You cannot charm your way into the lap of a greater family without jumping through a few hoops. When you want to do it properly, then come to me —" Spinel lectured.

"Today. Can you come with me today?" Silver tightened his grip on me as if I would flee.

Maybe he could read minds too because that's exactly what I was thinking about doing. "Silver," I hissed.

He stole a kiss and my eyes widened. We looked like two silly kids playing house.

"Do you want to marry my grandson, Ms. Tio?" Spinel asked.

It was such an unexpected question that my whole body went rigid. Instead of waiting patiently for my answer, Silver spun me to face him and bent his knees to look down into my eyes. His gold flecked chocolate eyes ensnared mine. I chewed my lip as I looked back. Gods, what was he doing to me?

"Yes," I whispered.

Silver's smile was blinding and infectious. I held myself away from him before he did something even more inappropriate like take me back to bed in front of Spinel. The girl wailed and finally, Silver turned towards her and made a face.

"Your wish is granted, Silver. I will join you for lunch at the Sumar palace today and we shall ask for her hand together." Spinel slid his scrutinizing gaze to me. "A Tio marriage. A greater family. I must admit, I did not count on you to find yourself an advantageous marriage. I will have to thank your Dagr friend for this one, I believe. Dress and join me for breakfast if you please," Spinel said, and he left with the two girls in tow.

The air whooshed from my lungs and I glowered at Silver. "Are you kidding me? You didn't tell me Spinel was a mind reader." He ignored me.

Silver attacked me with soft lips, peppering my face and every inch of exposed skin with kisses. It was very difficult not to laugh under his onslaught and I fell back on his bed.

"Silver, why did you do that?" I asked, trying to hold him back.

Silver looked down at me braced on his palms over me. "He is not stupid. He does not come in here. He must have seen you enter last night and wanted to know who you were."

I frowned. "Do you bring a lot of girls home?"

Silver smiled and seared one of his steamy kisses against my lips. "No, Dove. That is why he felt the need to investigate. By the by, I have no idea why that girl was crying."

"She's obviously sad you won't be sleeping with her anymore." I said stiffly.

His smile deepened. "I do not have sex with the staff. I have done things... but I try not to shit where I eat."

"Try harder," I said dryly, and he planted another kiss to my lips.

"For the life of me, I cannot figure out why you are still dressed," Silver said, pushing his pants over his trim hips.

After breakfast with Spinel, we immediately went with him back to the Sumar palace. I changed into a dusky blue strapless chiffon dress and met them at the portal room where Pearl and Hawk were already greeting Coyote Regn, the oldest Regn brother, Spinel, and Silver. Spinel had sent a messenger the moment he left Silver's room.

I slowed as I reached them and since Silver did not possess a modicum of decorum, he picked me up and spun me around before planting a full kiss on my lips. I was blushing a furious shade of purple. Pearl and Hawk gave me amused looks over Silver's shoulder and since

Silver had no mother or grandmother to entertain, I waited in the drawing room of the palace alone.

White, gold, and walnut decorated the drawing room. Sheer panels of white draped in front of each mosaic column that divided platform seating sections around the circular room. Food was set out around the small fountain in the center. It was softly lit by long, multilayered metal lanterns that hung in a ring at the center of the room and on each column.

The last time we had used it was for Gigi's baby shower. The time before that had been for my mother's funeral.

Fretting over the swaths of chiffon of my dress I waited nervously for what they would come back with. I heard footsteps and leapt to my feet in anticipation. I almost cried when I saw it was Scarlett.

"Is it true?" Scarlett asked with her very best smile that felt like the sun had risen just for you.

I nodded and bit my lip. She laughed and embraced me.

"You're going to be a double aunt. It's a little strange, but I plan on taking credit for the two of you getting together," Scarlett said.

She released me and swiped at a happy tear.

"Thanks," I said weakly, "It's going to be a long engagement."

More footsteps announced Silver charging in through the doors with Jett, Slate, Brass, and the girls in tow. One look at him told me all I needed to know. My anxiety melted in the face of his exuberance. His joy was contagious and he was flashing that smile around wildly as he glided over to me.

I expected him to scoop me up, but instead he fell to his knee. My head swam. I didn't like how traditional this was becoming. Silver and I were not traditional. We were anti-traditionalists. He held up a ring and I thought I would faint when he took my hand. It was a lapis stone in a silver bezel setting, a leaf was etched around the silver that reminded me of the tree of life, the Var sigil.

"Spinel had a damn good point. I cannot hardly expect you to act like my betrothed when I have not gone through the proper channels and done things the way the Guardians do them. Your family has said yes, Dove." Silver's devilishly handsome face was etched with anxiety and it looked so foreign on him that I couldn't understand what would have caused him to fret so much. "You are the only woman I see myself waking up next to every morning. I am the youngest son of a lesser family; you are so far out of my league I have to pinch myself while you sleep in my arms to be sure it is not a dream. I do not want to wake from my dream. My pinching stops today."

Silver slid the lapis onto my trembling finger. He didn't rise. He was waiting for my answer. My mind scrambled for words. Monosyllables. Even a grunt would have worked. Silver had lost his Gods cursed mind.

"Get over yourself, Regn," I said and Silver's mouth dropped open.

I grabbed his shirt pulling him to his feet. "It is likely *my* dream to have tricked the illustrious 'Quick' Silver Regn into my marriage bed."

Scarlett let out a little laugh and realization dawned in Silver's eyes that he narrowed at me. "Sometimes I think I hate you, you blasted Tio woman." He grabbed me roughly by the back of my head and crushed his lips to mine.

Jett chuckled.

TWENTY-TWO

"Tawny and Steel aren't going to make it," I announced to Hawk and Sparrow as they placed kisses on my cheeks.

I hugged Pearl and murmured an apology for the last-minute vacation. She said Orion came by himself and explained. I had a feeling Old man Vetr had a bit of a crush on my grandmother. So did a great many men if rumors were to be believed. She'd lost Flint young and didn't remarry, but she kept a healthy rotation of lovely men around if you paid attention.

"It was a very good idea, darling. Did you have fun? You look exceptionally beautiful this evening," she said, withdrawing from our embrace.

I left as soon as Quick made his proposal. It was so romantic I had to cry and refused to do it in front of Slate. I went to the Dagr palace until dinner and spent the last three hours starting to get ready for the play and then stopping. I decided I would get ready and go, then tell him I forgot I had something important to do and pray his pride was too wounded to question.

I wore a sparkling satin halter rose gown with pleated skirts, my hair was pinned up with a sparkling crystal comb and I'd lightly dusted my skin with a shimmering powder so it looked luminescent. Old habits died hard, so I wore all my fetishes in my hair tucked underneath where it wouldn't spoil the look. My stone pieces were tucked into my dress and sheath strapped to my thigh just in case.

"Where are *you* going tonight?" Gypsum teased.

I kept my eyes on Pearl as my cheeks flushed. "I did have fun. It was a much-needed break."

I was studiously ignoring Brass with his date. I couldn't believe he brought her. My *let's just be friends* sugarfoot must have been very convincing. At least Slate didn't have anyone on his arm, but he glared at me streaming a constant irritation through the bond.

Pearl looked about the room, her cat eyes seeing what I couldn't as she signaled to one of the staffers. "We shall sup on the balcony tonight. Bring the gifts, please."

Gypsum offered me his arm as we filed into the mosaic filled halls. We led the way out onto the balcony that overlooked the waterfall where the Rivers Mani and Sol met. The staff had a long low table set up with piles of cushions arranged for us to lounge on while wait ate at our leisure. Torches were lit along the massive stone columns as were the Moroccan lamps that were centered on the long table even though we were a long way from dusk.

Not the twenty-first birthday I had imagined growing up, but I had more fun than anyone should on Tawny's birthday. The last time I was out on the balcony, I'd been with Brass. We'd made love under the stars of Thrimilci. I looked up to the bright blue landscape, it was too early for stars. I had nothing, but good memories of Brass and I until recently.

I tucked my legs under me across from Indigo and was shocked when Slate sat down beside me. Gypsum sat on my other side and handed me my gifts while the staff brought out platters of eggplant turnovers, tomato rice, lentils and saffron rice, lamb with prunes and apricots, and finally coconut fudge cakes.

It became clear this year's gift theme was jewelry instead of last year's which was weapons — their subtle way of telling me to take it easy. I was feeling properly wealthy with a pair of emerald drop earrings from Pearl, a crystal encrusted gold head chain from Tawny and Steel, and a delicate gold ankle bracelet from Hawk and Sparrow. Even a ruby tennis bracelet was gifted by Quick and Indigo. Gypsum had given me a crystal collar, but it was for Tree. He said she liked it and I took his word for it.

I watched Indigo opening her gifts, instead of gold, she received platinum, instead of emerald it was sapphire. They treated us like twins in truth, getting us matching items in different colors.

When I'd opened the gift from Jett and the girls, my face had nearly started on fire with how uncomfortable I was receiving such creative lingerie that Cherry had no doubt chosen. Indigo and Quick were practically giggling over their box and I could only imagine what they had.

"I take no responsibility for whatever was in that box," Jett said and Slate slid it in front of him and peered inside despite my trying to keep it from him.

"You can wear it tonight after your date," Cherry chirped and my eyes went as round as saucers. I looked to my aunt and uncle who were thankfully distracted by something Gypsum was telling them.

"Where are you going, girl?" Slate rumbled and my ire raged.

"You have another gift," Amethyst interrupted, and I knew it was no accident.

I gave her a grateful smile as I reached for the last box. It was a long flat box that made me think of clothing. I untied the bow and lifted the lid knowing Brass would never get me anything as inappropriate as what Cherry, Amethyst, and Jett would.

I smiled and slid my eyes to Brass who inclined his head. I ran my fingers over the matte black metal scales, I pressed my fingertips into the padding underneath that felt like memory foam. Curse my hormones. I was going to cry.

"Well?" Jett asked peevishly.

I lifted the black scaled corset from the box. Intricate gold lacework that matched my wrist blades and sheath stretched across the breast of the corset. Dragon-like scale extended beneath it to the stomach that had a slight curve to it. From the way the metal pieces fit together, I could wear it early on as I was now and well into the pregnancy if I had a need for armor. There was a black linked skirt attached to the corset I could wear on its own or put pants under. I would wear pants.

"Thanks everyone," Indigo seconded my thanks.

Slate leaned forward; his long midnight waves brushed my bare shoulder making my skin prickle as he placed a little black box in front of me.

"What's that?" I asked, looking to the little black box on the table.

"Your birthday present. Open it and find out," he said nonchalantly and *called* it onto my lap.

I looked precariously at the little box as one might a bomb that needed to diffused. "Since we're already married, I know there can't be an engagement ring in here."

Gypsum and Quick were the only two who laughed at my little joke.

I opened the box and inside was a platinum ring. A square diamond cross was encircled by a ring of diamonds. It was a solar cross, the Dagr sigil. I rubbed my lips together and stared at the ring.

"The mother of the heir to the Dagr line should be properly adorned," Slate rumbled as his silver eyes glittered over his goblet.

I was speechless. "I don't carry our heir, Slate," I whispered.

"No, but you will," Slate said cryptically and plucked the box from my lap.

He took the ring out before setting it on the table and slid the solar cross diamond ring onto the middle finger of my right hand. It was delicate and feminine with a simple design that wouldn't take away from any other jewelry I wore. I could wear it every day.

I felt as if someone had transplanted me from another time. He could almost be *my* Slate.

I met his gaze for the first time. "Is that an apology?"

I could use a proper apology. It was the dabbling in whether he was my husband I had a hard time with. It was everything or nothing — no in between.

"You are my wife; you will have my heir. It is that simple," he said with gunmetal eyes over the edge of his goblet.

I shook myself out of the pit of misery I was teetering over. "Thank you everyone. I am getting the hint. Trust me. Although... with Brass's gift I'll be safe when I *do* train," I teased playfully and Gypsum and Jett threw pieces of balled up wrapping paper at Brass who deflected as he laughed.

Hawk offered to bring my gifts home, and I thanked him after slipping the ruby tennis bracelet over my wrist and leaving Slate's Dagr ring where he placed it. Gypsum saw me starting to get to my feet and helped me up with a lady killing smile.

"You met someone. You're being all secretive and mysterious," Gyps said making a face.

He was the boy I knew then, and it prompted a giggle from me. "A nice gentleman I met while shopping asked to take me out tonight. I was going to turn him down, but Tawny insisted."

"Truth. Do we know him?" Quick asked with a stern edge in his voice.

Indigo elbowed him in the ribs. "Where's he taking you?"

"No, I don't think you know him. I'm not sure, but we're going to see a play." The corner of my mouth quirked, unable to resist itself.

"An old man then, huh, girl?" Slate's rumbled.

I straightened my shoulder as I looked down my nose at him. "He's older if that's what you mean. I'm surprised you're here at all tonight."

I regretted snapping but held fast to my indignation. Slate got to his feet to loom above me.

"Come. Let us deactivate this bond and get it over with." Slate turned from me before I could claw his eyes out.

I said my goodbyes, giving hugs and kisses to everyone as I went and even said goodbye to the raven-haired vixen who'd stolen Brass away. Brass clutched my hand as I passed. He wondered if he could speak to me for a moment. I wanted nothing more than to wriggle free from his grip. Walking into the hall with Brass and Slate was not what I wanted to do in the least.

I folded my arms under my chest as I glowered. "Steal your kiss and be done with it. I appreciate you keeping it in your pants this week, but I never asked you to activate it," I said with clipped words.

Brass reached out and pressed his palm to my belly and *called*. He wasn't worried about me; he hadn't even said a word to me. He just wanted to know how his sons were. I could deal with that. I could deal with it *better* if Rosasite wasn't sitting and judging at my family's table.

I was about to thank Brass for inviting his child bride to my grandmother's home when Slate rushed me. I was standing against the wall as it was, but then he reached me, I was crushed. We'd deactivated our bond enough times that I knew one firm kiss would do the trick, but he had gone a full week without intimacy.

Parting my lips when Slate pressed his mouth over mine was an involuntary reflex. I felt Brass's hand slide from my stomach, likely because Slate's hips were pinning me in place. I pried my eyes open to find Brass hadn't moved a muscle. Internally, I groaned. As intoxicating as his kisses were, he was the memory missing Slate, not mine. This version of him cared nothing for me but my body.

I tucked my arms in between us and began to shove him, and his roaming hands, off. He growled deep in his throat so it seemed to reverberate off his ribs through his chest and only then rumble in his throat. It was not an amorous sound.

"Get off," I hissed. "The bond is deactivated."

His hands slapped the wall to either side away as I turned my face away.

"Gods' cursed woman. I have half a mind to take you to my room so we may celebrate your birth in earnest."

My body responded traitorously, but I slid along the wall from under him. "You *have* only half a mind if you think I'm going to sleep with you after you held my own seax to my throat and called me a whoring spy," I snapped.

I turned to Brass who was patiently waiting for our fight to wrap up. "The boys are fine. Tawny checked on them every day. At no point were they endangered. I'm glad you're both here, I don't want any spies tonight. I don't need them every night and if I get into trouble, I'll use the Shadow Breaker tracker."

Slate narrowed his eyes at me and reached for my chin. I expected the move and dodged his hand that sought to cut my lip on my own teeth to activate my bond.

"What's this man's name, Scarlett?" Brass asked coolly.

I inhaled deeply, trying to fight off a blush. "If I choose to divulge his name, it'll be because he's a part of me and my sons' lives. This is a single date."

I didn't know his name. He hadn't even offered it. What I *did* know was that Brass had no business asking me about my dates any longer.

Slate's nostrils flared, and he shifted as if he was going to grab me, making me take a step away unwittingly but was stopped by Brass's hand. "Okay, Scarlett. We can hardly blame you for trying to find happiness since you don't seem to find it in us."

My stomach churned. I was about to give him a piece of my mind when he knelt and ran his palms over the slight swell of my belly, catching me completely off guard and pressed a kiss to the left and then the right side. The insane part of me that crooned at this paternal display of affection caused me to lift my hands to cradle his face.

He was melting me. I needed that icy wall.

The side door to the balcony opened and my hands hovered near Brass's thick dark hair. I snapped them back to my sides and glanced to the door. The honey, deep-set eyes of the creamy coffee skinned girl were locked on Brass who slowly rose to his feet.

"Dare I ask?" Rosasite's voice sounded as smooth as her skin looked.

"I shall walk you out," Slate rumbled, grabbing my wrist.

"I know the way," I spat as I tried to match his long strides.

My heart wouldn't listen to my brain who warned not to look back. I did anyway and felt myself die a little inside when I spotted the vixen's hands laced around Brass's neck.

I couldn't believe he brought her.

Slate jerked my arm so my feet tripped in the pleated train and he caught me around my middle, never breaking stride as he guided me along the halls.

"If you're trying to take me to your room, you're wasting your time. I wasn't lying when I said I had a date and I am going to be late."

He was taking me to the portal room, the blue faux starlight shown through the doorway as we turned the corner into the hall. He arched a brow at me but kept going until we were at the door that bridged our worlds.

Slate stopped and pivoted to hold my shoulders. "Does this man know you are married?"

His fingers trailed down my arms over my elbows to my limp hands. "Yes," I answered hypnotized by those mirrored orbs.

"And that you carry —"

"He doesn't. I barely spoke to him. Tawny thought I should get out and negotiated the whole thing," I confessed and the corner of his mouth tugged up.

"Twist your arm, did she?"

I folded my arms petulantly. I didn't owe him an explanation. He'd made his stance clear.

"Go on, get out whatever you feel obligated to say." My tone was arctic, I hoped he felt it like ice water was dumped down the back of his shirt.

He pulled my hands to his waist and pushed my hair over my shoulders.

"The curious roamer, the hand, roaming all over the body—the bashful withdrawing of flesh where the fingers soothingly pause and edge themselves. The limpid liquid within the young man. The vexed corrosion, so pensive and so painful. The torment—the irritable tide that will not be at rest. The like of the same I feel—the like of the same in others. The young man that flushes and flushes, and the young woman that flushes and flushes. The young man that wakes, deep at night, the hot hand seeking to repress what would master him; The mystic amorous night—the strange half-welcome pangs, visions, sweats. The pulse pounding through palms and trembling encircling fingers— the young man all color'd, red, ashamed, angry; the souse upon me of my lover the sea, as I lie willing and naked, The merriment of the twin-babes that crawl over the grass in the sun, the mother never turning her vigilant eyes from them. The walnut-trunk, the walnut-husks, and the ripening or ripen'd long-round walnuts; The continence of vegetables, birds, animals, The consequent meanness of me should I skulk or find myself indecent, while birds and animals never once skulk or find themselves indecent; the great chastity of paternity, to match the great chastity of maternity. The oath of procreation I have sworn—my adamic and fresh daughters. The greed that eats me day and night with hungry gnaw, till I saturate what shall produce boys to fill my place when I am through, The wholesome relief, repose, content; and this bunch, pluck'd at random from myself; It has done its work—I tossed it carelessly to fall where it may."

Some things hadn't changed. I knew his game; we'd played it before. He used Walt Whitman and poetry to distract or seduce me. Slate couldn't remember that I also knew how to play.

"Five months ago the stream did flow. The lilies bloomed within the sedge. And we were lingering to and fro. Where none will track thee in this snow. Along the stream, beside the hedge. Ah, sweet, be free to love and go! For if I do not hear thy foot. The frozen river is as mute. The flowers have dried down to the root: And why, since these be changed since May, shouldst thou change less than they. And slow, slow as the winter snow. The tears have drifted to mine eyes; And my poor cheeks, five months ago Set blushing at thy praises so, Put

paleness on for a disguise. Ah, Sweet, be free to praise and go! For if my face is turned too pale. It was thine oath that first did fail, It was thy love proved false and frail. And why, since these be changed enow, Should I change less than thou."

The Brownings were my favorite poets. Whatever Slate was going to say faded with his deep inhale.

"I would have spent tonight with you," he said and I licked my lips before bringing my hands to the sides of his face.

"One night with you will never be enough for me."

I curled my fingers in his wavy hair at his chest and pulled his mouth down to mine, breathing deep his scent. He put up no resistance. Slate pulled me close, the charge between us crackled dangerously, and I pulled away before I melted against him.

"Goodnight, Slate."

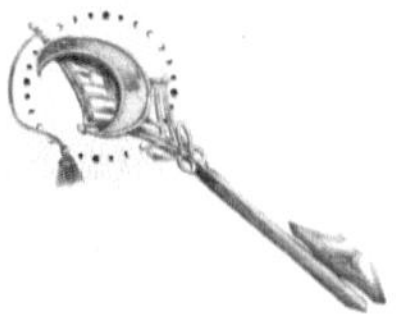

The mysterious man was waiting outside the portal. His lips curled as the white light faded behind me, and I gave myself an internal kick. I was supposed to be coming up with an excuse to leave. Slate and Brass had distracted me. He moved to take my arm, and I found myself being comfortable with his guidance.

I was back in his gilt carriage. With the two of us alone, I started mentally guessing his age. Guardians lived twice as long, matured faster, and started aging slower at about twenty. Some Guardians aged hard like Moon Straumr and Viper Enox, but others seemed to have found the fountain of youth like Cordillera who had to be in her mid-forties and looked about thirty. It was the same for my mother and Sparrow.

He leaned in the shadows of the carriage with the bright moonlight peaking under the partially drawn shades. I felt his eyes on the side of my face as our bodies swayed with the carriage's movement.

"You saw your husband tonight." It was rhetorical. "I shall strive to lift your mood."

Was I sulking? If I was, I couldn't put my finger on why I would take it out on a total stranger.

"Did his bed not entice you?" he asked and my head whipped to him.

I opened my mouth to begin a diatribe that would leave his ears on fire but stopped myself when I saw the ghost of a smile on his lips. He was goading me into speaking.

"If you wanted pleasant conversation, you could have asked a question I wouldn't mind answering," I said haughtily.

"You have a very alluring voice, young Scat. I do believe that is the most I have ever heard you speak," he mused. "Why are you here, young Scat?"

I'd nearly forgotten Tawny had lied about our names. If I was going to correct it, now was the time.

"My cousin thought it would be better than pouting at home alone, I suppose. Why did you ask me here?" I asked.

His eyes glittered in the darkness. "I think you know very well why I asked you."

I inhaled sharply at his scent which had spiked so suddenly, my inner fire went from match light to wildfire in a blink. I looked at my sweating balled fists and prayed we were close.

Tidings didn't have much for entertainment so I was astonished there was a theater in Ostara. I wasn't surprised to find that it only seated about a hundred people which included the two red velvet draped balconies. One of which we sat in... just the two of us.

There wasn't much to the upper crust of Tidings. There were two greater families on each of the islands except for Mabon where they had four lesser families instead of the three the other islands had. The mystery man was wealthy. He could have been one of the merchants that ran the notorious textiles. From the cut of his black embroidered waistcoat, my guess was he knew what he looked good in.

My fingers curled around the golden carved armrest as I settled into the gold and crimson jacquard seat. The mystery man took the seat beside me, there were only two, and the lights dimmed.

Everything was better with *calling*. The play took on a life of its own like a high budget movie right before my eyes. Three men changed scenes and props from the sides with their *calling*, never having to interfere with the actors. I found myself leaning forward on the gold railing.

Cymbeline was a beautiful play about deception, treachery, and love. It was brilliant. By the fourth act, I was on pins and needles, never having read that particular play by Shakespeare.

At intermission, the mystery man informed me there were five acts. He guided me from the balcony as I gushed about the play so far hoping there was a happy ending in store. He led me up a private stairway to the roof and I groaned when he held the door for me and I walked out into what had to be the most beautiful garden I'd ever seen.

Strands of lights hung from lattices that illuminated the cacophony of blooms that covered the roof. A few other couples strolled the garden finding their own secreted corners to seek privacy.

"A fan of flowers?" he mused.

"You'd be hard pressed to find a woman who isn't."

His hand slid over the skin of my back, coaxing me inside. He kept it there, his chest against my shoulder as we wandered the garden. let myself lean into the mystery man and enjoy the dreamlike surroundings under the starry sky. He had extensive knowledge of the blooms scenting the air. He identified each one literately stopping to smell the loveliest of flowers. I found it oddly soothing.

We sat on a stone bench together, my fervor eliciting the occasional laugh. I smiled at him; he was very easy to talk to; invitingly warm and an excellent listener.

"If I had known you enjoyed books and poetry so much, I would have brought you to my home straightaway. I have an extensive library. I will show it to you tonight. My chef is preparing a small repast for us once we return."

He brushed the back of his hand across my cheek and trailed his fingers down my hair. "That sounds nice," I said softly.

His rich scent swirled into my lungs and he held my chin tilting it up. My eyes slid shut. I hadn't needed to make a single decision all night. He tended to everything. I felt safe and cared for. What I loved most is that I couldn't see any strings that would complicate matters between us. I wanted this mysterious older man, who seemed to want nothing more than my company and all that entailed, to kiss me.

"Balas. She looks a little young, even for you."

I'd hear that voice in my nightmares. I immediately stiffened in the man's arms.

At least I had a name — Balas.

Balas stood, taking me to my feet and held me so possessively, I did a double take to be sure he hadn't been replaced by Slate. Balas's anvil jaw clenched and unclenched as he shown an easy smile at the approaching couple.

"Patriarch Haust, Willow. She is young, but all the rarest gems once were," Balas said smoothly.

Sterling got his features from his mother. Wide high cheekbones with deep set violet eyes and a pouty mouth. Her loose dark curls framed her fair heart-shaped face. Peak's bright green eyes flared in the dark as he set his intense gaze on me.

"Willow. Peak. What a pleasant surprise. Are you enjoying the play?" I asked in my most diplomatic voice.

"It is a wonderfully tragic production," Willow said in a steamy voice.

"I did not realize you had taken a paramour, Mrs. Tio. Was it not the younger Regn you were with before?" Peak asked, being antagonistic.

I bristled. "My sister, Indigo, is engaged to Silver Regn. None of the Regn men are paramours."

"Engaged?" Willow blinked.

"As of today. My family will send out a notice tomorrow with the Regn. Excuse us, I believe the next act has started."

I took Balas's arm and skirted Peak. I tried to control my scent, I tried to control my trembling — neither was working. Peak was going to make me pay for that.

Now Balas knew I wasn't Scat and my history. Balas was no longer string*less*.

"Would you prefer to leave?" Balas asked.

"I really am enjoying myself. I'm sorry if I was rude. The Regn are good friends of mine and I hate that anyone would think ill of them."

The lights flickered, and we went back down to our seats, watching the others gather. Balas angled his body towards mine and pulled my hair over my shoulder to run his fingers down my back. It could've been my imagination, but our seats seemed closer. His presence more difficult to ignore. The lights dimmed and the final act began.

"You fight for those you love. That is an admirable trait, young *Scarlett*. You interact with the greater families as if you have much experience at it."

"I'm sorry my cousin gave you a false name, and I didn't correct her. I thought —"

Balas pressed his finger to my lips. "We all have secrets. What is in a name?" he said teasingly.

I smiled. "In Tidings, everything is in a name, Balas."

His dark eyes were glittering again. He was a striking man.

"You are right."

His home was a short fifteen-minute ride from the theater. As we pulled away, I saw Peak's head shift with our departure. I was going to hear from him very soon.

Balas lived in a sprawling French chateau, its shrubbery along the crushed gravel driveway was meticulously shaped. We stopped beside a towering stone fountain that reminded me of the Buckingham fountain in Chicago. I was right about Balas being wealthy.

He took my arm and led me inside. Elaborate baroque architecture decorated the interior, the man had very ornate taste. He threw back a set of double doors to reveal a sitting room. Jacquard teal couches surrounded several low tables on a woven rug that looked very expensive. Everything looked expensive. Expensive and antique.

I arched a brow at him which he didn't acknowledge and led me to the furthest door. I saw the bedroom through an open door on my left. A tufted teal velvet headboard with silver tassels was intricately carved, it was massive. Even bigger than my bed at home. A matching teal tufted chaise rested against the footboard.

"A little further," Balas promised and dropped my arm long enough to open the French doors and step back.

I held my hands to my chest as I absorbed the beauty of what I could see. "Oh, Balas," I said breathlessly.

He bent down to my feet and removed my shoes and then his own boots so his feet were bare as we stepped into the garden. Diamond Frost flowers hung from planters down the walls, we followed a stone slab path over a small bridge that crossed a man-made stream at the center of the garden. Balas said it circled the entire room. He only grew red and white blooms there, the like of which I'd never seen. Kodupul flowers, campions, ghost orchids, chocolate cosmos, and the Middle Mist red which was my favorite, and the rarest flower in the world.

An antique white iron cafe table and two chairs were on a small stone clearing. Candles flickered on the table and a trolley with covered silver trays waited for us. My toes curled in the lush grass and I smiled like a fool as Balas led me to the table and served me himself. I noticed there were several covered trays. He intended to see me stuffed to the brim.

We started with a lobster bisque, then we shared a basil salmon terrine. He poured me a single glass of pinot grigio and made no comment on my switch to water. Dessert was crème brûlée that I had a hard time finishing with his eyes on me.

I sat back with my goblet of water in my hand. "That was delicious. You'll have to thank your chef for me."

His scent was simmering, I was practically wriggling in my seat from it. Peak was the last man who touched me. I wouldn't let Slate near me and now that Brass was with Rosasite, we were over. My stomach dropped a little. I couldn't believe he brought her to my birthday. Slate, now free of our bond, was probably off at the khoraz brothel.

Balas got to his feet and took my hand, lifting me from the chair. He plucked my skirts off the ground and led me off the beaten path. A squat tree with red blooms was spread above us and Balas turned to me. I swallowed hard.

He reversed me to a bed of the rare Middle Mist and gazed down at me. "I have waited to tell you how lovely you look tonight because every moment I spend with you, you seem to grow even more beautiful," he said silkily.

Balas slid his palms over my jaw and used his thumb to tilt my head back. My eyes slid shut, and I thought he was going to kiss me, but instead I felt the silky fabric of my dress slide over my skin. I inhaled sharply. The nude seamless thong was all I had left to cover me and it wasn't much.

"You are an exquisite creature," he said in the smooth deep voice and my skin prickled as his fingers trailed over my shoulders.

Balas lowered me down until the Middle Mist was all around me. He *called*. Flowers petals fell from the tree all around us as he unbuckled my short seax. He plucked one of the Middle Mist and held it before me.

"We're crushing your flowers," I whispered.

His lips curled. "*You* are the rarest flower, Scarlett."

"Balas, I've only given myself to men whom I loved," I breathed.

He took the flower and slowly drew it over my lips. "*I thought her as chaste as unsunned snow,*" he playfully quoted.

My chest rose and fell heavily as he outlined my curves with the petals tickling the fine hairs as he went. His *calling* unbuckled his waist-coat, and he shifted his shoulders to let it fall. He tugged his shirt over his head, careful not to muss up his dark coifed hair. His body had been hard muscled once. He was fit, but not as hard.

"You never asked my name," he whispered as the flower's petals ran below my belt line.

"What's in a name?" I asked, smiling.

Balas's fingers hooked into my last article of clothing and I lifted my hips as he eased it down over my legs. The flower slid to the apex of my thighs. My own flower blossoming for Balas as I curled my fingers in the soil.

"*Cytherea, How bravely thou becom'st thy bed! fresh lily, And whiter than the sheets! That I might touch! But kiss: one kiss! Rubies unparagoned, How dearly they do't! 'Tis her breathing that perfumes the chamber thus; the flame of the taper Bows toward her, and would under-peep her lids to see the enclosed lights, now canopied under these windows, white and azure laced With blue of heaven's own tinct."*

He quoted Cymbeline in a hushed tone as more red petals drifted down over me.

No wonder Tawny gave herself to Steel that first night in the greenhouse. I'd never felt more worshipped. I knew I was probably the hundredth woman he'd used the routine on, but I didn't care.

One night.

It *was* my birthday.

I could give him what he chased me for and erase Peak's touch from my skin. No one was waiting for me.

I nodded; the rain of petals fell continuously as he brought his lips to mine. My back arched. His kisses were moan inducing. I could feel him smile against my lips and withdraw. Now kisses and petals brushed my skin as he went ever lower.

The sounds of my own moans blocked out the stream. I supposed with some men, age equaled experience. It certainly did with Balas. Blades of grass poked between my fingers as they curled and my body went limp. Balas was using those skilled lips back up my stomach. If he thought my belly was a bit soft, he kept it to himself.

He'd pushed his pants down past his hips and hovered above me. "As I said before. Every time I look at you, you are even more beautiful."

Jacquard blankets were piled on top of me. I stretched my arms high above my head and curled my toes making sure I *could* still curl them. I shouldn't have spent the night, but I'd been too tired to go home even with a carriage ride to the portal. Besides, I wanted to spend the night in a man's arms who owed me as much as I owed him.

Nothing.

Balas wore a long navy robe with embroidered breasts. He looked as incredible in a robe as he did in a waistcoat. He rolled over a trolley himself with two silver trays. His lips curled when he saw I was awake and got into bed next to me, leaning against the headboard. He pulled back the blankets as I rolled onto my stomach and he traced the curve of my spine and over my backside.

I smiled lazily and folded my arms under my head. "Good morning."

He laughed. "*Afternoon*, young Scarlett."

I squeezed my eyes shut. "Sugarfoot. I've got to go."

"After breakfast."

I rolled onto my back and arched a brow as his eyes took me in again until I pulled the soft sheets under my arms. Balas passed me the covered plate so we could eat in bed.

I understood now why a woman would keep an older man as a lover. He was a combination of caring and lustful that made me feel special. Loved even. He made the choices for me. Every decision that needed to be made, was. I sat back and let him take care of things. It was a luxury I hadn't had before, or maybe it was because I didn't trust others to make the best choices for me.

Balas walked me to the carriage after breakfast and I was introduced to the real walk of shame in my clothes from the night before, dirt under my nails, hair untamed, smelling of sex and Balas's rich musk and subtle flower scent. He gave me a chaste kiss before I climbed into the navy carriage.

"Scarlett?" Balas said as he shut the door.

I lifted the shade to look out at him. Good gods, he was handsome.

"I am sorry if last night brings you grief. Sincerely."

"What —" He slapped the carriage as I started to speak and I watched him fade into the background.

TWENTY-THREE

I collected Tree from Gypsum's room and went back to the Dagr palace until lunch. I received a message from Tawny asking if I wanted to go check out the arena site.

I decided to have lunch at the Sumar palace where I kept catching myself staring at Quick and Indigo dreamily, knowing our father would approve.

I had raided the items we'd divided after our father died. He didn't have much for jewelry, but I had found something I thought Quick and Indigo would like. I turned Indi's palm over as we sat at the table and pressed the high polished, black tungsten ring into her hand. My father's wedding band from our mother rested with the pendant around my neck, but this one had been the one he'd gotten from Delta.

She looked at it and her eyes widened. "Was this in his things? I thought he'd gotten rid of it."

"I'm sure he cared about her at some point. You don't have a child with a woman and not have some sort of affection for them," I whispered.

"Thank you," Indi whispered hoarsely.

"You should go away for a few days. I've got everything going for the arenas. Go have a little fun," I said in a low suggestive tone.

Indigo sighed. "I sent a messenger to Sterling."

"All the more reason to get away. Indi, *please* act like a normal, wealthy twenty-one-year-old with an incredibly hot fiancée. Make love, drink, repeat. Food is overrated."

Indigo's powder blue eyes were watery as she nodded.

Slate and the guys wanted to go out to celebrate Quick and Indigo's engagement. While the girls decided to head to Elivagar to join us to check out the land for the arena and go dancing. Indigo and Quick's engagement had left me feeling like pieces of a puzzle that had been burned and left in the garbage had been restored and were fitting into place.

An hour after lunch, I had packed an overnight bag with a sexy little dress, some clothes to hike in, and pajamas. When I reached the Sumar portal room, the girls were ready and waiting for me and no Slate. Had he gone to the khoraz brothel last night? Was he spending the night with them now?

Balas's words had left me feeling unsettled, and it gnawed at me. I was probably over thinking it and he meant it about Peak seeing us together or the husband he'd heard little about.

The other women were wearing thick velvet dresses similar to mine. Elivagar's fashions were similar to Mabon's. My emerald velvet dress had long fitted sleeves and a high, pointed collar that came to a low neckline fastened by a serious of glittering ruby rose buttons. It came to my knees to reveal the crimson silk skirt I wore above the layers of petticoats beneath it.

Each girl carried an overnight bag that looked out of place with our ornate gowns. It really made me appreciate the thin gauzy materials of Thrimilci.

"Ready?"

Tawny's hair was parted down the center and fell in dark waves to her waist. Her fair cheeks were flushed on her heart-shaped face. Her wide eyes bright.

"Yup," I said, patting my necklaces, squeezing my torque, and twisting my ring new Dagr ring.

Damn Slate.

I crossed the portal with Tawny with Indigo behind us, and Amethyst and Cherry taking up the rear. The bright white light greeted us as we crossed through until the white and black of the Vetr greeted us on the other side.

We walked through the pristine fan vaulted hallways of white lace worked wood and echoing marble floors. Cold — the only word to describe the Vetr castle.

"Ladies, so grateful to have you here." Orion sounded more cheerful than I'd ever heard him before as he embraced Tawny and then to my surprise, me and Indigo. He nodded to the other girls. "A Vetr, A Geol, Two Tios and a Kaldr. We have half a council here."

We smiled.

Orion personally showed us to our rooms. He took us to the highest floor with huge sprawling windows. From one of those rooms, my mother had plummeted to her death on Tawny's wedding night. I tried not to think about that as he brought us to rooms that did not have balconies as if he knew my concern.

"Oh my goodness! This view!" Cherry threw the heavy blue curtains wide.

The snowcapped mountains surrounded the castle like a fairy tale hideaway, any minute now the snow queen would descend from a stairway made from pure ice. Puffs of smoke stretched to the sky from the far away village, it looked like the north pole, or a series of Thomas Kinkade paintings.

"We shall have lunch and begin our trek in thirty minutes?" Orion asked, and we agreed.

I roomed with Indigo, only because Tawny had her own wing there. Amethyst and Cherry shared the adjoining room. We didn't *need* to share rooms, but what was the point of a girls' night if we didn't end up giggling about the dumb things we'd done that night as we fell asleep about?

After we changed into our clothes for the hike, I put the fur lining in my mother's cloak for appearances. I didn't get cold anymore unless it was psychological now that I was a fire elemental. That would be like Indigo drowning in water when she was made of water.

Orion had his staff serve a thick stew to warm us before the trek full of veggies and beef, it hit the spot. He asked if Slate had made up his mind about wanting to try to get his memories back. I decided for him.

"Absolutely. I'll see if I can get him to come tomorrow," I told Orion.

Orion led us himself which alarmed me at first, but he was much more spritely than he looked. Hard unloved years made him look older than he was especially by Guardians' standards. Besides, if anyone got cold, the human torch was there.

I was armed to the teeth when we came through the portal in Elivagar's town heart. My heart hammered in my chest as I remembered the first time my father had spoken to me. I had fainted after overexerting myself while my mom had come through the Ragnarök. We would be back here in a couple months to do it ourselves. My father had been checking on me in the healing tent. It was also the first time Orion took an interest in me. We'd come a long way.

Two sleighs waited for us and I smiled wryly at them. They had no intention of letting us hike. Strong looking horses, Tawny told me were Norikers, pulled the sleighs. I climbed in with Tawny and Orion while Amethyst Cherry, and Indigo went into the second. We headed into the mountains, bypassing the cozy-looking town and away from the Ragnarök course. He warned me that it was on the other side of a mining town, but the scenic route was unparalleled. We'd have access to a portal from the ones he'd had commissioned.

It was a short hike after a long swift ride. We reached the top of a large hill and looked down into a valley.

Orion pointed to the side of the mountain. "No tribes, walking distance to the portal gate, and you can build it right into the mountain. As soon as you are ready, you may start building. We can create a smoother pass to flow with the hill to make it easier to traverse." He looked from Tawny to me expectantly, his blue eyes looked younger by several years.

It was really happening. Tawny looked to me and nodded and a smile stretched across my face. "It's perfect." I was positively giddy; nothing could ruin my mood.

"I shall leave you ladies and think on a list of possible vendors for cuisine and spirits, I do not have a preference for whom runs the arena as long as Tawny approves," Orion told us. "Tawny, perhaps you would like to take them to the water?"

Tawny nodded enthusiastically under her hood. "Thank you Orion, so much. I love you." She gave him a big hug, and I tried not to think about how different things were nowadays.

Tawny took us down the mountain to the water below. There was a worn path between the mountains we hiked where the wind ripped at us. I went full elemental, and the girls huddled around me. Indigo went full elemental as well and she was quite the sight. Her watery body turned to ice like a sculpture, except she moved easily in her own form. I could see through her; it blew my mind.

No one would ever accuse Elivagar of being ugly. Even despite the cold, you had to appreciate the beauty of the island. The water was actually the island's edge. Bubbles were frozen in layers in the water, I toed one with my boot and it bobbed before settling in the freezing water again.

"Pretty awesome, isn't it?" Tawny said with obvious pride.

"And you're going to rule it all!" I shouted.

She smiled back at me. "Everything the light touches."

We laughed as the other girls looked on, clueless. Few movies were available to watch out there.

"Tell me about last night. My mom said you strolled in after breakfast in your dress from the night before. Tell me you didn't give in to Slate."

Tawny gave me a side eye, and I laughed. "A lady never tells."

"I'll have to remember that for the next time I see one," she chided.

I told her about my night with the flower connoisseur and she listened with rapt attention.

"Are you going to see him again?"

"No. It was perfect as it was. Anything more and it becomes complicated."

I walked a little further back and sat on the shore next to Indigo. Icebergs poked up from the water like shipwrecks, the jagged shapes piercing the light blue sky.

"Brass will be commissioner; Quick will be chief of staff. Brass will run the arenas and deal with the greater families, while Quick will put his charm to use with the competitors and the individuals who run each stadium." My breath smoked in front of me and my skin steamed.

She smiled so wide I thought her face would split. "He'll like that. You really care about them, don't you? Is it hard with Brass and Slate?" I slung my arm around her shoulders as she leaned into me.

"Yes and no. I love them both." I sighed. "I want Slate, but I need Brass. Brass feels like a hot bubble bath after a long day. Slate is a glass of ice-cold water after walking through the desert. They're incomparable."

By the time we got back to the castle it was already dark, it got dark early in Elivagar. We stripped off our outerwear, and the staff brought it up to our rooms while we settled into a late dinner.

The walls were white with lattice work around the plaster sculpted walls and ceiling. Black glass plates lined the white marble table threaded with silver. Combined with white upholstered chairs made me afraid to touch anything or I might break it or stain it.

We ate the potato casserole with Salisbury steaks, it was hearty comfort food and I was stuffed by the time I was finished. Tawny kissed Orion goodnight, and he handed me the list he'd promised with the deed before retiring.

As Tawny led us back to the top floor of the castle she started to gush about the club we were going to. "Okay, try to keep an open mind. I stumbled upon this place during the day. I've never been at night, but it promises to be a very memorable night."

I gave her a questioning look and followed her into our adjoining rooms. She hand-picked our dresses for tonight. They would've made Lera proud. I wore a burgundy mini dress with long sleeves and black thigh-high boots, I paired it with my Deeply Adored lipstick and straightened my wavy hair in a triumphant return to the dark side. Cherry and Indigo wore red, Tawny was in a wine colored mini, and Amethyst wore black. Our dresses were short enough to keep things interesting but long enough to cover the important parts — the key to a good mini dress.

I seriously thought about taking my wedding ring off but changed my mind. Without my ring, I was still married to what I thought was a possessive animal, but it turned out that he was just like every other guy; didn't want me once he had me but didn't want anyone else to have me.

After doing a weapons check and patting my jewelry, we clasped our cloaks around our throats and headed out of our ornate rooms. They were the only rooms with color, favoring red and blue gem tones with stark whites. The beds were thick white square columns on either side of the room.

We took the castle's portal door into town and walked through the sleepy town. A sleigh pulled by reindeers wouldn't have been out of the question. Tawny took us to the outskirts where it got much darker on the road she took us down and as we approached our destination, I saw large shapes moving into the last building at the end of the road.

I gave Tawny a look, and she waggled her eyebrows; I wasn't reassured.

I'd never forget that club. It was like nothing I'd ever seen or experienced. I'd hung out with the Merfolk, and the Wemic on their lands, and gone to see the Jorogumo, but this was completely different.

As soon as we stood outside the far house, at least it was shaped like a large house. Tawny led the way in and gave us a wink before swinging open a large unassuming wooden door.

Bass slammed us as we entered the door, but that wasn't it. It was hot and musky and smelled like liquor. Not a classy joint, but the floors seemed clean and while the walls and columns were painted black and red lights streamed down from recessed lights while a strobe light pulsed on the dance floor, it all looked fairly well kept. Even the black shiny bar looked neat, all except for the huge hairy beasts sitting around it, dancing and laughing — at least I think it was laughing.

There weren't just hairy beasts either, Crathode were there, the crab human hybrids were scarier than my wildest dreams allowed. Even the Minotaurs with their wicked horns or Bjorn, the half bear hybrids were less frightening, except for those teeth of course. I even saw a few Lycans, which were known for their solitude. There were humans too and they were there with a purpose.

Humans and beast hybrids gyrated on one another on the dance floor. A girl with long, dark hair was making out with a Crathode at the bar. Its red claw pressing against her back as its too human eyes were closed, obviously enjoying itself.

"What the hell, Tawny?" I asked wide eyed.

It was a khoraz bar.

She gave me an apologetic look. "They said it was party central. *Animal Instincts*, it sounded like a change of pace. We might as well enjoy ourselves since we're here. Aren't you the one who is always trying to be diplomatic with the tribes?"

She got me there. If these beasts were human I would've seen a bunch of people jamming out to some heavy rock music, getting their freak on.

Fiddlestick. I was being judgmental.

I rolled my eyes. "Yeah, yeah. Let's get drunk and felt up by a ram man." Cherry laughed, but Indigo looked terrified.

Mental note: keep an eye on her.

Amethyst had the bearing of a queen as she moved past us to the bar sidling up to a Minotaur that looked like a yak man with long, black, wavy hair, and another that looked like a black kouprey. You would never mistake them for their animal counterparts. Their eyes were all human, and while they bore similar features to beasts, their face shapes were human, as were their bodies. Anything animalistic was an extremity or added attribute, e.g. claws, hooves, or horns.

They looked her up and down, clearly they knew it was our first time here. It was the type of place that had regulars, not a lot of new foot traffic. You came here looking for something.

If *something* was a tribe fetish, then yes, we found it. I knew the music playing, the club was being remixed by a dark-skinned man with dreadlocks. Rob Zombie's Feel So Numb pounded through the speakers and I was stunned. I expected some kind of bass-heavy tribal music, but this was music I knew.

"Oh! Let's dance!"

Before I could shout, *no, hell, no,* Cherry dragged me out onto the dance floor, but I managed to snag water from Amethyst as I followed her out staring daggers at Tawny. She had better be right behind me.

Cherry didn't have a problem elbowing her way out onto the dance floor until she found enough room for us, Indigo had followed us out while Amethyst had struck up a conversation with the yak man.

It wasn't so bad once you got used to bumping into six-foot-tall beasts, I realized after a while that there were females there too. They were exotic looking, reminiscent of the Wemic, but obviously female once you really looked.

Tawny brought out a tray of drinks and handed it off to some unassuming Bjorn that gave her a toothy smile. A quick glance at Amethyst let me know she was enjoying herself with the Minotaurs, it made me relax.

We were drinking and dancing the night away, it was a much-needed girls' night. Filthy Mind by Amanda Ghost came on and Indigo left the dance floor, but Cherry was a dancing machine so she wasn't going anywhere and Tawny was just getting in the swing of things.

Clawed hands slid around my waist and my first thought went to Slate, but the claws weren't charcoal, they were brown. I turned around and came face to face with one of the Lycans, I didn't do well hiding my surprise. He laughed when he saw my expression.

"First time here?" he asked in a rich brogue.

He had a muzzle and he looked way too much like Slate in his half beast form for comfort. His ears were longer though and his jaw fit perfectly so his fangs didn't show when his mouth was closed.

"Yes. Is it that obvious?" I asked with a shy smile.

"It is," he said with a grin that was well practiced. He must come there often. "I am Lorcan."

We were still dancing, his brown clawed hands on my hips. His words rolled from his mouth in a kind of purr that reminded me of a brogue accent.

"Scarlett. I'm here with my friends." I gestured to Tawny and Cherry who waved.

"I do not normally dance with the women here, but I had to come check you out," Lorcan said.

Wow. He could have come up with a better line than that, he wasn't even trying.

I was insulted. "You don't say?"

Lorcan nodded. "You smell different from any scent I have encountered before. The Bjorn and Minotaur have noticed it too. Their interest may be warranted."

I smelled?

Lorcan took my hand, and I dug my boots in. He looked back with a smile. "Just to the booth. I promise to return you in one piece."

Something about him made me trust him. I shouldn't go around trusting wolf-men in strange rock bars, but I was intrigued with what he might say.

The booth was black, like everything else, and circular with a round table in the center. The other two Lycans nodded at me, both male. One was black furred, the other grey, they all wore tartans of varying colors paired with woolen tunics and thick fur-lined boots. It was different from the Crathode who wore pants and boots which looked extremely weird to me with leather cuirasses or the Bjorn with their billowing pants cinched at the ankle and long tunics and the Minotaur who preferred thick fur trimmed vests with knee length hide skirts.

"This is Niall and Cabhan. Meet Scarlett." He pointed to the black wolf and then the grey and they nodded and smiled at me.

Niall leaned forward. "What have you been around to smell in such a way? It has vexed me since you walked in. I must know."

"You speak really well," I told him, confused at his curiosity.

Lorcan and Niall laughed. "We come here every so often. You are married? To a human?"

My eyes must have bulged in their sockets because the three Lycans laughed again.

"*Not* a human," Cabhan said. His eyes matched his grey coat, so he almost looked like a husky to me.

I would never have said that out loud. The rough burrs seemed to be a part of their local cadence.

"He's a human."

He was, right? Just because he can change into a barghest doesn't make him some sort of *were*barghest, did it?

Cabhan shook his head. "I smell animal on you. It is not strong but has been on you for some time. You do not even notice it anymore."

"It's not my secret to tell," I said and clamped my mouth shut.

I should get up and go back on the dance floor before my mouth got me into trouble.

I was going to do just that when Niall rippled. I gawked as black fur retreated into his pores of his face and faded into black skin, leaving waist-long waves that framed a ridiculously handsome face with bright green eyes glinting at me. He couldn't have been older than thirty, and he had dimples when he smiled.

I stared openly at him. The two Lycans next to me looked around and rippled. Cabhan was young too, and blonde, go figure, with grey piercing eyes. Lorcan had waist long chocolate brown hair and brown depthless eyes that twinkled with his dimples. I snapped my mouth closed, and they laughed.

They found me quite hilarious.

"Not many people know about our ability to transform. Here no one cares about us, but it is not something we want all Guardians to know. We value our privacy," Cabhan said.

His face was too intense to be called handsome, but he was striking.

"So why show me? You don't plan to kill me now, do you?" I asked, suddenly feeling like instead of asking I should have darted out the door.

Lorcan leaned in close so his chocolate brown hair brushed my shoulder. "Your husband. I think I know what he is. He may be human, but he is like us. Yes?"

I looked at the three men and wondered how I'd gotten myself in this predicament. I nodded.

"He's barghest."

Instead of running away or cursing me they seemed excited.

"Is he here?" Niall asked.

Maybe not thirty, maybe more like twenty I decided. His body was shaped like a man who fought for a living, scars ran up and down his arms from claws, no doubt.

"No. I came with the girls."

"Will you come back with him? We would like to meet him. Barghest... I should have known. He must be the last of his kind," Lorcan said his mouth turning into a frown, his dimples showed in his tan skin even then.

"One of. Um, bring him here, to this place? If he knew I was here, he'd probably kill me," I said, and I believed it.

They did too as they nodded. "We tend to be possessive. Barghest must be more so. It will only get worse. Do you have children? If you do, then you understand," Cabhan said.

"No, why? What happens when you have children?" I asked, terrified of his response.

"When my wife had our first pup, I could not stop myself. I drove her crazy keeping everyone away, wanting them all to myself. I felt the need to protect them, it was an instinct. It started while she was pregnant and became intolerable for her. Try to keep that in mind," Cabhan said with a hard smile.

"So what are you doing here?" I shouted over the music.

Baby talk was a sore subject.

"Same as you, relaxing... dancing. Since your husband is not here and he does not have a pack, you will be in our pack for the night. You can tell him we took care of you." Lorcan smiled, and it was a gorgeous smile. He must have known that.

"Is he an alpha?" Niall asked.

My, they were inquisitive. Every time I turned around they wanted to know more about him. I was only slightly disappointed that their interest in me was an afterthought.

Was Slate an alpha, hmm? "Yes."

Unfortunately.

"You are an alpha female?" Cabhan asked.

I shook my head. "Nope, just a regular girl."

Lorcan gave me a look and drank me in. "No, you are an alpha."

Okay, well I wasn't going to argue.

"Want to dance? I hope your mate does not mind," Niall asked as he rippled back into the big black wolf.

It wasn't so much as a ripple as it was a steady rapid growth of fur that pushed from every follicle all at once. His jaw smoothly extended from his face and his chest grew broader until he was sitting inches above where he had been. There was no sick crunching and popping. The whole transformation took minimal effort.

"He's seen me dance with other men before."

Not that it would matter since he'd been so mercurial about us. I took Niall's hand and when I looked back at the table, a grey wolf, and a brown wolf were left sitting there beaming canine like smiles at me.

The man version of the black wolf was smaller around the chest and about a foot shorter, so now I was dancing with a seven-foot-tall, barrel-chested, black wolf with dimples, whose green eyes glittered at me in the strobe lights. He struck me as one of those young wolves, always testing the limits of what he can get away with.

We danced a few feet away from where Amethyst and Cherry danced. Indigo and Tawny were at the bar assumably, that or the bathroom, the place wasn't so big that you wouldn't be able to see everyone, if you were tall enough.

"They are excited to meet you. We were sent out in search of your mate; I thought it was an old tale the ancient ones tell the pups as a bedtime story."

Niall's body moved easily with mine, that's when I decided that

Slate had ruined me for life. The barghest khoraz thought Lycans were attractive.

Keen was one thing; he had this sort of... innate sensuality to him. His every move had reminded me of a long-stretched purr. But Niall's fur was longer, not short and smooth like Keen's whose fur fit him like a second skin. Niall's was noticeably fur like and his muzzle was narrower, how Slate's got in half-beast form, not like Keen's where it was easy to forget he didn't have a mouth like a human.

Then there were the legs. I guess if I was really dividing Slate's form into stages, he had four; human, charcoal human with fangs and claws, half beast, and full barghest. All forms were terrifying, even the human form.

"What do you mean, a bedtime story?" I turned around to face Niall, I came up to his chest. Thank goodness for the super high boots.

Niall's green eyes glanced to where the other Lycans sat. "They thought it would scare you away, but I bet you are tougher than you look." His grin was decidedly wolfish. How apt.

"What would scare me away?" I asked, shouting over the music.

"We are here for you. Your mate will lead us to battle, he will save the tribes." His eyes almost glowed as the strobe flickered across his features. I stopped dancing and blinked at him a few times before walking to a table and putting my water down.

"I must have been drugged. Are you saying that my husband is in one of your prophecies?" I pointed from my chest to his, and he put his hands on my hips.

"Dance with me, alpha," he said with laughter glittering in his eyes.

Freak On a Leash blasted through the club. How did you dance to this?

I let the black wolf guide my body and I matched my movements to his. "You're trying to get your scent on me, aren't you?" I asked, narrowing my eyes at him. He was rubbing precariously close to me.

"Better my scent than your mate's in this crowd."

I gave him a wry grin. "You're trouble my friend. I have a special radar for these things, I seem to attract all things trouble. Curb that mischievous look in your eyes, mister, and tell me what the bedtime story is about."

He threw back his head and laughed. "Alpha." He raised where his eyebrows would have been at me. "I do not know if you can call it a prophecy, but our ancestors told us of a man who could become a beast that would rescue our people. They say it will be during the second Guardian war. That must mean now since here you are, and he is out there, you confirmed it."

"A Guardian war?" I asked. Niall had moved very close so he could whisper in my ear over the loud music.

"Storm and Wind, the Natt and Dagr tale of old? By the Mother, girl, do you not know your own history?" I didn't need to see Niall's face to know he was giving me sugarfoot.

"I *do* know it. I didn't know it was called the Guardian War. What's that have to do with anything?" My boots were starting to stick to the floors from all the spilled drinks.

"Nothing, that was the first war, that is all. You will bring him to us, will you not? We need him. He will save us." His whisper was fervent, and it gave me chills. Niall honestly believed it.

"What if it's not his prophecy? It's hereditary in their males. His father was one as well and there was a massacre by the Red Kinds in Valla. That could've been it," I said, pointedly checking for Crathode nearby.

Their red and brown bald heads were hard to miss even if you could miss their claws, or their shelled backs.

Niall shook his head. "It is you. That is how we knew."

"Me? Am I wearing a sign that I didn't notice that says *Wife of the Barghest of Lycan Prophecy?*"

Niall smiled wolfishly again at me. He was a handsome man, *er,* wolf.

Slate had broken me.

"No. You remind us of the Freya — beautiful," he said, grabbing a lock of my hair and trailing his claws through it.

I wasn't buying it. "That's ridiculous."

"*One* Grar Dyr. One whose wife who is fire of body and soul. That is you. I can smell it in your skin."

Niall nuzzled at my neck and I took a step back. His words had floored me.

"Can everyone smell the, *um,* fire?" I asked watching his expression, half his face was red from the recessed lighting, the other flickered. It was like a live action horror movie.

"No, I am unique. Be careful. Some might try to kill your unborn pups so they may claim you for themselves. You should take your friends and leave." My stomach dropped.

"They would do that?" I asked, gripping my stomach protectively.

Niall stepped close. "Yes. They would fight to sire children on you. They would challenge your mate for the right to claim you. Elemental pups would be a highly sought after privilege as would barghest."

What was with people and our fertility?

"Thanks. I'll take you up on that advice."

I pushed through the sweating, furry bodies and against the hard shell of a Crathode and it made me want to gag. I was more afraid of them than I was of Jorogumo and I had no idea why. They'd never done anything to me, while Jorogumo had repeatedly attacked me. I supposed their history preceded them.

The Minotaurs friends Amethyst had been talking to were trying to get the girls to join them off the dance floor and gesturing to a booth in a shadowed section of the club. They were starting to make a scene.

I pushed past several irritated club rats as I reached the dance floor and jabbed the loudmouth water buffalo hybrid.

"Hey, cud breath, let go of my sister!"

His slate grey hand had a death grip on Indigo's wrist, if we started *calling,* things would get really messy.

The water buffalo stared at me with beady, brown human eyes. Its horns stuck out at angles behind animal-like ears. I should've said he stared down at me since it was like, *oh,* seven feet tall and about as burly as an actual buffalo. It grit flat teeth in a snarl from its muzzle.

"What are you going to do about it, little girl?" the buffalo asked, his voice was deep, and he pulled Indigo closer.

She looked afraid, but not of the buffalo.

I gave him a lazy smile and cocked my hip. "She wants to leave. Are you saying you're not letting her?"

I noticed a handful of lackeys walk in behind the big mouth; I counted seven total. We could take seven, but we *could* end up in a local lock up for brawling.

Fiddlestick it.

"If I am?" Buffalo was getting in my face, but he had let go of Indigo.

I smiled sweetly as my eyes shifted to Indigo. She knew to start towards the door, but I also knew that behind me Tawny would be ready to have my back, Amethyst would follow Indigo outside.

"Then we have a problem Buffalo Bill." We stared at one another a second longer and I started to back up without taking my eyes off the bully buffalo.

It all would have been fine except someone decided they'd much rather see a fight, so they threw a mug of beer at Buffalo Bill and I was the closest jerk to him.

Even though I knocked aside his first attempt to grab me, driving my elbow into his stomach afterwards was probably what triggered the full-blown knock-down-drag-out fight.

We were brawling.

Buffalo Bill wasn't very fast, but he was as strong as his ox brethren and the glancing blow he landed on my cheek made me see stars. Luckily, when I went down on my fanny pack, I found his manly bits and kicked them with my thigh-high boots so hard he fell to his knees.

I was on my feet and found Cherry and Tawny wrestling around with a Bjorn. How did that happen?

I fought my way through the crowd of punching, biting, kicking limbs — doing a little of each myself. I stalked up behind the black bear they were trying to beat away and kicked him right between the legs, sweet and simple. He dropped like a sack of potatoes.

They saw me and smiled; I hoped I looked better than they did. Cherry had a black eye, and Tawny's lip was busted, not to mention their wild hair and torn dresses.

"Party time's over," I said as we hopped over a falling Crathode being followed by a Bjorn.

We got to the door, and I cursed myself, Buffalo Bill had seen my escape plan and regrouped with his six buddies.

"We just want to leave," I said, holding my hands up placatingly.

They weren't about to let us leave, seven on three weren't great odds. I was going to have to nip it in the bud. I let my eyes flame out.

"You're gonna want to move," I said, low and dangerous, something I'd picked up from my errant husband.

The buffalo laughed and their line exploded as they surged forward. Three shapes erupted from behind us and collided with the Minotaurs.

The Lycans. I wasn't about to leave them to fight our fight.

"The Lycans are on our side!" I shouted at Tawny and Cherry.

I saw Cherry grab a stool and crack it over a Minotaurs head. I almost laughed; it was kind of fun as long as we didn't get pulverized.

Buffalo Bill was gunning for me, so I evened the odds with a heavy glass mug cracked over his head, which did little but break on his horns and piss him off super bad. Lorcan came into view and knocked the buffalo out cold with a rapid succession of punches to its face.

I would've gaped, but then he wrapped one arm around me, and the other around Tawny and hurled us out the door past the line of fighting Lycans and Minotaurs. We skidded over the icy road using one another for balance until Cherry knocked into us both a second later, making us all fall gracelessly onto our backsides.

We scrambled to our feet and found Amethyst and Indigo huddled by the shadows with our cloaks in hand. They beckoned to us frantically, and we clasped them around our throats in a hurry.

"Gods," was all Cherry said before she wrapped an arm around the other two girls.

"Come on. We need to get out of here, running would be best." Indigo and Amethyst nodded and let Tawny lead them away.

I looped my arm through Cherry's just as the doors busted open. The wood ripped from the hinges as three wolves started strongly — the most ridiculous grins on their wolfish faces.

"Come!" yelled the grey one I knew as Cabhan.

"Get them first!" I yelled back.

Cabhan ran ahead, and I watched as he slung Cherry around his back and grabbed Amethyst in an arm. Lorcan grabbed Tawny and Indigo who yelped and took off after Cabhan. Niall ran to me and I shouted.

"Careful of my babies!"

He gave me a roguish grin as he swept me off my feet just as the Minotaurs poured into the street and started to chase us. I *called* a wall of air which they ran into at full force, knocking them all on their fanny packs.

The big black wolf laughed as he looked over his shoulder. "Should I ask why you are starting brawls while pregnant?"

"You shouldn't. We have to get to the portal." I clung to him like a monkey on his hip, his strong muscles moving beneath me.

"Whatever you say, Alpha. Does the fighting arouse you?" Niall's green eyes flitted to mine.

"Excuse me?" I asked as incredulously as possible given I had my legs wrapped around his waist and clung to his shoulder.

He chuckled. "I can smell it. Either the fighting does it or maybe you are attracted to dark beasts?" He gave me a rakish grin, and I narrowed my eyes at him.

"My blood is high, it's the fighting," I said stiffly.

The snow-covered roads were empty, I could make out Cabhan and Lorcan ahead carrying the other girls until they turned the corner and stopped at the portal. We caught up quickly and Niall set me down.

"I'm all partied out. Too much excitement for this lady. Anyone else want to head back to the palace?" Tawny asked, straightening her dress.

"I'm going back to the Sumar palace. Quick had better turn up tonight," Indigo said and thanked Lorcan for the lift before they went through the portal.

Cherry and Amethyst looked at me, probably wondering what Jett would say if he found out I was cavorting with Lycans after having married a barghest. Probably nothing good. I waved goodbye to them and Amethyst sighed and took Cherry by the arm to leave.

"What do you three have planned?" I asked the Lycans.

"We are coming with to meet your mate," Lorcan said matter of fact and it almost made me laugh.

"Thanks for helping us out back there, but I don't know where he is. He went out with his friends in Valla or Thrimilci." I might have known if he'd bothered to tell me.

Lorcan smiled. "It was fun. We should go again sometime."

"Do you not have some way to find him?" Cabhan urged.

I pulled my lips between my teeth. "I do, but there's no guarantee he'll answer it."

Niall's body rippled back into his human form. "Please."

The other two shifted. They each grinned at me and I groaned as I held out my hands for them to take. They couldn't get through the portals without me.

TWENTY-FOUR

Three Lycans walking around would have been spotted immediately, but three strangely dressed men, not so much. Niall had given me a puckish grin when I'd tried to free my hand from his. I growled unwittingly, but that only made him more insistent.

Trouble.

I bit down on my lip hoping Slate would feel the bond and wouldn't be too drunk to respond. I wasn't even sure if he was in Thrimilci. They could have been in Valla celebrating.

"I guess we can just walk until he responds. *If* he does," I said, feeling ridiculous as I strolled with the three human formed Lycans.

Niall and I looked like young lovers out for a midnight stroll. Except I looked more like a woman of the night in my thigh-high boots and mini dress. The Lycans would not stop asking about Slate. I told them stories about his fighting skills which seemed to be all men wanted to talk about anyway; fighting, weapons, and women. I didn't know much about weapons and I wouldn't be discussing women my estranged husband had been with.

The Lycans were enthralled by how hot it was in Thrimilci. None of them had been off of Elivagar and its island of perpetual winter.

A few buildings down one of the shimmering roads had people drunkenly talking out in front of it and the Lycans stopped.

"We might as well get a drink while we wait, yes?" Niall asked.

I shrugged and Niall shot me a dimpled smile. If I was single, I might have let myself get carried away with a smile like that. Instead, I only let him lace his fingers through mine as he led me towards the bar. He sniffed the air and smiled at me again. It was a lecherous grin.

"I smell mating," he said, showing far too many teeth.

The other two Lycans didn't smell it yet and the closer we got; I realized why Niall had scented it. It was a khoraz brothel. I stopped walking making Niall jerk my arm. If Slate was there and I saw him, it would tear my heart asunder *again*. Niall looked back at me.

"Come. We will protect you," Niall encouraged.

The two-story buildings were side by side with people going in and out of them both. Some people laughed outside who were obviously intoxicated. One of the men made the mistake of letting his eyes linger a little too long over me and Niall snapped me to him and growled with bared teeth like an animal. The guy held up his hands and laughed, but Niall had taken offense and stared him down until he turned away.

"Niall, you're not my mate," I said pointedly.

Niall was pressing me to his warm body that smelled like pine sap. "I could be. He does not know that. You did not catch his scent —"

"I can catch scents. Lots of men smell that way around me. Do I need to point out your scent?" I asked and Cabhan and Lorcan chuckled.

Niall's faced relaxed and he laughed a way that made me think he was like Tawny; hot tempered but cooled just as quickly. Lorcan led the way into what I hoped was the bar. It was packed with scantily clad women in gauzy skirts and barely-there ruched cropped tops. There seemed to be a denser concentration of women near a back booth that was partially cloaked in red slinky fabric.

I could recognize my brother's laugh anywhere.

The bastards. My blood boiled and Niall turned down to me.

"What is wrong? Your fire..."

Niall saw I was glowing. The heat from my power igniting in my veins from my anger. Niall's scent spiked.

"Wildfire," he whispered as he searched my eyes.

His eyes seemed to spark heedless of some warnings coming from Cabhan and Lorcan who had stepped up to us. Did one of them say to back away? Niall had wanted me from the moment he saw me. Whether it was because he was the kind of guy who wanted what he couldn't have, or if he was always testing himself against the best — it didn't change the fact that if I let him, he would take me home tonight.

Niall placed a finger under my chin and tilted it up as he cocked his head to place his mouth just above mine. I inhaled as he exhaled stealing his breath and the back draft of my anger burned itself out.

"If your den is near, I can teach you how to pet a Lycan so he purrs like a Wemic," Niall said in such a suggestive tone I thought my elemental powers had flared again.

My mind was somewhere far away. His words barely reached my ears.

"Over there. My estranged husband, the barghest," I said distractedly.

I saw inside the closed off room where Brass and Gypsum looked to be so inebriated they couldn't sit up while Quick was privy to a partnered dance from the half-dressed women. Coyote was passed out next to Steel and Jett, who had a scantily clad girl dancing for him. My husband had two girls in his lap. Lynx was one of them.

I pulled myself up and took Niall's arm before leading past the gauzy fabrics to the long couches. The sheer material brushed over my face like the veil I never wore at my wedding until I stood before my debaucherous family and the Regn.

"Niall. This is who I was telling you about," I said amidst the glares from the girls and the straightening up of the men.

Niall looked down at me surprised and back at Slate to let his eyes roam over him in a scrutinizing fashion. He pointed. "This one? He has tried to tame you?" Niall scoffed. "Come, Wildfire. Let us see how hot you can burn."

From his scent I knew he was saying those things to test Slate. Cabhan and Lorcan flanked Niall, and Slate took them in as well before growling deep in his chest.

"Grar Dyr?" Lorcan asked and looked to me.

I nodded hoping the more levelheaded Lycan could stop this before it became a fight. Another girl went into the back room and I saw her straddle Brass's lap. I grit my teeth. I shouldn't be there. Brass's eyes widened when she started to move and he unceremoniously pushed her off and got to his feet. Slate's arms were wound around the girls' bare waists, more skin was exposed than covered. Jett had finally noticed me and Brass had moved to stand in front of me.

"He's Grar Dyr. I'll wait outside," I told them and started to walk away.

Brass darted forward to grab me, but Niall jumped in his way. I spun back.

"Niall, don't. He doesn't know who you are. Why don't you guys all talk? They can bring you back to Elivagar when you're done," I told them and Niall wrapped his arm around my waist, keeping me in place.

"Remove your hands from her," Slate ground out.

"If you cared, she would not have been in the tribe bar alone," Niall growled.

"I wasn't alone," I countered.

"I do not like where your thoughts lie, Lycan. She does not belong to you," Brass said in a low rough voice.

Slate narrowed his eyes at Niall and the other two. Lynx had a very low neckline and a bosom that would have made Dolly Parton's eyes widen, she pulled Slate's mouth to hers. Niall turned back towards me and I looked away, feeling my chin wobble. It was one thing to know it was happening, another to see it.

My eyes were still closed when I was lifted off my feet and I used a hand to cover my backside as we rushed out into the street. Niall cupped my face.

"That was your husband? Do you allow him to spread his seed with —"

"No! We're not really married anymore. We can —"

My sentence ended in Niall's mouth. His kiss wasn't as aggressive as I would have suspected. It was sweet, in truth. I could not start dating a Lycan so I had to put an end to it right now. Right *now*... okay, now...

Lorcan ran out of the bar laughing with Cabhan on his heels. Niall tossed me over his shoulder, ending our kiss and began to run. Sounds of a fight and glass breaking came from inside the bar.

"Guardian, you are a lodestone for trouble." Lorcan laughed.

"What happened? Are they okay? You didn't hurt them, did you?" I grunted as Niall jostled me.

"Ha! I saw a man break a mug over his head and he kept coming after us. That was the barghest, yes?" Cabhan, who was normally intense and serious, seemed positively riveted.

I groaned. "Yes. My *slutty* husband."

I saw Steel, Slate, and Brass explode out of the bar with two other men I didn't know. Jett fell through the door backwards and Brass caught him under his arms but was plowed over when Gypsum was tossed out feet first. Their heads swiveled until they spotted us and I shook my head since I was the only one facing them and gave a little wave.

"*SCARLETT!*" Slate's inhuman roar boomed down the road to us and the men ducked, covering their ears.

He had bellowed that way for me when he was captured. I patted Niall's back.

"Niall, put me down. He needs me. You guys need him. I'll calm him down."

Niall skidded to a stop and looked back to where the guys had started to come for us. Cabhan and Lorcan noticed we weren't with them and trotted back. Niall set me down on my feet.

"I hope you have a plan. He is very angry," Niall said and nodded to where he was charging down the road at us.

"Get behind me. He won't hurt you if that means hurting me," I told them and Cabhan grimaced.

"Cower behind a woman in front of the Grar Dyr?" Niall asked disgustedly, and I flared to life.

My fire burned like a pyre and the Lycan men stopped arguing. "Shift," I said in a disembodied voice and they listened.

I stretched, *calling* my fire. I became a flaming wall they'd have to jump over to get past. That or slam me with something that would knock me unconscious as Peak had done.

They started to approach and Slate didn't stop. Did he think he could jump five and a half feet high? *Could* he jump five and a half feet? Nothing surprised me anymore. He called my bluff, and I winked out just as he reached my wall, the smell of burnt hair wafted to my nostrils. It had been close.

Slate saw the three men were Lycans, but only slowed once he had me in his grasp. I cried out from his uncompromising hold on my arm.

"Stop, Slate. They wanted to meet you. They don't mean any harm," I said in a rushed tone and he looked at me and then at them, and back to me.

"What are you wearing?" he growled.

"I was out. You'd know that if you cared to speak to me," I said and tried hard not to sound petulant.

"Werewolves!" Gypsum slurred.

"Lycans. How did they get here?" Steel asked me even though they were fifteen feet away from where he stood.

"I brought them. I met them at a bar in Elivagar and —"

"We were looking for a woman. Fire of body and soul whose beauty rivals the goddess's." Niall wasn't doing himself any favors.

"They're looking for a barghest with a *wife* who is fiery," I said, trying to yank my arm free. I was going to have a bruise. "Here he is. The infamous Grar Dyr. I've done my job. One of them can bring you back to Elivagar." I freed myself from Slate and stumbled back in my heeled boots.

"Which one of you was touching my mate?" Slate growled.

Niall stepped forward in his black wolf form before he finished his growl. "She said you are not her mate anymore. I would have challenged you for her before I marked her if you were." His tone was almost differential.

Marked? Did he mean rub his scent on me?

Slate snarled exposing fangs not like a man's at all. Not even close.

"I do not give a shit what she says. She is *mine.*"

I blinked at Slate and then at my drunken family members and the Regn brothers. Quick had stumbled up at some point and was laid out on his back in the middle of the road with Gypsum sitting slumped at his side. A variety of bloody cuts and bruises marred their skin. Brass was the only one looking at me, but by the glassiness of his eyes, he was wasted.

"Are you okay, love?" Brass slurred.

I nodded and shook my head. Steel and Slate seemed the most sober, which didn't make me feel any better. Lynx and the other had been draped over him and he wasn't even drunk.

"I'm my own. I don't belong to anyone. I did what I came to do. You can leave with me and I'll bring you back to Elivagar or you can try to have a conversation with him and maybe Steel, my uncle there, can bring you back. Make your choice," I said, crossing my arms.

Cabhan and Lorcan shared a look while Niall and Slate continued to stand nose to nose, ready for who would flinch first. I was through waiting. I started to walk down the road on my own and Slate spoke up.

"Where do you think you are going, girl?"

"Back to Elivagar to pretend I didn't see my family and my sister's fiancée getting felt up by khorazes. Why? Do you have something to say about Lynx who had her tongue down your throat? Or was that a different khoraz you frequent?" I asked dryly.

"We will talk about this later," he ground out, and I shook my head.

"Nope. We won't. Niall?" I called.

Niall backed away from Slate and kept his eyes on him as he came closer to me. "I will make sure you get back safely since your mate is busy tomcatting."

Cabhan and Lorcan hadn't moved. They wanted to speak with Slate and he knew it.

"Stop that pup from leaving with my mate and we can speak back at the brothel," Slate said, and I glanced at him over my shoulder.

I placed my hand on Niall's black furred elbow. "Go. It's your people's future at stake. I'm just a foolish girl who makes very bad decisions."

Niall finally dropped his eyes to me and started. Niall's eyes caught at my breasts and Slate growled. Niall closed the distance between us as if in a trance and blatantly gaped at my neckline.

"Daughter of spring and summer. Night's child," he whispered reverently.

The other two rushed to stare at my chest too and then gasped.

"I knew you were a rare woman." Niall's green eyes glittered at me.

"Watch yourself, whelp," Slate growled.

Niall seemed to remember him. "Grar Dyr. You and Night's child must come with us. You must speak with our sagamore." He pointed to my chest. "She is the access key. She must have the pieces. Your son grows in her womb?"

Slate's silver eyes regarded him above his snout.

"No," I answered, avoiding the men's eyes.

Lorcan whispered a prayer of protection. "Then we still have time," he stressed.

"How far is your village from Elivagar's town?" I asked, feeling unnerved.

"A few days through perilous territory, but you must make the journey to save the tribes." Niall hadn't taken his eyes off me.

I frowned and looked to Slate. "We will have to return to do it. We will meet you in less than two months. I will have my people find you at *Animal Instincts* during Yuletide. That is the best we can do," Slate argued, and the Lycans frowned at one another.

"Done," Cabhan said.

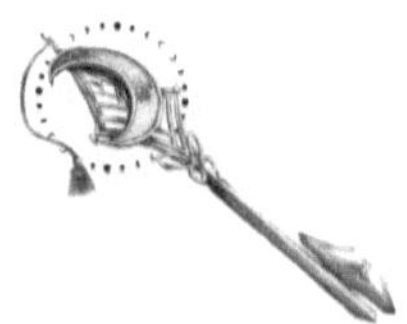

The discussion they needed to have had taken a lot less time than I thought it would. After they worked out a few uneasy details, I walked with them back to the portal in their human forms. Niall saw how tired I'd become and cradled me in his arms despite my protests.

Slate and Steel had been put in charge of getting everyone home. In their rush to chase down the Lycans, Coyote Regn was back at the bar and they had to collect him.

"If you lay with dogs, you wake up with fleas," Slate had growled as he passed me.

"I won't bother asking you not to do anything because how I feel doesn't matter to you." I'd retorted, and he'd stopped in his tracks, but not turned around.

The snow glittered like piles of spilt sugar crystals in the moonlight in Elivagar. The Lycans shifted back into their natural form. A black, Gray wolf with green eyes, a grey Arctic wolf with grey eyes, and a Eurasian brown wolf with warm whiskey-colored eyes said goodnight, and I promised I wouldn't let Slate back out of our meeting this Yuletide.

Lorcan had pulled me aside before I went back through the portal door to head back to the Vetr castle. "Wildfire, your mate did not want that khoraz. His scent was for you. As was the other man's with the tiger eyes."

I gave Lorcan a dry smile. "Your input is noted. Goodnight, Lorcan. We'll see you the month after next."

I waved to Cabhan and Niall before entering Elivagar's portal gate. It was a free-standing iron gate with square pillars on either side. I could see through the iron bars, but every time a person would cross, it would light up. It lit for me.

I felt lost, and then I was lost. As I wandered around the Vetr castle, I took stairs at whim as I padded barefoot carrying my boots through the pristine halls. Servants weren't around so early in the morning. The castle was asleep. Since no guards were about, I assumed the other girls got back intact.

I wasn't sure how I felt about seeing Slate at the bar next to the khoraz brothel. Why did they even have those things here in Tidings? We were supposed to be Mother Nature's Guardians, balancing the world for her. It was our purpose, our reason for existence. What did overstimulated prostitutes have to do with nature? Was it human nature they cared for?

It was a safe bet that where the guys had wound up tonight would be the equivalent of a strip club back in the States. Unfortunately, there were no laws against selling your body in Tidings. Was that what I would be like if I sold my womb to Moon for little elemental babies?

I found myself having gone down so many flights of stairs; I must have been in the bowels of the castle. Sporadically lit by pure white globes, I continued down the low wide hall whose floor was so cold I thought it was ice at first. At the end of the hall was another square doorway and only darkness beyond it.

Curiosity got the better of me and I stepped through the doorway. The temperature dropped noticeably from one side of the threshold to the other. Likely because this room was a massive cavern. I couldn't see five feet in front of me, but I could feel the change in the air.

A ramp wound down without railings and darkness fell to unknown depths on either side of me. My feet stuck to the ground, and I realized it *was* ice now. Very slippery ice, very high up. I sent a globe of light in front of me to light the way and divided my *calling* so three more globes were constantly lighting each of my sides.

My *calling* was more powerful than anyone had heard of. Too bad I only had two years' worth of using it and was learning new things every day at Valla U. My father once told me that I could do anything I could think of *calling* to Nature's elements. One only had to be creative enough to find an answer.

Ice stalactites and stalagmites met to form towering icicle columns. More ramps flowed from the one I walked, but I stayed on the path. A pull, like the string tied around my heart to Slate, tugged me forth on its invisible thread. I needed to be there, to do something. I just didn't know what yet.

Slate. Had I changed so much I couldn't play his game to win him back or was he who he'd always been and I'd been too blind to see it? I didn't know anymore.

Letting Niall kiss me had been a mistake. It was just a kiss though; I wasn't planning on seeing him or taking it any further. Besides, *he* had been in a bar, next to a brothel with his khoraz lover. Honestly, what I did was one star in Slate's Thrimilci night sky.

A steep winding ramp almost forced me into a jog as I went down until I came to a pit. A towering oak tree was at its center.

The funny thing was, the tree was chained on six loops embedded in the walls to wind around its trunk. Orion had chained a tree in this ice prison? It didn't make any sense.

Then it moved.

My scream came out as a squeak as the being swiveled around its chains to face me. My boots dropped from my forgotten fingers as I stared at the bark knoll formed eyes and a long pointed nose. It had no mouth to speak of, but where there should have been one two patched of moss parted in what I thought must be a toothless smile.

What I'd taken for roots were actually long twiggy fingers and toes. Its arms and legs were chained to its sides. The being was trapped. I recognized the pewter colored metal for the material they made nix torques from. It was a Leshy. The original Guardians of nature before humans became too many and them, too few. The Mother had enlisted their help to create us enchanting the first Guardians with our elemental powers and the ability to *call*.

Here was one imprisoned in Orion's ice dungeon. They hadn't been seen in fifty years. My own great grandmother being the last to see one when she was only a few years old, lost wandering in Valla. She'd come back fifteen years later and fell in love with her younger brother; Pearl and Reed's parents. That was how we were the only line to have both male and female Tios. When she was lost the name became a patriarchal line, after she returned they had no other name to give her.

It had been a very big scandal. Our great-*great*-grandfather was Prime at the time and allowed it to go on. It was good to be Prime.

"Ah, daughter of spring and summer. The Mother's night child. It is our time to meet."

The leshy had a grandfatherly way about him I hoped I wasn't just imagining because if he managed to break those chains, he could squash me like a bug with one of his big tree trunk legs.

"You knew we would meet?" I asked in a squeak.

The mossy lips parted and the head of oak leaves bobbed causing a breeze that ruffled the leaves. "Why, of course. How else would I escape my prison if not for a powerful Guardian? You are the most powerful born in a century. Your family is very strong indeed. Very strong."

My mouth popped open, but no words came out. He wanted me to break him free? He could be a murderer! Did I look that naïve?

"I think I'll have to hear your story before I decide whether or not to free you..." I didn't know its name, and it seemed to know mine so it felt rude to ask.

"Ah, my name. It cannot be pronounced in the human tongue, but you may call me John."

I laughed, but he only smiled back at me. "You're serious? John?"

"It is a good name, is it not? Millions of humans could not be wrong, could they? Perhaps so," he said breezily.

I had a feeling; he could talk like this for an eternity. "Why were you imprisoned?"

"Only leshys can make enchanted items since Mother took away the Guardians ability to shift. Here you are though. Returned to the world at long last. You need only be trained and you can enchant them yourself with help from your sister of course. Everything must have balance."

"Orion imprisoned you so you could make things for him? So he could sell them? Did you make the portal doors?" I asked in a squeak.

I desperately wanted him to say no, but I already knew the answer. I may have known the answer to every question I thought to ask John. I only needed it to be repeated to me like a parrot.

"Ah, you know. Clever girl. Are you still deciding? Time has almost run out. Mother needs your help. She cannot do it alone this time. The families must unite. Only balance and unity will win this fight. That is what you must do."

My thoughts slipped like sand through my fingers as I tried to process what he was saying. "Where is the works or is it a project? Where can I find the other pieces? I only have three. Who took the one from the Anguillan? I need help. I can't do it on my own." My voice had risen to a pitch only dogs could hear, but John only smiled.

"I can tell you where it is not. Do not go to the sixth island. You will not find it there. I am not all seeing, I do not know where the other pieces reside only that you cannot do it alone. Trust those who love you. You have all the skills that you require to be successful. Mother would not send her daughter into battle ill prepared."

He looked like he wanted to embrace me, but the chains stopped him short. "What sixth island? The prophecy. The one that claims my husband. Slate Dagr will die, is that the only ending to it? I have this dream... and... I can't lose him. Even if he's a horrible husband... I can't lose him." I repeated.

If the leshy could sigh, he would have, but I suspected he didn't have lungs to swell. "The less you know about the sixth, the better. What has been written, cannot be erased. We all follow the paths to our destiny. What we do along the way determines our happiness. Make your decision, night's child. They are coming."

I had so many more questions, but the urgent tone in his voice made me do the unthinkable. I jumped blindly into the pit and caught my hands around the chain. It nearly tore my arms from their sockets as I dangled seven feet above the ground. I let go and hit feet first plopping onto my fanny pack on the ice floor.

I couldn't use *calling* on nix chains so I shifted into my elemental form and pressed my hands to either side of the loops that were embedded in the ice. The ice melted quickly against the inferno of my skin. The first loop fell with a crack to the ice floor and I ran along to the second.

By the fourth loop, I noticed fractures in the ice floor. We were on water, and I was melting the ice. I immediately stopped my heat from going to my feet and focused on my hands.

"Make haste daughter of spring and summer. They are nearly here." The leshy whispered in a way that made my mind's eye see birds soaring through a clear blue sky high above a cliff side, a nest in the limb of a tree that wasn't a tree, and then the image was gone.

The fifth one fell to the floor and a crack shot across the pit. I stopped. The leshy watched the crack climb the wall of the pit and water started to seep through the floor. Murmured voices echoed through the ice cavern and my heart thudded loudly in my chest.

I'd come this far, I wouldn't fail. I got down on my hands and knees and used a gust of air to slide me across the ice until I hit the wall below the final loop. I pressed my fiery hands to either side, and the ice began to melt.

The voices were closer. I could clearly hear Orion's voice now and any doubt that he wasn't involved in the leshy's capture went out the window. The sixth loop fell, and I nearly punched the air in victory. That was until the leshy shook off the chains and cracks fissured through the melting floor all around us.

"Don't move," I whispered as if the power of my shout would do in the rapidly thinning ice.

"Thank you, night's child. When you need me, I will be set upon your path." John said cryptically and tossed a stick at me.

My reflex to catch the stick caused me to jerk on the ice and I slipped, crashing onto my side. I turned to the leshy which demateri-alized before my eyes. I had no time to gasp as the floor gave out and

I was plunged into icy waters. I shoved the stick into my bra as I flailed.

The serene ice floor was above a roaring river that was trying to drag me with it and under the ice floor of the cavern. I twisted and rolled, kicking as my hands slid over smooth cold ice until my finger caught on a link and I gripped on for life. Before my calling allowed ice to form the rushing water knocked it away.

The nix torque chain had saved my life. The hot link had found a new home lower in the wall. I began to pull myself, hand over hand up the chain. My arms burning from the effort until I was against the far wall. I'd dropped my boots on the rim of the pit before I jumped down so I stuck my big toe in the link and tried to get purchase to climb higher.

I was strong in *calling*, but not strong enough to propel myself twenty feet straight up against the force of the river. It was no use. I twisted on the chain and looked alarmingly at how it was starting to wriggle free from the ice. John might have to come right back to save me.

I needed to *call*, but I couldn't while I held onto the chain. The chain was the only thing keeping me from going under. I was swallowing water every time I spun on the links and getting nowhere. I had to let go.

I shut my eyes and sucked in a deep breath before I released my fingers. A large splash tossed me under the water and I flailed. Arms banded around me and we hit something solid. I coughed as we broke the surface and I heard the sound of blades or claws crunching into ice *shing CRUNCH, shing CRUNCH* as we climbed higher as I hacked and coughed.

I was unceremoniously dumped onto the hard ice and I scrambled clumsily to my feet and pulled my short seax from my thigh sheath. Slate glared at me at the dried a shirt with his *calling*. His hot skin steamed in the cold. Orion was with him; his brow drew down with his lips pinched together as he looked me over.

I didn't sheath my knife, and it seemed to irritate Slate more than anything. He stalked over to me, ice freezing in his wet hair, and plucked the knife from my stiff fingers before ramming it home in my sheath. He roughly touched my hip instead of my belly and I felt him check on the babies, then suck in a deep breath.

I moved to place my hand on him and he shrugged me off. Orion stepped up and healed Slate who would have probably died of hypothermia if he didn't. The only reason I wasn't dead was because the cold didn't affect me as intensely as it did them. I was starting to feel it though, drenched and exhausted in the pit of ice after almost drowning.

"When he told me you were down here, I thought it was a ploy to investigate the castle. You are lucky you are bonded or you may not have been alive for him to be angry at. What happened to my guest? Did you free him?" Orion said in a croaking voice.

I found my voice worked just fine. "I did. All the good it did me, he left me to die! What were you doing with a leshy?" I accused and thought better of it.

I was not in the position to be yelling at the Patriarch Vetr, ruler of Elivagar even if my cousin was heir. I might not live long enough to leave the dungeon. Orion thick snowy brow quirked. Slate was still drying his clothes but listening intently and furious with me.

"I dabble in black market goods. Has Tawny not told you? I suppose she wished to protect me; I could be in a great deal of trouble if it were discovered. I am the richest man in Tidings with the richest lands from the mines we have here. I am greedy. It is my flaw. I enjoy having things others do not. A leshy with the ability to enchant items for me so I can trade to black market dealers is a valuable commodity. *Was* a valuable commodity," Orion said with a wry smile.

I narrowed my eyes. "Things like what?" I asked, and wondered if Slate would help me if Orion attempted to keep his guest from getting out, i.e. kill us both.

"Secrets, my dear. Nothing more valuable than knowing the secrets of others. You can predict how people will think and react if you know all there is to know about them. For instance, I know my daughter's husband has taken a fancy to you and has visited you on a few occasions. An unwelcome suitor when you have his younger, more virile counterpart at your fingertips."

Orion gestured with a sweep of his scarlet robes to Slate who had stopped to snarl while putting his shirt back on. Whatever suspicion Slate had; Orion just confirmed it.

"Does she know?" I asked stupidly and shame reddened my cheeks. I hoped he thought it was the cold. He shook his head.

"It does not benefit me to see harm come to you. Quite the opposite since your well-being is directly related to my granddaughter's happiness and her ability to run this island. Because I know secrets, does not mean I tell them. I store them like nuts for the winter." He smiled at his own joke and I sucked in a breath now that my lungs had thawed.

"Black market dealers... like Styg, Civet?" I asked.

Orion's brow quirked. "Why, yes. Civet, or Styg as he likes to be called, works for me."

I frowned and took a step back. "Do you work for the Stygians?" I asked point blank and felt Slate come up beside me, his muscles bunched ready to spring.

Orion looked at us both with an amused smile. "Why dear, I used to run them."

"Used to? As in a long time ago, or like last year?" I asked as Slate positioned himself between me and Orion.

Orion tucked his hands in his sleeves. "Come upstairs. It is cold and I do not believe you are too old for hot cocoa."

I could hear Slate's teeth grind. "Answer her question."

Orion pursed his lips and followed Slate's movements with blue hooded eyes. He was so calm, so relaxed. I wondered if he didn't have some secret army hidden only a few feet away that could kill us before we knew what happened.

"When Ridge was murdered, I changed. The leshy and my secrets are all I kept from that life over twenty years ago. I have not been involved in the Stygian Knights' goings ons since. If your next questions are if I had anything to do with your parents' deaths, Scarlett. The answer is, I did not. I am responsible for a great many deaths I expect retribution on, but not your parents'."

"Why would men coming to capture Slate have a note that read Stygians on it?" I asked a question that had been bugging me for the better half of two years.

Orion smiled ruefully. "A mix up. I believe you were lucky or rather unlucky. It was Styg whom those men bought black market items from. His name happens to start with the four letters of the guild's name.

Coincidence. He was not out to capture you, but they were. The Norns are fickle."

My shoulders slumped as I ran out of questions to make me feel better about freeing the leshy other than the obvious one, that no innocent creature should be tied up in an ice dungeon. Though I was doubting its innocence after it left me for dead.

"How did you find the leshy?" I asked finally and Slate returned to drying his clothing, apparently satisfied with Orion's answers.

Orion noted Slate's change in opinion and relaxed. I hadn't noticed he'd tensed.

"Trapped it in the woods in Valla. I was a much younger man and happened to have a nix chain with me. Back then, leshys were uncommon, and I had gone hunting for one with my servants," Orion informed us.

"Did you have them all killed once they brought him back here?" Slate rumbled without looking up.

Orion's jowls shivered with a suppressed laugh. "I only hire servants who are willing to swear blood oaths never to betray me. Saves me the effort of having to burn bodies."

"Is this what you meant at Slate's wedding to Amber when you said there might be things that come out about you... and for me to help Tawny through it? Or is there more?" I asked and Slate placed his palm at the small of my back.

Had I been swaying?

Orion's face was grave. "No. There is more. Stories for another time. You know enough to restore your faith in me even though it is you who should owe me since you stole my leshy."

"I didn't steal him. I freed him. He was a prisoner for...How long?" I had thought twenty, but that was wrong. It had to be longer.

Orion smiled. "Five decades, Mrs. Tio. Additionally, I have bad news I am afraid. With the leshy's freedom, you have released the only way I knew how to retrieve his memories."

I wished Slate had let me drown.

Orion had the servants bring me with my hot cocoa and a thick cotton nightdress. I climbed into the big bed next to Slate, who was still not speaking to me. He wore a thick cotton pair of pants to bed but left off the nightshirt.

After he'd dried his hair, I had the privilege of watching the big man drink hot cocoa. I didn't know anyone could look so sour while consuming chocolate.

"I thought I was onto something when I found the leshy, but it's just more of the same. More questions and very few answers," I told Slate's back, wondering if he was still awake.

The stick the leshy had given me was a hair fork with an oak leaf carved into the top. I left it on the nightstand with my other fetishes and hoped the peacock feather I got from Pavo and Aeetus's white eagle feather dried without looking too rumpled so I could keep wearing them.

"I think Orion was telling the truth. Nothing he said sounded like a lie to me but there's one thing I've learned about Guardian men, is that they like to bandy their words."

I ran my hands over my face, glad I had a chance to wash it with a hot cloth since I was too tired for a shower.

"Do you think it's worth telling Tawny about? She should know what she's set to inherit, but not knowing doesn't hurt anyone, does it?" I sighed when I didn't get a response.

As long as I didn't think about how the leshy basically told me Slate was going to die and there was nothing I could do about it, I'd be fine. It had to be wrong. It *had* to be.

"Thanks for saving me, by the way," I whispered, thinking he was sleeping since he was already breathing steadily and his body rose and fell in rhythm.

"You could have killed your bairn. Risking your life and theirs for a tree. A tree that did not hold you in the same regard as you held it since it left you there to drown," Slate ground out.

He was right, but it wouldn't change anything now. "Did you expect to find me with Niall? Is that why you came looking for me?"

I'd forgotten I'd activated the bond, then I'd forgotten to deactivate it. Thank the gods I didn't.

"No. You did not want to lay with the wolf. I could sense that much. A distraction because your *feelings* were hurt. What I sensed was your exhilaration. Then fear. I do not think Orion wished to show me the leshy. Perhaps he did believe I lied to investigate his grounds. He was shocked to find you drowning in the pit of his dungeon, that much was obvious or I would have torn out his throat before I pulled you out."

I swallowed. "I didn't know what I would find there. If I thought I was in danger, I wouldn't have gone alone. I don't mean to put their lives at risk."

Slate shifted to face me in the bed. This would be the first time we slept the night together since he came back. I didn't count that first night, because we did very little sleeping.

Moonlight lanced through the great windows that lined the wall of the room. His grey eyes regarded me in the relative darkness.

"I believe you. It does not make it any less fool hardy," he rumbled.

"Did you..." I trailed off not wanting to know the answer. "Did everyone get back safely?" I asked instead.

"Quick, Jett, Steel, and Gypsum are back at the Sumar palace. Coyote and Brass went to the Regn manor. Everyone was good, girl, even the single men. You should not have been there."

I pinched my lips together to prevent something biting from coming out. If I'd had men straddling me and he'd seen, he would have thrown a fit. His hypocrisy knew no bounds. What they were doing couldn't be considered good behavior. Just because something is not bad, did not mean it was good.

I shifted in bed giving him my back as he'd done me. "I am glad everyone returned safe. I am sure Indigo is happy Quick came to her rooms tonight."

Slate chuckled. "Without the bond, I know when you are angry now. You go from your American dialect to the Tidings way of speech. It is very amusing."

I boiled inside. Gods, I was that pathetic girl I hated. Chasing after a guy who threw her breadcrumbs, and she followed along like a brainless dolt.

"Whatever," I said maturely and shut my eyes.

"Did you lay with the old man?"

I knit my brows and stared at the shadows on the wall. "Do you really care, Slate?"

John said he would meet me again on my path. When I envisioned a path, I thought of the yellow brick road with Judy Garland in pig tail braids with lots of singing and dancing. My path was more of a slip and slide over a rocky cliff face. When I reached the end of the figurative path, I'd be beaten, bruised, and probably left disoriented. There was no way I'd survive unscathed if I survived at all.

Sleep hit like a truck. One minute I was awake, the next an earthquake wouldn't have woken me. My body was exhausted and Slate's warm body, curled along mine as I faded away, only made me fall deeper.

CHAPTER 25
INDIGO

It was our last day of sleeping in, making love, and eating hardly anything otherwise known as harvest break. I finally drummed up the nerve to give Silver Alder's ring. I leaned back against his chest in the jasmine scented bubble bath. We spent our nights making love until we passed out from the effort. I'd never known a man's body could make me feel so good. That Silver was multi-talented was undeniable.

That we had crossed the threshold into a sexual Utopia was indisputable. The water steamed as Silver ran his palms over my stomach to my breasts. For once, he didn't grope. He was blissfully sated and drowsily sloshed water over me.

"I blame you," he said in a voice thick with contentment.

"For?" I pondered.

"Awakening me to the possibilities of monogamy. I do not believe I have ever been so relaxed. I am spoiled. We should not go back to classes. We could stay here in the tub — never leave."

Now he groped with a rocking of his hips. I smiled. He never stayed sated for long, but I liked him ravenous.

"Mmm."

I *called*, sensing it was the right moment before his amorous intentions distracted me. The ring stealthily slid into my outstretched palm from my robe pocket and I licked my lips.

"I don't know what the future holds for us, Silver." I sucked in a deep breath.

"I do. Marriage. Children. More of this." He purred as he kneaded my breasts with more purpose and kissed the side of my neck.

"Whatever it holds. Right now, you mean more to me than I ever would have predicted," I whispered feeling emotions cascade down on me.

"Are we speaking of whom-we-will-never-speak-of, Dove? Do you intend on still seeing him?" Silver muscles flexed beneath mine as he tensed for my answer.

"I sent him a messenger after we returned from Ostara."

"What did you say?" he asked in a grave tone.

"That we couldn't see one another now. I didn't specify a date when we could again. We'd had a similar discussion when I told him I wanted to marry," I honestly answered.

Silver let out a breath and he relaxed again. "A scroll will be waiting for you after our bath. I know you do not believe I can faithful, Dove, but I intend to prove you wrong. Perhaps then you can stop seeing him and focus on more important things like my all-consuming pleasure."

I smiled. He understood all too well my reservations.

"You're distracting me from what I wanted to do," I chastised him.

Silver chuckled darkly, and I understood why as he impaled me with a little lift of my hips. I gasped at the sudden invasion.

"By the Mother, Silver. Does your desire ever ebb?" I moaned.

"Let us hope not." I heard the smile in his voice and tried to regroup.

"Stop moving for the gods' sakes. I can't think straight when you do that."

I snatched his hand away from my breast and slid the ring over his finger. More than the part that was sheathed in me stiffened.

"It was my father's. Now it's yours. Try not to make a big deal about it," I said self-consciously as I returned his hand to my breast.

"Freya's burly boar," he whispered. "You are really coming around to this. I thought it would take months to get you to accept that we are together."

He shifted so he could spin me around in his lap and we faced one another. It wasn't the first time we'd done that maneuver.

"I do not want to wait two years, Dove." Silver searched my eyes.

I would have scoffed in his too handsome face except for the sincerity in those gold-flecked eyes. "Silver," I started in my most patient tone. "If we can maintain fidelity for six months, I will gladly have your children. One step at a time."

CHAPTER 26
SLATE

Orion words rang true last night, but something about the way he phrased them had unnerved me. He was hiding much more. Now was not the time to be making powerful enemies and while Tawny was his unexpected heir, he would remain on our side or more appropriately, his own side. We were not a threat to her or their dynasty.

The girl had been reckless. Leading on Lycans, running around the streets in the dead of night, fighting, and then she had nearly drowned. Did she have a death wish? I worried she might. Had she given up on this life deciding it was too much pain worth living? Was I partially responsible or had she always been this way?

Peak would die; for touching a woman he knew was my wife and for claiming a barghest's life mate. He would wish he had never set a finger on her caramel head.

I had been distracted last night — angry and distracted. Lustful, angry, and distracted. It was the first time in my memories that I had slept with a woman and not *slept* with her. The first time I had spent the night with a woman at all.

Ripe supple curves and lean tan muscles. She was beginning to show. There was a soft swell to her belly that was not visible before. That she was gaining weight after so long hinted at her possible peace of mind and put my own at ease after her stress from worrying for me.

She was not trying purposefully to hurt herself. Her oval face was sleep flushed or perhaps she was nervous, afraid of my rejection. Her lips swollen and green-blue eyes bright with possibility as she rolled onto her back and pushed herself up against the headboard.

She bedded another. Not Brass. Not forced like Peak. Freely. I knew his scent now; I would remember it when I saw him... or if she did.

I had felt her the moment she awoke. Happy, then wary.

Since I had lost two years of my life, the others thought it had affected my ability to remember every detail of what I saw or heard. It didn't. She had mentioned her birthday at lunch and I had heard. I did not choose what I remembered; it happened as easily as Brass received mental images.

I had been ready for her the moment I felt her awaken in my mind. I braced my hands on the bed as I pushed myself up and she bit on her full lower lip. I wanted to catch one of her heavy breasts in my mouth that swayed when she moved her loose nightgown. She was admiring me, she wanted me.

Pregnancy suited her. A smart man would keep her in this condition.

She was looking into my eyes for what? Permission? I did not want to give it. I wanted her to take what she wanted like I knew she could, but she was unsure of us. Unsure of where she stood in my eyes.

"Good morning," she said shyly.

She pushed her long waves over her shoulder and I drank her in. She had been mine — all mine. I had made one mistake after another to drive her away, some of which I could not recollect. I would have to start small... if I wanted her.

She would not meet my eyes. I started to lift my hands to pull her closer, but she went rigid so I let it fall to her thigh. She sucked in a harsh breath but accepted it.

"Good morning."

Her pupils dilated. She liked my voice almost as much as she liked my hair. It was a wonder Brass had let his grow out. I lowered my face, her cheek brushed mine as I placed a kiss to it. I wished I had shaved so my stubble would not scratch her soft flesh.

She held her breath and scooted up further giving me a glimpse of her hips where the night gown had bunched and the two Celtic "X"s on her left hip bone.

"The inguz? Brass's blood or mine?"

The Shadow Breaker tracker would need a breakers blood to work. She also had the tiwaz with him. We had the EH rune bond. That Brass had two, and I had one would nettle me to no end.

"Brass," she said in her gravelly voice as she let her nose brush my cheek.

She had not turned from me after my lips grazed her cheek, she seemed to be taking in my scent. Running her lips along my jaw teasingly, driving me mad.

It was a foolish question. The beast rattled his cage. Her thigh flexed beneath my palm as I slid it over her skin, she could sense my anger.

"Close your eyes," she breathed against my cheek.

She smelled like warm spiced apples and vanilla. Fucking delicious and she tasted just as sweet. I growled.

"No."

She pulled back. Red marred her cheek from where she rubbed against my face. Her skin had tightened so goose bumps covered her flesh. Her lips pouted as she scanned my eyes. Doubt and hurt poured through her bond.

"Is something wrong?" she asked.

Gods, the girl thought that she was the problem. It was what she was *not* letting me do that was. She intoxicated me with her scent.

"I need a new Shadow Breaker tracker. I will use your blood for it."

That was not what I should have said. A muscle in her chin twitched.

"I did not lay with Lynx or anyone else at the brothel."

Her face darkened, but she did not move. Would she shift and sear my cock? She had already.

"You Tidings men and your words. Did you do other things with them? No. don't tell me." She sneered, angry with me and herself.

She was going to flee. I held her in place and she clenched her narrow jaw.

"After the Merfolk, did you bed Brass on rousen?"

I could not help the question. I knew Peak had drugged her, but had she done it for pleasure with Brass? My jealousy over their kinship kept me from getting close to either of them.

She started to push away from me, but I held tight. She cocked her head, spilling her waves back over her shoulder and she frowned.

"No, we never did."

She blushed. The color crept all the way to her chest. Now I wanted to leave. Curse the blasted woman.

"Slate." She shifted to me leveling her eyes to mine. "When I was on rousen, deep, well into the first hour when I could hardly manage coherent words, you gave me a choice. You and Brass stupidly stood in a room with me and let me pick. I don't know what would have happened if I'd chosen Brass over you since we were already married," she emphasized.

That was news. It was extremely difficult to control yourself on rousen. Anyone else would have tried to take us both. Likely we would have let her. She chose me. She was choosing me. The beast growled at me. Good point.

"Nothing is worth doing if you are not going to do it extremely well," I said, giving her a lecherous grin that made her pupils widen to saucers.

Yes. I liked that reaction very much.

I gripped her so she couldn't wriggle away and flipped her onto her back. I planted a kiss to her throat and ran my tongue along her throbbing artery. Her breaths quickened. I waited for her token protest as I tilted her chin up to mine.

Her eyelids fluttered to slits. I brushed her lips gently so our bond would not deactivate and she looked at me through her long brown lashes. She lifted her hands to my face and curled her fingers in my hair.

"Just a kiss. Nothing more... unless you want *more*," she whispered breathlessly.

If I pushed, she would succumb, even if I promised nothing. Not for me but for the man she loved.

The beast whispered in my ear to take her. Fuck her rules and wishes. She would love it. The man pushed from the bed and walked away.

I could not fill the shoes of the husband she lost. If I laid with her now, she would hurt when I left her. I would leave her…. eventually. Being close to her would assure my death, perhaps sooner than later.

TWENTY-SEVEN

I was trying to think like I did when we first met, but yelling at Slate and trusting he'd return was too hard for me now. I wanted him around. Old Scarlett did whatever she could to get rid of him.

Brass had come for lunch at the Sumar palace and seemed to be surprised Slate and I arrived from Elivagar with the girls. Slate and I hadn't spoken since he rejected the kiss when we'd woken up together. I tried to view it as a positive thing. He wasn't going to toy with my emotions. He knew what I wanted and because he wouldn't give it to me, he was staying away.

When Orion said that he had planned to use the leshy to retrieve Slate's memories. My mood plummeted from hopeful to dismal.

Slate sat back and drank from his goblet. "Brass, would Dhole be around tonight?"

"During harvest break? Of course. Thinking about branding your name across her forehead?" Brass asked with a sly grin.

No need to ask whom *her* was.

Slate scoffed. "A new tracker and perhaps another would like to get something."

Dhole didn't seem to mind that I brought a small army of people with me. Dhole's bald head opened the slot in the metal door down an unsavory part of Valla and smiled when he saw me. Then his thick eyebrows slowly rose as he saw the troop behind me.

Tawny had brought Steel and Gypsum, we couldn't leave out Jett and the girls, and Brass *was* a part of the family. Indigo and Quick dragged themselves out of their sex induced coma to come along too. Eleven of us waited on Dhole's doorstep.

"Not very covert," I said, giving my most apologetic smile.

"We are here all week during harvest break." Dhole let out a breath that blew the long goatee around his mouth. "Better come inside before you draw any more attention. This place is supposed to be exclusive."

Dhole closed the slot and after several locking mechanisms moved, opened the door wide enough for us to follow him in single file. Brass stayed back to close the door after us.

"Tell me some of you are here to have work done," he said, cocking an eyebrow at me as we trailed behind him in the high stone ceilinged hall.

I shrugged. "I will."

We entered the carpeted room of the parlor. Four cubicle like sections divided the space behind a stone counter, and images of tattoos cover the walls. It had an industrial feel to it.

Slate licked a full bottom lip as he watched me. "Myself as well."

I followed to where he sat in a chair and a woman stuck a syringe in my inner arm and withdrew blood without preamble.

"May I?" I asked as Slate sat, straddling the chair.

He raised his scar brow at me and gave a curt nod. I braided his hair and tucked it up into itself so she could tattoo the scar where they'd flayed his last tracker from. Tawny gave me a look when I turned around. It was hard not to try with them.

"Tawny, you want to get a bond with me?" Gypsum asked as he perused the walls and we all smiled.

"Pick one for both of us."

Tawny was shirtless and blushing fiercely as Steel stood in front of her, daring anyone to watch as she leaned against the reclined chair. Dhole was readying his equipment. I leaned into the little cubicle and saw what Dhole drew, a pair of wings with Celtic ropes in each segment that looked almost like talons. Feathery, circular braided ropes would lay over her shoulder blade, and between the wings was a blazing sun with an auseklis in the center. The Sumar symbol blended with the Vetr for the man who sired her and the man who raised her.

The whole tattoo was done in black and reached from her shoulders to her waist. Tawny's face paled as Dhole transferred the image onto her back. Since we could heal at will, he could do the whole tattoo in one sitting.

"Ready?" he asked as the machine started to buzz.

Tawny looked to Steel who gave her a reassuring squeeze, then to mine. I gave her a thumbs up and she smiled weakly and pulled her hair further over her shoulder before settling her face against the back of the chair.

"Let's do it," she replied and Dhole set to work. After an initial stiffening, Tawny relaxed and Steel scooted closer to talk to her during the long process.

Jett sidled up to me. "We're getting some bond tats."

"You and the girls?" I asked and Jett bumped me with his hip.

"Indigo! The three of us can get one." My brother smirked as he jutted his arrogant jaw looking as smug as ever.

"You think she'll let him bond her?"

"I *think* Quick isn't going to let anyone get a chance to get to her before he can force her down the aisle. I wouldn't be surprised if he pulls a Slate."

"What's that supposed to mean?" I placed my elbow on the counter and glanced to where a tattooed woman inked Slate.

Brass walked to my other side. "I wish I could say Silver won't do the same, but Indigo ties him in knots. He would fight dirty to keep her."

"Maybe," I said, thinking back to the night we spent in Mabon with the Centaurs.

Brass had told me Amber was pregnant that day and I had been distraught. Slate had wanted me the moment I told him my fertility was back. He had wanted to fill me with his child. I was too blinded by him to even contemplate it.

"My ears are ringing. I've decided this was a terrible idea. Silver has ribbons with him," Indigo said, resting her chin on my shoulder.

"Scar. This one. We can each get different ones. Yeah, well, you should have thought about that before you came. What are you bonding her with, Quick?" Jett said smiling at Brass who gave me a wry grin.

I looked where Jett pointed. It was a greater than symbol, the rune kenaz. It literately meant *torch*. I loved it.

"What about you?" I asked, looking down the sheet to where Jett pointed and burst out laughing.

Brass leaned in behind me and pointed over my shoulder to the gebo rune. "This one?"

Jett nodded with a smirk and the girls came over to see what we were all laughing about. "Gift?" Gypsum asked, shaking his head ruefully.

Quick wrapped his arms around Indigo's stomach and pulled her close. "EH rune for cosmic union, though if you and Slate are any indication, we should get something more like love. The ribbons for a hand fasting, Mrs. Scarlett. I do believe they are the same ones Brass tricked you into using — our sigil colors."

Only Brass and I saw Slate glancing over his shoulder at us with a glare that could melt all of Elivagar. Brass chuckled and took a step away from me. After he moved and I felt the absence of his body heat did I realize how close he'd been. His chest had been pressed up against me, his front to my back and I hadn't thought twice about it.

"I'm getting the laguz rune," Indigo decided for our bonds.

Jett took our hands, and we showed the other two artists our rune choices and decided to get them on the skin between our thumbs and index fingers on our right hands. Jett and I were sitting in reclined leather seats staring up at the overhead lighting as two unfamiliar tattoo artists drew some of our blood and exchanged it before mixing it with black ink.

"You know, they say tattoos are the kiss of death for relationships. Are you going to disown me after this?" I teased Jett.

"I think it works opposite for you, baby sis. Any man who you bond is leashed to you. I should probably run for the hills."

"Touché," I mumbled grudgingly, turning back to the tattoo artist.

Her nose was pierced at the bridge and her arms were covered in vivid sleeves that spanned across her chest.

"This will be quick," she told me.

Amethyst sat on a sofa at the front of the shop with Cherry while Steel and Gypsum watched Tawny get her tattoo. Indigo and Quick were getting their bond together. Quick couldn't keep his hands off her. I'd never seen him that way. She finally let herself be happy. I was practically jungle green with envy.

I didn't have time to think about pain. She drew the outline of the greater than sign then, she shaded it in with the Celtic designs that would allow us to bind one another. In about ten minutes, she was done.

I was astonished to see how much detail she managed to fit into the small space of my skin. Slate met me on the other side of the stone counter. He'd taken down the braid so his hair was in its usual plaits and beads with fetishes.

His grey eyes glittered as I stepped closer. I breathed in the scent of him; fallen leaves and a crisp wind mingled with the spicy scent of man and cloves. He was nearly my Slate. He'd used my blood for his new tracker. Maybe I was reading too much into it, or maybe I didn't like him denying me.

I placed my hands on his abdomen bunching his shirt in my fingers.

"Are you smelling me?" he asked amusedly as his lids lower.

"You smell like autumn in Chicago, like a gust of wind through the changing leaves." My head leaned back to look up at him and his dark eyebrows rose.

When he blinked, I thought his lashes must cause a breeze they were so long. "Touching is allowed?"

I blushed, and he lifted me up effortlessly lacing his fingers at the small of my back.

"No," I whispered, knitting my brow.

Slate let me slide to the floor and I felt dizzy.

I turned to lean against the stone counter next to Jett who bumped me with his hip again. The tattooed woman appeared beside Indigo and Quick holding up two ribbons, one that was navy with a grass green border and another that was gold with silver trim.

Regn and Tio colors. Sometimes, I was a complete idiot.

They held hands and moved so they faced one another before the woman. It was hard not to think about.

"Will you honor and respect one another, and seek to never break that honor?"

"We will," they said.

The woman draped the navy ribbon over their hands.

"Will you share each other's pain and seek to ease it?"

"We will," they said in unison again and she draped the second ribbon over their hands.

"Will you share the burdens of each so that your spirits may grow in this union?"

"We will." She draped the third end over them.

"Will you share each other's laughter, and look for the brightness in life and the positive in each other?"

"We will."

The woman wrapped the fourth end over our hands. "And so the binding is made. As your hands are bound together now, so your lives and spirits are joined in a union of love and trust. Above you are the stars and below you is the earth. Like the stars you love should be a constant source of light, and like the earth, a firm foundation from which to grow."

Quick gave no kiss on the cheek as Brass had done to me. He yanked their bound hands as Indigo giggled and shifted so her bound arms were behind her head as he kissed her. I sighed so deeply the papers fluttered on the countertop.

I shifted my eyes to Brass to find him looking back at me. Balas had been a nice distraction for a night, but my heart was already too full.

Dhole was leaned over Tawny's bare back, her arms crossed under her head, one hand in Steel's as he chatted her up. I noticed not for the first time how fit Tawny had become, she was never the joining type in high school so any muscle she had was from daily use, but now I could see the tone in her back the way it was stretched in the seat and her arms as she squeezed Steel's hand. Her cheekbones, like mine, stood out more. I did sigh then realizing we had both lost the softness of our teenage years to become warriors.

She had adjusted to finding out about her father so well. Better than I would have suspected, I found it jarring whenever I realized we weren't actually related. Not by blood anyway, but she would always be like a sister to me. I didn't have a single memory without her until we moved to Tidings. Then we both had made lives of our own. Her quest was much more successful than mine.

Jett leaned in close to us. "We've started to plan the Ausa Vatni. Scar, we won't let you go along with Moon's request," he told me.

"I know," I told him and looked to Slate who stood on my other side. "I'm not going to. I don't know how I ever thought I could."

Brass leaned next to Slate and me on the counter. Tawny's tattoo was finished and now she was getting a bonded tattoo with Gypsum. A simple Dagr sigil since they both were Dagrs on the inside of their index finger's knuckle.

Her back was completely covered with awesomely bad-fanny pack dark, Celtic wings. She sat up with her forearm to her chest while holding a mirror in the other as Dhole lifted a second mirror so she could see her back. Steel was turned towards us, scanning faces in case one might be sneaking a peek. I thought the only one who had was Jett.

I smiled at Steel and thought he must know that almost everyone here had seen Tawny undressed in the showers or in the prep rooms. I fought off the inclination to say those very words and realized Tidings must be rubbing off on me if I would say something so inappropriate. That, or Jett's debauchery was rubbing off on me through osmosis.

I heard Brass chuckle.

... Always rifling through my thoughts...

Brass's eyes slid to mine with a smile playing on his lips. "Feeling nostalgic?" he asked in a hushed whisper.

... Did you want me so badly you were willing to risk my anger to trick me into hand fasting you?...

"Don't I?" he confessed.

Jett had gone to sit with Amethyst on the couch and Brass had moved into his place. He slid his hand over the counter and I met him halfway. Letting him brush my fingers so he wouldn't involuntarily receive my memories.

I pulled away aware of Slate's eyes on us and met Indigo at the door to congratulate her.

CHAPTER 28

INDIGO

"I am not letting you out of my sight, Dove. You may come to your senses and run off."

The insatiable Silver Regn unabashedly groped me as I tried to get ready for dinner. We had returned to wait for Scarlett and Brass to return from the contractor.

He turned me around now that I was ready and slid a hand into my hair kissing me so my toes curled in my heels. "I want you," he breathed, and I melted.

Cursed Lothario.

The fragrant smell of the morning glory vine mixed with the feats of lemon chicken, pitted olives, crunchy asparagus, and couscous. A crisp white wine was served with the uncomfortable meal.

Scarlett looked radiant, her belly was starting to look more like someone who was in her second trimester with twins rather than say, myself who wasn't pregnant at all. I had Silver check that morning. She wore a shimmering aquamarine charmeuse halter with a platinum hair chain.

What was odd was that Brass sat next to her with a pile of what looked like swatches of fabrics. Slate sat across from them and looked to be studiously ignoring that they were even in the room. Occasionally, Brass would glance up with a little crease between his thick brows. Scarlett kept her face placid except when she spoke to Brass.

The family noticed the strange interactions as well. I would have to get her alone to ask her what was going on. That was if I could break free of Silver long enough.

Scarlett ran a hand across her stomach and Brass put down the swatches to press his hand beside hers.' Slate went rigid, but quickly recovered.

"They're fine, I think there was just a little too much zest on the chicken for my fickle stomach." She sighed. "I want to stay true to the local architecture, but I also want it separate from the greater families." She bore a look of consternation then smiled at Brass. "How on earth do I accomplish that?"

Pearl looked down the table at the swatches and papers they had set around their plates. "Please excuse us." Brass said. "Details need to be finalized so we can go over them tomorrow. Scarlett, we can go over them after you eat. I don't have anywhere to be. We'll bring these back to your wing and get some ice cream for your heartburn," he said with a warm smile and she blushed glancing away.

He'd hurt her with Rosasite. She would never say it out loud, but her excursion with the older man was completely out of character. I knew it had to do with Peak and those two scoundrels, but she seemed somewhat healed today.

"She won't mind." Brass assured her after whatever she said using telepathy.

There was a brief uncomfortable silence and Brass stifled a sigh as he nodded. "Whatever you wish."

He missed the glare Scarlett shot him and quickly masked.

Yikes.

Slate returned to his meal with a self-satisfied smirk on his lips. It was apparent to everyone that while she was putting away her personal feelings to work with Brass, she in no way had forgiven him for Rosasite.

"So… you and Brass?" I asked Scarlett when I brought her back to my rooms for a brief tête-à-tête.

"What about us?" she asked, rubbing her ring finger.

"You nearly had a public fight."

Brass was with Silver now updating him on the arenas and no doubt gossiping about us. Scarlett's face flushed and she rubbed her hand over her heart.

"It wasn't a fight. I don't want to get too comfortable with him… again. He's with Rosasite."

I gave her a dry look.

She sighed and leaned back in the chaise. "I want ice cream. We're going to spend days together working on arena business," she said bitterly.

"And Slate?"

"He hasn't come to the Dagr palace or asked me to come over…. he hasn't even taken an interest in the arenas. That's my whole life right now, and he doesn't want any part of it. It's time I face facts, he appreciates my body, and that's about it." Scarlett's weak smile broke my heart.

"He looked really jealous at dinner," I offered and she sniffed derisively.

"I miss *my* Slate. He never would have done this."

I changed the subject. Watching her moon over Slate pissed me off. She deserved better.

"What about mystery man?" I asked, leaning back in my chair.

"Balas. It was a onetime thing. I didn't ask any questions. I didn't want to know him. I wanted one uncomplicated night, and that's what I got, for the most part. You're happy, aren't you, Indi? After everything, you're good?" she asked, trying to avoid the topic of her onetime lover she wasn't entirely comfortable with.

"Great. Silver's keeping it in his pants for the time being. Balas sounds really familiar. I can't think of all the gem years. How old is he?" I asked her.

She shook her head. "No idea. Guardian ages are tricky for me. I'd say like fifty?" A bubble of laughter burst from me and she scowled wryly. "He was cultured... and extremely good looking with a great body," she said defensively. "It was more romantic than anything I'd ever experienced."

I scrunched my face. "Did he need *help*?"

She spluttered. "No! It wasn't what I was used to with...others, but he had ways of continuing things when he... couldn't." She folded her arms and glanced away with a burning red face. I started giggling uncontrollably, and she gave me a wry grin. "*Nothing* was lacking."

"I believe you. Just giving you a hard time."

I sighed, thinking about how handsome Silver would be when he turned fifty. He'd turn women's heads for the rest of his life.

"Are you nervous about the competition Friday?" I asked her and she shook her head as she swallowed. "Silver said Cordillera got you a special outfit?"

"A fat suit," she said with a strangled laugh.

Scarlett got to her feet and hugged me. "I have a lot of work to do. We'll talk more tomorrow. I'm glad you're happy. Silver's a good guy."

CHAPTER

TWENTY-NINE

I stood with Cordillera as I delegated to the Breakers. The music was altogether different there. There were two different levels, one where a food and drink spread was set up and the second level carpeted in deep red with plush seats spread out before the glass to see the entire arena. From her suite above the arena, the greater families and the other patrons would have an unobstructed view of the Crash Course.

The room was dimly lit with gold sconces along the walls. Soon the room would be filled with the glittering dresses of the women gathered, and the satin embroidered waistcoats of the men. There the Guardian upper crust would gather. Only about fifty people would be in the room, all wearing masks.

Chafer was there alongside Cordillera in her black slinky gown. He cleaned up well. His short, dark hair combed stylishly to the side reminiscent of a nineteen thirties playboy. He stood sipping from a glass as Cordillera directed a breaker to move an appetizer table.

I walked to the two-way mirror. All walks a life came to watch the competition and with the arenas more people would know about it. Average Guardians would sit in the stands as if it were a sport to watch. Loud music with a heavy bass played in the background, it matched the adrenaline amped crowd's mood perfectly. The arena was brightly lit by wrought-iron chandeliers that matched the railings lining the wall to keep the crowd from falling onto the Crash Course.

The Guardian high class had seats at the end of the arena, you could tell by how well they were dressed and some of them wore masks as if they didn't particularly want to be recognized. Some were well-to-do merchants and lesser families that were going to bid on the competitors. As soon as the arenas were built, we were putting an end to the patrons.

"Wildfire," Chafer called.

The greater families had started to arrive. I straightened the golden paisley mask encrusted with emeralds and pearls over the cascade of curls that fell down my back. My green velvet dress was in the Elivagar bell style. Topaz buttons plunged along the neckline down to the hem, trimming embroidery that wound around the collar, embedded with pearls.

Orion and Tawny had arrived. They both wore the scarlet red of the Vetrs. While she wore a red mask tucked into her up-do of big dark curls, he wore a plain white satin mask. I kissed them both on the cheeks in greeting.

Ruby Geol, in all black, came with Jett, who also wore black. They were all recognizable to me without their masks, but for their sake and the patrons who didn't know them I thought it best they not reveal who they were.

Breakers passed out drinks as Pearl entered with Gypsum and Reed. Gyps's eyes were wide with delight as he took in the rich atmosphere.

"Scar, this is awesome. Is this what your arenas will be like?" Gypsum said with a dimpled smile.

"That is the plan," I told him.

The other greater family members gathered in a group, having recognized one another. They were the more amenable heads of the families, but there were even more coming. Spinel Regn had become the most influential lesser family patriarch overnight with two of his grandsons having marriage contracts with greater families. I had invited him so he could see how well his grandsons were doing...and to visit his daughter Cordillera. The notorious Spinel had eluded me on previous occasions and I was intrigued to meet the man Brass said had raised him.

The usual patrons mingled in with my guests and Cordillera entertained with Chafer on her arm. I tried to keep a bird's-eye view of the gathering so I knew everyone was having a good time. Belatedly, I thought I should have hired someone since I'd have to go to the prep room soon to get ready for the competition.

My stomach flipped when I saw Peak and Sterling enter. I thought Peak might bring Sterling, but hoped he wouldn't. Things only got worse when Moon arrived with Ash, Crag, and Fox. Where the hel were the wives?

Cordillera met my eyes over the crowd and looked to the corner nearest the entrance. While I squinted in vain, a hand pressed possessively to my back.

"You are starting to show, sweet Scarlett. Should you be competing?" Peak's deep voice was close to my ear.

I turned to remove his hand that sent a chill up my spine from my back. "Patriarch Haust, thank you for coming. I'll take that under advisement."

Try as I might, I couldn't keep my hand from covering my stomach as I faced him. I hated that he and Slate so closely resembled one another. His lime eyes popped from beneath a silver mask that highlighted the silver in his short blue-black waves.

"To ensure the best preview of what your arenas can deliver you would have to partake in the demonstration." Peak's full lips pulled into a wry smile.

"My last and final show," I told him as Moon wandered near with Ash and Fox in tow.

I greeted them as I would an uncle with kisses to their cheeks. "I hope your escort was pleasant."

They had to be blindfolded. It was Shadow Breaker policy until you signed the blood contract that bound you from revealing their secrets. I had sent a team of attractive female breakers to escort them.

Fox smiled brightly at me.

"I think my escort was a bit grabby," he said with a wink as he leaned into whisper.

I returned his smile with my very best one. Normally, if the Prime and Ash weren't there, we would've engaged in a flirty banter. A number of retorts about the true identity of his escort came to mind, but other than the twinkle in my eye. I let it go.

"It is true? These people bid on the victors for their company?" Ash asked, glancing about the room.

"Ninety minutes in a prepared room supplied with appetizers and drinks. The arenas won't have patrons. The whole point of charging an entrance fee is to make them obsolete," I explained.

"Pity. Have you competed before?" Ash asked, and I noticed the men's interest.

"I have. Twice. I had a lot of catching up to do when I arrived at Tidings, they allowed me to train with them."

"You have been in the patrons' rooms?"

I tried not to purse my lips as his glittering celadon eyes watched my reaction carefully, his tone filled with innuendo. "I'm undefeated. I've had two patrons and hold the record for the highest bid placed for a competitor. I dislike being required to spend my time with someone because they bought it rather than have it be my choice. Our lives are made up of our decisions. When someone takes that choice away from me, I find it suffocating."

"Careful. When my wife is cornered, her claws come out."

Slate's arm slid around my waist and I wondered if I was standing straighter or if I looked as if I would float away. As anxious as Slate made me, my relief was palpable as was the men's' irritation. All except Moon and Fox. I hadn't expected him to come. He was competing and after the last few uncomfortable days, I didn't think he had any interest in the arenas.

"Only to those who mean my loved ones harm," I said coyly, and Slate chuckled as he greeted Fox and Moon.

He held onto Peak's hand a moment too long and Ash's not long enough. Sterling had wandered off, and I spotted him near an older man whose back was to me. He turned around, and I gasped.

Balas. I recognized his date, Firefly from the gift shop and my heart lurched. I squeezed Slate's side and hoped he couldn't hear what they were discussing.

"Have you made a decision on my proposition?" Moon's seamed ebony face hadn't so much as cracked a smile.

He was all business, and I was grateful Slate had shown up out of the blue.

"What proposition is this?" Peak asked with a stony face.

"We included your family in the bargain, Peak. Scarlett's elemental abilities could be bred into the other greater families after she has a Dagr and a Tio." Moon answered so nonchalantly I blinked.

I was not some broodmare. When would they figure that out?

Peak's face darkened. He cast Ash a side glance and looked to Slate for the first time since shaking his hand.

"How does my nephew feel about loaning out his wife? I do not think I approve of the use of his wife in such a manner," Peak said, and I wanted to scoff so badly it hurt.

"What can he say about it when the khoraz he beds is coming this way now, no doubt at his behest," Ash interjected and I went rigid.

I shouldn't have looked for her. I saw Lynx's thin brunette hair and expansive chest sidestepping patrons with her luminous aquamarine eyes set on Slate. The men had caught my gaze and had all turned to watch her approach. I could *feel* the smugness coming off Ash. Peak turned back to me and I could sense his disapproval at Slate taking such a lowborn lover. The hypocrisy was staggering.

"I will take care of this," Slate whispered in my ear.

"I will return after the competition gentleman, I'm afraid I must prepare. Enjoy yourselves," I told them and left without another look back.

I made one last round to visit Ruby, Pearl, and Orion before going to the prep room, carefully skirting Balas. Partially because it was proper, and it gave me time to speak to Lera to make sure it was all going smoothly and partly because I wanted to watch Slate with Lynx. They had disappeared into the hall and my heart constricted painfully in my chest.

I had to focus. My errant husband would have to wait. Quick slid into my peripheral vision and an idea struck me.

"Quick! Come with me. I have something for you." Quick looked dapper in his navy brocade waistcoat and cravat. "Escort me to the prep room, please. I want to give you something for later. You'll understand when you need it. Did you see Indi yet?"

"She is nervous. She thought I would distract her." Quick's eyes were straight ahead down the hall, but he smiled as if she stood before him looking enchanting.

Quick missed a step when we turned the bend and saw Lynx sauntering our way. "Let me handle this," he said, and I let him think I would.

Lynx hazel eyes settled on me and she smirked. "I remember you. The *fat* wife, you work here. The one who told me Savage Storm was unavailable."

"Pregnant. Still is," I retorted coolly, and she laughed with a hand to her chest meant to draw the eye there.

"I bed to differ." She clicked her tongue. "I meant *beg*. Same difference. No matter. He has been in my bed every night and will be again tonight. He has only been with me since he left you. All mine." Lynx sauntered away, and I didn't rise to her nettling.

I would not fight for a man who wouldn't fight for me.

"Does he always sleep with crazies or do they go in search of me?" I asked once we started moving again.

"I hate to be the bearer of bad news, but I have questioned your sanity a time or two," he teased, trying to boost my mood, but I could *feel* how he pitied me.

Him and I both.

The crowd's roar shook the building as the first competitors exited the prep room. Slate was in the process of getting oiled by Cricket with Brass. They both wore the standard black leather briefs with greaves and bracers. I had to keep a tight rein on my eyes as well as my emotions as the blonde hairdresser tipped the glass pouring oil into her palms and then began to rub it on my husband and former lover.

I sat at the vanity next to Indigo. Quick had pulled up a chair next to her as Katydid did her hair and make up for the competition. She was already wearing her black leather tankini and thigh-high boots with a hint of heel. If Quick was a khoraz, his eyes would have been pure obsidian from his scent. He couldn't stand that he couldn't have her right now.

Katydid was in her third trimester, her older sister Cricket who also ran the salon trio, patted her on the back and pushed her big curls away from her hazel eyes as she began to dust Indigo with shimmering powder that made her luminescent.

Bronze, the voluptuous brunette, didn't have as much to dust with the shimmery powder since Cordillera had been true to her word and gotten me a long sleeve one piece. However, the neckline plunged precariously low and the bottoms hardly covered my ever-expanding backside. Bronze opted for a natural look with my hair down and my make up subtle so when I returned it wouldn't take as long to remove.

Dark Shadows was the underground club the crowd went to mingle with the rest of the competitors and I had planned to host a small gathering of the greater families who wished to stay and let loose.

Slate and Brass took the center black marble benches with white skein and faced the polished metal doors that led out into the arena. Normally, the section the vanities stood in was occupied by massage tables, but those were pushed up against the wall. I checked the zipper on my one piece willing it to go higher before frowning and thanking Bronze for another job well done while she adjusted my plain black mask. Indigo wore one just like it as she stood from her seat.

Quick was whispering fervently in her ear and she was shaking her head. Tweedledee and Tweedledum were smiling and laughing beside me, even if they hadn't, Quick's scent told me what he was trying to convince her to do. Her scent told me she was going to let him.

"Nervous?" Brass asked as I frowned at my boots.

I'd crossed my legs in front of me and leaned back my palms on the cool surface and realized I had a gut. A genuine baby belly as small as it was, it was there. I found it daunting and I was going to run around like a lunatic performing impossible feats for people I didn't like all that well's amusement.

"I'm getting big," was all I managed to say, thinking of Lynx's words.

Brass laughed and I avoided looking at him. His white flash of teeth in my peripheral against his oiled skin was sure to incite my senses if I managed a peek. Of course, Slate was in the same direction. It was twice the torture.

"Fat with his child is how he likes you best," Slate rumbled and I could hear the smile in his voice.

I heard Katydid gasp, and I whirled in the seat to face Slate. Brass was looking at me, waiting for my move. I got up and crossed to Katydid.

"It was after you two broke up and only a few weeks. I'd really appreciate if no one else found out," I said the last part loud enough so they all heard me.

"That is okay. Solder and I are happy. I was only surprised. I knew he... had a crush on you. Who does not?" She offered me a weak smile and rubbed her expansive belly as she set about cleaning the cosmetics she used on Indigo.

"It's good to see you two together again, but maybe next time you feel like announcing something so personal wait until fewer people can overhear you," I snapped at Slate as I walked past to the bench.

I tossed my long hair from my face and after a moment of silence I looked to the two men. They were both watching me with dry expressions. I gave them a questioning look keeping very careful not to let my eyes roam.

"Even a woman such as you could not come between us, love," Brass said smoothly.

The crowd roared. The first match was over. A screen in the right-hand corner beside the doors blinked to life. It would read the Vegas room number and the amount the patron paid for their company. Vegas was what I called the patrons' rooms — what happened there, stayed there.

Quick and Indigo emerged from the aisle to sit down next to me. Quick was buttoning his waistcoat with a flush of red across his olive cheeks. A hint of a smile played on his lips while Indigo was acting as if she'd been sitting there all the while.

"That is not a bad idea," Slate rumbled and my heart twisted.

When I left him, I had uncharacteristically pulled him into a bathroom stall and seduced him with little effort. I had developed a fetish for bathroom stalls after that, as Brass well knew. I couldn't wait until Slate retrieved his memories if he got them back.

"Good luck, Dove. I hope you lose," Quick said, planting a kiss to her forehead, and she scowled at him.

"Thanks for that," Indigo said dryly with a purse of her pretty pink lips.

The competitors from the first match burst through the doors and immediately began stripping as they headed into the showers. Modesty was not an issue for Guardians. A wave of heat rolled through me as the women showered within full view of us. Slate and Brass would do the same. Freya's burly boar, my hormones were wildly out of control.

... Sorry...

"I'm flattered," Brass murmured even though Slate would hear him.

... You have reason to be...

I wondered if he could pick up the playful tone in my mind, I knew he had when he laughed.

Slate growled deep in his chest.

"Your topic of conversation is transparent, as is your decision not to say it aloud."

As the bright red numbers climbed on the screen, my anxiety grew. Brass placed his palm to my stomach and *called* settling the boiling churn but couldn't ease my mind.

"Thanks. I'm not nervous about the Crash Course. Not really. I'm afraid I'm going to hurt myself. Why did I agree to this again?" I asked, running my hand over his.

"I think it was because you are a thick-headed woman who set her heels in and refused to listen to reason," he offered.

"Oh, that's right. It was so much easier to not think of the lives I am responsible for when there wasn't any evidence of their existence, but now with this gut, I'm all too aware of how real this is." I wiped my hands over my face, careful not to shift my mask.

"Brass will be here to heal you when you win," Slate reassured me.

"Thanks," Indigo and Brass both said and Slate chuckled.

"I go in trying to win every time we compete. I might actually beat you one of these days," Brass mused.

"By the way, Slate. We ran into Lynx. She intends to make Scarlett's life hel," Quick said as he walked through the metal doors.

I let my face go blank and guarded my thoughts. I'd never ask Slate to lose, but it'd be nice if he didn't win. The red numbers read *100-2*, one hundred gold daymarks for an opening match competitor was good. The woman walked out to the cheers of her fans.

"I have no desire to be with Lynx again," Slate rumbled so only Brass between us would hear.

Whatever they discussed in the hall after she so boldly approached him while he was with me must have gone sour. "She made it quite clear who you've been frequenting and why you are never around. She also called me fat," I said flatly.

... Words. Show me...

"You're supposed to say it out loud when you speak to him. I'm the one who reads your thoughts." Brass said with a warm smile.

"Maybe I didn't want him to hear it." I replied and turned to Indi. "You're going to do fantastic. Do you want me to settle your nerves?"

"I think I'm going to stumble through the doors or somehow rip this asinine outfit. You're not going to make your competitors wear this are you?" she asked making a face.

"I have Solder on it. Each arena will have a different uniform, but I guess they will be a little revealing. More clothes on the men though, that's smaller than their underpants," I said with a coy smile.

Indigo leaned forward to look at Brass and Slate and it took all of my will power not to admire them with her. She tilted her head so her chin rested on my shoulder.

"Frigga's sweet grass, Scar. I think most women would have killed to have been with those two men of yours. Might've killed *you*," Indi said with a waggle of her brows.

We both knew she thought Slate was intimidating, and he was, but he was also straight out a woman's wildest imagination. If that woman dreamed about being kidnapped by a barbarian raider who tames his savage heart to win the love of his once victim.

Brass was an entirely different story. His would be of a lowly peasant who finds out the prince she spied bathing nude in the stream and had thereafter pined after the highborn man, had fallen in love at first sight with the village girl.

"They're not *mine*. Gods, it's hot in here," I said, lifting my hair from the back of my neck and she blew on it for good measure.

"Quite the imagination," Brass said with barely contained mirth.

"Shut your mouth, Regn. I sometimes hate that you're a filthy mind reader."

"It's the mind that's filthy, love. Not the reader," Brass countered, and I aimed a scowl at his face, careful not to let my eyes shift.

"Must you call her love?" Slate grumbled.

"Deal with it," Brass retorted.

The announcer came on, I had not missed the booming man's voice. *"For our second match, our first competitor... the ladies' favorite.... HEAT!"*

I'd forgotten they said that about him and my lip curled in disgust. I'd folded my arms in a pout when Brass leaned down.

"Kiss for luck," he said, stealing a kiss of my lips.

I rocked back and then swatted forward trying to land a slap, but only succeeded in connecting with his backside. Brass's corresponding laugh with the look he shot me over my shoulder made me whip my face away.

"I'll get you for that, Regn," I said with a moronic smile.

"Looking forward to it, love," he called back as he strode through the doors to the screams of hundreds of women.

Slate had arched a brow in my direction and I scooted down to him, so close I could feel his body heat where our skin nearly touched. "I never have to wish you good luck."

He looked down his nose at me with an unreadable expression. Part of him was angry at me for some reason, but there was always that other part of him that wanted me no matter what I'd done. His bone deep lust.

"It is not luck, but skill." He bent his head close to my ear. "I will take a *skilled* kiss if you can manage."

"Gods, Slate —"

"Our second competitor and undefeated champion of the Crash Course... SAVAGE STORM!"

My tongue fell leadenly in my mouth and Slate took my face in his hands. I placed my own over his as he gazed into my eyes. Slate took my hand and placed it to his hard sculpted and wonderfully oiled chest.

Was my hand over his heart?

Then he was gone.

Slate's body moved with fluid like grace, every single muscle in his carved body was highlighted by the oils and spotlights as he walked through the doors. His wavy mane of hair spilled down his back, pieces of silver catching the light. He entered the arena like a bronzed god and had every right to be that arrogant.

The bastard.

I moved back to where Indi sat and rested my head on her shoulder. "His old lover wants him back. They always do. I should know."

"I'm so glad Silver isn't competing tonight. I couldn't stand knowing he'd be stuck in a room with some woman fawning all over him. His ego is monstrous enough as it is without any added encouragement." Indi's pink lips smiled impishly at me, but it wasn't in her eyes.

"You never get used to it. It's part of the reason I chose the arenas out of all the excuses I had to insinuate myself on each island when I was going to search for Slate."

Her nails sparkled under the lights, they were painted a glittering silver and gold which hinted at the dress Cordillera had chosen for her to wear afterwards. Mine were a white shimmering satin so it would go with anything I wore and complimented the jewelry I had put on for tonight.

The crowd's stomping of their feet and the energy from the excitement signified the end to the match. I would be astonished if Slate had been beaten. His emotions before he left were high, he had been in a competitive mood and eager to prove himself after his imprisonment.

"You didn't kiss him," Indigo murmured.

"I trust him with my life, but not my love. There's no such thing as just a kiss with Slate Dagr."

Brass and Slate burst through the metal doors and headed directly into the showers, stripping as they went. Indigo's cheeks flushed as they ducked their heads under the showers streams and turned to rinse water over their heads.

I straightened and slid my hand into hers.

"Dear Frigga's sweet grass, I hope Silver never asks me if I think his brother is well formed," Indigo breathed. "He is... beautiful."

Brass was gorgeous. He had likely grown his stubbly beard in order to make him less so, but the ruggedness of his unshaven face did little to hide how attractive his features were. Everything about him was disarming and invited you in.

I bit my lip, but it didn't stop the snicker.

She looked at Slate's rippling bronze body and his patch work of scars I knew were there, but never actually saw. I saw through them, I supposed. It was the same with the weight he'd lost in the month they'd had him. He'd never been thin, but muscled that border lined on bulky. Now, he'd lost some of that softness so his muscles resembled Quick's slightly trimmer form, but I would work on him and feed to the point of bursting. Not that he looked bad, he was just so hard.

"Not so much. When he gets his memories back, I'll plump him up with sympathy weight." I sucked air into my cheeks to puff them out and Indigo giggled.

"I would *love* to see you try to fatten him up. I could help," she offered.

The men had finished washing and the numbers on the screen started to climb. Brass and Slate dressed without speaking while Cricket and Bronze moved about combing and moisturizing as they went.

"You both realize his hearing is unparalleled and *I* am a mind reader," Brass said, slipping his copper waist coat with black brocade embroidery over his broad shoulders.

"Mind your own business, Regn," I said jokingly and Brass lifted his head to give me a quick smile.

I checked the screen and then quickly looked away. *500-3* the bright red taunted. My good mood, that had been so difficult to force to begin with, faded to the gloomy melancholy that kept threatening to pull me under. No Ama, no Shale. It felt impossibly wrong for one of them not to be there with me. I hated grief. She was a sneaky carrion feeding on me at the least opportune times. Tears burned at my eyes making my nose tingle. I didn't understand the anatomy of it.

"She trembles her fan in a sweetness dumb. As her thoughts were beyond recalling; with a glance for one, and a glance for some. From her eyelids rising and falling; speaks common words with a blushful air. Hears bold words,

unreproving; but her silence says — what she never will swear — and love seeks better loving," I whispered.

Abruptly, Slate was before me and before I could lift my eyes, he knelt down and took my face in his rough hands and molded his lips to mine.

"Be careful," he whispered before brushing his lips over mine once more and walked through the metal doors to the roar of the fans.

Brass sat down next to me and let his shoulder touch the thin leather that covered my arm. "I know what you're thinking," he murmured.

"You don't say?" I whispered.

He wrapped his arm around my shoulders and leaned his head against mine. "I'll be here as soon as you get back."

"He still thinks I'm going to kill him," I whispered.

Brass's gusty sigh ruffled my hair. "He's dealing with it."

"We have a special main event planned for tonight," said the announcer. *"Pitting twin against twin, the ever alluring and undefeated female champion... WILDFIRE!"*

The announcer interrupted us. Brass let his fingers run down the length of my arm before it fell from my shoulders. I knew what he was going to do, Indigo was doing a good job to ignore us as Brass ran his thumb along my cheek bone. His amber eyes flitted between mine.

"We'll never be as we once were, will we?" I whispered.

He smiled ruefully and leaned forward. "A kiss for poor luck," he whispered so Indigo wouldn't hear.

I almost laughed before he pressed his full lips to mine. Brass's kiss was sweet and warm. I sighed and withdrew, letting my fingers brush his hand. I took a fortifying breath and headed through the metal doors.

The spotlights were swirling, my shimmering skin glittered under the bright lights. The crowd was deafening. I sashayed onto the course raising my chin and letting my hips sway as I walked. When I got to the start of the Guillotine, instead of waving I bent over dramatically over one leg to check my boot. The cheering grew louder and I let my fingers trail back up my leg and flipped my hair back dramatically before I'd fully straightened. It was my move. Belatedly, I remembered all of my invited guests and family members in Cordillera's suite.

The crowd went wild.

"Our second competitor, our newest recruit and rising star. Please welcome to her very first match... DOVE!" The announcer's voice echoed throughout the arena and Indigo trotted out and smiled, waving her hands through the air.

She spoke through gritted teeth. "I'll kill him. If he thinks he's ever getting me into bed again, he's sorely mistaken."

Wildfire was my competition name to hide my true identity. Wildfire was cold and calculating, but with my twin competing next to me my mood had bolstered substantially and I was having a hard time maintaining my cool demeanor. She wasn't my competitor; she was my sister. I wrapped an arm around her waist and waved with a megawatt smile to the fans.

The announcer tried to start the match but gave up when the crowd's elated cries reached a fever pitch. "Lera didn't tell you beforehand what Quick had begged her to let him name you? She has a soft spot for Quick and Brass," I told her speaking through my teeth.

Indigo snorted, and we both stopped waving and gave one another a hug before the announcer tried to speak again. *"Ladies! Are we ready?"*

The crowd cheered again and Indi gave a thumb's up. The fans already loved her.

I never got used to the sound of the boom. A sound like a cannon firing shook my entire body. My instincts took over, and I was running into the Guillotine before my mind could catch up.

I was fluid. My feet were featherlight on the arena floor. The world outside blurred. Sounds and faces faded into white noise. I had gone through great lengths once I had learned the course to make it a choreographed dance for the crowd. My every movement was intentional. I slithered between the blades, rolling and leaping to best display my body's natural gifts. I didn't stop moving when I came to the treetops. I could flip from treetop to top; I stopped my usual dramatic backflip to a simple leap because my center of gravity was off. The fans didn't seem to care.

I started at a run and flew through the air across the earthquake section. I made landfall five times instead of my usual three as I twisted and turned, leaping gracefully through the shaking grounds and falling boulders. When I reached the lava and I leapt onto a lava rock passing by. The crowd hadn't even noticed I was pregnant, but I was never more aware of it as I was then.

Again, I mentally chastised myself for the needless risk.

I checked for Indigo. Indi was a second behind me, reaching the end of the earthquake zone so I leapt to the next rock, and kept at it until I reached the end, twisting midair to avoid a geyser of molten lava. Indi had caught up.

At a jog, I propelled myself with the force of both of my feet off the edge of the lava rocks spinning until I landed on a raft going by. Indi was a raft ahead of me. Quick and Brass had taught her well. She'd picked up nearly as fast as I had without the motivation I'd had to urge me forward.

I kept my stance wide to maintain balance. Another raft came around and I hopped over letting myself teeter. One thing Slate and Brass hadn't taught me was the art of showmanship.

It was time for the win.

I didn't want to miss it. I was neck and neck with Indigo as our rafts came around the whirlpool and I put more weight on one foot, then the other, causing the raft to lift from the dangerously churning water. The crowd gasped, but I was focused on Indi as she landed lithely on the dock. I righted the raft, holding back the tears of pride and joined her on the dock.

She blinked at me in disbelief until I grabbed her hand and held it into the air so her fans could greet their new undefeated female champion. She was swept up in their emotions. Indi started waving numbly at first and as her win began to process, she blew a kiss towards Cordillera's suite. Whether for Sterling or Quick, I didn't know.

I wrapped my arm around her waist and led her towards the prep room around the track that would pass along the high walls of the arena where fans had begun to throw golden roses. I smiled and scooped up three. Indi was in a daze, basking in the adoration of the fans. I broke the stems off two of the roses as I always did and tucked one behind her ear, one into my own, and handed the third to her.

She knew what to do. She pressed her lips to its lemony petals and smiled before she tossed it into the crowd. The wrought-iron railings barely kept the fans from falling into the arena as they rushed forth to catch it.

"Our new undefeated female champion... DOVE!" the announcer blared.

I led Indi back to the prep room at a trot. My days of performing were over. I was looking forward to the next chapter of my life. I wanted to be a mother, to find the stone pieces, and put things right. In my life and in the world. I wanted to be a wife, to run the arenas, and to work on Tidings from the inside out. I was done marching to the traditional tune just because that's the way it was always done.

We pushed through the metal doors and before I joined Indigo in the showers, there was Brass. He got to his feet and smiled warmly at me. I gave a little shrug.

"That was nice of you," he said in a low deep tone.

I held up my ring finger with the tiwaz tattoo. Success through sacrifice.

"Motherhood means more than the glory. I'll work from behind the scenes now," I murmured.

Brass placed his hand on my stomach and *called,* healing my aches and pains, but otherwise I was unharmed if a bit wet. Indigo was showering behind me, Brass could have easily glanced over my shoulder, but he never would.

"I had better go. Watching you shower may prove more temptation than I bargained for and Slate will not forgive me for what I would do. He's coming around to the new terms of our relationship. I won't give you up, love. Not all of it," Brass said, and I tried not to notice Katydid eavesdropping.

"Me neither. You should probably run very far away from me. I mean that," I told him with brutal honesty.

Brass looked out towards the arena doors. I reached up to run my thumb along the stubbled jaw and he shut his eyes.

"I am still seeing Rosasite," he said.

"You should probably stop kissing ex-lovers then," I said weakly, unable to make myself stop touching him.

He took my hand from his face and kissed the inside of my wrist before raising his eyes to mine. Brass gave a small, sad smile.

"I can't stop myself."

"Goodbye, Brass," I said, hoping he would walk away.

A lump swelled in my throat. Saying goodbye to Brass was like cutting off both my own arms. How does one accomplish that? He nodded.

"I'll see you in Dark Shadows," he murmured before leaving.

He let our fingers slide through one another's and I watched him leave before I walked into the showers. Slate would be with his patron for another hour. Ninety minutes with another woman. Even noble Brass slept with a patron or two.

I tried to focus on scrubbing myself down. Indigo finished and hurried to sit in front of the vanity with Cricket and Katydid drying her hair and doing her makeup in tandem. I shut off the shower spray with a slap to the energy plate and took my time drying off as I walked to Bronze with a fluffy white towel.

"Tough luck, hun," Bronze said, and I offered her a smile.

"I don't mind losing to my sister. I had a good run," I said, sparing Indi a glance.

Indi narrowed her powder blue eyes at me. "Promise me I beat you fair and square."

"I'm not as fast as I used to be. The pregnancy has thrown off my balance." I hated lying, I was terrible at it, everything I said though was true.

She pursed her lips to the side s she contemplated this, then her smile dropped. "I'm terrified. Silver was right. I don't think I can do this."

I placed my hand over hers and gave it a squeeze. "I promise it will work out, Indi. Trust me."

She knit her brow and sighed. They finished her make up and helped her into a metallic gold gown that was sheer from the knee down and glittered under the lights. They placed a matching gold mask over her eyes and set her sky-high gold pumps in front of her. She stepped into them and wrung her hands as the bright red numbers of the screen stopped at *1000-1.*

"I thought you would win. I didn't get this far in my hypothetical," she mumbled absently as she stared at the doors.

Bronze was finishing my make up as Cricket begun to do my hair. Katydid was starting to pack up their things and hung my dress on a hook against the wall.

"Wave, smile, don't let them grope you as you go. Throw elbows if you have to, there will be two bodyguards, Breakers, who will help you reach the hall. Above all, have fun, Indi." I told her and she nodded before pushing the doors open with her out flung arms and was greeted by her awaiting devotees.

I had several reasons for throwing the competition tonight. It wasn't simple. Peak was there. He would have bid on me, if not him, then Ash. With Slate, Brass, and Jett all under one roof and I trapped in a room with one of those men, they'd lose their minds.

I'd given Quick all the daymarks I had on me to ensure he would beat out Sterling who would have likely bid on her unable to watch her go to another man.

"Thanks, Bronze. You're a magician not a beautician," I said with a smirk.

Bronze chortled. "Need help to get back into your dress?"

I was putting back on my rich emerald velvet dress with all its petticoats and corset. "No. I can manage. Go ahead home. I'm going to take my sweet time. Thanks, ladies," I said, casting a smile at the three talented women.

When I finished all of my topaz buttons, I put on my emerald earrings and the rest of my newly acquired jewelry. I straightened my dress running my palms along the ornate golden threads of the embroidery and the pearls before slipping my gold mask over my eyes. I was twisting my diamond solar cross ring when I pushed through the metal doors that led to the grey stone steps on the other side of the prep room. One hand slid along the polished wood railing of the wrought-iron balustrade while the other lifted my skirts.

Headquarters smelled like leather and metal. A scent that once made me nervous probably because it reminded me of Slate and Lera — now I found it reassuring.

I was preoccupied with reminiscing and didn't see the man waiting for me on the next landing as if he'd known I'd come that way.

"Sweet Scarlett," Peak purred.

THIRTY

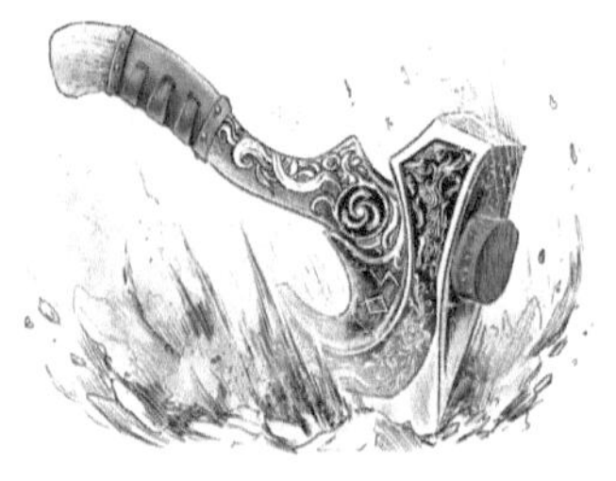

"Freya's burly boar! What did Scar get Indi into?" Jett exclaimed.

"You're an idiot. Look who else is missing," Tawny whispered in an amused tone and Jett's head whipped around the room.

"Quick is gone," he said stupidly and Tawny smiled knowingly at him. "Quick paid three thousand daymarks for an hour and a half of her time when he sees her every day," he realized aloud, shaking his head.

"*Love*. Slate did it for Scarlett for her first competition. This has Scarlett written all over it." Tawny was smiling enchantingly as she thought about Scarlett and her hopeless romantic tendencies.

If they weren't married, and she smiled that way at him... Jett would've made a play for Tawny in another life. Her wide hazel eyes came into focus and whatever she saw in his face made her narrow her eyes at him.

"I told Steel about that kiss. He said it wasn't the first time you kissed someone he was with," she said imperiously.

Jett couldn't help his smug grin. "I think you kissed me, Tawny." He gave her a wink and her wide mouth tightened.

Divine Beauty got them every time. Unfortunately, it was indiscriminate as to whom it attracted.

Brass came over with drinks for the lot of them and they thanked him as he sat on one of the purple velvet couches in the black tiled V.I.P. section. The ultra-chic night club was like all of Tidings, modern with a flair of older times. The DJ booth was just off the dance to the side of free-standing tables and more purple velvet couches. Below the raised V.I.P. section, a black-tiled dance floor teemed with people that had been in the stands and now hoped to rub elbows with the competitors. They didn't know that it was a mercenary guild or at worst an assassin's guild.

"Is your girlfriend here?" Tawny asked with uncharacteristic equanimity.

Brass shot her a wry smile. "Rosasite is here. She is not my girlfriend."

Tawny looked out to the crowd. The older guests Scarlett had invited were sitting at another table at her reserved sections with Cordillera. Oddly, Chafer wasn't with her. He usually followed her like a shadow. Fox, Ash, and Sterling were at yet another booth being entertained by pretty young women without masks. Gypsum stumbled over the velvet rope and knocked into Tawny as he sat, making her brace against him.

"This is awesome. Scarlett and Indi were awesome. You and Slate were awesome..." Gypsum said, sweeping a narrow braid from his dimpled face as he addressed Brass.

"It was awesome. We get it," Tawny said, rolling her eyes.

Gypsum rolled his eyes dramatically back at her. "Hey. Where is she anyway? This is her party." Gypsum sat up and swung his head around. His face paled, looking like he'd maybe had some bad shellfish.

"Dude. If you're going to barf, aim away," Jett said, leaning back.

"Peak. Where's Peak?" Gypsum asked soberly.

Jett, Tawny, and Brass shot to their feet to look about. Jett cursed a colorful stream of words not often said all at once.

"What on earth does she see in him?" Jett ground out.

"Don't be stupid. She wants nothing to do with him. I'll check the prep room." Brass said, already leaving.

"What does that mean?" Tawny asked hesitantly, looking at Gypsum.

"What do you think it means?" Gypsum's brows pulled together as he looked about.

"I'll go back to Cordillera's suite," Tawny said, picking up her scarlet dress so she could move more nimbly.

"Chief, you stay here in case she gets back and send Tawny a message through the bond if she gets here. I'm going to head to the portal and see if she went home, maybe she was feeling sick, and it's a coincidence," Jett said hopefully and Brass shot him a worried look.

"I never should have left her alone. She would have told us if she was going to leave. These arenas are her world. She would show," he said.

Brass walked briskly until a gorgeous woman with a head full of inky curls grabbed his elbow to try to pull him into a dance. The girl wrapped her arms around his neck and he gently took her hands away as he spoke quickly and left her standing there staring after him.

Jett walked through the darkened cobbled roads of Valla towards the portal gate. It stood at the center of the star formation that made up the once fortified town. Stone buildings, never higher than three stories, lined the streets. Glass store front windows, reminiscent of a European town, were to either side lit by low globes of light from lamp posts the Guardians kept energized — no power plants in Tidings.

Jett sucked in air sharply at the knot of pain that bloomed in his mind. Scarlett's bond had been activated and she was in pain. Something nightmarish was happening to her. Jett broke into a run to the free-standing stone gate with sculptured tree branches twisting up it, a sculpture of a woman, hands extended forming into branches crested the top.

Hold tight, Jett wanted to tell her. He was coming.

He'd be the closest one to the portal unless Slate or Brass had been activated as well and they could use the 'secret' portal on the top floor of headquarters.

The sky opened up as the buildings vanished in the empty town hexagon. Pain and shame poured through the bond like it was his own. She was fighting. Jett could feel Scarlett's struggle. Her indomitable will. It reassured and scared Jett. Was she fighting to the death, is that why she was so resolute?

Agony.

Gods, she was in so much pain. Jett's arms pumped and he didn't pause to explain to the Guardian on duty why he was running. He dove through the portal with one place in mind — Mabon.

On the other side of the portal, in the land of perpetual fall, Scarlett's bond was stronger but still further away. The arena site had to be it. Jett had never been there, he'd also never portal jumped without a clear destination in mind. At worst it would spit him out in the same spot. He charged back through the portal thinking of a construction site in Mabon.

By some miracle, he plowed through a copse of trees and ran right into a neighboring red wood. Jett pulled the only two blades he had shoved into his boots, not anticipating a fight at the competition. He whirled his head around to be sure he was in Mabon. Lush green grass and a crisp breeze reaffirmed the island.

Jett sucked in a breath. He had to keep his head. Follow the bond, no need to hunt. Keep low, keep quiet. Jett trotted forth at a crouch and saw the clearing and campfire the moment he climbed the low hillock. Jett's hands tightened on his daggers. A man's body was sprawled about ten feet away from where a barghest was ravaging a woman who could only be Scarlett.

Jett would hear her screams in his nightmares. Her bare hands limply struck at him. He'd knocked her blade away, and all she had left was her fingernails and teeth. That wasn't stopping him as he wasted an occasional moment to bat away her hand.

"My babies! Heal them!" she screeched hoarsely.

The hulking, heather-grey, seven-foot-tall barghest sneered with a snout full of teeth as long as Jett's fingers. Two sets of horns formed from his scalp. One set slightly curved back from his long-pointed ears as a second pair curved around like a ram's. A pair of tusks that glinted red from the flickering fire light extended from its jaw.

"Please!" Scarlett screamed, "I'll be good. I promise."

Jett had ducked down low as he climbed until he was close enough to charge, taking Peak off guard. It was Peak. Those lime green eyes shone at her. She was crying and Peak sneered.

"I cannot do that. You will never learn. A little diffidence would go a long way, sweet Scarlett." Peak spoke in a rasped cultured voice at odds with itself.

Peak had a great deal more control than Slate had in his barghest form. Jett couldn't stand another second of hearing Scarlett whimpering. He realized his mistake too late. Peak's head lifted with a grim smile. Scarlett cried and tried to roll away, but Peak put a foot on her back as Jett charged.

Jett almost faltered. It was too late. Of course Peak knew Jett was there, Slate could hear a whisper in a crowded room of conversations. Peak had heard Jett panting the moment he'd slammed into the redwood. Jett shot a fire ball into Peak and gasped. The fireball evaporated as it hit Peak and he laughed. Scarlett lifted her beaten face.

Blood matted in her hair and her face was mottled and swelling. "He's a void! Please, blessed gods save him!" she shouted, her voice cracking.

A void.

No wonder her *calling* didn't work on him, why her elemental powers didn't affect him like they should've.

Shit.

Jett came at him anyway. He wouldn't run out on Scarlett. They would die together. Peak *called.* Jett was wrapped in ropes of air and fell to his knees less than twenty feet away from them.

Jett grit his teeth as Peak laughed. The man lying in a pool of his own blood was Chafer. What the hell had happened?

"It is unfortunate you came upon this man taking advantage of your sweet sister. At least you killed him before he could finish you off. Do not worry. I have no intention of killing my mate, but she *will* leave here with my seed sown in her womb."

Peak lifted his paw from Scarlett's back and Jett finally saw her.

Tears burned his eyes. Hadn't she been through enough? Her corset and petticoats were slashed through exposing bloody gashes of her skin. She crawled on her hands and knees to get away from him gritting her teeth and coughing up blood that spilled over her narrow chin. Her breaths wheezed from her chest. Her emerald gown was carefully folded over a log. She was crawling towards Jett.

"Why did you come?" she cried, raising one good eye to him, her mouth pulled down like the Greek mask of tragedy.

Jett was gagged with air, but he fought against the ropes trying to *call* to break their binds. Peak watched Scarlett with contempt and kicked her backside making her hit the soil face first. Jett groaned and struggled all the harder testing every call he had against the ropes.

Scarlett gritted her bloody teeth, bits of grass stuck to her broken lips and the bloodied side of her face where he had split the skin under her eye.

Bloody lip. Slate.

Any minute.

Peak grabbed Scarlett. Jett squeezed his eyes shut as she wailed.

Tears poured down Jett's face. He could hear the short struggle that ensued and the air that rushed from her lungs as Peak hit her. Closed fist. Then the whimpering again.

Useless.

He'd gone there rashly, guns blazing, not a single intelligent thought and now he would watch her children forcibly aborted... again. He might kill her in the process. They'd both die. His children raised without a father.

The family would know Chafer would never have hurt Scarlett. For some reason, Chafer and Scarlett were friends. Chafer didn't have a single friend outside of Scarlett, but for Cordillera.

Peak roared and Jett winced. A roar answered Peak's and Jett's eyes shot open to try to look into the woods where the roar had come from. A charcoal grey barghest bounded into view.

Slate had finally come.

THIRTY-ONE

My life was slipping through my fingers. Darkness beckoned, and I reached with open arms for it to take me away from this horrible life.

I had a plan.

Chafer was to follow Peak via the cameras throughout headquarters. If we left HQ, I would take him to Mabon where we wouldn't be seen. If Peak tried to corner me, Chafer would mind blast him and I would use the dagger I'd concealed in my heeled boot. The trick was, I had to do it before he turned into a barghest or resisting him would be impossible.

Maybe I could have gone along as I had the last time with Peak's affections, but he was in a foul mood from me having been with Balas. I knew it was going to be painful from the moment Peak began painstakingly unbuttoning each topaz button himself. It had given me plenty of time to think. If I could distract Peak while Chafer snuck up, it would be over in a matter of seconds.

Peak's head had whipped around when Chafer emerged from the shadows and Peak had instantly shifted into a barghest. That's when we discovered why Peak had so easily taken advantage of me. His skin wasn't thicker as I'd thought, he was immune to *calling* unless he willed it. He was a void. Peak had swiped his claw across a stunned Chafer and I heard a crunch as the barghest clouted him in the face. Chafer hadn't stirred and Peak turned his wrath on me.

I pulled my blades struggling with my will to give into him as his mate and he had beaten me until I couldn't move. He'd clawed off most of my under garments as I huddled in a ball trying to protect my stomach. He was practically foaming at the mouth. I'd given in and started to beg for the lives of my children.

Then Peak had smiled from above me. A brief respite from him as I tried to get away. I would never stop fighting in one way or another.

Agony. Such an act that could give life changing pleasure was not made to be such nightmarish pain. I would always remember Peak's brutality.

Jett. Gods, no.

I didn't warn him in time. Jett had shut his eyes away from my humiliation but I knew he could hear everything. Peak said he was going to kill my sons. He might've already.

I wouldn't give up for Jett's sake. For the lives of my children. For Gigi and his son who hadn't met him yet.

Begging and pleading would allow me to fight another day I told myself. Peak roared as he claimed me. A roar had answered and the eye that wasn't sealed shut searched for Slate. Panic and relief intermingled. He couldn't see me like this, his memory would prevent him from ever erasing it. I tried to buck away from Peak, but my body was broken and weak. His clawed hands dug into my hips and I cried out feeling the hot blood pour down my thighs where his nails bit.

A huge beast charged into sight from the portal with Brass on its heels. Peak didn't let me go as I thought he would to face Slate. The bastard and gripped my hair and held me over his body like a shield while we were both on our knees.

Slate's bunched muscles rippled under his skin in his hybrid form, he skidded to a stop when Peak used his other hand to grip my throat until my eyelids began to flutter. Brass cursed.

"He's a void," Brass said roughly.

"Come to watch me mate, nephew? You do not want her. All of

Tidings knows you have left her. No need to fight over a woman. Take your companion and find a new one. This one will not carry your bairn anymore. I have seen to it," Peak said. "I fill her womb as we speak."

Hysteria gripped me. "No!"

The word ripped from my throat in a bloodcurdling scream. I did what I said I wouldn't do, I mewled pathetically as I tried to get my fingers to find my stomach.

Through my tears, Jett lurched to his feet. Brass must have cut the *call* Peak had on him. Then Jett was luminescent. Divine beauty — gods, he was so beautiful. His tan skin glowed golden and resplendent. I forgot my crying and suddenly I was face first on the dirt again.

The light went out and a dark shape sailed over me. Roars tore through the silent night. Thunder rolled as if beckoned by their calls. Arms gently turned me over and I could only blink at them as I laid in the dirt. Brass and Jett placed their hands on me and I stared at the churning clouds watching the lightning strike through them.

"Chafer. Go. Chafer," I croaked like a ninety-year-old smoker.

Brass disappeared and Jett held my head in his lap. He was crying. His head whipped up, and he threw his body over me as two shapes rolled over us. A flashing of teeth and claws reminded me of what was happening. I braced my hand on Jett's thigh and pushed myself up despite Jett's fervent words of warning.

Slate and Peak were tearing one another part. Claws sliced through blood-soaked furred flesh. Fangs gnashed and bit into bodies. Peak was just as big as Slate and even more skilled in his barghest form, but Slate was much younger and trained daily as a man.

Lightening flashed. The surreal scene brightened, and I saw spots before my eyes. I clambered to my feet to find Chafer. Brass had the other man lying on his back now, alive, but unconscious.

"You need to lay down, Scarlett. That or come home. Let's get out of here. Slate can handle this," Jett urged from my side and reached for me.

I recoiled.

The thought of anyone touching me — of *them* touching me after what they saw... I couldn't bare it.

The barghests stumbled a few feet away from us landing clawed blows on one another as a light splattering of rain began to fall. It was always raining in Mabon. I blinked at the drizzle collecting on my lashes.

I wouldn't leave. Not until I saw it through. It was all my fault, and I was useless. I had found my blade as I'd stumbled to Chafer and wondered if I could throw it into Peak.

No shot was presenting itself. Jett had managed to temporarily captivate Peak so Slate could knock him away from me.

Lightening flashed again, and it wasn't two barghests fighting. Peak held his throat as blood poured from between his fingers. He was nude, half resting on a cut down tree, gouges wounded his bronze body and his chest heaved.

"I could teach you things your father would have," Peak ground out in pain.

Slate shifted into his male form wearing shredded pants and the remnants of a waistcoat. "Teach me how to rape women and kill bairn?" Slate snarled.

Peak spat and the effort caused blood to surge, it coated his arm to the elbow. Slate had nicked his artery. "You did not see her the first night. She wanted it. A barghest khoraz. You should have a better wife than that, nephew."

I struggled to my feet and scorched Brass and Jett as they tried to grab me, not bothering with a warning. I staggered over to where Peak laid and Slate stood over him.

"Barghests mate for life." I said hoarsely, my throat had phantom soreness from screaming despite their healing.

Peak's lime eyes peered up at me from a face who looked eerily similar to Slate's. I didn't wait for him to affirm what I already knew.

"I hope you understand the privilege I bestowed upon you. Your life is a small flicker of a flame I can extinguish as easily as breathing." I repeated words he'd said to me the first night he'd drugged me and leaned in. "A little humility would have gone a long way. I'm afraid I will not be forgiving this transgression," I said in a harsh whisper.

Our eyes locked. He thought he could talk his way out of it. He hadn't lost hope. I had been reluctant to kill him. I liked Sterling. Peak was his father. I had lost my own father less than a year ago. Then he promised to kill my unborn sons.

Before he could say some snide retort, I threw the weight of my body behind my blade as I lunged. My blade pierced his hand into his throat and he jerked violently to throw me off. I took hold of his short waves as I grunted, pressing my chest into my own arm so the blade bit deep and I felt it lock up against his spine.

His hot blood welled up over my hands and against my chest as I took ragged breaths, refusing to move until I watched the light leave those cruel lime eyes. His mouth tried to work as blood spilled forth running over his full lips and went slack. I took a shuddering breath as his head slid to the side.

Peak was dead. I'd killed Slate's uncle.

Slate tried to help me up, but I yanked my arms away from him. "Don't touch me." I hissed.

I rolled off Peak and onto my back beside him letting the splattering rain soak my skin. From the way my skin dampened, I knew there wasn't much left of my corset and petticoats.

No more Peak. It was over.

No one would convict me for defending myself. The council would have to see that even if they all thought I was a khoraz.

I shifted into a sitting position and saw that Chafer was getting to his feet if a bit unsteadily trying to shake Jett off his arm.

Slate tried again to reach for me, but I yanked myself away. I thought better of it and turned around staring past him and only grazed his hot flesh long enough to heal him. If I saw what I was afraid I'd see in his eyes, I'd never be able to look at him the same way again just as he would never be able to look at me the same way after tonight. After watching me beaten and forced by his uncle.

I made it to Chafer who gripped his hand around my bicep to steady me. We were quite the pair. The other men got to their feet, but we ignored them.

"Fuck, Delegate. I failed you," Chafer said, his sharp features pinching.

I shook my head and braced my hand on his arm. "No. There's no way we could have known. I led you into a trap. I'm so sorry."

Chafer hadn't seen what happened after he'd been knocked unconscious. I could talk to Chafer. He wouldn't be looking at me like a poor, broken, wounded girl like the others were. His eyes scanned me; the corset and skirts showed much more than they covered. He looked to where my dress was laying and helped me over to it.

The other three stayed silent and hung back as Chafer held up the dress to shield me. I stripped off the torn clothing, wiping blood and dirt from my skin and using the warm water from my *calling* to rinse. I even worked it through my hair until it ran clear. Then, I slid my arms through the sleeves and began to button the topaz buttons. Chafer turned me around by my shoulders and started from the bottom so we met at the middle.

Chafer acted like an annoying older brother who could barely tolerate me, that meant we got along. Chafer didn't get along with anyone. That he helped me said a lot about how he felt for me.

When I was dressed and he helped me rid my hair of tangles Chafer leant me his arm as we walked back to the three men. I couldn't meet their eyes. Not after what they'd seen. Before I could open my mouth, another figure rushed up the hillock and Chafer pushed me behind him.

"Is he dead?" Orion said, panting as he climbed up the hill.

His scarlet robes dragged through the mud as rain flattened his snowy thin hair to his scalp.

"He is," Slate growled, watching with silver glinting eyes as the old man came to a stop and looked past to where Peak's body lay.

"Get back to the party. No one must know you were ever here. They will send someone to look for him soon. Go. *Now.*" Orion started towards my discarded clothes and set about burning them to ashes.

We stood, dumbfounded, as he churned dirt covering signs of a fight and started towards Peak. Old man Vetr cast a glance at us from his hooded blue eyes and looked aggravated we were still there.

"Do you know what happens if Willow finds out her husband was having an affair with a Tio? She will hire as many assassins as it will take to kill her. Now go! Tawny would be heartbroken if you were murdered." Orion started back towards Peak under the drizzling rain.

Chafer grabbed my elbow and started leading me towards the portal gate. Jett came beside me and I cringed. I heard Jett sigh and fall back with Brass and Slate who were having a conversation in low tones. Chafer seemed to know I wanted nothing to do with those three and led me back to headquarters himself.

Cordillera met us at the top level of headquarters through the studded wood carved portal door. It lay against a plain dark grey wall with no other adornments. Chafer opened the door on the opposite end that led to the golden sconce lined hall with navy walls. Our feet sounded on the polished wood floor. Lera heard us coming and opened the door as we reached it and hurried me in.

Jett cleaned his pants as he sat on the maroon couch in the sitting area across from the sprawling cherry wood bed.

Brass found new clothes for Slate as Lera herself did my hair and make-up, then found me a new corset and petticoats to go under my emerald dress that Chafer was drying after he'd cleaned and changed himself.

She stood back pursing red lips and lifted her thick manicured brows. "That will have to do. Smile. Flirt. Be your clever self. You can grieve at home in bed, out of sight. Right now, you entertain. You show no weakness. You understand?"

I numbly nodded. All emotion had fled me. I wouldn't grieve or be sad, I didn't think I could *anything*.

"You were tired because pregnant women tire easily and laid down for a moment to shut your eyes and fell asleep on the massage table in the prep room. Jett, Brass, you two go down now. Act happy. Slate found you and escorted you to the party. Chafer and I had a rendezvous of our own for an unrelated purpose. Understood?" Lera finished, swinging her chin length dark waves to the men in the sitting area.

My voice choked in my throat. "Lera, I lost the babies. I'm not —"

"No, they're okay, Scar. The babies are healthy. He lied," Jett interrupted, and I felt my eyes start to brim with tears.

Lera cracked me across the cheek so it stung and I gasped. Brass shot to his feet as Slate growled and Jett shouted out. Lera held out a hand to them.

"If you want some jealous wife sending assassins after her because she cannot act, then by all means attack me now. If not, get downstairs and drink. Dance. This is a party after all."

That was why she was the Grand Mistress.

Jett and Brass hurried from the room both trying to catch my gaze, but I wouldn't meet it. Lera and Chafer left next leaving me alone with Slate. I heard the door shut at the end of the hall meaning they'd gone into the stairwell and I rose to my feet.

Hopefully, Orion remembered my dagger I'd left in Peak's throat. It was pretty incriminating.

Slate moved alongside me wearing a black waist coat over a long, black sleeved shirt. The cravat and waistcoat had a deep, bright green paisley embroidery that complimented his complexion. His hair was plaited back away from his face as he looked down at me.

"Scarlett —"

I held up my hand to silence him. "I need to get through tonight. Don't touch me, don't try to make me look at you, just be there. Try to manage that much."

I should have said thank you.

The night was a blur. I was so tired from fighting and healing, the competition and stressing out about the greater families being there. I would have been exhausted without everything that happened with Peak.

I'd gone to every table to make sure I was seen laughing and joking with Slate by my side, but keeping a safe distance away so he wouldn't accidentally graze me. Everyone except those who knew me best were fooled by my cavalier attitude and schmoozing. The spiky-haired DJ Haarder was there spinning my favorite modern music when Cocktails asked me to dance. I went out there and pretended I was a twenty-one-year-old girl who'd been asked to dance by a sweet young man.

My mind was clear. I had a hard time following along conversations I hadn't initiated. Moon, Fox, and Ash left with Ruby and Sterling. Sterling asked if we'd seen Peak, but he was only half interested since Quick and Indigo came down from the patron room glowing with their infatuation for one another. She could be seen with him; she could hold him and kiss him in public. She never could with Sterling. Quick had taken advantage of her euphoric mood.

Reed escorted Pearl home leaving Gypsum, Jett, and Tawny with us. Tawny and Gyps hadn't been fooled by my act. I suspected Pearl hadn't either, but she was better at feigning ignorance than anyone else I knew.

Orion never returned. I'd killed Sterling's father. He deserved it and would have killed Jett, Chafer, and me if Slate hadn't appeared with Brass.

"Scar, did Orion find you? He said he had to check on something, but he never came back. I'm worried," Tawny said, her face a mask of consternation.

"I didn't see him. Don't worry, it's late, or early, he probably went home. I don't think this is really his scene." I offered her a smile.

"You look exhausted, Scar. You should have gone home yourself. Come on, I'll walk you," Tawny said, looping her arm through mine.

"Wait up." Gypsum jogged over to us.

We waited to the side of the dance floor. The club would be open for hours after we left. Chafer had retreated into the security room and had likely fallen asleep from the all the healing. Lera was entertaining the crème de la crème of her patrons. Jett, Slate, and Brass had gone up to the bar once the Straumrs and Sterling had left. I didn't have the luxury to drown my memories in liquor.

Gypsum walked on our other side looking drunk and carefree. I became irrationally jealous and my temper flared. I kept myself from lashing out as we passed into the stairway where Breakers waited to blindfold people and lead them back to the portals. I took two blindfolds and helped secure them to Gypsum and Tawny's faces before looping an arm through each of theirs.

By the time we walked through Valla to the portal gate and I brought them both into Sumar palace, I was ready to sit on the floor and call it a night.

I trudged on and went to the Dagr palace. The warm air blanketed me as I passed the statues of the former matriarchs of the Dagr family. One of Sparrow had been added, and I thought it must have been sculpted by trolls by the intricate detail the artist managed to capture. Could a sculpture have an attitude? Sparrow's did.

One foot in front of the other, I kept telling myself. That's all I could manage.

Right foot, left foot, repeat.

Sparrow had gone home before I'd returned from Mabon, probably already in a deep slumber next to Hawk. I was feeling bitter.

Bypassing my nightly routine of growing the morning glory vine and confessing to it as one would a priest or trusted confidant, I opted for a long hot shower. I walked through my wing unbuttoning my gown with trembling fingers. I never wanted to see another topaz button in my life. I slowly removed my fetishes, hair fork, and beads before removing my corset and petticoats.

The heads of shower could swivel. I pressed the many heads to aim at me as I took my soaps to the floor and leaned against the wall. The water should have burned. My elemental power absorbed the heat internally, so it had no effect. I wanted it to burn, to scour. I could've used a steel wire pad to scrape away the layer of flesh Peak had tainted with his touch. Could someone hate their own skin?

I did.

Snakes writhed over my body. My skin crawled making me feel nausea rise and fall like an ocean's tide. I would be fine for a moment and then a memory would trigger the feel of Peak. He was dead. He couldn't hurt me again.

Lethargy and exhaustion weighed me down like leaden chains. I climbed out of the shower and completed my nightly routine of teeth brushing and moisturizing that would have made me frown on other nights but tonight I would go to bed with wet hair and likely sleep until noon.

The telltale sound of men's boots over the tiled floors outside the bathroom made my heart skip a beat. Were assassins there? Had Willow found out? Maybe I wouldn't make it through the night after all. I heard the soft creak of my big white bed and frowned. I doubted an assassin would be making himself comfortable in my bed.

I opened the door, prepared to berate Slate into leaving, and stopped. Not just Slate. Brass was making up a cot next to the bed while Jett and Slate were already laying down.

Determined not to speak to any of them, I went into my small room of a closet and pulled on a pair of bubblegum pink boyfriend sweats and a white, crew neck, long sleeve shirt. Not a single mark remained on my body that would denote the night I had.

My palms ran over my stomach. My babies were okay. Gods, if they weren't... I didn't think I could keep going. Not again. Not after everything.

"Scar? You coming to bed?" Jett called from the bedroom and my anger ignited in my veins.

I would not acknowledge them. I let my eyes slide over them as I came back into the bedroom and saw that they had each settled themselves into their respective sleeping spots. Two six and a half foot tall behemoths left a spot between them that I assumed they meant for me.

Didn't Jett have two wives to get back to? Nothing had changed that Slate needed to start sleeping there.

I was about to say these very things when Slate patted the bed next to him. "We could not decide who would watch over you tonight. To avoid a fight, we all will be staying. Do not bother trying to get us to leave."

They had left a separate blanket and pillow at the center for me. If I argued, I'd have to speak to them. If I looked directly at any of them, I'd likely see myself reflected back. Their version of me, damaged and frail. I kept my eyes lowered as I climbed up the center of the bed and slid my hand under the pillow.

Slate picked up the edge of the blanket and pulled it over me. I laid on my side facing Jett with my eyes shut. I didn't want to be alone. I felt cocooned by their warmth and love so I could safely sleep because the three of them would be there to protect me.

Damn the lot of them.

Jett hovered above me, dressed and giving me a small smile. "I've got to go, but Brass is taking my spot. Love you, baby sis," he whispered, pushing my hair from my face and planted a kiss on my cheek.

Jett was moved away, and the bed shifted as Brass took his spot on my left. My brain wasn't fully functional. Brass's hair hung loose brushing past his collar bones as he ran his thumb over my jaw. Brass leaned forward and brushed his lips over mine. I found myself kissing him back as my eyes slid closed. My hand placed over the one he had on my face when another hand over my stomach flexed.

"I am not in the mood to be forgiving," Slate said in a voice thick with sleep.

Brass withdrew from my lips and sensed his warm smile.

"Scarlett! Orion's been arrested."

Tawny's voice broke through my melancholia. I'd been drifting in and out of sleep all morning. Slate and Brass had stayed in bed with me unwilling to leave my side. I hadn't spoken to either of them. They tried to get me to eat, but I had no appetite. I was just so tired.

I rolled over away from Brass where he sat reading a book he'd gotten out of the Dagr library and turned towards Slate who was going over Dagr palace information, the day to day running of things; staff information, the small village that the Dagr oversaw just outside of the palace. I didn't even know the name of it and I was supposed to be the wife of Patriarch Dagr.

Tawny stood at the edge of the bed almost leaning over Slate's legs, heart-shaped face fraught with worry. I blinked at her, my mind numb and heart dead and unfeeling in my chest.

"Scarlett. Snap out of it. What's wrong with you? I said, Orion's been arrested for Patriarch Haust's murder. Did you know anything about this? Were you really asleep in the prep room last night or were you with —"

"What has Orion said?" Slate interrupted.

He wore a pair of drawstring maroon pants, loose and comfortable with bare feet above the white sheets. His mane was loose, free of beads and fetishes that fell over his shoulders just past his chest. Brass was dressed similarly though Brass's pants were a forest green. They must have picked up clothing while I was asleep and returned to annoy me. They seemed content just to be there and relax, which was completely out of character for both men.

Tawny didn't look to Slate but kept her eyes on my blank face. "He's confessed," she choked out. "They're still looking for Karkinos. They're going to put him on trial, if they find him guilty, they're going to execute him. Scar, he's saying he's guilty. What *happened* last night?"

Tawny was dangerously close to losing composure. That she hadn't noticed Brass and Slate were both in bed with me spoke volumes about her state of mind... and mine. I opened my mouth to test my voice and found no words at the ready. I had no opinion. It felt as though I'd been dropped into a sticky batch of tar. Blind and deaf, when I opened my mouth the thick substance filled my mouth leaving me mute. I wasn't panicking. I accepted, even welcomed it.

"Have they let you visit him yourself? Scarlett isn't feeling well. We're taking care of her," Brass reported before he picked his glass up from the white distressed night stand next to the vase of peonies.

Tawny noticed the two men for the first time and frowned. "I did. He said to let it go, but Orion doesn't benefit from killing Peak. He wouldn't. You don't understand how his mind works. He doesn't *do* things without a reason. *Please.* If you know something that might save his life... he's the only tie I have to my birth father, Scar," she pleaded.

"I'm sorry," I rasped and felt both men stiffen.

"For what? Scar, Orion said he went in search of Peak and found him with a young girl and grew enraged that Peak was cheating on Willow. Orion's claiming it was a crime of passion." She shook her head. "I don't believe it."

"If he is found guilty, you will take his place on the council," Slate noted and tears rolled over her fair cheeks.

"I'm not ready. Help me, Scar. I know you know something. Did Peak find you last night? Are *you* the girl?"

The tip of what would be a very long lance of pain, pierced me and I tried to keep my lips from trembling. "I'll talk to him."

Slate looked down at me. "I do not think that is wise."

"The trial is Monday. Peak's funeral is tomorrow. The council will be out for blood. Sterling is livid. I ran into him at the jail in Valla, he was visiting Orion. By the Mother, Sterling is his grandson. Have you spoken to Indigo? Has she seen Sterling yet?" Tawny asked.

I hadn't so much as moved my head. She knew I hadn't spoken to anyone, she needed to speak and wanted comfort. I could understand that.

"No. I'll go now." I started to push myself up with all the energy of a sloth and Brass tried to place his hand under my arm to help.

I yanked away using my precious energy to do so. "Don't touch me," I whispered harshly and Tawny started.

Brass froze and I could feel his wordless communications with Slate over my head as I scooted down the bed. I flexed my feet that hung over the side before stepping onto the floor. I couldn't bring myself to stand up straight.

I tottered into the closet and shed my pajamas before dressing in a moss taffeta gown with a pleated skirt and over my bustle. A velvet trimmed jacket that hugged my waist with pearl buttons. I wore the emerald drop earrings from the night before with my usual emerald wedding ring.

Under my bustle, I tied up my calf high brown boots and tucked a knife into each. Ignoring the men and Tawny in my Mabon styled clothing, I went into the bathroom.

My tan face had an unhealthy pallor. My normally bright turquoise eyes looked dull. After I wiped my face with a warm washcloth, I began to apply makeup so I could at least fake a warm glow. I pinned my unruly waves in a top reverse roll that sat low on my nape and secured the fork the leshy gave me into it as my only adornment.

I exited the bathroom to find Slate and Brass both dressed and armed as Tawny furrowed her brow at them. They must have changed right in front of her by the way she was blushing. I clenched my jaw but didn't say anything as I walked to Tawny.

"Lead the way," I told her, but she didn't move.

"Did you eat?" she asked, looking to the full tray one of the men had placed on the nightstand when I'd rejected it.

My annoyance piqued. "I go now or I won't go at all," I said brusquely and Tawny hazel eyes widened.

"You know what would be easier? If you told me what was going on," she said, fisting her hands on her hips.

For someone so petite, she had always had a mouth on her. I didn't have the energy to argue, so I left them all standing there to find my own way.

I knew where the jail in Valla was, it was in the university on the same floor as the hearing room. It was a temporary place for accused criminals until their trials or until they were transferred to Karkinos. With no Karkinos, there was nowhere to put the criminals. We'd destroyed the portal door when we rescued Slate. When Guardians tried to access it from Moon's office, it spit them back out.

Black cloaked Guardians with the silver interlocked triangles on their backs met me, Tawny, Brass, and Slate at the set of doors past the hearing room. A rose marble counter spanned the hall with a series of carved arch doors behind it. The Guardians recognized Tawny immediately and widened their eyes in exasperation at her presence.

"I want to see —"

"We *know*. Right this way. Two visitors at a time. Two of you will have to wait," a blonde bearded Guardian said, interrupting Tawny.

Slate and Brass didn't like the idea and glared at the Guardian wardens. "Just us two," I said in a peremptory fashion.

The Guardians took me in and I slid my blank gaze over them. "Prick your finger and press it to this. It says you will not attempt to break out the prisoner and will be peaceful during your visit. It is enchanted, so you will not be able to break it."

The blonde bearded Guardian pushed forward the contract that Tawny had already signed. I took the athame blade and pricked my index finger with its razor-sharp tip watching my blood bead over my skin and pressed it to the blood contract.

The man filled in my name and filed away the paper before the grey-haired Guardian led Tawny and I back.

The halls were unremarkable, but practical. We were led through a doorway that held a length of plain cells with an intersecting pattern of metals like the ones in Karkinos, but with larger slits so a man could fit his entire arm through, up to his elbow.

At the end of the hall was another door. Greater families had better cells. Thick glass pans barred visitors from a small luxurious room complete with full sized bed, a small table and two chairs. Orion sat at the mahogany table reading a copy of *Animal Farm* I was sure wasn't his. When he saw us approach, the Guardian left us alone, and we each took a heavily carved, wooden chair placed in front of the glass.

Only the nix torque around Orion's throat revealed that he was a prisoner. They must have let him dress before they took him, he wore a pristine white thick jacquard jerkin that made his blue eyes pop with color. He smiled broadly as he moved his chair closer to the pane.

"I expected to see you, Mrs. Tio. Are you well?" Orion asked, crossing his ankle over his knee.

"As well as can be expected." I told him straightening my skirts over the chair. "Is it safe?" I asked, needing to know if we could speak candidly. Orion dipped his head. "Why?" I asked.

Orion sucked in a steady breath. "Tawny, my dear. You know I have a great many secrets. When Ridge died, I gave up my position running the Stygian Knights, but I had bigger aspirations. I wanted to rule Tidings. The massacre the Red King Crathode executed was arranged by me. Ridge and Sparrow's carriage ran into the Crathode on their way to the induction ceremony. It was an accident — a terrible accident. I may not have killed Peak, but because I was deep in my grief, I did not abort the attack against the Guardians. All of those deaths fall on me. Peak drugged the drinks of his family. His own parents, Robin, who took her drink to the Geol table and shared it with Opal Geol enough to render her helpless when the Crathode attacked. He did not want to wait to inherit Mabon. He knew about the attack and set his own plans in motion. My goal had been Moon, but when you release a group like the Red Kings — I did not care until I lost Ridge."

Tawny and I sat stunned. My hand found hers, she didn't clasp it so I held on for both of us. Orion searched her face that had lost all color. She was too shocked to even cry.

"I told you this because I owe your family and Slate's. Pearl had her suspicions. She never liked me much. I suppose Ridge warned Sparrow, and that was why she took you and ran. This is the only way I can attempt to redeem myself. Nothing stays hidden forever. I do not expect you to forgive me. My only hope is that you will not hate me," Orion said, leaning forward as if he wished to hold Tawny.

She spluttered. "All of those people. For power? Hawk's father, Moon's wife, Slate's father, grandparents and aunt... Brass and Quick's mom. Scarlett never knew her family because of it. Her whole life... my whole... everything could have been so different." Tawny jumped to her feet and ran down the hall with the rapid click of her heels and slammed the wood door behind her.

I swallowed and sat back. Orion met my eyes. "How are you really, dear?"

"Not good," I breathed in a rough exhale.

Orion took a heavy breath. "I thought not. Do not let his actions define you. You are stronger than you think. I have never been a good man. I took Ridge for granted, and when I lost him, I became bitter. It was not until Tawny came into my life that I found happiness again. I would do anything for my granddaughter. Please help her through this."

I nodded. I would. Even if he hadn't asked me, I would always be there for Tawny.

"Why now?" I asked.

Orion's mouth quirked. "Canis is looking for pieces of Storm Natt's great work. I made an unforgivable mistake twenty years ago. I have a chance to help now. I believe you are the key to the puzzle that Canis is missing. Stay away from your uncle, dear. My wife has told him a great many of my secrets. I resigned as of today and Tawny will be the councilor for Elivagar and the Matriarch Vetr."

"Did Canis have my parents killed?" I asked, feeling my chest tighten as I waited for his answer.

Orion sat back on his chair and gave me a sorrowful smile. "I do not know for certain. If Canis had anything to do with their deaths, it was trivial. As much as Canis disapproved of Alder's choices, he would not have gone out of his way to kill his nephew. I believe someone else is the culprit, Mrs. Tio."

I rose from my seat and faced Orion. "Thank you. No matter what you've done in the past, I know you care about Tawny and I'll try to help her see that if nothing else." I started down the hall and stopped.

"Do I need to warn you against making accusations against Canis before you have all the evidence?" he asked, getting to his feet.

"No. Even with Sterling and Tawny on the council, I don't think Moon would give my hearsay a second thought. You were the one who gave the portable portal doors to the Stygians. Weren't you?"

I listened to Orion release a whistling exhale. "Yes."

I nodded at nothing in particular. "Thank you for taking the blame for Peak."

"It is quite literally the least I could do," Orion replied, and I thought he must be pressed against the glass behind me.

"I know. I still appreciate it. I won't let Tawny confess your sins. I think it would reflect poorly on the Vetrs and I need her. As my cousin and friend and as a council member."

"Welcome to the game, Mrs. Tio," Orion said, sounding regretful, and I heard him slide the chair back.

Slate, Brass, and Tawny were waiting outside the room with the rose marble counter. The yellow stone hall of Valla U was empty on a Saturday morning except for the four of us.

"What did he say?" Tawny said, wiping at tears.

Brass had wrapped his arms around her as she cried. He was good at that. Quick was notorious for his own version of cheering women up when they were down.

"My uncle is the other one searching out the pieces. He did not, however, kill my parents or order them to be killed. Orion's taking the blame for Peak. I can't talk him out of it. He's resigned already. I think he wants to die, Tawny. Without Karkinos... I think he's been waiting for something like this but didn't want to rot in one of those cells," I told her, tugging on my jacket hem.

Slate moved to place his hand on the small of my back and I started forward so his fingers missed me by a scant inch. "I'm going home. I've done all I can for now. I'm sorry, Tawny or should I say, Matriarch Vetr." I glanced up to give her an apologetic smile.

The tip of her nose had reddened from crying and she released Brass to loop her arm through mine. It felt good to comfort someone rather than receive it myself. I pulled her close as we walked through the halls of Valla U and we took her to the Sumar palace where Steel was getting ready to hunt for her.

I said my goodbyes once she was in safe hands and went back to the Dagr palace hoping Slate and Brass would stay, but once I was walking in the covered walkway they were walking a few paces behind me. I growled internally and started to devise ways to rid myself of my shadows.

Once I got back to my wing, I walked into the closet and changed out of my dress. I would ask Pearl about what Orion said later. For now, I had wasted my cherished energy and needed to recharge. I tied my champagne half robe around me and took my fresh pajamas into the bathroom for another shower.

Whenever I thought I was getting some semblance of normalcy to my life, the Norns threw me a curveball. I wasn't surprised that Canis was the one collecting the pieces. He was the Anguillan ambassador after all. A part of me was relieved he wasn't responsible for my parents' deaths. Who had hired the Stygians was still an issue, as were the Stygians in general. Did they want Slate back or were they through torturing him?

My brain hurt from so many questions. I wrung out my hair and got ready for bed though it wasn't even noon. My body was exhausted. All my sleepless nights were catching up in one single day it seemed. In my PINK sleep shirt and leggings, I went back into the bedroom with my wet hair braided in two to keep it from tangling.

Slate and Brass had made themselves comfortable in my bed *again* and I frowned. Were they waiting for me to have a break down? For me to talk to them? There was nothing to discuss. Brass and I hadn't been lovers in weeks and if Slate had wanted to be with me, I'd given him plenty of chances. I didn't want him to come crawling back because he felt sorry for me.

The best route was to ignore them until they went away.

CHAPTER 32
SLATE

Deflecting Lynx had been easier said than done. She had been stark naked when I had entered the patron room. I told her to dress and I would return what she paid for my time, but she rejected my offer. She wanted me, not coin. Lera's dirty secret was once we signed our blood contract, we had signed on to participate in the patron rooms. I had to stay in the room unless the patron released me early.

An hour and a half and she had stripped me down to my undergarments, eating delicacies off my body, *still* undressed. She had kissed me several times, and I had to push her away every time. Lynx was livid that I was rejecting her again.

The girl would be disappointed when she found out.

Brass was waiting outside the patron door and I had been furious. Was he spying for her to get back in her bed? Then he told me that she was missing, as was Peak.

Her bond was not active, and we had begun to search the bedrooms at headquarters until we felt her bond ignite with an excruciating amount of pain. She must have wiped her hand over her mouth to ignite the bonds all at once. There must have been a great deal of blood.

We could feel the determination and fear of her battle. Then there was shame and humiliation. It took all of my considerable will not to shift into my barghest form and crash through the floors at headquarters to get to the portal. The girl's emotions changed and she was terrified. It was not for herself; Jett was the only logical reasoning. If Jett had gotten to Peak and her before we had, she would be afraid for his life.

Her body had been incredibly beaten. If she had not been wailing and whimpering, I would have thought she was dead. That body I worshipped; her face mangled. It had not been a long enough fight. Peak had died too quickly; she had done it herself. She had to if she would ever recover.

Her macabre speech, Brass later told me, were words he had uttered to her when she defended herself against him. I had known and I had done nothing. I was the only one who would have been able to defeat the barghest void. If Brass had attempted with his team, they would have all likely died unable to meet the strength of the barghest hybrid void.

She was not recovering well. The girl would not eat, she was not speaking to those of us who witnessed her abuse. Our bonds were all active. Her emotions were scattered except for the constant shame. Jett, Brass, and I had gotten into a heated if short argument as to who would stay with her. No one would back down. Jett had to leave to take care of family matters but would return as soon as he could.

No one was to know what happened that night. Orion was taking the blame. Scarlett knew more but had gotten good at hiding pockets of her mind from Brass unless she was touching him.

She had been delirious with exhaustion when Jett left and Brass had taken his spot on the bed. The girl had kissed him. What had started as a friendly peck from Brass shifted as she'd run her hands along his hand. The scoundrel had gone along with it with me sharing the bed. She had yet to kiss me or so much as touch her. I had managed to hold her as she fitfully slept. Brass and I had slept little and decided to call a truce until she was better.

She had not said much of what we did not already suspect about her extended family. Brass had comforted Tawny when she had started crying. The girl did not have a flicker of jealousy when she saw them embracing. She trusted them both. I was not afforded that trust.

I ordered one of the staff to bring her lunch. Sparrow and Hawk had come by to check on her and saw Brass and I in the bed. Admittedly, it did not look wholesome, but they only inquired about her. Once they were reassured she was doing well, only feeling tired from the pregnancy, they left.

Now the girl was back in her pajamas and Brass and I had gone back to trying to stay near, but not underfoot. She might explode if we got in her way. Every time she looked at us, but did not meet our eyes, her fury surged.

Her loose shirt occasionally rubbed against the swell of her belly in a pleasing way that reminded me she carried bairn. When she had thought she'd lost them at Lera's, we thought she would give up. We should have told her right away that Peak had lied.

I picked the tray off the nightstand. Grilled chicken smothered in feta over a bed of leafy greens, tomatoes, cucumbers, and black olives with a chicken broth and noodles. She looked coolly at the tray and ignored it as she climbed the long way up the bed.

"Eat or Brass will hold you down while I shove it into your mouth," I growled.

She had the bairn to think of. She would eat. We would make sure of it.

Brass raised his gaze from his copy of *The Count of Monte Cristo* to her, letting her know he would do just that. She didn't meet our eyes, but we felt her aggravation as she snatched the tray away and leaned against the headboard as she began to eat.

Such a trivial thing, watching a woman eat, making sure she keeps herself fed. It satisfied something primal in me and I sensed it did for Brass as well. She finished every crumb and leaned past me to return the tray to the nightstand so she would not have to address me.

It took a great effort not to look down her shirt as it leaned from her skin. She had two braids in her hair like a young girl and one slid across my chest until she sat back down. The girl rested back in the bed and *called* water into her mouth.

Brass absently pulled her blankets up over her shoulders as she faced me and shut her eyes. We could feel her exhaustion through the bond. It had been effecting us as well making it difficult to not sleep as we watched over her. We felt the moment she dozed off.

"If you need to get more clothing, I will take first watch," Brass said in a low murmur.

"I had the staff bring over a bag." I slid off the bed. "I will shower first."

When I exited the shower, Brass was curled around her. Had she put her hand over his intentionally or while she slept? They were both asleep. Damn them both.

I climbed into the absurdly white bed and faced her. She murmured in her sleep and her lips curled. I knew that smile and with her in Brass's arms, it made the beast roar.

Then her hand left Brass's over her belly and I watched it slide over the narrow space of bed between us. I held my breath as her hand grazed me under the sheets. Nothing good would come of that right now.

She moaned and curled her fingers to cup me. Freya's burly boar, had she done this to him last night? I carefully unfurled her fingers in case she had a nightmare and fisted her hand while she clutched me.

She slid her hand over my waist and urged me closer with a hand to my ass. I did as she beckoned, only in her sleep would she allow herself to be vulnerable to me.

"You cannot go. I forbid it, Scarlett."

Forbidding the girl from doing things goaded her into doing them out of spite. I meant it though; she would not go to Peak's funeral and mourn him. He did not deserve her to feign missing him. All she did was scoff. Not a single word since her competition.

She slept in Brass's arms, but I had woken up to her forehead pressed to mine. When I raised my mouth to hers, she had kissed as if on reflex. Her body had squirmed on the bed as she began to awaken and I had withdrawn. It would have to be enough.

Jett had shown up to check on her and hung around until she fell asleep for the night. She was not speaking to him either. How does one argue when the other person refuses to engage?

I looked to Brass for ideas. He gave a slight shake of his head. I cornered her in the bathroom and stood behind her in the mirror as she applied cosmetics to her face. She would have to face me when she looked at her reflection.

"Do not go. It is not right. We can go to Chicago instead, order a pizza and rent movies — you, me, and Brass. We could invite Quick and Indigo if you wish. We will make a day of it," I urged and raised my hand to run it down the curve of her spine.

She nearly hissed as she side-stepped my touch. That was getting old fast. I wanted to grab her and shake her. To lay her down on the bed, kiss every inch of her skin and erase Peak's touch. I hated that he was the last man with her. It never should have happened. I should not have been with Lynx. When she found out Lynx was naked, licking juices from my body while she was fighting for her life she would despise me.

Brass had said he would not be the one to disclose what happened in the patron room. I could not tell her now and risk her not letting me stay close.

She wore a silk jacket in the Mabon fashion of a modest cut that covered her cleavage entirely with a ruched bustled skirt. She'd curled all of her hair, pinning it up with a small hat tilted towards her jauntily folded and blusher veil.

"Knock, knock. Is she in the bathroom?" Indigo's voice came from the bedroom.

"She is with Slate. Perhaps you can persuade her not to go," Brass said irritated, his patience was as low as my own.

She had refused breakfast and dared us to hold her down. We did not. All without words of course, but her emotions made things crystal clear.

"Do not count on her persuading her not to go. Indigo is going though I begged her not to." Quick's tone was hostile.

"Gods, not this again," Indigo mumbled under her breath so only I heard it with my heightened hearing.

The smell of freesia and honey preceded Indigo as she swept into the bathroom and offered me a small lift of her lips before she turned towards Scarlett.

"Hey. You don't have to go," she said, picking up a tube of lipstick and admiring the color.

"Peak was my business associate. He was supposed to be with us when he was killed. How would it look if I didn't show up? I'm the wife of the Dagr patriarch, my personal opinion of the man doesn't matter. He was killed at *my* construction site. It's bad enough my cousin's grandfather murdered him. I won't let these arenas die with him," Scarlett said firmly and Indigo held up her hands in surrender.

"I'm with you. I think we should all go, but I'm saying you don't *have* to," Indigo stressed and gave the girl a grin that quirked her pink lips.

Quick leaned in the doorway looking unamused. "I am not going and he was my uncle. Indigo should not be going, and neither should you, Scarlett. Since when you care about Guardian politics?"

Scarlett pursed her lush full lips that glistened with a shimmering pink gloss. "It's not politics, it's smart business. My absence would be noticed. Besides, Tawny has to go and aside from Steel, she needs someone to lean on."

"And who do you lean on, girl?" I asked too angrily, and she ignored me as she swept past Indigo and Quick.

"Do you suppose I could be content with all if I thought them their own finale? This now is too lamentable a face for a man; some abject louse, asking leave to be — cringing for it. Some milk-nosed maggot, blessing what lets it wrig to its hole. This face is a dog's snout, sniffing for garbage; Snakes nest in that mouth — I hear the sibilant threat. This face is a haze more chill than the arctic sea; Its sleepy and wobbling icebergs crunch as they go. This is a face of bitter herbs — this an emetic — they need no label; and more of the drug-shelf, laudanum, caoutchouc, or hog's-lard. This face is an epilepsy, its wordless tongue gives out the unearthly cry. Its veins down the neck distended, its eyes roll till they show nothing but their white, Its teeth grit, the palms of the

hands are cut by the turn'd-in nails, The man falls struggling and foaming to the ground while he speculates well."

Her brief pause was the most acknowledgement she had shown all day.

Indigo glared at me. Blue eyes liquified into icy depths. "What did you do now?" she hissed.

"I cannot keep up with you two," Quick said, shaking his head and holding out an arm for Indigo to follow.

"He hasn't done anything to her. Neither of us have. She is giving us the silent treatment. Jett too," Brass defended.

"I felt you. Through the bond," Indigo said suddenly, making Scarlett freeze in place. "I started looking for you with Silver, but then Lera told me to go mingle that it was under control." Indigo pressed her hand to Scarlett's and let out a heavy exhale.

"I'm sorry you had to feel that. I completely forgot about our bond," she said stiffly.

The girl sat on the bed and laced up her boots. Brass came around the side and knelt before her to help her buckle on her short seax and she placed the boot on his chest to keep him away before she shot to her.

Quick frowned. "Who did you bed? I have only seen her mad at you over women."

Brass got to his feet. "I have not bedded anyone except Rosasite which Scarlett knows about."

Quick chuckled. "Rosasite is pissed at you for ditching her Friday night. She has been to your rooms the last two nights and said you were not there. Where *have* you been? This is why you should never date Shadow Breakers."

"Just sleep with them," Indigo amended with a derisive sniff before she followed Torch out.

"By the Mother, how am I in trouble now?" Quick cursed.

Peak's funeral was a long affair. We sat between the Dagr family and the Sumar's as what remained of his body burned to dust. The girl sat with her fists balled between Brass and I, her jaw clenched as a muscle twitched above her eye. Quick did not come and Sterling had gone off with Indigo for a short time but did not return smelling like sex. They had gotten into an argument if the flush of her cheeks was any indication.

It had been a strange affair in which only his daughters had shed tears. Willow Natt sat with Sterling and her sister Delta stone faced. Rumors had begun immediately about Orion's accounting of the young girl he had found with Peak. The girl who had run off before Orion could identify her. We did not stay for the reception and returned to the Dagr palace seven long hours after we left. The human body took a long time to burn even with help from our *calling*.

She went straight into the shower; she had been showering at least twice a day. Brass and I suspected it was because she felt Peak's touch on her skin even now. Brass and I changed out of our clothes and used the guest bathroom to ready for bed. I thought about asking him to leave, and then I thought about Lynx. If the mulish woman was here alone for even a moment it would be unacceptable.

We both climbed into bed and I thought I knew what he was thinking. It was the same as what I had thought since the first night. Who would she face tonight? Who would get the kiss and who would get to hold her?

She opened the bathroom door, and I jolted from the bed, *calling* her robe, which she defiantly batted to the floor.

"Put some clothes on!" I shouted at her.

She emerged from the bathroom; hair dried in waves down to her elbows. Her lean muscled body on display, meticulously manicured and glistening with a sheen of moisturizer. The swell of her belly did nothing to diminish how breathtaking she was. On the contrary, it was a badge of her fertility and pure femininity you could not help but appreciate.

She ignored my outrage and leaned into the bed, her breasts like ripe grapefruit ready for the squeeze — or the taste. She purposefully prowled up the bed knowing full well how alluring she looked with her curvy backside in the air.

Damn the blasted woman.

Brass had frozen, apprehensive about his next move and decided closing his eyes was the best recourse. I picked up the tray of dinner and held it out to her, she ignored it and the beast growled deep in my chest.

"Eat your dinner, Scarlett. Under the blankets preferably," Brass said, sticking his nose in his book.

"You will not sleep until you finish your meal," I growled, seething with anger.

She laughed and I groaned internally at my body's response and caught Brass's scent spike.

"Who is going to make me eat it? You are both welcome to try," she said with a purr in her gravelly voice.

So that was her game. She thought she could rid herself of us if she could get us angry with one another or jealous. It would not work.

"Don't do that, love. This isn't you," Brass said in a soothing tone and her eyes flashed dangerously as she made eye contact with Brass for the first time in three days.

"Get out of my room. I never asked either of you here. It's my bedroom. You *both* are the intruders. I won't do anything stupid. I have my children to care for."

"*Our* children. I am as invested as Brass," I told her in a measured tone.

Brass momentarily looked as surprised as she did. He got off the bed and went into her closet and grabbed a long silver nightie then tossed it to her. The dress landed in her lap and she looked down at it. Hurt and rejection quickly masked by frustration stemmed through the bond. How I wanted to comfort her in any way she wished.

She pulled the nightie over her head and when I grabbed the hem to pull over her breasts where it had bunched, she cringed, but did not hiss. How she thought she would play Brass and I off one another when we were not allowed to touch her was anyone's guess. She held out her hand, and I passed her the tray.

A summer vegetable tian with melted cheese and a side of wild rice was licked clean. I took the tray from her without her having to ask and then she slid down against her pillow facing the ceiling.

"I'm sorry," she said thickly.

We had been waiting for her to talk about it. Bottling it up would catch up to her. I put down the Breaker updates I'd been shuffling through.

"No worries, love," Brass said with his endless patience.

I waited for her to say more. "I want to deactivate the bonds now," she said, swallowing.

Brass offered her his hand, and she slid her knuckles along fingers so their tiwaz tattoos touched. She dropped her hand back to the bed and Brass placed his book on the nightstand before he went into the bathroom to offer privacy.

With a snick, the door shut.

I shifted on the bed, careful not to touch her. My hands braced my weight to either side of her and she shut her eyes as if the sight of me pained her. The light kiss she had given me in her sleep had not deactivated the bond. The silver satin fluttered as she let out a deep exhale and licked her lips.

She was wide awake now. I lowered my head to slant my mouth over hers.

"Lynx was your patron, wasn't she?" she whispered.

"Yes."

Her eyes moved beneath her closed lids. "Did you sleep with her?"

"I did not," I whispered a hair's breadth away from her lips.

"You kissed her though, what else?"

She was rife with anxiety and I could practically feel how lightheaded she was. She was upset, *deeply* upset. Nausea was causing her stomach to churn and her dinner might not stay down.

"She had undressed before I arrived. She dined off of me, but I did not allow her to take it further," I told her firmly.

"She put it on herself too?" she breathed.

"Once," I confessed.

As soon as the word was out of my mouth, she grabbed the back of my head, deactivating the bond, and rolled away. "Get out. I made myself perfectly clear that when you left this bed, you weren't welcomed back to it. Please leave," she said in an even tone.

There it was.

Without the bond I could not tell how bad the damage was. Only Jett maintained his bond with her. Brass emerged from the bathroom and I began to collect my things.

"Sleep in the next room. She said her bed, not the wing."

Brass spoke so low; a human ear would not have heard him. He was one of a few people who could communicate with me in front of others and not be heard.

"What happened to you was not by choice, Scarlett. It does not count," I rumbled before I took a pillow and blanket and left the room.

CHAPTER 33
INDIGO

Never having said no to Sterling before and turning him down at Peak's funeral, when all he wanted was to get lost in me, had been one of the hardest things I'd ever done. I'd wanted to comfort him in any way, but I owed Silver at least a few weeks of fidelity. Besides, his betrothed was there as was half of Tidings. Not that that had ever stopped us.

He had been furious and wanted to know if I still loved him. Of course I did.

Then he'd gone on to accuse Scarlett of being the woman Peak was with even though he'd seen her himself at the Dark Shadows night club. I told him she couldn't be in two places at once. Peak had obviously had other lovers which wasn't that big of a surprise. At least two of the attractive staff members had been crying at the funeral in the bathroom and not in a way that bespoke of their respect for him as the ruler of Mabon.

I knew Sterling was right. I felt Scarlett's pain and constant abyss of shame until we deactivated the bond. Silver had darted out into the hall to see Slate and Brass running, likely to her rescue and he'd made sure I drank so much our bond was numbed. When I saw her at Dark Shadows

"

an hour later, it was as if it never happened. Her wounds weren't visible from the outside.

Sterling was the patriarch. He ruled Mabon. Tawny had taken Orion's place. Overnight, everything had changed. Scarlett wasn't speaking to Slate or Brass. Slate didn't surprise anyone, but Brass did. I wanted to be sympathetic to whatever they were going through, but Silver had been keeping me very distracted.

Since we announced our betrothal, he invoked a *No Clothing Once We Are Alone* rule. It was silly and childish, but the moment we entered either one of our bedrooms, or prep room, he began stripping me of my clothing. We were in what others called the honeymoon stage and it was fantastic.

Monday, Valla University classes were called off for Orion's trial. The entire family went to show support while his wife and daughters had shown up to watch Orion fall from grace. There hadn't been an execution in anyone's memory, not even the leader of the Red Kings had been executed.

The hearing had been horrifically short since Orion stood and entered a guilty plea saying when he caught Peak with the young woman, he'd *called* a blade to Peak's throat killing him. The girl got away and Orion had left his sigil ring with Peak's body so the Guardians knew who had done it. Orion was waiting in his portal room fully dressed and drinking wine when the Guardians came to arrest him.

Other than Tawny who couldn't bring herself to condemn her grandfather, every other council member voted for his execution. Orion was allowed to say his goodbyes since he had given himself over willingly, Guardian arrests could be brutal affairs.

To my surprise, Scarlett had hugged Orion when his own daughters had merely spoken a few stiff words. They were their mother's daughters. Cassiopeia hadn't even gone up to gloat. When everyone had returned to their pews, Orion was allowed to say a few words.

"Please forgive me, Tawny."

Orion's eyes gleamed as he slapped a hand to his mouth. Tawny was crying openly from where she sat in the Vetr council chair, wearing her newly fashioned scarlet robes with snowy white trim. A white auseklis emblazoned the back to match the carved chair and sigil that hung over her table edge.

Everyone was distracted by Tawny's uncharacteristic out pour in the hearing room until she cried out and the thump of a body hitting the tiles sounded. Orion had fallen over. Whatever he had in his palm had killed him on his own terms. Orion was dead. Tawny clawed her way past the black cloaked Guardians to get to her grandfather, but she was too late.

Steel had hopped over the railing that divided the pews from the dais and elbowed his way to Tawny. Sparrow and Pearl were already there trying to pry Tawny from Orion's body. Scarlett stood hands on the railing with Brass at her side and Slate on his side. They were both looking at her as she watched Cassiopeia who sat with Canis. A tangled web indeed.

Since the trial was over and there was no way to detect who gave Orion the poison, and perhaps because they were afraid to find out what an interrogator would discover, they let everyone return home. Orion's funeral would be the following day.

Tawny and Steel were officially residents of Elivagar. The matriarch and her consort. The staff finished moving them into the Vetr castle that very night. They were only a portal away and yet it seemed so final. I, Gypsum, Jett, and the girls were the last of them. Jett, Amethyst, and Cerise would leave us eventually too.

Silver hadn't said where he wanted to live once our two-year engagement was up. I hadn't planned on moving, but would he want to leave Pearl and Gypsum too? His family was all men, Coyote and Butterfly lived there with their two kids and she was pregnant with their third. Brass wasn't going anywhere even if he spent all of his time at Shadow Breaker headquarters, as did Silver. We should stay. I would have to find a way to bring it up.

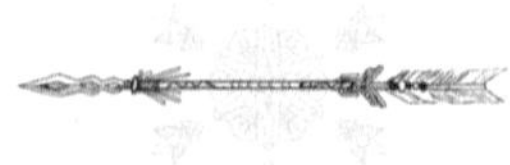

Jett and Scarlett were holding hands in Tawny's wing in Elivagar. Sparrow and Scarlett had taken on the task of getting her ready for Orion's funeral. It was being held on the lowest balcony where our mother's body had landed after her plunge from the bedroom.

Tawny was inconsolable. Steel was having a hard time getting her to do anything other than cry. Only Ruby and Jackal had shown up from the Vars, none of the Hausts had come, but the Straumrs and Tios were there. A few of the lesser families had arrived — it was a very small gathering for a greater family patriarch.

Hawk had set up extra Guardians to protect Tawny and Steel temporarily, since they were alone in the enormous castle. Knowing Orion from the time we spent together doing the arenas, he had already set up extra guards, the kind that weren't visible, like the Shadow Breakers.

Slate and Brass were still hanging around Scarlett to her consternation, but Slate had fallen further from grace so he wasn't allowed to be near her.

Fluffy white snowflakes fell from the grey sky as they sat on pristine white chairs to watch over the pyre. Tawny sat between Steel and Scarlett sobbing with them both cooing softly to soothe her. The only other noise was the crackling of the fire.

Silver held my hand directly behind them with Brass and Slate sitting together beside Silver speaking in hushed tones. The cold breeze kissed the gatherer's cheeks with frozen lips. All except Scarlett whose skin held a red tinged glow like burning embers whose heat I could feel where I sat.

Steel helped Tawny ascend the steps they had erected to send Orion's ashes into the wind.

"Lo, There do I see my father. Lo, there do I see my mother. My sisters and my brothers. Lo, There do I see my people. Back to the beginning. Lo, there do they

call to me and ask me to take my place in the halls where the brave may live forever."

Tawny spoke the traditional words with a trembling voice as she held out the white marble urn. Steel held her wrist as she walked back down the steps. The small crowd stood to move into the reception area and a Valkyrie spoke gently to Scarlett.

They were the only organized spiritual group in Tidings since the disbanding of the Brotherhood of Paragon. The all-female sect similar to nuns who worshipped Mother Nature were the ones who helped with funerals and took in orphans. They wore plain flowing robes of cream that covered their bodies loosely cinched at the waist by a brown silken rope.

"May I?" The woman's hood protected her shaved head from the biting winds on the mountain.

Scarlett nodded, and the woman placed her hand on Scarlett's stomach. She was an older Valkyrie, most of them were Pearl's age or older. This one's brows had lost all color and were now a shining white above big green eyes. The woman's wide mouth smiled.

"Two boys. Your husband?" The Valkyrie shifted her eyes to Slate who stood past Brass.

Scarlett's full mouth puckered as if she'd sucked on a lemon. "Estranged," she said in a tone so cool a sliver of ice must have pierced Slate's heart.

The Valkyrie smiled sadly. "Not his. You plan to keep them?"

Scarlett's hands shot to her stomach so abruptly I jumped. The Valkyrie's eyes glittered as Scarlett acted as if the woman would try to steal them.

"They would have to pry them from my cold dead body to take them and prepare to fight my spirit," Scarlett said with vehemence, and Jett sidled up beside her to lead her away.

The Valkyrie followed Scarlett with her eyes as Scarlett cast another suspicious glance over her shoulder. The woman placed a gloved hand on Slate's arm as he passed.

"To tame any animal, it must grow accustomed to your touch. Too soft and the animal will think you weak, too hard and the animal will fight. Time and care, and above all, trust. You have a long road ahead of you with that one," she said cryptically with a smile that led me to believe she was trying to lift his downtrodden spirits. She began to dismantle the steps, leaving Slate looking flummoxed.

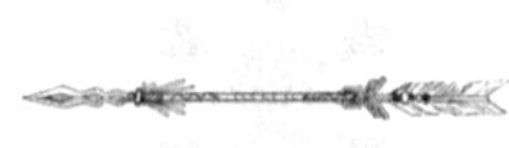

Steel and Scarlett spoke in rushed whispers in the hall when I came around the corner. He was a thinner, shorter version of Jett's gigantic form. His tan cheeks had blooms of red as they argued. Tawny came from the bathroom across the hall and inserted herself into the conversation. They hadn't noticed me yet.

"Do what she asks, Steel. If you don't, she'll do it anyway. With you at least an ambassador will be there so they're less likely to do something stupid. *Please*. For me," Tawny urged, barely coming up to his chest.

Steel ran his hand over his dirty blonde hair and nodded. What had he just agreed to?

THIRTY-FOUR

Tawny had decided with less than seven weeks left of classes before the Ragnarök challenge, she would return to Valla University. Since I would not be spending the night at the Dagr palace, I managed to ditch both Brass and Slate. Slate was in all my classes, but I could ignore him.

I'd dumped all of Slate's things outside of my wing. All the things he'd slowly been bringing in until I found out he'd been with Lynx

How that had hurt.

Lynx had been right that night, I wasn't sure about him. No matter how much he looked like my Slate, he wasn't. *This* Slate only sullied my loving memories of him.

My desperate attempt to be rid of both of them when I'd climbed into my bed naked had only succeeded in making me look stupid. I thought Slate would get mad at Brass and throw him out, then I could easily rid myself of Slate. It was Brass who I had a hard time throwing out of the room, not Slate. I had ample reasons to toss him out.

After Orion's funeral, I put my foot down with Brass and spoke to him for the first time since my naked night. He had a girl he was seeing and sleeping in my bed wasn't acceptable behavior. He'd said they were still getting to know each other, but I told him it didn't matter and to take Slate with when he left. Slate didn't listen, but it didn't matter. I was going to stay at Valla U during the week.

I had slipped Orion the unknown poison. He told me where to find it in his private office and how to slip it to him knowing the Guardian traditions when a man was convicted. A hug, a slip of my hand into his and the deed was done. When did I become this person? I understood wanting to die on his own terms and I trusted he wouldn't be slipping the fast-acting poison to someone else.

The arenas hadn't caught any flack in the trial, thank the Gods. Selfishly, it was what I had been most concerned about after Tawny's wellbeing. She'd be okay. She had already forgiven Orion and Steel was taking good care of her.

The whispers about our family that never seemed to cease and now included my supposed paramour, Brass and the continued fear of the vengeful Vetrs. Ash had to be the one who leaked the information about Brass. It helped that Brass and Slate were on the same side again, it didn't help that rumors about Slate carousing were everywhere I turned.

It had gotten so bad that my red headed extended Tio provosts had taken to giving me marital advice holding me after class while Tawny, Quick, and Slate waited in the hall. Slate had made me into what I hated most, a victim.

Tensions had grown between Sterling and Quick. Sterling was beginning to realize that the former playboy had set his sights on Indi and fully intended on taking her away from him. What Sterling had dismissed as a pointless fling had taken on meaning, and more than he could ever give her.

I left Magnolia Rot's Arithmetic class after a five-minute conversation about seeing to a husband's needs in barely contained rage. She was Crimson Rot's mother! Her daughter had slept with Ash when he was my fiancée! She had no right did she have to offer me advice. As well intentioned as it was, it wasn't welcome. I could tell Slate had heard it even through the door by the way he seemed to be looking everywhere but at my dagger eyes.

"What did she want?" Tawny asked in a hushed tone.

The yellow stoned walls of Valla U were beginning to feel like a prison. Just over a month, that's all we had left. I hated being pregnant there.

"I'll tell you in the prep room," I ground out as Quick fell back to find out from Slate.

Those two would go to Hawk's American History class while we would skip to an extra Battle Training course, though these days I'd done little more than practice with the dummies so I wouldn't get hurt. My sparring was restricted, and since the competition, I swore my belly had grown substantially. It was going fast and slow at the same time.

"How are the bairn today?" Slate attempted to engage me in conversation and it was exactly the worst moment.

I stopped in my tracks so Quick bumped into me, then grabbed my shoulders to keep me from bowling over. I turned around, startling them all. It'd been two weeks since I last spoke to him. He had spent last weekend on my couch since I banned him from the bedroom. Brass had stopped coming by after last Tuesday and aside from the weekend which he happened to be visiting the Sumar palace when I went for my Sunday dinner, I hadn't seen him either.

Being alone suited me just fine.

"Why are you wasting your time? What do you care? Unless I say otherwise, assume they are fine. All of us. Without you. Does that answer your question?" I seethed, craning my neck to glower up at him.

His face darkened. Slate was not used to people speaking to him that way. I wanted to argue so he would do what he did best and let some woman lick his wounds. I'd know my decision to push him away was best then.

Slate lifted his hand to where my black caftan hung from my slightly protruding belly catching me off guard with his tenderness and *called*. "You are right. They are growing strong," he rumbled.

My eyes widened in surprise. That hadn't gone as I'd hoped.

"Do you have everything you need for the challenge...or for the nursery? Is Indigo planning a baby shower?" he asked, making me feel like I'd fallen into an alternate universe.

Had he been storing up all of these questions for a time when I would start speaking to him again? I wouldn't let him reel me in. Two weeks hadn't erased the feel of Peak on me. I showered at least twice a day, in the mornings and after training, it wasn't enough. His filth was all over me. I was Lady Macbeth with blood on her hands.

I broke our gaze unable to hold up under that rare tenderness. What did he see now when he looked at me? Was it Peak, and the broken bloodied girl? Was that why he was afraid to fight with me — because I couldn't handle it anymore?

I itched to slap him. I spun on my heel and looped my arm through Tawny's and hurriedly led her down the grand staircase that led to the first floor.

"*Um...* that was weird," Tawny said, looking at me out of the corner of her eye.

"He won't even argue with me. Like I'm made of glass or something," I said peevishly and Tawny scoffed.

"I think he was trying to be nice. Are the rumors true? He's been sleeping with khorazes in Thrimilci? Is that why you guys are fighting?"

"We're not fighting. I don't have any use for a man in my life right now. He's stalking me again. Showing up where I live, sleeping on my couch... I don't need him looking after me, I do a fine job of it myself."

"Scar, I think ever since you had to take the rousen, your needs are different from other people's..." Tawny started, and I knit my brows as we entered the prep room.

"What does that mean?"

She slid her arm out from mine and wrapped it around my waist so she could lean in and speak in a hushed tone. "I'm not judging, I just think that... when your needs aren't met... you get kind of testy and irritable which is exasperated by your hormones. No offense."

"Oh. Well, since you said no offense... Are you telling me I need to get *laid*? I don't need to get laid, Tawny." I opened my cubby door muttering to myself.

"Why don't you call on one of the men who worship you to have a wild-no-strings-attached fling?" Tawny offered, putting on her black-on-black training clothes. "OH! What about Balas?"

"With my luck, I'll somehow get *more* pregnant and be some kind of human anomaly." I sighed.

The thought of any man touching me made me sick, but I couldn't tell Tawny that. She'd ask questions.

Diamond Natt passed by our aisle and I gave her a little wave. She had looked up to me at one point, I didn't know if she still did because Indi was sleeping with her betrothed. Though, I was that introduced her and Gypsum. She looked so much like Ash; the family resemblance was unmistakable.

"Hi, Scarlett. How's the pregnancy going?" she asked with that girlish tone she hadn't lost yet.

"Good, getting bigger every day. No more nausea, which is awesome," I said giving her a self-deprecating smirk.

Diamond giggled. "I am not looking forward to it. They will likely expect me to be pregnant this time next year," she said, twirling a chestnut lock of her hair between her fingers. "Do you have a minute?"

I gave Tawny a look, and she left the prep room giving Diamond a friendly smile on her way onto the battle grounds. Diamond was built soft, but curvy. Her full head of hair tumbled down past her caramel shoulders worn long in the Tidings fashion for girls our age.

"I do not know how to put it delicately, so I will just blurt it," she started, and I sighed.

"Go ahead. I doubt you have anything to say I haven't heard before," I said in an exasperated tone.

Diamond shook her head and knit her brows. "It is not bad. I heard that Slate lost his memories, or he has a block? My father has Alzheimer's. Ash keeps it at bay because he has a talent for mental manipulations. Did he not treat you a time or two when you were together?"

My mouth fell open, but I promptly shut it again. "He did. I probably didn't think of it because there's no way Ash will help me, let alone Slate. He hates us."

Ash had hinted at what he could do the first time I saw my father after I ran into him and my mother arguing in the hall at Valla U.

There was no way, it was kind of Diamond to think of something for us, but asking Ash would be making a deal with... whatever the Tidings version of the devil was. I was still updating my colloquialisms.

Diamond looked away with light green eyes the same shade as Ash's. "He does not hate you, Scarlett. He is angry you did not choose him. If you were to choose him... once or twice... he may help return Slate's memories to him."

I scoffed. "Sleep with him?"

Diamond shrugged her shoulders. "Maybe you have a better option. It was only a suggestion. Gypsum told me things have not been good between you two. Slate would forgive you if you got your memories back for him. Would he not?"

I licked my lips. *My* Slate. The man who made me fall in love with him, who had to be forced into dating Amber because he didn't want another woman other than me. I missed him so much it physically hurt. I would do a great deal to get that man back.

"Ash!"

All it would cost was a piece of my already stained soul and I might get my Slate back. The tricky part was navigating through Ash's sugar-foot to get what I wanted and make him think I would give him what he wanted.

Ash walked with Sage, Hunter, and Sterling from the prep room on their way to the dining hall before they went home for the weekend. I saw my opportunity while Jett, Tawny, Slate, Quick, and Cherry ate dinner and took it.

Ash's winged brows lifted as I approached on a mission. Sage and Hunter said some snide remark that made Sterling frown, but Ash only raised a hand to silence them. Ash was the leader of the mean cool kids. I liked to think we were the nice cool kids, but in truth we were a rag-tag band of misfits. Jett was adored by guys and girls alike and Tawny was respected as the heir, now Matriarch Vetr, but Slate had grown up as an orphan and womanizer. Quick was a known seducer, and Cherry hadn't been well known until she started dating Jett. I wouldn't begin to run down my laundry list of known faults.

"Scarlett? This is a surprise," Ash said smoothly, his sensual lips curling as his celadon eyes glittered.

"May I have a moment alone to speak with you?" I asked, seriously considering using my emotional manipulations to hurry it along but decided against it.

I checked over my shoulder down the long hall to make sure none of my family had followed me. "We can speak in my room." Ash watched carefully for my reaction.

I nodded, and he offered his elbow in a gentlemanly manner though the snickers from Sage were anything, but. Sterling placed a hand on my forearm and I paused to look at him.

His violet eyes scanned my face. A whirlwind of emotions soared through Sterling. He wanted to ask me if I was the girl his father was with, to know if Orion told the truth, to ask if I was all right. He wanted to be mad at me and to tell me not to go with Ash.

He shook his head as if to clear it and let his hand fall. I appreciated the sentiment and gave Sterling a reassuring smile as I let Ash lead me to the men's second wing of the massive, colossal castle.

When we were dating, I had strict rules about coming to his rooms in Valla U. I didn't want a reputation. Gossip was the number one currency.

I knew he wouldn't make it easy and having me up in his room so there was a chance I might be seen leaving it would benefit him and sully me. I didn't care. Not anymore.

He closed the door behind us and leaned against it, watching me. His room was set up the same way as ours; four beds spanned the square yellowed stone room with a stained-glass roof that cast brilliant shades of color across the room despite the brightly lit sconces. I sat atop his bed and waited for him. It was a Friday night, most of the students had gone home so there was a chance no one would see me leave.

"I did not expect you to come to me so soon," Ash said, taking in the sight of me on his bed.

"I didn't come here to sleep with you, not now anyway, but maybe soon if we can come to an agreement."

His eyes narrowed as he contemplated my words. "You put a high value on what many men have had."

I smirked. "But you still want, if I'm not mistaken."

Ash sniffed a laugh, and he walked over to his bed to stand less than a foot in front of me, his hand resting on the cherry post of his bed. "What do you want, Scarlett?"

I looked at him through my lashes with one of my smiles that made Jett curse. "I know you're very talented at mental manipulations. I want you to unravel the block on Slate's mind. I'm flexible on your price," I said nonchalantly as if we discussed a bag of apples to barter over.

"I want an elemental," Ash said in a measured tone.

"I thought you might say that. I don't plan on taking Moon's deal. What I am willing to bargain is a weekend after my children are born. You will have two days to try. That's it."

Anxiety ripped through me. I would have to sleep with Ash, but I would get my Slate back. What was two days when I would have Slate every day before and after that?

"A blood oath. Your first ovulation after you birth your twins. Three days," Ash said and then gave me a cocky grin. "And a small taste now."

"I need to think about it." I held out my hand then pulled it back. "*If* you can remove his block."

Ash's eyes slid to slits as he looked down his nose at me. "I can and will. When we are agreed."

"I swear I will spend a three-day period during my first ovulation trying to conceive a child *if* Slate's memory is returned to him. *When* I've made my decision."

Ash smiled. "I am looking forward to our practice."

It had been a very long time since I'd used *calling* on Ash for what we had called practice. He was as tall as Brass with chiseled hard caramel muscles, all the greater family sons had leaner looks compared to Slate and Jett. I imagined he spent a great deal of time to achieve his look until he was what he believed perfection should look like. It was spoiled by how ugly he was on the inside.

There were worse things I could do for love. I'd worry about our bargain after I had the twins, not before. I wanted my Slate back. Ash walked me back into the hall.

"Let me know what your decision is. The longer you wait, the longer it will be until your husband's memories are returned," Ash said smugly.

"You will be the first one I tell."

Slate had hated when I used *calling* on him. Brass was indifferent, but felt *calling* was an addition to the physical not a supplement for. Power of any kind stimulated Ash, he liked what my *calling* could do to him.

Men heading home for the weekend walked through the halls. I was one of a handful of girls in the men's' wing tonight. Sterling and Hunter were hanging out against the stone wall outside the door and straightened when we exited the room. They weren't the only ones I recognized. Dinner had already ended and Jett, Quick, and Slate were coming from the wing entrance to their shared room. They were standing stock still.

"Can you do it now?" I asked Ash, not taking my eyes off my brother whose chiseled face was darkening.

"I suppose," Ash said as if I bored him.

"Are you coming with me tonight?" Sterling asked. "My sister is expecting you."

I cringed inwardly at his blatant insinuation. "Thanks for your time," I said to Ash.

Hunter chuckled amiably and Ash shot him a glare that made his laughter taper off into coughs. "Excuse me, gentlemen," I said

Quick's upper lip curled in a snarl as I approached. Slate's face looked sculpted of actual bronze it had gone so stony.

Slate went rigid. "Did you fuck him?"

I swallowed praying my traitorous cheeks wouldn't flush. He knew I hadn't. "He might be able to help us."

"Scar. Please tell me you did not promise that asshole anything." Jett spoke in a tone reserved for insolent children. I was in no mood for his criticism.

"No promises yet," I said and my cheeks finally gave in.

"No use in arguing in the hall," Quick muttered and pushed past us to go to their room.

Since Quick and Indigo got together, he was treating me like the sister he never wanted. His grudging support constantly shocked me at unexpected times. Slate and Jett folded their arms and stared broodingly at me.

"I'll see you guys later. Nothing happened. No promises were made," I said leaving the men's wing.

It was dark when I awoke. I tried to shoot out of bed. Nothing about my senses told me where I was. I woke up with anxiety ripping through me more often than not since Peak first forced himself on me.

Arms banded around me and lips pursed shushing me in my ear.

"You are in our bed," Slate rumbled in my ear.

My stomach flip-flopped. "You snuck into my bed?" I squeaked.

"Our bed. Brass tells me you do not like to sleep alone," he said, shifting on the bed.

My chin wobbled as I suppressed tears and I realized whatever walls I had built around me were starting to crumble. I should have made the bargain with Ash. This could be my Slate I was in bed with.

"Is it so bad you cry?" he asked.

"I miss him," I squeaked.

"He is me."

I swallowed.

"Your scent says I am enough of him that you would bed me. You *have* bedded me. Quite enthusiastically, I might add," he purred.

The room was too dark to see much, but I could feel him. "My Slate would understand why I would've made a deal with Ash. He wouldn't like it, but he would do the same for me. He'd sacrifice a great deal for me," I whispered thinking about all he had done already.

"Like save you from a barghest?" Slate asked.

My body went rigid. Slate's hand had been tracing the swell of my stomach and I hadn't realized it. His palm went flat to my skin.

"Thank you... for saving me... and letting me kill him." I sighed, hoping he didn't want to talk more about it.

"I only regret I could not kill him once more after the deed was done." His hand heated against my skin as he delved to check on the babies. "I care a great deal for you. Did your version of me not make mistakes?"

"He's made his mistakes. I can't *live* through them all again as you fall back in love with me, it nearly broke my heart the first time. A second time is too much. I wouldn't be the same once it was done," I whispered.

"After you lay with Ash? You will be unchanged? That is the deal you made, is it not? He wants your bairn," he asked.

"Three nights of my life to have you back for the rest of my life."

"The rest of *my* life, girl. Which may not be much longer with the prophecy. It was a foolish deal, and you were a fool for thinking of it," he chastised and I rolled in his arms to face him.

His silver eyes glinted like a creature of the night from the sliver of moonlight. No other feature of his face was visible in the dark.

"Even this version of you, I never want to hear you talk about it." I couldn't stop myself from cupping his face.

"You love me more than any one man deserves," he breathed.

"I should have loved you *more*. I never should have left you."

His hand closed over mine. "Did you not learn? You should trust me now," he insisted.

I bit down on my lip and he eyes flared. I sucked in a sharp breath.

"Goodnight, Slate," I whispered. "I am glad you're here."

Slate seductive scent made my head spin and insides pulse. The part of my mind that the rousen enhanced became intoxicated on his pheromones and I had to stop him before it started. He may not be my Slate, but my body knew no difference.

"What did you do with the Straumr boy?" Slate growled frustrated with me.

"I didn't touch him," I swore.

Slate leaned his head forward, hair scratching against his pillow until his lips brushed mine as he spoke. When I licked my lips, I caught one of his with my tongue and froze.

"There's no such thing as just a kiss with you, Slate Dagr," I said, feeling the tug to him.

"Have you tried enough times to be certain?" he purred and sucked my lower lip into his mouth, running his tongue along it.

I pulled my lip back. "I have. If I am going to stay in our bed tonight, you can't be doing that."

I slid my palm up his jaw and fisted his hair close to his nape and claimed his mouth with my own. My tongue found his and his arm pressed my back so my belly rubbed against his muscled torso.

"I need you to stop," I breathed between kisses.

"Hard... when you have my hair," he growled, and I kissed him again, sliding my leg over his.

"Okay," I said, releasing my grasp and throwing my hands up in surrender.

Slate pulled his mouth away with a growl of a groan.

"Soon," I said, climbing between his legs and resting my cheek on his chest.

He folded me into his arms. "Better be."

CHAPTER 35
JETT

Cherry's libido was always a bit more desirous than your average woman's, but with her pregnancy Amethyst and Jett were pressed to keep up with her need. Another benefit of multiple spouses illuminated. Jett landed a satisfying smack to Cherry's backside as she bucked against him.

She would have giggled, but her mouth was otherwise occupied. It was a particularly strenuous midday adventure while Gigi took her nap. Jett couldn't think of a single way he'd rather be spending the glorious Thrimilci afternoon.

The door to their bed chamber crashed open and Amethyst yelped at the intrusion. Cherry was undisturbed, but Jett released her hips out of propriety's sake. Jett tossed a blanket over Cherry who laid on her stomach next to a furious Amethyst.

"She is gone. We ate breakfast. I told her I was training at headquarters and asked her to meet me here for a late lunch. She is not here; she is not at the Dagr palace and she was not at headquarters. Would she have gone to Ash?" Slate asked, not registering Jett's two naked and ready wives on the bed, nor Jett's total nudity.

"I was kind of in the middle of something. Can you come back in say five —"

"Fifteen," Cherry shouted.

"Fifteen minutes?" Jett asked.

"Brass said she has not been there. Her bond is not active and Indigo had not seen her either," Slate said, taking up the decanter of a sweet red wine and pouring himself a goblet.

Jett blew out a gusty breath. "What about Gypsum, Quick, or Tawny?"

"Quick was with Indigo. It did not look like they had left the bedroom today. Gypsum is not here and Tawny is in Elivagar. I will check there." Slate guzzled the last of the wine and slammed the glass on the pedestal table.

"Indigo and Quick were in her bedroom? Did you walk in on them too?" Jett asked coolly.

Slate looked to the bed for the first time and grunted when Cherry waved. "My apologies, ladies."

Jett looked at the girls and Cherry grinned. "Wait, a moment. I'll join you."

Cherry pouted until Amethyst pulled the blankets over her head and a fit of giggles bubbled up. Slate cocked his head like a dog.

"Does that make you jealous?" he asked.

"No. Why would it? They don't use up all of their pleasure before they get to me, I bring something completely different to the table. Don't even think about trying for a second wife. Scarlett would never go for it. Now, a second husband should be fairly easy to persuade her of. So, you spent the night? Knowingly or unconscious the entire time?" Jett asked as he dressed.

"Knowingly. She said nothing of Ash at all in this bargain she is contemplating. Only that she must spend three nights with another man during her first season after the bairn are born before we are able to have more of our own. In truth, if we did not wish to have any children, she would not need to fulfill the oath at all," Slate said in earnest.

"Scarlett can be dangerously clever at times and at other times she lets her passion get the best of her. With you she hardly ever uses her head. Where do you think she's run off to? Did you get into another fight? Should we go to Chicago?"

Jett was dressed similarly to Slate. A black sleeveless linen shirt with two wooden toggle buttons on the left side of his shirt tucked into black fitted pants paired with black calf-high boots. His boots had golden tree of life buckles while Slate's had a matte black solar cross. Slate wore his wrist blades and the crossing of dagger belts over his chest while Jett strapped his two long seaxes over his shoulders so the pommels peeked out. A dozen other knives were hidden about their persons as well.

"No fight. Last night went well, she stayed. I do not think she ran either. She is hoping I get my memories back soon."

"She'd do anything for you. Foolish girl. Tawny first. She hates Ash, she won't be with him," Jett told him. "I bet she can't stand giving him ammo to taunt you. We might catch her flogging herself somewhere or doing something else to punish herself." Jett shook his head.

"She is not dealing with things. It is bound to catch up sooner or later. I need to be there when it does. It is the only way she will trust me again."

Jett smirked as he led them out of his wing. "I was meaning to ask you. Is it strange to have her love you, but not you. To have her miss you and wish you weren't yourself? It gives me a headache just thinking about it."

"You are a smug bastard," Slate growled as they walked to the portal door.

"If you won't tell us where Scarlett is, when it's obvious you know, could you kindly lower yourself to inform us where your brother or Steel went instead?" Jett asked in a sickly sweet voice.

Tawny sat in her white office behind a big black marble desk going through all of Elivagar's day-to-day paperwork. Jett was not looking forward to the day he would take over Ostara. Her fair heart-shaped face appraised them both. She had Guardians trailing her everywhere, not to mention the Shadow Breaker that was hiding in the darkest corner of the room cloaked in shadows.

"They're all together. To tell you where one is, would be telling you where they all are. Scarlett isn't stupid, she knows she can't do things alone anymore. She asked Steel to help her days ago and Gypsum happened to come over and Steel asked him to come with because she forbid the two of *you* knowing where she was going. The Regn too, that's why Indi doesn't know so she wouldn't have to lie to her fiancée." Tawny picked up her pen again and began to scratch on the paper.

Jett counted to ten. A matriarch already so he couldn't throttle her for the answers. Those Guardians would kill him or try before he came around the desk.

"Tawny, if you don't tell me, I'll have to use my superpower. We both know what happens when I do that. What will Steel say when he finds out you've had your tongue down my throat again? What will the girls think? They'll probably think that you've wanted to get me into bed all along. They're probably right," Jett taunted and her face turned an alarming shade of tomato red.

Divine beauty strikes again.

Slate was doing a good job of keeping out of her striking distance. Those two got along like oil and water.

"You *wouldn't*. Steel trusts me, and the girls know I would never ever have had sex with you. I've only been with Steel!" she said, looking to the Guardians to see if they were smirking or laughing at her, but she would soon find out you did not laugh at a Vetr unless they laughed first.

"You're sure, are you? I don't know if I could stop you if you tried to take advantage of me. Then you'll have been with two men, Tawny." Jett gave her a smug grin and she spluttered indignantly. "Slate, Tawny wants to test her will against my wiles. Please close your eyes so you don't try to bed me as well."

"Done," Slate said, promptly shutting his eyes and Tawny gaped.

"They're with the Merfolk," she said defeatedly and slumped in her chair. "They're probably there already. They left late this morning."

Tawny ran a hand over her long dark waves looking much too grateful for not having to fight herself from jumping Jett when he used his talents. Jett had a mind to do it just to vex her, but he was too angry.

"The Merfolk! Is she out of her mind? She's completely lost it this time. She's gone crazy before, but this is too much even for her!" The Guardians looked uneasily at Jett who paced the marble shouting into the air. "What was Steel thinking? Dion're and Non're will never let her go. She was trained by them on rousen for *days*! She'll tear off her clothes and beg them for it within fifteen feet of a Merfolk. Look how she is with Slate! If she's not screaming at him then she can't stop herself from trying to lay with him. She doesn't even *like* this version of him!" Jett shouted and dry washed his face crouching.

"Thanks," Slate said dryly. "Come. We can go now."

"You're serious? She's probably already..." Jett trailed off after one look at Slate's glower. "Steel might be able to hold her off for a little while. We don't have much time. She might be a barghest khoraz like you say, Slate, but she's definitely a Merfolk one. She won't be able to get near one without wanting to... Okay, okay. Never you mind. Thanks, Tawny."

Behind the Sumar palace, Steel kept his rafts docked for travel. Down the river Sol under the high afternoon sun was no picnic. The last time they were making this trip, Ama and Shale were with them to rescue Scarlett. Most humans died after being on rousen for so long. They didn't crave food or drink or even sleep, only pleasure. To give and receive it. Slate had found a way in a rewards-based system to get her to take care of herself, but she was never the same again. A door had been opened that never closed.

Jett steered with the tiller as Brass used air against the small sail and water in the river to push them along. Typically, the race along the desert landscape took about three hours. With their combined *calling*, they might make it there in two and a half. Thrimilci fishing villages consisting of small adobe houses in creams and browns lined one side of the river. Canyons sprang up shortly after, red rocks that looked like they erupted from the earth. Coconut trees, cacti, and scattered greenery sprouted along the shore.

Brass had remained silent for the ride to the Merfolk. For once, Jett was glad Slate didn't have his memories. If he had, Slate would have been murderous, now he was only violent. Violent was manageable.

After all, he had controlled himself enough not to shift in front of Ash yesterday.

That was enlightening. He was none too happy about being left behind, but if he couldn't rein in his temper, bad things would happen.

They pulled into a dock where several other rafts were and handed a man a rope to tie off the raft. Docks and rounded thatch huts lined the coastal white sand beach. It was a trading post of sorts. Humans accustomed to Merfolk, mostly men, and Merfolk alike traded within huts. The Merfolk had strategically placed shells, scales, star fish, kelp, and other ocean debris. Otherwise, they were completely nude with purple and green, even blue tinged skin.

They had gills under their chins and angled features with pointed ears, eyes that tilted up that were all iris and pupil. Women were a rarity around Merfolk because their bodily fluids were toxic to humans. Especially women. Guardians *calling* didn't help against it. Merfolk were addicted to humans, their warmth in particular.

A lone woman ran changing huts, Brass and Jett put on their swim shorts and checked their things with the woman so they wouldn't have to dry all of their weapons and would have clothes to wear when they returned.

Brass and Jett had strapped short seaxes to their biceps before heading into the ocean.

Merfolk had a sixth sense for "gifts" they had received before. Slate had not been gifted but taken by their princess Larn'ra when he was fourteen. He had shifted into a barghest for the first time afterwards. The Merfolk that walked about stared openly at them like choice cuts of meat for their devouring. The way they behaved with Scarlett would be worse because she was a woman and had been with the Merfolk for days longer than Slate had.

In the water was a highway of sorts, Merfolk transformed the second they hit the water. Gills flared, where there should have been a nose was a flat mound blended along with the cheekbone. True forms were revealed. For some that meant iridescent fish tails, others it was tentacles. They all had long flowing hair in the water, or tentacles that coiled from their scalps.

The king's coral palace was deep in the water. Its spires wound high above the ocean floor; the coral palace was alive with creatures. Fishes swam in and out of little coves, its colors brilliant. Merfolk were swimming through what appeared to be an entranceway. Jett had seen it a dozen times and it managed to take his breath away every time. The Merfolk were the most seductive of Tidings' tribes.

There was a standing wall of ocean water where the entrance met it like a window, you could stand with one foot in the ocean depths and the other dry inside the palace. Brass and Jett's air bubbles, that allowed them to breathe under the water, burst upon entering the dry sand.

"We'll go to the court first," Jett said, wiping droplets of water from his face.

Brass's silent contemplation extended to the palace. "I am surprised he stayed behind. It wasn't as easy last time." He sighed, swiping his hair back. "This could be bad."

"I know," Jett said solemnly.

Slate had been irate when the Merfolk had Scarlett last time. If Scarlett were to lay with one of the Merfolk, it could cause her to miscarry just from their seed alone.

The floors were sand, the walls were a porous sea foam rock. Enormous pearls hung in strands along the walls attached to globes of light and star fish chandeliers. Pearlescent clam shell doors lined the halls. There were no guards. Everything about the Merfolk drew you in. They wanted you there, they wanted *you*.

Merfolk were pouring into the court and Brass and Jett shared a panicked look. The others had to be in there. The court was where the Merfolk king sat. Pillars ran from floor to ceiling; the floor looked like polished marble and had the feel of ancient Grecian design.

Jett's breath caught in his throat. Steel and Gypsum stood at the foot of the dais where three thrones sat. Sear're the king's advisor and enforcer of Merfolk law, held back Steel and Gypsum with arms outstretched in a friendly, but firm manner. What was a shark on one side, was a man as tall as Steel on the other. Sear're had long black hair peppered with silver streaks, his skin had a blue tinge and around his large pupils was bright blue. He was Steel's friend and the easiest Merfolk to deal with.

In the throne to left was Larn'ra. The princess had long blonde hair like her father with strands of pearls that dangled down the length of it. Her top was even made of pearls, her skirt though shimmered with diamonds. Her green eyes stood out against her peach skin and her eyes were focused on the actions before her.

Non're sat to Dion're's right. His powder blue tinged fingers clutched the arm rests of his pearl throne as he watched Scarlett, barely able to contain himself. He had a skirt made of kelp and pearls that did nothing to hide his arousal for her.

Powerfully built, like all the Merfolk, the Merfolk king was putty in Scarlett's hands. Dion're wore a skirt of sapphires and pearls and didn't look a day past forty. Merfolk were long lived, even longer than Guardians. The young princess herself was over fifty.

The gathered crowd of bright Merfolk seemed to roll and lean towards Scarlett. She had pulled the stopper on the purple vial of rousen when she reached the top of the dais and nocked it back into her mouth. Groans and moans were emitted, knowing the royals would be first to have her.

Scarlett wore an iridescent shimmering white bikini that did little to hide her body or the swell of her stomach. She turned towards the king whose lips were parted visibly from his long blonde beard. Her skin glowed a warm red and The three royals squirmed in their seats eager to touch her.

Jett put his hand on Brass's shoulder to stop him from moving forward. Scarlett threw the glass vial, so it shattered on the dais and her fingertips grazed along Dion're's thigh. Steel called out something to her that was hard for Jett to hear from too far back and Jett looked to Brass.

"He said not to do it," Brass said.

Everywhere her fingers grazed brightened his peach skin to salmon as if heat infused her touch, which it did. Dion're's bright blue eyes stared at her as if she was his own personal deity and would take him to the halls of the afterlife if he could only touch her. Scarlett ran her palm up his chest and along the glossy blonde beard at his chest until her hand twined around it. Her mouth moved with unheard words before she crushed her mouth to his. Light illuminated Dion're's skin as her heat warmed his cold blood. Jett watched, mesmerized, as her heat unfurled in his taut stomach that heaved with his heavy breaths.

"She said, 'If you had kept me all three nights, they never would have hurt me,'" Brass said, not taking his eyes off Scar.

She deepened the kiss fisting her hand in his hair in front of the entire Merfolk court and Dion're shuttered with a low moan heard even where Jett stood in the back. Brass pushed up against Jett's arm.

"Wait," Jett said in a hushed tone.

Scarlett pressed kisses along his cheek to his ear and whispered. Jett looked to Brass.

"'If you had made the effort to seduce me, I may have gone to your bed willingly. I am sorry for what I have to do now, but a lesson must be taught. No one takes from me what is not freely given','" Brass repeated for Jett and his stomach dropped.

It happened in a blur. Scarlett twirled away from Dion're and her blade flashed in Non're's lap. She was already at Larn'ra when Non're started screaming, his blue tinged legs and polished white chair colored by his blood. Larn'ra never saw Scarlett coming as she yanked back the princesses head and shoved the sliced off appendage into her mouth. Scarlett held her mouth closed and ground something out.

"You can go fuck yourself," Brass said, and Jett glanced at him to find him smirking.

Larn'ra spat as soon as Scarlett released her jaw. Steel ran forward and did the dirty job of healing the Merfolk prince as Larn'ra wretched. Scarlett looked unsurprised as if she planned for Steel to do just that. She held up two more vials of rousen and faced the crowd.

"You all have seen; I am capable of great pain and great pleasure. If you care to take a gamble on your most prized organs, I will take rousen every three hours and if you make it past me, you can have me. If not, you will *never* take another Guardian against his or her will even if they're on rousen and think they want you. Non're, you owe me something." She sauntered over to where the seething prince had been reattached and held out her hand palm up.

"'Give me the piece or I'll incinerate all Steel's hard work','" Brass repeated as Scarlett's mouth worked.

Non're glared at Scarlett and for a moment, Jett thought the prince would attack her even with Steel standing right there. Sear're was standing next to Gypsum as entranced as the rest of them. Non're wore a clamshell necklace and yanked it from his neck with a fist and thrust it at Scarlett.

She said her thanks and descended the dais with Larn'ra retching and Non're glaring. Dion're was completely enamored and hadn't moved since she'd withdrawn from him. Not even when Non're had screamed.

Scarlett's hips rolled as she sauntered with Sear're, Steel, and Gypsum barefoot, but somehow regal. Her swollen breasts jiggled in her bikini top from before her pregnancy. The Merfolk didn't care about her threat, they looked as though they planned to test her before she made it from the court. It was lucky Jett and Brass came when they did.

Scarlett was giving cool looks to the court when her nostrils flared. Her head whipped around and her eyes settled on Brass and her lips parted. Turquoise was swallowed by the black of her pupil as she neared with a fluidity to her steps.

"I thought you said your boyfriend was not coming," Sear're said, flashing three rows of sharp teeth as he spoke.

"He shouldn't be here," Scarlett ground out. "You have to leave. *Now*," she said to Brass and moved past him, but not before she breathed a lungful of air as she came near him.

Jett knit his brow at Brass and saw that he too was staring after her. They fell in line behind Gypsum and Steel.

"What were you two thinking?" Jett asked, following them up flights of porous rock steps.

"She was going to come without us. There wasn't much of a choice. Either that or Tawny would come with. I never want her to come here, no offense Sear're," Steel said.

Sear're sniffed. "None taken. I cannot believe you brought *her* back here. They will be lining up to try you even if that means you chop their cocks off. Out of curiosity, what will you be chopping off of the women?" Sear're asked wryly.

Scarlett's profile smiled at Sear're and she glanced at Brass out of the corner of her eye. "I don't plan on dismembering any of your people, only beating them senseless. I need a room with only one way in and out and preferably available from intersecting halls so there are several directions for them to move about. You have to leave, Brass," she said, casting him another glance, her pupils were the size of saucers, her movements slinky.

"I'm not leaving, love. This wasn't smart," Brass said in a smooth soft tone and Sear're smiled.

"I see nothing has changed or has it? Where is Slate?" Sear're chided.

"It's a long story." They came to a room at the end of a long hall with another bypassing it. "This will do," Scarlett said and Steel groaned aloud.

"I don't like this plan. Sear're is right," Gypsum said, wrinkling his forehead but wary of her.

"Me neither. But look."

Her provocative smile made Jett curse. She cracked open the clam shell around her neck and pulled out a rigid piece of stone triumphantly holding it for them to see.

"Five pieces left. Four still need to be discovered, but I have a good feeling about the Lycans, so that makes three. Mabon has to have at least one, I plan to find Lewt, the Centaur chieftain, and see if he offers any information on it. I promise, I have a plan. First things first. You guys go have fun. I'd appreciate dinner brought up with an empty goblet, I won't be drinking anything here in case someone tries to drug me. I have everything else I need as long as there is a chamber pot in the room." She looked to Sear're who chuckled.

"Garderobe," he answered, and she wrinkled her nose.

"Wonderful. Everyone knows the shave and a haircut knock, yes? Since Sear're is the only Merfolk, I trust not to take advantage of —"

Sear're cleared his throat. "If it is all the same to you, I will take my leave before I find out what this 'shave and a haircut' is. You may prove too much temptation for me after what I saw you do to Dion're. I will see you in the morning, Scarlett."

She pressed her lips together in consternation but nodded. Scarlett turned to the four remaining men.

"Gypsum and Steel can take the room on the left, Jett on the right. I'm serious Brass. You can't be here, it's not that I don't want you here." She was anxiously rubbing her arms now, the first sign of the rousen in her system.

"Because you do not want me to stop you from —"

Jett wiped a hand over his face. "Because you're too much temptation. By the Mother, you can read minds, but not body language? She doesn't want *them* so she fights it."

Scarlett's high cheeks flushed as she averted her gaze and looked to the clam shell door. "This is the knock. I'll only take food from one of you." She demonstrated a beat of knocks as a code for their entry so she wouldn't blast one of them into smithereens if they opened her door. "I'm not asking you don't hook up with anyone while you're here. They're not all bad but be smart about it." She said looking at Gypsum who blushed.

"Not going to happen, Scar. I am staying in the room until morning unless you need me. How are you going to sleep?"

Her tan muscles flexed and relaxed, then flexed again as she tried to control the rousen's effects. It would start to hurt her soon. Rousen could feel like raw nerves as if burned when at its height when you weren't receiving pleasure.

"I won't. I'm not worried about that. I'm concerned more than one will come at a time and I won't be able to deliver wounds that will incapacitate them as opposed to kill them."

She let out a shuddering breath. Her eyes blatantly scoured Brass and her fingers curled as if she itched to touch him.

"*Gods*, get him out of here," she ground out as she let her head fall back as if the Gods would listen and he would be beamed from the Merfolk palace.

Scarlett reversed into the door shutting her eyes and Brass's hand snapped out to run a thumb over her tiwaz tattoo. She groaned.

"In case one gets by," Brass said roughly as if the rousen in her system affected him too.

Her laugh is low and throaty making the men she was related to uncomfortable. "You're going to want a separate room, Brass. Not a lot of foresight put into that, was there?"

Her gravelly voice had dropped in a breathy tone best reserved for bedrooms. Scarlett opened her eyes and Jett was thrown back to the day they rescued her from Non're's pleasure. Her full lips seemed somehow plumper, almond eyes glassy, skin glowing. She smiled knowingly at them.

"I didn't think so," she said when Brass only stared, obviously struggling with his own demons. "Food. Please. I don't plan on being dressed so perhaps Jett should bring it. He's used to it. Not Brass. I cannot stress that enough."

With that, she slammed the purple iridescent clam shell door but didn't lock it.

"Do any of you have nix torques?" Brass said through a clenched jaw, staring at the door.

"She thought it would be a good idea, just in case." Steel held up two sets of nix cuffs with the chain that led to cuffs for ankles as well, their pewter metal shone dully in the globe lights of the hall.

Brass nodded. "Activating the bond may not have been my best idea. I dare not touch her again. If I become... difficult, you have my permission to cuff me."

Jett and Steel shared a look. That must have been hard to admit for Brass.

THIRTY-SIX

After the first twenty Merfolk tried to get into the room, they started to get smarter. The last four had come in two at a time. My nudity on the satin circular bed wasn't helping matters, but I couldn't stand my clothes touching me. Poor Brass would be having a time of it wherever he had chosen to wait out the night. I could not stop touching myself.

I was mostly knocking the Merfolk unconscious and Gypsum or Steel would drag the bodies away to be healed. I expected a lull at some point and then it would be hard not to fall asleep after using so much *calling*. Luckily, I was stimulated beyond reason and practically clawing the walls in aggravation.

Tossing and turning on the bed with my blades unsheathed beside me, I wondered for the millionth time what room Brass was in. They were my worst-case scenario safety nets. Not a single Merfolk had made it past the thresh hold, but it was early.

My empty tray sat on the floor beside the door. I didn't risk losing myself in the palace. My theory was correct. I was a Merfolk khoraz, but

I had also developed a high tolerance to the sweet concoction. The vials I had were actually watered down from when Chafer gave them to me the night of my last competition. It had been a friendly gesture in case I wanted to back out of killing Peak and tolerate his touch better. Three full vials would have lasted a long time, but he hadn't been sure how high my tolerance was.

Performing a penectomy on Non're had been horribly satisfying. Shoving it in Larn'ra's mouth was even better. I wished I could've thought of something of hers to chop off, but it had been a spur-of-the-moment kind of thing. Kissing Dion're was not nearly as bad as I had thought it would be. He was a good-looking hybrid, and if I was the kind of girl who had meaningless flings, I *might* have welcomed him into my bed before he took what wasn't offered.

The knob began to turn, and I didn't bother sitting us when three Merfolk shadows were cast over me. With a flick of my wrist, I sent two men and a woman flying down the hall. I started to use my *calling* to shut the door when two more coming from either side of the hall charged through the door.

A challenge.

I sat up and rolled away relishing the feel of the satin on my skin while blasting them with water forcing them to shift into their fishy forms and then knocked them from the room like swiping dust from my doorstep.

I slammed the door behind them and sighed. As long as they didn't touch me, I would be fine. I had to keep the room dark so I wouldn't see them, their scents alone was enough to keep me dangerously close to the edge. I ran my palms over my skin feeling it prickle and tighten deliciously, I rolled back and forth tangling my hair around my face. Gods, that felt good.

The shave and a haircut knock sounded, and I stopped. "Who is it?" I asked in a voice way too throaty to be mine.

"Steel. Just checking. Need anything? That was five at once this time, they're getting more organized," came his muffled voice through the door.

"No. Thanks. Is Brass still here?" I asked, unable to stop the thrill that ignited at just his name through my veins like lightening.

"*Um*, he's right here," Steel said hesitantly, and I shot to my feet and pressed my body against the concave door.

I imagined I could catch his scent, that his body heat could penetrate the door. Fiddlestick the door, what about me? I groaned and thought I heard someone inhale sharply on the other side. Brass?

"Is there something you need?"

Brass's smooth deep voice vibrated through my bones sending a wave of pleasure crashing over me. I wanted him to keep talking. I didn't think I could get the word out since my mouth had desiccated from his satiny smooth tone best left for a more sated mood.

"No," I whispered.

"I'm going to talk to Sear're and see if we can get you a short reprieve," Jett answered.

I nodded at the door. "They won't but thank you. Don't drink anything you didn't get yourself. Non're and Larn'ra will want revenge."

I waited hoping Brass would speak again, but he didn't.

Hours.

The Merfolk were coming less frequently and dawn had to be right around the corner. It was impossible to tell under the ocean if the sun had come up. I was exhausted, but mostly, I needed the rousen out of my system. I had just taken the final vial when Jett had let me know it was time, and another strategized attack of four had come hoping to catch me off guard.

They were wrong.

No one had died, but a few had been seriously injured after hitting their heads the wrong way when I flung them back. I ate another meal, steamed salmon and kelp which never failed to surprise me with how good it tasted. Then I laid down on the bed and talked to the twins about nonsense. I sang and drew over my skin with my fingertips and then grew too frustrated to come up with words until I satisfied my urges for a short time.

The shave and a haircut knock sounded, and I steadied my idle hands. "Yes?" I squeaked, irritated, trying to even my breaths.

"Love?"

I sat up and licked my lips. "You can't —"

"Dion're proclaimed any Merfolk found guilty of taking a man or woman against their will would be castrated or the female equivalent. You can relax now. He also banned any others from trying you. Dion're wants to offer you a formal apology in the morning once you have rested," Brass said from behind the clamshell door.

I'd won. What had happened to me would never happen again without serious consequences. I got to my feet and turned the doorknob, too happy with the news to think.

Brass.

My insides coiled painfully just by the sight of him, dark honey, sculpted muscle from head to toe and amber glittering eyes that saw through to my soul. I felt weak and invigorated at the same time.

Time slowed.

I *called* as my mind fell away. I'd been doing so well.

Suddenly, I was back on the shore the morning they'd rescued me from Non're. Brass understood what I was going to do a second after I'd already done it. Ropes of air bound his arms as I pulled him into the room shutting the door behind him.

"Scarlett," he said huskily, but I had already slipped those tiny swim shorts over his hips.

I straddled his powerful thighs as I licked along his chest dusted with silky dark hair and traced hard brown nipples as his breaths came shallower.

"You're not thinking clearly... you should stop."

I smiled devilishly at him as I scooted up his body and claimed his mouth. Not once did he say no or don't, or even that one of us didn't want it. They'd all be lies. He wanted it. I wanted it.

Brass moaned against my mouth as I wrapped my fingers around him not able to touch fingertips to tips. He had come like this knowing it could happen. I yanked back his head and seared his throat with open-mouthed kisses, swirling my tongue along his skin that radiated its own heat.

My ache consumed me as I lowered myself onto him. I moaned aloud and Brass's muscles flexed against my ropes. With our bond, we wouldn't last long. My lust was his, and his was mine. I'd been on the brink all night; I just needed that push.

"Release the *call*, love," he said with emotions that ran from guilt and self-disgust to love and desire.

I didn't release him. I could barely find words once my free fall began. I had almost begged for him to leave. He shouldn't have been there. I was attracted to him on my best days, this was far from my best. My muscles clenched around him and my *calling* slipped as I threw my head back and let out a high-pitched moan. I was just getting started. Brass's body had stiffened beneath me, but he was rousing and held tight to me as he rolled us over the floor so my back was against it.

"You're going to regret this," Brass said breathlessly.

I shook my head and ran my fingers along his stubbled jaw and into his hair so it fell free around his face. I fisted my hand in it and dragged his mouth to mine. He sucked in a sharp breath but let me kiss him as I squirmed with him between my legs. He caught my wrists and pinned them gently above my head.

"I can't read your mind when you're like this. What do you want, love? Besides the obvious. Are you sure you want —"

My wrist slipped free of Brass's hand and I ran my palm along his backside as I rocked my hips. Brass's lips parted as he tried to steady his breaths.

"*Shit*, Scarlett. I'm not a strong enough man to deny you. Slate. *Shit*."

Brass was talking too much. I wrapped my legs around his waist and hooked my arms around his shoulders as I moved beneath him. He groaned. I could tell he was debating whether to let me use him and he'd be utilized like a tool, or if he would be a participant. I knew what Brass could do. I wanted a very active participant.

"Brass," I whispered, finding my voice and sucking on his earlobe.

The spike of his scent that I was lucid enough to remember words much less his name was as much as me declaring my undying love to him.

We all allowed ourselves a lie or two now and again.

Brass unwrapped my leg and pulled it up as he began to kiss me deep and passionately as if we hadn't done it in ages. As if I was some long-lost love he'd found again and he wanted our first love making after our absence to be the best we'd ever had. Brass was a mind reader and he was nothing if not a sensual man.

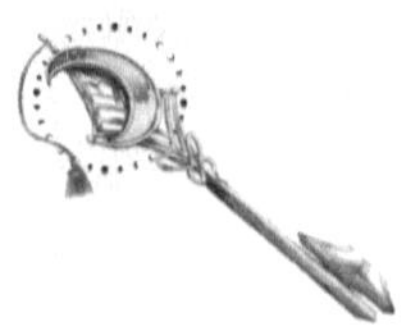

No move or touch or taste was wasted. Brass hadn't lost the road map of my body and knew every turn to take by heart. The rousen certainly made his life easier, and I wondered if he could still climax by the time I'd fallen out of his lap and sprawled on the bed.

I doubted he could. My whole body was deliciously sore and my throat dry from my cries. Brass was like an artist in the bedroom. My body his blank canvas.

He fell back and pulled me up the bed so he could hold me, tugging the dusky pink sheets over us.

"That was very brave what you did. Do you feel better?" Brass asked.

I exhaled. The rousen had begun to wear off a while ago. I was not going to divulge how I was feeling about myself at that particular moment so the distraction was welcome.

"I do. I feel like I'm taking charge of my life again. I didn't realize how sweeping what happened under the proverbial rug would not let me get on with my life. Now I just need to find those four pieces, steal the fifth from Canis, and find the works."

"But first, sleep." Brass's hand emanated warmth through me and I sunk into darkness.

Cinnamon and fresh rain on a field of wildflowers. I heard a door-knob turn and stretched. My cheek stuck to the chest of a man. Brass. I heard a gasp and a curse.

Brass's muscles went rigid under me and pulled the sheet up to my shoulders where I laid between his legs.

"*Uh*... you're here." Jett cleared his throat awkwardly, "I wasn't sure if you had gifted yourself."

"We wouldn't have come in; except we've been knocking, and we were worried." Gypsum stepped around the bed and faced the wall so Steel could come in after him and shut the door.

I rubbed my eyes that felt dry and gritty. Brass *called* and handed me my discarded swimsuit.

I felt sick. "Actually, Steel do you have the... thanks."

Steel handed me a taupe colored tankini halter top with a metallic white trim. I slipped under the dusky pink sheets and my eyes widened. How did I forget Brass's splendidly naked body? Times like these made me hate that Brass could read my mind. Brass did not have the same issue I had, he slipped off the bed and pulled on his shorts in full view of my brother, my uncle, and my cousin.

"I wouldn't be anywhere else," Brass said as he started buckling his blades around his biceps after he pulled his hair back into a knot at his nape.

Jett looked between Brass and I making me feel ashamed. "My mistake."

"Are you ready to accept your apology? There will be many very sore Merfolk attending," Steel said with reddened cheeks as he tried to look anywhere, but at us.

"I am. I'd rather just leave, but that would be rude. We should go right after." I stopped short of saying I was exhausted and further shaming myself.

"So... this is happening again?" Gypsum asked deliberately.

I stood tossing off the sheet and running my fingers through my hair. I needed a shower, but it would have to wait until we got back. I rubbed my wedding ring and bit my lip.

"Can we have a moment?" I asked, wishing I had more clothing to wear.

Slate would smell Brass all over me the second I saw him. They left the room leaving me and Brass alone. The tension was palpable. We both started speaking at the same time.

"Go ahead," I said sheepishly.

"I'm a mind reader," Brass said, giving me a slow, warm smile.

I sat on the bed and smoothed my hands over my hair. "Freya's burly boar. I don't even know what to say. He'll never forgive me."

"He loves you. If he had his memories, he would have been with you and if he wasn't, he would forgive you. You were on rousen. He might kill *me*," Brass said sinking down next to me.

"He loves you. You're his brother. He loves me, but he's not *in* love with me. I'm sorry, Brass. I couldn't help myself. You'd think I'd get sick of screwing up all the time." My brow furrowed as I shifted my head to look at him.

Brass cupped my face. "I'm sorry."

"Don't be. I forced myself on you." I fell back on the bed; Brass fell back and met my eyes. "*I'm* sorry."

Brass slid on the bed so our noses touched. "I wish I could regret it. I could not stop myself either, love."

I felt myself sinking into his amber eyes. "That's the problem, isn't it? I don't feel regret. I'm only upset that Slate will be hurt, or angry, or... he might kill you. I'm only partly joking."

His plump defined lips brushed mine as he spoke. "I'm in love with you, Scarlett. I'm sorry if that makes your life more complicated. I knew what might happen if I came to this room and I hoped that it would. I've missed you."

"You shouldn't say those things," I whispered.

Brass tilted his lips to mine. "Say it out loud. Just this once."

My breath hitched, and I shut my eyes as I swallowed. "I'm in love with you, Brass," I whispered, feeling a thrill shoot through me and instantaneous guilt the second after sinking like a stone in my gut. "I'm a terrible person. I fell in love with my husband's friend. This is an affair, isn't it? By the Mother, I am such a bad influence on you. What about Rosasite?"

Brass looked away and ran a hand over his face. "I had not thought of her until now. It is not an affair, love. It was one night. You will tell Slate and deal with the consequences. I will be there to help you. That might have to be in the figurative sense."

I scoffed. "We should go. Are their thoughts as horrible as I fear?"

Brass looked back and rolled over me so his forearms were braced to either side of my head. I should've felt more guilty. Since I was going to hel anyway, another kiss wouldn't make it any worse. Brass slanted his mouth over mine and my skin tightened all over my body.

"Their thoughts are not as bad as my own," Brass purred.

The vibe was very different from yesterday. I walked with Brass on one side and Steel on the other with Jett and Gyps behind us. Dion're still wanted me, even after what I had done to his children. Granted they deserved it. His bright eyes followed me as if was the only person in the room as I approached the dais in a much more modest swimsuit than I'd worn yesterday.

"Guardian Tio. It grieves me that you felt the need to defend yourself and the honor or your people against my subjects. I would like to apologize to you formally for the suffering you have endured.

Dion're beckoned to a pair of his subjects who carried in a treasure chest. Dion're kicked open the lid to reveal pearls and all kinds of colorful ocean baubles. Steel leaned into me.

"It would be an insult not to accept it. He means to make amends," Steel whispered.

"Thank you, your highness. I humbly accept," I said in a clear voice.

"Scarlett." Dion're lowered his voice and stepped off the dais. "May we speak?"

I nodded despite Brass's rigidity.

We walked a little ways away. Not too far that Brass couldn't read our minds.

"You do not have to leave," Dion're began.

We walked in the narrow hall behind his dais the court visible at either end. "I do have to leave. I'm pregnant, Dion're."

"Then return once you birth your children. You may bring them here with you."

I looked to him to see if he was joking. I would never get used to their nose-less faces. A beard should have a nose to top it.

"And do what, Dion're?" I asked, shaking my head.

Dion're stopped me and we faced one another. He smelled like the ocean. They all did. Not like fish at all, but of cool waters and hot sand.

"As my Queen. It is allowed by our laws," Dion're said with his large pupils scanning my face.

"Dion're, you don't love me. You love how I make you feel. I'm already married. My sons have a father who loves them. Your son and daughter…"

He held up his hand to quiet me. "Yes. It was my mistake. They have their mother's cruel streak. I thought Larn'ra would stop Non're from harming you. I was wrong. She harbored hate for revealing her involvement with the traitors," he explained and I nodded.

"I know. I have a feeling… if you knew about the situation on how I arrived in your bed chamber that day, that you would've freed me. I *do* know that you didn't believe that I truly wanted to be there, otherwise you wouldn't have kept it a secret from Sear're," I said dryly and Dion're's lips quirked from within his long beard.

"As usual, you are correct. Have a safe journey, Guardian Tio. You are always welcome here," Dion're told me, looking like he very much wanted me to kiss him again, but I didn't.

THIRTY-SEVEN

On the shore, they collected their things and waited to eat a late breakfast until they got on the raft and were on their way home. Scarlett sprawled out on the front of the raft to soak up the sun. A little vitamin D and some quality thinking time. Gypsum soon joined her on one side while Steel perched by the tiller.

Brass had heard what Dion're said and had not been amused, Jett and he were on the second raft behind the others. Jett guided the raft while Brass sat, leaning against the short wall, *calling* the wind into the small sail.

"Go on. Let it out," Brass said as the desert whisked by.

"You are undoubtedly better for her. Stable, even keel, love her without all the extra lovers even though you have one right now," Jett said without looking back at Brass. "Which we all know, in some backwards way, is for Scarlett's benefit."

"*But...*" Brass urged in an amused tone; he already knew what Jett was going to say.

"But you and Slate struck a deal even though he doesn't remember it. She's going to grow old with you, you are going to have children with her. We're not all blind, we know she loves you. She also loves him... very much. His time is limited. That he fell for her is a miracle. You couldn't have let him have her *now* as your creepy plan dictated? They were getting back on track." Jett exhaled gustily. "He isn't there yet. He's going to lose it. Old Slate, maybe he would've gotten over it because he was crazy about her. *Seriously* crazy. You should've stayed away last night. It was a dick move."

"You're right, on all counts. It was a Silver move. I lose my head when it comes to her. Selfish, lustful, even a little manipulative. If he wasn't going to die soon, he would understand." Jett turned around, and they shared self-deprecating smiles.

"She's going to tell him, and you're going to have to be far away when that happens," Jett said in total seriousness.

"I can't leave her."

Jett looked back at Brass again. "Frigga's sweet grass. What does she do to you idiots? No offense. You, Slate, Ash, the fucking Merfolk King, that Lycan... Keen, well, he's married now... that asshole she killed." Jett sighed and faced where Scarlett laid on the raft. "You have to back off. Give them a fair try, Brass. I know you love one another. You'll get your chance, but not now. Not while he's alive. She's his wife, he *needs* her. If all this prophecy stuff is true, they're meant to be together."

"It's their destiny," Brass agreed.

CHAPTER 38

INDIGO

A single choice could change the trajectory of a life's path, of many paths. Within an hour, you could go from having the world at your fingertips to having lost everything.

Amethyst and Cherry were in their rooms. They'd been there since the messenger in the Straumr's livery, the deep purple cloaks swept through the Sumar palace. Bad news shouldn't be brought with grown men who wear purple velvet.

A bedraggled-looking Scarlett had returned from the Merfolk with Brass, Jett, Gyps, and Steel. Slate had taken one look at them, nostrils flaring. There were a few growled words to the top of her hanging head, but the only ones who would have heard were Brass and Scarlett. Brass left shortly after. They had been vague on the details. Scarlett clammed up and put on her brave face.

It wasn't until Pearl handed Jett the scroll from the messenger that they were yanked from their own pondering. Jett had dropped the scroll and ran from the dining hall to the girls and Steel had picked it off the tiled floor.

"Moon Straumr is dead. While he was out riding, his horse led him right over the cliff side. Reed is acting Prime until another can be elected. The funereal is in two days." Steel said swiping a hand over his face. "It happened this morning. I've got to go to Tawny. Gyps..." Steel shook his head. "Not this time, chief."

Gypsum drew down his thick raven brow looking defiant. Diamond. He would want to comfort her. Sterling would be with her.

"The Hausts and Straumrs will be mourning together," I said cryptically but knew he would understand.

Huge white silk tents had been erected on the front lawn of Valla University the same way they were for the induction ceremonies. The Guardians were a sea of black clad bodies in the forward-facing rows of seats.

Sparrow insisted on sitting next to Slate and I thought it took all of her will power to not try to hold his hand. Slate was acutely aware of her and it was hard not to snicker.

The family had sent a messenger to Amethyst and Diamond at the Straumr palace and received one in return, it was vague and I guessed that a lot of people had sent messengers and they had someone else writing their responses. It was the first time I'd seen any of them since the messenger arrived. They had moved into the Straumr palace temporarily to help with Moon's arrangements. Jett held Scarlett and I for a long time when he saw us.

"This has sucked pretty damn bad," he said as he leaned against me.

"Don't worry, after this we'll get you guys home and take good care of you all." I tried to soothe him, and I heard him sigh.

"Thanks for watching Gigi for us, it's been crazy," Jett said, releasing me. He looked like he hadn't slept in days. His watery eyes were bloodshot.

"She's a sweetheart. It's no problem. You're giving Silver ideas though," I told him with a smile.

Sparrow and I were watching Gigi during the day and Pearl had moved her bassinet to her room. Gigi was getting a lot of family time in.

I was holding her during the funeral. Poor Gigi was pooped. She slept with her head on my shoulder, my forearm under her backside. It was probably the sad songs the choir was singing on the dais that did her in. At least she wasn't crying.

We sat in the third row with the other greater families all around us, I had to dull my borrowed empath abilities because the emotion in the room was a depthless ocean of grief. Pearl and Scarlett's mouths were pulled down in permanent grimaces. Moon may not have been loved, but he was respected. The choir's sad song ebbed and flowed like the tide. The power of music never ceased to amaze me, the effect it can have over a person's emotions. You could feel the crowd's response to the doleful song.

I could see he back of the three Straumr brothers' heads. Crag, River, and Fox sat together with Amethyst. River's wife and kids on Fox's right side with Nova, Jett sat on Amethyst's left with Cherry and Jackal. In a surprising turn of events, Basil was made patriarch of the Straumr's being the next oldest Straumr and Crag having rejected it. Ash's father didn't look like he wanted to be wearing his brother's mantle.

We had been sitting there for an hour when the choir sang their last song and lit the pyre behind the dais. An emotional surge through the Guardians caused bile to rise into my mouth and I swallowed it back. Silver looked down at me, but I shook my head. I leaned forward and saw Pearl frowning as well. It was too much for empaths. Scarlett held her hand over her mouth as if she might empty her stomach in full sight of them all.

The cool fall breeze brought fresh air into the cramped tents every once in a while and gave new meaning to the phrase 'breath of fresh air.' The tents had grown stuffy with all the people crammed into it and more waited outside to pay their respects. We were obligated to stay until the end because we were members of a greater family, that meant another six hours.

Another singer came up and belted out slow heart wrenching ballads. It was going to be a long day.

I started to get antsy around hour number three but didn't want to move around and jostle Gigi. A crying baby in the middle of a funeral wasn't entirely out of place, but I didn't want to place any undue stress on Jett and the girls. My head started to swivel around looking for familiar faces.

I spotted Sterling and ducked my head. We were best friends as well as lovers. We were always together, all our classes together, ate lunch with one another until Diamond came to Valla U and then in one night it was all over. I was glad Silver had been staying with us. Even if he was making it too obvious, our family was used to seeing him in the mornings and since we were formally engaged, it wasn't as unseemly as it could have been.

Six hours, two diaper changes, and a bottle later. Gigi was wide awake in my arms as Crag *called* Moon's ashes into a silver brushed urn with an embossed crescent moon. A set of stairs had been constructed on the hillside and those of us who had made it through the seven-hour ceremony filed out of the tent to the hillside where the branches of the Yggdrasil held up Valla University. There were hundreds of people gathered.

We spread out around the Straumrs as Crag approached the stairs. I bit my lip to keep it from wobbling, I was being swept away with the sorrow. Tears came unbidden and Silver put his arm around me. The Valkyries in their plain robes hummed and swayed with their hoods pulled up.

"Lo, There do I see my father. Lo, there do I see my mother. My sisters and my brothers. Lo, There do I see my people. Back to the beginning. Lo, there do they call to me and ask me to take my place in the halls where the brave may live forever."

Moon's ashes poured from the urn and into the air swirling away into the waters below the Yggdrasil. A melancholy fell over the last of us as we filed into the tents which had been transformed into a reception area. Silver and I turned and saw Brass stride up to Slate and we held our breath. It was the first time they had seen each other since their return from the Merfolk.

Rosasite was on Brass's arm. Scarlett looked like she wanted to find a rock to crawl under from where she stood on my side. She placed her hands on her stomach, the dress jacket in the Mabon style she wore curved over her small belly.

Slate and Brass spoke while Rosasite looked about coolly, she was the anti-Scarlett. From where I stood, I could feel the girl's dislike for Scarlett. I could only imagine what Brass was seeing in her mind. Brass and her still weren't a couple, but he had been honest about his affair with Scarlett. It was a secret; I only knew because Silver had gotten it out of Brass when he stopped coming around.

Slate had left her. Scarlett knew I knew. The guys knew as well since they were there when it happened. She wasn't doing so hot in private, but in public, she was a rock.

Classic Scarlett.

She and Slate hadn't spoken a word since he caught the scent of Brass on her when they got into their confrontation. It had been blessedly brief and Scarlett had steered clear since.

Rosasite was an astral projectionist, she could leave her body and travel unseen. I wondered if she had done that at some point and spied on Brass and Scarlett. She'd like Scarlett even less if she had.

"At least you're still speaking to me," she said wistfully speaking to Silver.

I handed her Gigi; it was impossible to feel gloomy while holding our gorgeous niece. She smiled gratefully at me with big sad turquoise eyes.

"Ah, yes. Brass does not have many exes. You are the ex that never leaves and Rosasite knows that. You did also sleep with him last week, so don't expect her to be gracious. I am shocked Slate is speaking to him so soon, but you know how it goes, bros before —"

I looked at him dryly. "Finish that statement and you'll find yourself very cold tonight and not in Thrimilci." I sniffed.

"Rosasite is as much for you, Scarlett, as she is for Brass. She is a beautiful girl who enjoys Brass's company. She is not his type, him parading her around is completely out of character for him. That is how I know it is not for him. 'Look how happy and normal everyone is having moved on. Now we can all hold hands and skip like best friends again.'" Silver used a high mocking falsetto that made Gigi giggle as

Scarlett bounced her. "Rosasite is beautiful, but cold-hearted. He offered to stick by you, but you wanted distance."

The longing on Scarlett's beautiful face was heart wrenching as she linked her arm through mine. "I didn't want Slate to think we were having an affair. It was one night." She paused trying not to stare and failing miserably. "I didn't think he would stay with Rosasite. Not that he shouldn't be happy... I just... I don't know what in the world I'm talking about," she said almost to herself.

Rosasite was an exotic beauty, she smiled, and I imagined if she had a tail it would be twitching ready for the pounce when she turned to look at us. A calculated move to let us know she knew we were watching. Scarlett slowly turned away to face me and nuzzled Gigi's cheek.

"You're in love with both of them," I said to her.

I wouldn't wish that on anyone. I lived it. In love with Sterling since I was twelve and having fallen in love with Silver the past year. My heart had been torn in two. Each man had claimed their portion and constantly rivaled for the other half. Of course, I wasn't married or pregnant... yet.

Scarlett pulled me close.

"I hate her," she hissed and Silver raised his brows at her making her blush. "Gods, did I say that out loud?"

"I feel as though you could use Indigo's knowledgeable advice on the topic. I would say you have to make a choice, but I do not think you have one any longer. Brass is with Ro and Slate will not speak to you."

I elbowed him in the ribs. "How about a little optimism, Silver? Slate will forgive you. He has to. After all the crap he'd put you through, it's just a little pay back."

Scarlett gave me a rueful smile as she knit her brow. "When he caught Brass's scent on me, he didn't outright call me out on it. He said Quick and you had a three-some. His exact words were, Quick and Indigo were bored so I fucked your sister with him. I thought I was going to die. Like one of the Risar had kicked me straight in the stomach. Then he said, imagine how I feel now knowing mine was a lie, but you really did fuck my brother. That was the end of our discussion. What does one *say* to something like that?" She sighed and I could feel her tears wanting to spill forth. Her laugh was forced, and she pressed her lips to Gigi's raven hair. "I love the smell of babies. Quick, smell the baby."

Silver leaned past me and took Gigi from Scarlett and inhaled deeply with a smile. "I look damn good with a baby. Would you not agree, Scarlett?"

She smiled. "You really do, Quick."

"Truth," he said flashing his fabulous smile.

THIRTY-NINE

Seeing Brass with Rosasite and her rude demeanor to me had stung, as I'd expected. She didn't like me, and for good reason. She was my subordinate, so she was not outright rude, but as close as she could be to it. I couldn't figure out what he saw in her besides her looks. She wasn't very nice at all.

Slate hated me. There was nothing more to say on the matter. I kept my head down and got through each day and spent my nights with Tree in my big white bed alone.

Classes were cancelled until a new Prime was elected at next week's end. The staff was getting used to seeing me in my robe when they brought me my meals. I had fallen back into old habits not showering, not doing much besides sleeping and eating. At least I *was* eating, but it wasn't for me, it was for my sons.

My dresses started to hang off the curve of my stomach and it was hard hiding that I was pregnant.

I had my solitude for nine days before the council called for an election of the new Prime. Sparrow had forced me to leave the palace, which meant leaving the bedroom and have new dresses commissioned to accommodate my expanding tummy. The seamstresses and tailors of Thrimilci were a talented bunch and by the time I was showered and ready to dress, the new gowns had arrived.

Tawny had chosen most of the gowns, she was the fashion merchandising major and fabric guru. Pastels, whites and golds she'd chosen with a handful of darker richer materials for my Mabon and Elivagar styled gowns. The Ostara caftans were easier to adjust with their wide decorative belts so there were less of those to order.

I had only gone through the front door of Valla University a handful of times. Maybe two or three times a year at most. It was a shame too because other than the ballroom, the entrance hall was really something.

A sundial symbol greeted us on the polished granite floor below the beautiful stained-glass windows that lined the room above stone pillars. Banners bearing the sigils of all the greater families hung before opening up to a wide staircase that spanned most of the opposite wall. It was used to get to the first floor where all of our classes were held. The dining hall was directly behind the wall of the stairs.

We walked up the stone stairs and then down the hall to the next set that led all the way to the top floor where the council held their hearings. My family swept into the pews to await the voting process. Basil sat in Moon's seat, my great uncle Reed sat next to him, he'd lost his closest friend and it showed.

"We take this moment to mourn our fallen Prime. May he reach the halls of the Gods and rejoin the Mother," Basil said in a voice so thick with emotion his every word strangled forth from his throat.

A coo from Gigi broke the silence and heads swiveled to us with small smiles playing on their lips. The reminder that life goes on. Moon's granddaughter, the only Geol grandchild, was there as living proof. She made everyone's mood rise considerably, I could breathe again.

"We are here to elect the new Prime, may they bring balance and peace to the Mother." Reed's voice rose over us, his eyes scanning over the crowd.

"Would Sky Tio and Ash Straumr please approach the council?" Fox asked.

Nausea beat through me like a hailstorm. "I didn't know Ash was being considered. Isn't he too young?"

The idea of him running the Guardians until he died was unacceptable. My stomach kept contracting, begging to empty itself.

Jett grunted. "They prefer young Primes to old, Tio and Straumr descendants have always held the position. Even though Ash is not a Guardian, he will be soon and they all know he will not allow himself to fail. He would have made a good Prime if he was not such an arrogant ass and did not want to make you his paramour."

Jett's almost compliment made me forget myself and stare open-mouthed at him. "If I had a choice from any known family to become Prime, I would vote for —"

Jett looked down at me with a mocking lip curl. "If you say Brass, I will throttle you."

An inappropriate laugh bubbled up and I repressed it. "I was *going* to say Hawk... and if not Hawk then Steel. Neither of them want it, they're both mild mannered with high morals. Of course, I also think River should have taken the Straumr nomination." I leaned in. "If Ash becomes Prime, he'll never leave us alone."

"Your former fiancée will make our family's lives hell until you give him what he wants. You will. You may hold off, but we both know, as does he, that you sacrifice yourself to save them from harm. Once he gets what he wants, he will demand it. It would help if you perhaps stopped showering, rub a bit of dirt on your face," Jett said, leaning his head towards me.

"This is not a laughing matter," I said, fighting a smile.

"Council will put it to a vote. The candidate must have five of the nine votes to become Prime," Reed said in his most official voice. His small mouth moving below his thin mustache.

"Five out of nine? Does it ever get that close? The Prime would always remember who voted against him," I asked.

That seemed like a terrible idea, it should be anonymous like in the states.

"It does not. Three votes was the most ever against an elected Prime," Jett whispered.

I chewed the inside of my cheek. It didn't look good. The voting started, it was over in a blink and left my mouth dry. My mind reeled.

"All those in favor of Sky Tio?" Reed asked.

Four hands; Pearl, Sparrow, Reed, and Tawny.

I gasped. Ruby had voted for Ash. Sterling had as well, but he knew better than most what kind of man Ash was.

Reed stood with the black sleeveless robe of the Prime trimmed in silver and gold, the three interlocking triangles on the back. Ash stood behind the horseshoe table as Reed slipped it onto his back. Basil stood and shook his hand and joined Dahlia in the pews.

I found Jett's hand and slipped mine into it. He gave it a squeeze. It may have been my imagination, but it felt as though Ash's celadon eyes zeroed in on me with a cocky smile. Tawny sat in the Vetr seat with her scarlet robe and frowned openly towards me.

Movement caught my eye to my right. Canis's round face didn't hold a smile. His prominent round blue eyes gleamed. Something about his surrounding energy disturbed me. I looked at his chest to see if he wore the stone piece as I did mine but found no hint of the piece there.

Ash was taller than Moon, but the robe settled on his shoulders as if it was made for him. There should have been a crack of lightening, boom of thunder, *something* to signify the beginning of a tyrannical reign — at least where I was concerned. I'd settle for an ominous cackle.

He stood next to Reed before Reed made his proclamation. "I present to you, your Prime of the Guardians, Overseer of Valla University for Guardian Mastery, Ash Straumr."

We all stood in recognition of our new Prime. My former betrothed who hated my family with the fiery passion of a thousand suns and felt as if I owed him my body. I closed my eyes. It had to be a nightmare, I was still in bed and this never happened.

When I opened my eyes Ash was making a speech. "Guardians! I thank you for your confidence." Ash sat in Moon's seat and we all sat with him.

Diamond stirred on the pew and shot me a sympathetic look past Jett. Nothing would be the same. I killed Peak only to replace his lusting by Ash's. Jett would kill him before he let Ash take me. What Peak did with threats and beatings, Ash would do by torturing my family. He'd grant reprieve once I gave in. Jett was right. I was willing to take a beating when it was only myself being injured. Once my children came into the picture, or Slate and Jett, I surrendered. I wouldn't put my family through Ash's prejudices. He wouldn't beat me, but he would taunt Slate and my brother to no end.

Indigo sat with Quick on my other side and she gave my thigh a pat. "Quartz won't let him do anything too stupid. She's a Natt. Natt women don't tolerate paramours."

"I know. They kill them."

The trudge back to the palace was somber. Amethyst decided to spend more time with her brothers so Jett and Cherry returned without her. Sparrow and Hawk came to the Sumar palace so we could have supper together. Things were made exceedingly awkward when Silver asked if Brass wanted to join us and Rosasite happened to overhear. Tawny came over with Steel so the entire family was there.

The table was set with lamb with dauphinoise potatoes, parsnips with a mint sauce. We retained our old seats at the long silver and gold light carved wood table when we were all gathered.

"If no one else is going to bring it up, then I will —" Jett started and Pearl interrupted with a graceful raise of her long-nailed hand.

"Darling, for propriety's sake." She gave Jett a wry smile and set down her cutlery then looked to me. "Scarlett, darling, our new Prime likely harbors resentments towards you. It may be prudent to avoid attention for the time being."

Jett gave a derisive grunt.

"That'll be hard to do when the arenas are set to open next month." I sighed.

"Let Brass and Silver handle it," Hawk said without looking at me.

"What?" I knit my brow at my uncle leaning my palms on the carved table. "I've —"

"We will take care of things. Brass and Quick are the faces of your arenas, they were your choice," Jett pressed.

I frowned at my plate. Slate hadn't said a word from where he sat across from me in the dining hall next to Brass. As if to rub in my face that no woman, no matter who she was would come between them. Point taken.

Peak had cornered me getting the arenas together. I put myself in the debt of the greater families to secure the deeds and convinced them to trust me. It had not been cheap. Now I was supposed to back off?

"I can't do that," I murmured.

"You're going to have to, young lady," Hawk said, dropping his tone.

I gaped at him. I couldn't remember the last time he spoke to me in his disciplinary tone. Tawny and Gypsum seemed to shrink unwittingly like we were little kids he'd caught playing outside before we cleaned our rooms.

"But..."

Telling him it wasn't fair was the first thing that came into my mind and I snapped my mouth shut. I was a grown woman. He couldn't stop me. That I had to remind myself of those facts counted against me.

We all turned at the sound of footsteps marching along the tiles in the hall. Ash, Sterling, and Sage came around the corner and entered the dining hall without breaking stride. None of the men grabbed for their weapons as Ash came around the side of the table where I sat, eyes fixed on me.

"Prime, Patriarch Haust, Sage, to what do we owe the pleasure?" Pearl asked.

"I have need of your granddaughter," Ash said, smiling at me. "In an official capacity as Prime, I require her presence."

Quick eyed Sterling as he came to stand behind Indigo's chair while Jett's red-faced glower was barely contained as he looked upon our half-brother. Sage stood behind Ash who placed himself beside my chair. Disobeying a direct order from the Prime was an arrestable offense.

"May we use the drawing room?" I asked, pushing back from my heavy carved chair with a weighted resignation on my shoulders.

"Of course, darling," Pearl said, signaling to the staff to ready the drawing room.

"Prime." Hawk began, "My niece is pregnant and her nutrition and health is of the upmost concern. I hope if you feel the need to call on her again, it will be at a more suitable time." Hawk's dark gaze lifted to Ash and Sterling side stepped with an incline of his head.

"Provost, how right you are. Our apologies." Sterling said smoothly, "We shall only keep her for a short time."

Ash regarded Hawk and gave him a nod. I tried not to wring my hands or look to Slate or Brass for reassuring glances, feeling my family and friends' eyes on me as I was led to our drawing room flanked by the three men.

Sage and Sterling stood outside the doors like guards and shut them behind us.

The staff had readied two octagonal tables with fresh fruits and cheeses with no notice. The fountain bubbled water from the center of the room and I walked to the ledge not wishing to sit next to Ash in one of the sheer paneled alcoves.

"Wine?" I asked, pouring myself my glass for the day.

"Please," he said amiably, and I turned with his glass and he grasped it from me so his fingers slid over mine with a smile.

We watched one another over the rim of the glasses as we drank and sat on the fountain's ledge. Ash sat next to me and placed his glass back on the table.

"Are you not going to congratulate me?" Ash asked with a cocky twist of his sensual lips.

"Congratulations, Ash. You have the potential to be a great Prime. I have never had any doubt of it." I raised my glass to him and drank again.

"Thank you. You did always believe I would be Prime, did you not?" Ash favored me with a genuine smile and my brows quirked.

Ash's genuine smiles were like Slate's cheek creasing ones, very rare.

"No matter. Since you were raised with myopics, I will explain. With the election of each new Prime, a new Second is chosen. Straumrs and Tios have always worked hand in hand since the beginning of our people. Reed will be the Patriarch Tio, my father will retain his position as the Straumr patriarch. *You* will be my Second."

Ash took my glass and placed it on the table next to his and held my hand. "This was always my intention once I became Prime. I am the most powerful Straumr to be born in a century and you, likewise, for the Tios. We belong together, Scarlett. I never should have broken our marriage contract. Our bargain will bring us closer together once we have blood to bind us. The most powerful child born since the age of elementals. A return to the days when Guardians had real power."

Butterflies beat in my stomach and his pause seemed to last a lifetime.

"We are not husband and wife, but I will make you the first female Second in the history of the Guardians. You and I will rule the Guardians together."

I was swept up in his impassioned speech. It had been his plan for us. Why he had been willing to forgive me for my love child with Slate and why he pushed so hard for our marriage. If I was the kind of woman who craved power, Ash would have been the man for me.

I would have to be with Ash the way Reed had been with Moon; always at his beck and call, his voice of reason. To help him with his ceremonies and the running of Tidings. I would have allies. *Powerful* allies. While Ash might still try to get me to be closer than I was willing to be, when he tried to use my family against me, as his Second, I would have ways to counter him.

"You don't even like me," I said, unable to pry my hands away from his in my shock.

Ash leaned forward, and I thought he would kiss me, but instead his lips pressed to my cheek, lingering. "I love you, Scarlett. From the night I met you, I knew, we are meant to take this journey together."

"Yes," I exhaled and started to hear the word squeezed from my own lungs.

All the good I could do as his Second. My family would no longer be the black sheep of the greater families. I could reunite the islands, teach the Guardians to respect the tribes instead of treating them as problems to be dealt with.

Yes.

I would find a way to manage Ash so I could do good for all of Tidings.

Ash released my hands and pulled me into an embrace. I was still reeling when I loosely held him back. By the Mother, what was going on? He withdrew, hands on my shoulders and his eyes darted to my lips.

"*Yes* to your Second, not your paramour," I said, feeling the need to clarify.

Despite the heat of the moment, an icy chill passed through his eyes, but was gone just as fast. "Believe me. I know, Scarlett," he said as the temperature dropped in the drawing room.

"You'll send word when you have need of me?" I asked, not fully comprehending what was required now that I had accepted the position.

"Meetings are held at Valla U. It will not interfere with classes. We have ceremonies on each of the islands this coming week and I have arranged so the final day will be in Valla. There, Quartzite and I will marry so all of Tidings will celebrate the marriage of their Prime. Reed will help us with the transition until we pass the Ragnarök challenge. I have it handled. If something arises, I will send word to the Dagr palace. You are still there?" Ash asked, getting to his feet.

I followed suit. "I am." I bit my lip.

Ash pursed his lips and looked to suppress a snide comment. "I am sorry you have been left in such a vulnerable state. As my Second, I promise to take care of you, Scarlett. We will find you a suitable second husband. Greater family women have taken two husbands in the past, one for lands and another for love or to propagate the lines. You need to look strong. An advantageous man on your arm to support you. It will look better than having a lone woman with no husband and with child."

I thought I already knew what man he would help me find. "One errant husband is more than enough for me to handle at the moment. Besides, it's not his fault. It was mine." I sighed and Ash saw I wasn't going to divulge any more.

"Men flock to you. Power seeks power. I will have a comprised list of possible suitors for you sent over," Ash said simply, he hadn't meant himself after all.

I followed Ash to the doors and Sage's round blue eyes scrutinized me before he followed Ash towards the portal room. Sterling hung back just long enough to lean into my ear.

"I know it was you," he whispered before following after them.

My blood ran cold. Sterling's tone had no inflection either way. There was no way he'd let me become the Second if he thought I'd murdered his dad, it had to be that he knew I was the girl. That Orion was protecting *me* with his lies.

I returned to the dining hall to find that no one had moved. Quick stood to help me into my seat and I smiled graciously at him. I looked at my half-eaten plate and sucked in a steadying breath. Not having an appetite didn't mean I had the luxury of not eating. I picked up my fork and began to shovel food into my mouth.

"You're kidding, right? Tell us what he said. *Our* Prime." Jett sneered.

"It's been a long day. I think —"

Tawny interrupted me. "Don't give us that crap. Spit it out, Scarlett Tio.

"I'm the Prime's Second. He's finding me a second husband." I confessed and rubbed my fingertips at my temple. "Please, before you all tell me the position I know I'm in now... How much worse would it have been if I'd tried to say no?"

"By the Mother," Tawny whispered. "He wanted to be married to his own Second. That was his plan, wasn't it? I don't mean to admire his foresight, but it is kind of spectacular."

Jett leaned forward, so his head almost touched the table, to glare at Tawny who shrugged. "Congratulations. The arenas seem like a small feat now that you're Second only to the Prime. Your ex. Let me guess, he wants you to marry *him*? You don't need two shitty husbands." Jett shook his head and knocked back his drink.

"Manners, darling," Pearl said, tossing her coppery hair from her deep tan face. She was trying to process everything I'd just told them.

"Not him. He's... going to send me a list of pre-approved men." I laughed and shook my head. "I don't even know what that means. One of his lackeys that want and elemental child, I assume. I was a little blindsided." I called over one of the staff and asked for a pen and paper so I could remind Ash that I was blood sworn as Slate's wife before he started to make promises to some man.

"He cannot force you to marry, darling." Pearl's emerald eyes glittered at me.

I shrugged. "This was always what it was going to be anyway, wasn't it? If I had just done what I'd promised to do to begin with, I'd be married with at least one child already." I knew my smile wasn't pleasant by the way Steel frowned. "I should have married Ash. I'd be the Prime's wife now." I pushed back from my seat and placed my fingertips on the table. "I'll pick a good one off his list. Don't worry."

"By the Mother, Scarlett don't be an idiot," Quick said, almost startling me.

"I'm not being cynical. I'm being practical. I don't belong to myself anymore. I belong to the people and my children. Arm candy is necessary in my position. Besides, Ash is nothing if not thorough. He'll find me a better choice than I could ever provide for myself. Probably a greater or lesser family son who prefers men but needs an heir," I said, chuckling.

My stomach relaxed, and I felt like slumping in my chair.

"Did you speak to anyone else?" Indigo asked in a casual tone that fooled no one.

"I did, but it was... personal," I told her.

...Sterling knows something...

Brass would tell her. I'd avoided both of my exes at the table. Indigo being able to absorb Quick's lie detecting abilities had put a damper on my white lying. I didn't want the family knowing the truth about Peak. That was one step away from Willow Natt finding out. I believed Orion, she would hire assassins on principle. Once things had settled, I would come clean. I was done with secrets that could put me or my children's lives in jeopardy. I might even tell Tawny I helped Orion poison himself after all this.

"Be careful with Ash. It's redundant to warn you, but he irked you before, now it will be worse. You will have to join him for the festivities all week. When a new Prime is elected, we have a week of feasts and celebrations in his and his Second's honor. Moon was elected when I was just a girl. This will be interesting. Wren and Alder would be proud," Sparrow said, and I sighed.

Would they? If they knew that the Prime thought he loved me. Wanted me as his Second because he had deluded himself into thinking we were meant for each other. *That* was the only reason I was to be the Prime's Second, would they really be proud?

Hawk shifted. "You could marry a second husband in the way of the Guardians."

I furrowed my forehead. "No, I swore a blood vow. I can't say the words to anyone else."

Hawk nodded. "You can say them if your first husband said them with you. That would mean the other man would also be his husband as well though."

I guffawed. I couldn't help it.

"I do not care. The Straumr boy can pick her husband. She can be legally married to whomever they choose. Have a messenger inform me where and when I am needed for your vows," Slate rumbled.

All heads swung to him but mine. I nodded looking down at the beautifully carved table as I held my breath to stop the torrent from springing forth.

"No," Brass said and seemed to be as surprised as the rest of us that he spoke.

"Congratulations, Scar. To the new Second!" Gypsum raised his glass to me breaking the awful uncomfortable silence that the second from Brass's single word proclamation lent. "You're going to be really busy now, aren't you? Do you want me to look after Tree for you?"

"I won't *stop* sleeping, so I'll be home every night. Tree will be fine, Gypsum. Better than fine, she has all my attention these days," I said, flashing my very best smile even if it was forced.

"Gypsum the mineral? You will be inducted into Valla University this year as well?" Rosasite spoke for the first time.

As well? What did the infant think about Brass's outburst?

Indigo raised her eyes to me and Tawny shot me a cool questioning gaze. Their looks and nudges said, *Just how old is Brass's little girlfriend?* It was none of my business anymore.

Gypsum leaned forward so the copper beads in his long raven hair clicked. He flashed her a dimpled smile.

"Yeah. Rosasite is a mineral? I guess I didn't really know."

Gypsum warming up to her vexed me.

"Call me Ro. I start this year, too. I suppose your cousin will induct us in now." She tossed her glossy curls with a lovely smile for my not so little chief.

I winced. I would help Ash induct the new tyros into Valla U, one of which was Brass's girlfriend. I'd be even rounder by then.

"All this excitement has left me exhausted," I said, getting to my feet.

I looked too Quick to dare him to call me a liar. I *was* exhausted. The babies sucked the energy right out of me. It wasn't from the excitement, there was an array of sugarfoot that attributed to it.

Hawk got to his feet as well, and I almost laughed as Steel, Jett, and Gypsum had the same idea. "I'm no one's delicate flower. I'll talk to Lera about getting someone to watch over me while I sleep. Stay. I'll walk myself out."

Hawk leveled his eyes at me and cupped my face in his long pianist's fingers. "Second to the Prime, but you'll still be the little girl I helped Wren raise. My daughter just as much as Tawny is and *my* delicate flower."

I would not cry.

I looped my arm through his as we left the room. "Will you help me in choosing a second husband so I don't screw it up, please?"

I heard Jett curse as Hawk nodded.

My first week back at Valla University with Slate's hatred burning as bright as ever was...interesting. I sat in our classes with Tawny and Quick between us, I walked the halls with Tawny ahead of the two men and sat with Quick between us at lunch.

My nights belonged to Ash. The ceremonies for the new Prime and his Second were celebrated on each island starting with Elivagar and ending in Valla. I spent all of my time by Ash's side when we attended the feasts held at each town center. By the time we made our way home at night, I was exhausted and usually passed out the moment I entered the bedroom of my wing.

Classes all day, ceremonies until I was dead on my feet.

I had sent a messenger to Lera asking her if she would prefer me to resign my position and to my surprise she asked me to keep it for the time being. She wouldn't relinquish having the Prime's Second on her staff so easily. Brass had chosen my bodyguards, Styg's cousins. Pewter was an animal controller, which I was sure not to tell Gypsum about, and his sister Siren, had supernatural flexibility. They looked like Styg, tall, slender, with narrow noses, gaunt fair cheeks and brown hair. Brass had trained them well. Most of the time, I wondered if they were really there or not.

In Elivagar, Tawny and Steel were the ones who planned our feasts, and it had been a great start to the five-day marathon. Ostara was next and while the Var's were all there, the up-and-coming Regn family were as well. The illustrious Spinel was unavailable which I found extremely odd and Lera sat as the matriarch of their house even though she was a Blomi. After all the effort I went through to elevate their family, I had been looking forward to meeting the Patriarch and felt snubbed.

I'd avoided Brass. I could sense he wanted to speak to me, but if he asked me to consider him for my second husband, I might cave and destroy his and Slate's relationship irreparably. I managed to spend a few minutes with Indigo while we were there since Ash and I could not reinstate her to her classes.

In Thrimilci, my family had been in the seats of honor at the festivities and it had been the best day by far. Normally, I danced with Ash mostly, but that night my dance card had been filled by an array of men from Hawk to Solder and all in between. It had been a long time since I'd had fun.

I was already being approached by the wealthy families that were not part of greater or lesser ones for favors. Not to mention that twice I had been cornered by very attractive young men looking to have bragging rights for having slept with the first female Second. Ash had put those men down fast enough. Not even he was tempted by the attentions of young women who went atwitter when he visited their islands. Quartz was with us too and not many would cross a Natt.

One of the immediate perks of being the Prime's Second was Ash had agreed to make this year's theme precious stones instead of minerals, to satisfy his need not to do exactly as I asked. Jett and the girls were getting their Opal Geol after Amethyst's mother.

CHAPTER
FORTY

On the fourth night, Ash and I went to our ceremony in Mabon. It was my first time coming back since Peak's death.

Bronze canopy tents were set up in case it rained, strings of lights lined the poles with leafy garlands. Throne-like chairs were set on a dais for Ash, Sterling, and I while the spouses had to sit at a table at the front of the tent.

The Haust castle loomed behind the tents, they had leveled the lush grass with temporary panels so there could be dancing. Fairies had threaded their glowing mushrooms through the leafy garland. Fairies were bits of nature shaped like people with wings, their eyes were green and blue glowing slits in their tiny twig and grass faces.

Trolls beat on drums as Guardians danced with fairies flitting between the twirling people to the ethereal music. Wide tanned faces with skinny limbs and round bellies, the trolls grinned, big wide smiles, on their wrinkly faces as they moved their skinny limbs. The trolls were about waist high with tufts of hair that stuck straight up from their heads in an array of colors.

Centaurs cantered around the outside of the tents. I wanted to see if Lewt was with them, I needed to ask about the stone pieces. The Risar, the warm-blooded giants of Mabon, were the only ones who didn't attend. They hadn't expected them to. The Jotnar of Elivagar, the cold-blooded giants, didn't come the first night. Neither had ambassadors nor wished for them. It was one of the many things we needed to address in our management of the islands. No one knew what the giants were up to.

Sterling finally took my hand and led me onto the dance floor. He had been stealing glimpses of me all night. Our impending altercation was unavoidable. The topic of the altercation was yet to be determined. The blues and greens of the fairy lights gave his violet eyes an other-worldly glow when he spun me into his arms.

"I think I'll finally have to relent and take much needed dance lessons," I mumbled, hoping it would lighten his severe mood.

We were being watched.

Willow, Ash, and both of Sterling's sisters sat at tables facing us on their thrones. Idly, I wondered what Sterling's barghest form was like. He wasn't ridiculously tall like Slate or as muscled. Sterling was fit and trim with broad shoulders like Ash, though a little shorter. Slate and Jett were just freaks of nature. Gypsum was catching up.

"Quartz is pregnant," Sterling said abruptly, and I tripped over my own two feet on the wood paneling.

Sterling alone kept me from falling face first. "I had no idea. I'm surprised. They aren't even married yet."

He had a low rasping voice that reminded me of how Orion must have sounded when he was Sterling's age. "I did not think he told you. Nova is pregnant as well. I am sure you know Fox Straumr is too old to be able to conceive. You are in the lion's den now, Tio. Ash owns you. If he had not been with me all night, I would have thought *he* had killed my father for having been with you, but I believe it was your husband. Orion was too old to fight Peak. My father would have torn him to pieces. You and I know that very well. The only way I could divulge this new information would be to reveal myself as a barghest. I know you were there."

I stared at him trusting he wouldn't let me trip up and embarrass us both. What did he want? Sterling slid his hand into his pocket and pulled out a feather. A single white Aves feather from the sachem's son Aeetus. I always wore the feather in my hair, but Peak had torn it free that night. The white feather had mud and blood on it. He tucked it back into the pocket of his jerkin.

"He was going to kill me. Call me crazy, but I don't like men forcing themselves on me," I said coolly.

Sterling shook his head with a nasty smile, "You are in over your head. Ash may have been able to keep Peak away, or vice versa, but Slate does not play the same games as the rest of us do. He is prone to violence. How long until Ash does something that incites him? Ash is looking for any excuse to arrest him. He wants you to himself. This ploy about husbands... has he sent you the list?"

Sterling didn't mention that I had likely killed his father. Were things that bad between them? Indigo had mentioned they didn't get along, but to not care? Even as terrible as Peak was, shouldn't Sterling care a little?

Sensing my hesitancy, Sterling smiled. "I do not have any proof about my theory. Just a feather. You should have stayed in Chicago."

"I'll have the same contacts as Ash once I do a little networking. He did me a favor by bringing me closer. Friends and enemies and all that. Slate will be smart. He left me. I appreciate the warning though. I received the list," I told him with a snort.

Hunter and a few other candidates from the lesser families were on the list. He had even included distant cousins from the Tio male line. All in all, no one I had even the slightest interest in. Ash wanted me to test the waters, let them court me properly, under his supervision of course. The whole thing was laughable.

"My sisters are not as covert as my mother, but they have people to handle their dirty work. If Quartz or my mother find out you have been warming Ash's bed, well, I hope they do not."

"Is it because you love Indigo that you try to remain neutral?" I asked, curiosity getting the best of me.

Sterling gave me a lopsided smile as he twirled me and brought me back. "If I had known she was a greater family daughter, I would have married her against my parents' wishes. I could not do it if she was adopted and against their wishes. It was one or the other. She stuck by me even after Diamond had more… adult interests. I would never have completely disobeyed my parents, but in this they were wrong. To compete with what that Regn can offer her, I must be able to help her as well or I will lose her to him."

"Love isn't about what you can get from one another. It's about how they feel, how you feel, what you bring out in one another," I said, creasing my forehead.

"And what does Slate bring out in you? To be fair, you seem worse off with him than Quick's brother. Or is it all about *feelings* with you two?" Sterling asked in a condescending tone.

I pursed my lips. No one needed to tell me that Brass was better for me. That Slate and I were little better than two animals when we were together. That other people noticed it though was news.

Before I could come up with anything remotely clever to retort, a hand tapped my shoulder. "May I cut in?"

In roughhewn pants and tunic, a stunningly beautiful man stood with sapphire blue eyes that dazzled against his golden skin framed by his waist long sunny waves of hair. The Centaur clan leader was in his human form and I was amazed no one recognized Lewt just because he didn't have a horse's body. Not many knew they could shift into a human form.

Sterling looked affronted that such a low born man would interrupt his dance with me. I placed a placating hand on Sterling's.

"We know each other. Thank you for the dance…and the advice. I will do my best to heed it," I told him before spinning to Lewt.

I embraced him with a laugh and his usual rakish grin appeared as he held me out to admire the small swell of my stomach. "You were not with child when you visited us, Scarlett."

My cheeks flushed, and I ran my teeth over my lower lip. "Do you dance?" I asked, gesturing to the swirling people around us.

Lewt snaked his arm around my waist and twirled me impressively and I laughed. He caught me and we started to move with the other dancers.

"I shall take that as a *no*. That mongrel must have scented your season. He did not leave you alone for long, did he?" Lewt teased. "He had asked for any items we might have to increase fertility. The stew he gave you had cassava root for twin fertility. Many Guardians put it in their everyday foods." My eyes widened, and he laughed. "I take it you did not know. We also gave you a balm to... *encourage* you."

I spluttered. "Fert told me it was for abrasions! Plotters!" Lewt laughed again, and I sighed. "They're not his. Mission accomplished — twins." I smiled ruefully at him. "What are you doing here in your man form? There's only a handful of Centaur around, aren't you needed?"

"I find human women are intimidated by my horse anatomy. This form is preferable for tonight's agenda," Lewt said with the rakish grin and my cheeks flamed.

"Dear Gods, Lewt. I thought Guardians had no modesty. Do you frequently come stud yourself out when Guardians gather?" I asked dryly.

"No, but I heard the Prime's Second was a woman." Lewt's sapphire blue eyes glittered at me and I shook my head.

"You are not the first, and I doubt you will be the last. I'm becoming something of a novelty."

"Congratulations, Scarlett. It is good to know I have a friend high on the council," he said with complete sincerity.

I gave Lewt my best smile and his brightened. He couldn't help the way his eyes dropped to the way my cleavage seemed to be in every-one's face with the corset. Green light from the fairy mushrooms colored his face and his eyes flitted up to mine.

"Where is Slate? I need to speak with you, but I do not want your mate trying to tear my throat out," Lewt said in a rush.

I knit my brows but took Lewt's hand as I led the way outside of the canopied tent. I followed checking to make sure we hadn't drawn anyone else's attention. Ash would be upset I left early.

We stopped a little ways away from the tents so Sterling couldn't hear us. "Slate and I aren't an item any longer. How are you, Lewt?"

"Very well. Karkinos has reappeared. I thought you should know. I am not sorry about the mongrel, barghests are not good for women." Lewt said in a tone so casual I had to blink a few times before I could speak.

"We've been looking for Karkinos. I have to send people there first thing. Slate was imprisoned there for a time and Karkinos is injured."

"You have such a lovely pout," Lewt teased, and I narrowed my eyes.

I was *not* pouting. "What did you want to discuss?"

"What you have there in your bosom," Lewt said, nodding to my chest, and I frowned.

Lewt hooked his finger around my silver pendant chain that kept my stone pieces. "I get sick of men looking down my dresses." I grumbled and Lewt laughed.

Mabon should have held bad memories for me, but it also held the memory of where Slate and I had made love in the Centaur village. Where I had rode Lewt's back and felt like the wind. The smell reminded me of Slate and how could I possibly dislike *that* even if it felt like my nerves had been flayed and everything held an impossible hurt.

"I know where another piece is," Lewt interrupted my pity party.

I tucked the pendants back into my corset.

"I took your advice and united the herds. I am the all-clan leader. We have a piece on Mabon, but it will be difficult to convince the Risar to give it up," Lewt said, looking to me.

"The Risar!" I almost shouted, and he gave a dry look. I grimaced. "Sorry. Where is it? Any help you could offer retrieving would be welcome."

Lewt took me in. "If I had known you were the ones that would come for the piece, I would have begun to plead your case beforehand."

"Why does that sound like it will take a long time?" I asked, leveling my eyes at Lewt.

"Can you ride? Your event is over, yes? I will take you to the trolls' hamlet." Lewt pulled his shirt off and I couldn't help my blush.

I had seen Lewt naked before when he shifted. He was very much a man in this form. Pants were thrown over my shoulders and I neatly folded them with the shirt and the rest of Lewt's garments. The surrounding air seemed to change, a certain pressure to the air as Lewt shifted. I heard his hooves stomp and turned around picking up his boots.

Lewt was a shimmering palomino with a man's glorious torso. He smiled tossing his mane of hair over his shoulder. He leaned down offering me his hand, and I happily took it.

"I do enjoy when you ride me, Scarlett," Lewt joked, making me blush so heatedly my ears burned.

Sitting on Lewt's back pushed my dress and petticoats up to my thighs. "Please don't go too fast. I don't want to fall. My balance is all off with these babies."

Without any word of warning, he started forward, and I yelped.

Trees and shrubbery flew by as indistinguishable blurs. Lewt in his Centaur form leapt over rivers that required stone bridges in over places. His massive paws kicked up chunks of lush grass over the rolling hills and scraped on the rocky landscape. Lewt was having the time of his life if his hearty laughter was any indication.

Three more Centaurs burst through the brush at some point and I recognized them as Fert, the female Centaur had long brown hair with barely a scrap to cover her human breasts, Goep, the Clydesdale Centaur with flowing brown mane, and Hute, with black curls that fell to his black stallion waist. Their eyes twinkled in the moonlight as they tried to keep pace with Lewt.

Ambient light coming from the dozens of trees ahead signified the fairies and trolls homestead. The green and blue glowing mushrooms lined the trees and walkways that were barely a foot wide that connected the trees in a way that reminded me of the Aves but on a much smaller scale. Knolls divided the trees where dirt paths linked the trolls homes. A small clearing where they held their bonfires rested in the center that was only big enough for a hundred humans.

Fairies and trolls shrieked as we came into view. Lewt and the others laughed as fairies flew into trees and trolls dropped their instruments to crawl into their knolls.

"Sorry! We're just visiting. We don't mean any harm. Lewt is with us, we're friends."

Trolls and fairies crept back on of their hiding places when the Centaurs' robust chuckles greeted them. To my chagrin, Lewt started to shrink between my legs until I could easily swing over him and he was in his human form. I thrust his pants at him with a frown and heard Fert catcall just to vex me.

"I will go to the Risar and bring them round. They do not like guests otherwise I would have brought you there." Lewt handed back his clothes. "Give them to Baboo. She keeps spare clothing for me when I come this way." With that, he shifted again and his herd galloped away.

A little wrinkly faced troll with a puff of white cottony hair sticky straight up stared at me. She wore a shirt and shorts made of moss and leaves with grass blades in a crown around its head. Baboo's face split when she saw me and I crouched down to hug her.

"Baboo! It's been too long. I've been in Mabon several times, but I never have a chance to visit. I hope we're not intruding," I said, hugging her frail body.

The troll shook its head comically, it's little tuft of hair shaking. "Not at all. I am always happy to have a friend over." Her small voice that managed to be high and croaky at the same time.

"I have to wait for Lewt to return. May I camp by your home?" I asked, handing her Lewt's clothes.

Baboo laughed holding her moss-covered belly. "Why of course! Come along."

Baboo led us over the knolls, it wasn't far until we reached a large knoll, larger than most of the others. The door was *maybe* two feet wide by three and a half feet tall, but there were stairs as soon as you opened the door that opened up to a five-foot-high ceiling.

Baboo hummed a merry tune and walked inside putting Lewt's clothes on her table. "Come in, come in. It will be a few hours."

I climbed in and ducked my head. Baboo walked back, and I helped her push the table to the wall so I could stretch out my legs and she handed an empty jug that I filled with water and sat down next to the steps.

"You are tired, Scarlett?" Baboo asked, and I sighed.

"I operate at a constant level of exhaustion these days," I said, sounding weary.

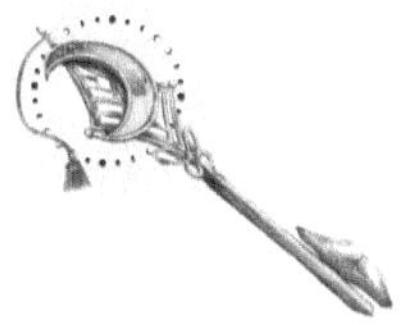

Baboo and I were speaking like longtime friends. Discussing wood carving of all things. I flipped through paintings Baboo had handed me when I awoke.

"This one," I said, showing her a painting of a troll made crib, which meant it was exquisitely carved with care. "I have cribs, but..."

"You do not have troll made cribs. Everyone knows we do the best woodwork," Baboo replied.

I almost guffawed, but I swallowed it back and looked at the other crib she selected. The cedar wood would match what we had in the nursery.

I took out a pouch of coins I carried tied inside my skirts and counted off gold daymarks and silver crescents handing them over to Baboo who bobbed her grass ringed head and collected the coins. "Two of the first one," I told her.

"They are back," Baboo said with a wide smile at me as the muted rumble of their galloping hooves trembled the small knoll.

Baboo was climbing out behind me as Lewt returned with his herd. The horse hybrids stomped their hooves and looked towards the trees.

Mabon's portal gate hung between two trees, carved on the massive doors with fairies, centaurs, and trolls carved along with a pair of giants. The two Risar that emerged from the shadows and were *not* the whimsical creatures from the portal carving.

I wished I could shrink behind Baboo, my feet moving me of their own volition. They bent trees as if they were twigs as they emerged from the woods. I noticed they were being careful not to step on any of the knolls, probably because their weight would crush the homes of the trolls if one of the Risar were to put their foot on one.

Several feet above where Slate would stand, and twice his weight at least, the sienna toned giants were to us as we were to the trolls. I couldn't help but notice that their fists were as big as my head. I expected them to lumber, and they did move in a slow careful way, but it was out of awareness not a lack of grace.

I suddenly wished it was daylight. Risar hadn't been seen in ages, likely, Viper Enox had been the only one to see them in the last two decades. Cherry's dad was the Centaur ambassador. From what I *could* see, they were both male. One's wide head was completely bald while the other had a white strip of hair that covered him from ear to ear around his head. Their eyes were beady and dark in their wide craggy faces, but they looked human if an off color and very large and bulky. That was the other thing, they seemed overdeveloped with thick necks and barrel chests, one hit from them and I would undoubtedly die.

The two Risar wore fur vests and thick belted skirts that fell to their knees, met by thick furry boots wrapped with leather straps to cinch them. They weren't carrying weapons that I could see, but then, they were the weapons.

Beady eyes peered down at me and I made a mental note never to look like I was going to eat Baboo, because it was terrifying. "Is this a jest?" the one with the white band asked as he leaned down to look at me.

The Risar's voice with deep and guttural, and he rumbled something in Risar that left me feeling unsettled. The other Risar boomed a laugh that caused the Centaur to skittishly stomp their hooves.

"I am not fluent in all the languages of Tidings's inhabitants," I said. "I am Scarlett Tio. Daughter of spring and summer."

"This is Anundr, I am Brusi we are the sons of Edda the seidkona. You do not look like a gray beast; I expected you to be older. Grayer. Manlier," the bald one said, shifting his beady eyes to me.

The seidkona was a sorceress that led the Risar. It was a good sign her sons were there, that meant at least I was being taken seriously.

"My husband is the Grar Dyr." As if he didn't know.

"This is Night's child? She looks like someone gave a sunbeam skin and a plump set of lips."

I stood my ground against their ridicule. "Where I come from, people are not very polite either. I believe when introducing oneself, you should not ridicule and judge them in the process. I was raised better than that. So I would never say that those furs you're wearing smell as though you forgot to skin the beast you stole them from and perhaps their rotting corpses rest around your chests instead. I would never say such things. I expect others to treat me with equal respect because this what you get. I am destined to save Tidings and the Mother. You want to waste time with physical descriptions? Be my guest, but I'm pregnant, tired, hungry, and have classes in the morning. Not to mention I have not lain with my errant husband in months while I am trying to win him back and I am wasting time here listening to you. So unless you're going to give me the piece I need to help save these islands, don't squander my precious time."

The others had turned to gape at me. I had said much more than I had intended to when I opened my mouth, but once I'd gotten started I had a laundry list of grievances. I had held back from saying my feet hurt, but they did. I had set my jaw and was staring at the giant brothers and imagined it must be how Tawny felt on most days.

Brusi started laughing and Anundr joined his great bellowing belly laughs that made them sway dangerously, being as close to us as they were. Lewt and his Centaurs started laughing and even I let my lips quirk.

"By the Mother. The barghest created a monster," Lewt said amusedly and my fierce expression slipped.

Brusi made a gesture as if he relented and his laughter tapered off. "My mother taught me never to anger a pregnant woman, no matter her tribe. You have spirit, woman. I can appreciate a woman with spirit. Come. The piece is not with us."

I sighed. Of course it wasn't.

Anundr's wide round head split with a lipless smile.

"It is a short walk, Night's child."

Lewt trotted to me and reached down after giving me a smirk. I took his hand gratefully and swung up onto his back and pulled my skirts down over my legs as far as they would go, which wasn't far at all. The umber skinned giants started barking laughs again at my modesty.

Baboo was lifted onto Fert's bay horse back. Brusi and Anundr shared an approving look and gave me an expectant one as if they were waiting for my magic transformation. I happily obliged whispering in Lewt's ear just before I became a fiery inferno in lady's wear. They sucked in satisfying sharp breaths and even Lewt strained to look at me with wide nervous eyes. I quenched the flames so he wouldn't have to worry about a stray spark burning his backside.

The Risar spoke in their guttural rumbles. I had passed the Risar's test.

The Risar were wary walking around hillocks that formed the trolls' homes, Lewt shot me a rakish grin over his shoulder when we heard the babbling of the swirling stream. It was where Baboo had taken Indi and I when we first met her and Lewt had seen us swimming in our undergarments. It was also where Slate had watched Ash and I go as far as we ever had. I had come dangerously close to giving myself to Ash that day.

The warm water swirled looking like giants much bigger than the Risar had pressed their thumb prints into the water, leaving their permanent marks. The glowing plants that the fairies grew also grew under the stream's constant flow. The waterfall poured over shelves of rocks to head past where we stood on the shore.

The herd came up alongside us Fert and helped me off Lewt as Anundr stepped into the spring, the water didn't even come up to his waist as he trudged to the waterfall bare chested and bootless.

"Have you found the works yet?" Brusi asked in a casual tone as we watched his brother stir the water.

"No," I grumbled. "Help would be appreciated. Elivagar is impossible to traverse. Ostara likewise for different reasons. It is not on Thrimilci. That much we know."

"It is not on Mabon. We know every inch of this island," Brusi said, crossing his arms over his chest and giving me a sidelong glance.

He was daring me to question his surety. Lewt stepped between us.

"I have ridden this island all my life, so has my clan. We would have found something amiss. I did not expect this prophecy to come true in my lifetime," Lewt said, and turned his stunning blue eyes on me. "A son, then?"

"Two sons," I told him, placing a palm to my belly.

"You should only activate Storm's project while you are pregnant with the Grar Dyr's son," Brusi noted, and I started.

"I'm not even four months along. This is only the fifth piece. We have four more pieces to collect and we have no clue where this *works* is. I don't even sleep with my husband anymore."

I chewed on the inside of my cheek. With Slate's hatred for me, there'd be no way he would have children with me even if I begged. I wasn't above begging.

"It looks like you shall have time to seduce him until you find it all," Brusi joked and I gave him a dry look.

Anundr was reaching into the falls and I knit my brows. He leaned back, as rocks grated on one another and a portion of the falls parted around a hidden hollow. Anundr's bulky arm plunged between the exposed rocks, water dripping from his pointed elbow as he removed something that fit in his palm from the hollow. The rocks shifted again, and the waterfall poured into the stream as if nothing had happened.

Anundr made his way back to the shore and the fresh water ran over him in buckets forming his own stream on the land. I imagined if he'd had his heart set on it, the giant brothers could indeed make their own stream in short order.

A cool breeze made Anundr's scalp prickle under the moon's beam. The rustling of leaves and coursing water being the only sound in the dark night, lent gravity to what he held in his outstretched palm. A small square stone piece, wet and gritty from its previous home, now rested in my palm.

"Thank you, Anundr," I said as I unclasped my necklace and slid the piece on with the other four I already had. "As well as being forced to save Tidings, I'm also the Prime's Second. Since you're here..."

I lifted my gaze to the Risar who had knowing smiles on their faces. "We will bring word of the new Prime to Edda. Dagr, you live on Thrim-ilci?" Brusi asked.

"Yes. At the Dagr palace, but I spend a lot of time at the Sumar palace as well. Will you seriously consider sending someone to treat with us? Relations between all the people in Tidings is important for balance," I implored.

Anundr appraised me with his dark beady eyes. His head was the size of a boulder and he could easily have swallowed my head in a single bite as he lowered it to meet me at eye level. "Are you pure of heart and conscience, Night's child?"

I knit my brow as I gazed into his pits for eyes and wondered if any part of me was pure anymore. His teeth were flat and each one was the size of my palm in his lipless mouth. There was no gleam to his teeth, they were dull and crooked. I sighed.

"I was before I met my husband," I said, running my teeth along my lower lip.

Anundr and Brusi guffawed so abruptly I jerked back when spittle hit me in the face. I wiped it off with the back of my hand.

Anundr straightened. "My brother and I will come ourselves on one condition."

"What condition?" I asked.

Brusi pointed a thick finger at me. "We deal with you *after* you complete the works. We will know when it is done. Goodnight Guardians, you are free to return home and lay with your husband," Brusi said, laughing again in his deep bellowing voice.

Brusi and Anundr ambled away and walked into the woods. They were quiet for two beings who weighed as much as a car would. I walked over to where Baboo sat on Fert's back.

"I won't wait so long next time for a visit," I told her and her wrinkled face grinned back at me.

"I know. I am making your babies' cribs, four weeks at most until I see you again, Scarlett," Baboo croaked in her high pitch voice and I gave the tiny troll a hug.

Lewt appeared at my side and I took his hand as he helped swing me onto his back. I was getting better at it but Lewt still had to help me balance with my ever-growing belly.

The tents were dismantled, and the feast was over when we returned. Lewt dressed in the trees and we walked to Mabon's portal. I embraced him tightly and caught the smell of wind in his golden mane.

"You do not have to go home to a husband. I am in my human form..." Lewt said suggestively, and I found I didn't want to leave, but not to lay with Lewt, but to be held.

"Goodnight, Lewt. Thank you for all your help," I said, giving his cheek a kiss.

Five down four to go.

FORTY-ONE

The final day of feasts had finally arrived, and I was deliriously tired. As an added bonus, Ash and the Straumrs had arranged his and Quartz's wedding during the same time so all of Tidings was invited, not just the greater families and the residents of Valla. It was a great idea; his marriage would be celebrated with all the pomp and pageantry that would dazzle the average Guardians. They would fall in love with him, the Straumr golden boy.

Platforms were built behind the free-standing stone gate with sculptured tree branches twisting up it, a sculpture of a woman, hands extended forming into branches that crested the top. On the top platform sat Ash and his bridal party which consisted of who's who of Guardian heirs and future ambassadors. Sterling, Sage, Hunter, and the three Straumr brothers were the men in Ash's party. Nova, Diamond, Amber, and River's wife were seated alongside Quartz.

Attending my ex-fiancée's wedding as an honored guest was not something even Slate's prophet abilities could've foreseen. We sat on the platform below his with Amethyst, Jett, Cherry, and Gypsum to my right and to Slate's left were Tawny and Steel, Indigo and Quick. Ash had done it as a favor to me, reuniting the greater families through their children. He was off to a great start as Prime, with my arenas to keep the ties knotted, it was as close as the islands had been in decades. It was the closest to Slate I had been since I returned from the Merfolk. We both did a good job of ignoring one another though electricity crackled between us oblivious that it was not supposed to while we were on the outs.

The older greater families sat at tables around the platforms. Guardians in black lingered, their sole purpose was to keep the star formation town center comfortable for the guests in the cool autumn weather. Straumr jewel tone purple and glittering white silks decorated the long tables backlit by twinkling lights. Elaborate crystal candelabras sat on each table with purple and white orchids. The Straumrs had spared no expense.

Ash had color coordinated the honored guests' clothes with his wedding party's so once again, I was being dressed by Ash. While they wore deep purple, our dresses were a light thistle color that the men's waist coats matched. Slate was forced to wear purple. If he wasn't so angry about it, it would have been hilarious. If I'd had a right to cheer him up, I would have. I imagined Pearl and Sparrow had been the guiding force behind his presence.

Each of the honored guests' dresses were cut in different Mabon fashions so all of us wore flattering cuts. I wondered how Quartz liked me being included in her wedding, but I had a feeling knowing Ash, he did as he pleased and she went along.

Dancing. My goodness, all the dancing. I wore practical shoes with my glamorous gown, but it did little to alleviate the pain I was feeling in my lower back. The spiced wine called wassail was flowing freely, and the guests were getting drunk to the beautifully ethereal music of the Guardians.

I danced with Ash at his wedding. I wanted to laugh at the irony. He was as light on his feet as ever and I was swept away in his arms.

"This should be our wedding," he mused.

My stomach dropped, but I kept my tone light. "Quartz looks beautiful. Congratulations on the baby, Ash... and Nova's baby. You must be very happy."

Ash didn't miss a step. "Yes, my love, but it *our* child I look forward to most. You have done well this week. A lot of late nights, I expect they will continue. How is your estranged husband adjusting to your new position? He had not been back in the brothels has he? Husbands with too much time and busy wives will seek comfort elsewhere. Have you considered my list?"

"Spouses will do what they will, I have no hold over him. I'll let one of the men on the list court me. Set it up, I don't really care who, I'm not interested in any of them romantically. It is a business arrangement. Are you worried about Quartzite?" I asked, ignoring his jibes.

Ash's eyes flashed with anger. "Quartz is firmly in hand." He spun me around and leaned in close to my ear. "Who *are* you interested in, my love? A marriage out of love was foolish, but this one will benefit you. A mutual agreement to be a man's spouse, produce him children and support one another's careers. That is what you need. We could have been that for one another."

Well, that only took five days. I was about to say something clever when I was tapped on the shoulder. Brass smiled warmly at us both and offered me his hand.

"Excuse me, may I please dance with my business associate?" Brass asked in his smooth deep voice and my lips quirked.

"Be my guest, Brass... the middle Regn," Ash said coolly.

I released Ash's hand and slid my palm against Brass's. "Congratulations on the wedding and becoming Prime," Brass said, holding my hand.

"Are you here alone or have you maintained a special interest in my Second?" Ash asked coolly.

That was subtle for Ash and I had almost forgotten how easily he angered when he didn't get his way. Brass laughed as if Ash had been joking.

"I doubt my love interests are appealing enough for your attention. Scarlett?"

Brass's amber eyes slid to me and I gave Ash my very best smile, no sarcasm whatsoever. I would walk this fine line with Ash for the rest of our lives. I placed my free hand on Ash's forearm.

"Thank you for the dance, Ash. You may send me your choice of men to court me for a dance tonight to see if we are compatible but be sure to let him know it is nothing beyond a dance that I agree to." Ash's eyes glittered and his sensual lips quirked as he inclined his head to us.

Brass took me into his arms. Cinnamon, spring rain, with a touch of fall that threw me. "Are you sniffing me?" Brass asked in an amused tone.

A self-deprecating smile lit my face as I peered up at him. "Maybe."

"Be careful with those smiles, love," Brass said wryly as we moved along the dance floor they constructed for Ash's wedding.

"I thought you liked my smile?" I teased, and Brass's trimmed stubble rubbed against the side of my face as he leaned in.

"You have the female equivalent of Silver's smile. Don't pretend you don't wield it intentionally; I saw you diffuse Ash with it."

I laughed and reined it in wondering where Slate was. "My smile hardly has the effect that your brother's does. Otherwise I'd be decorated in men's undergarments as we speak."

"Don't tempt me," Brass joked and his fingers flexed on my hip pulling me closer.

"Now who's smelling who?" I said ruefully, and Brass's lips grazed my temple.

If I shut my eyes, the world would know I was enjoying this dance more than I was supposed to. "You should take dance lessons, if you have the time."

I scoffed. "By the Mother, Brass. Don't bother sparing my feelings or anything. Is my dancing really that bad?"

Brass chuckled softly. "No. You let me guide you with almost no effort, but I am a mind reader. You want to be able to hold your own as the Prime's Second. Language classes would not hurt either. Not every tribe will have English-speaking representatives available."

"Are you offering to teach me to dance? Slate is not inclined to teach me much of anything these days, but perhaps my second husband will be more amenable to me stepping on his toes and teaching me to speak in tongues," I said, tilting my chin up to his cheek.

"Are you asking?" Brass inhaled deeply and twirled me. I smiled ruefully at him though my heart had flip-flopped.

"Pushing me away? Literally? I thought that was my job. This is not smart, Brass. I've been keeping my distance for a reason. How is Rosasite?"

Brass caught me and pulled me tight against his body. In the mass of bodies we went unnoticed, but Slate and Rosasite would be out there somewhere watching.

"I miss you, love," Brass whispered and my heart lurched.

I took a shuddering breath. "What about Rosasite and Slate? This isn't like you," I said breathlessly.

Brass confessing his feelings would do me in. Things weren't the way they always were. Brass and I had a relationship, we made love, we were going to move in together. There was no big blow out ending, no fights. The most we disagreed about was where to get delivery from when we weren't discussing Slate. When Slate was out of the picture, as much as he was ever out of the picture, we were going to spend the rest of our lives together.

By the Mother, what did I do?

He looked away. "I know. Are you happy, Scarlett? I know you are torturing yourself. Contemplating marrying someone you couldn't possibly love. Not when your heart is spoken for."

I bit down on my lip as I knit my brows. There was no answer that wouldn't hurt someone I loved. If I told him I missed burning his breakfast because he would make love to me on the kitchen counters, or I missed how he cuddled with Tree on my couch more often than he cuddled with me. Or that I missed our wordless conversations when I told him I loved him without having to say the words and he knew I meant it.

"Loud and clear," Brass said roughly, and I swallowed hard.

Gods forgive me.

"Brass Regn, if I am not mistaken."

My blood turned to ice in my veins when I heard the stiffed lipped words of Canis Var. Our last interaction was broken up by Slate when we got into it at my father's funeral. No place was sacred.

Brass didn't release my hand. People moved about us as if every other person was his polar opposite and was forced to circumvent him.

"Ambassador Var," I said, resisting the urge to step in front of Brass as if I could protect him.

Canis's white hair was spiky on his round head, his blue round eyes bore into me. He was huge. All the Var's were.

"Brass, the year of the alloy. You will make an excellent paramour for my grandniece. Unfortunately, you will never have any heirs of your own. In her present condition, your time has nearly run out. I can hear the clock tick ticking away on your virility. It has the same lifespan as your honor. Laying with married women when your family has so much riding on their reputation." Canis gave a slow shake of his head. "Not smart. Men do uncharacteristically mindless things when women are involved."

In less than a minute, Canis had spoken to Brass in a way he had never been spoken to before. No one had reason to. I had done this. I had confronted Canis about his affair with Cassiopeia and now he was taking it out on Brass. We were beneath his notice. He was up to something bigger.

I realized it too late. When Brass had twirled me, my necklace had spun free of the dress and laid over my chest. Canis's eyes ran over it greedily and I stilled my fingers from tucking it away. I took the opportunity to look for his as well.

"Ambassador Var, you misunderstand the nature of my relationship with Mrs. Tio. Paramour is too inadequate a word to describe it. She is far enough along where her next child can be mine with time to spare. The Regn reputation cannot be sullied when we are already hand fasted." Brass held up my left hand and slid up my emerald ring to show my tiwaz tattoo. "She will make an honest man of me yet. No bastard children will be put in her womb but thank you for your concern. Scarlett? Are you ready to return home?"

I didn't see Canis's reaction. I was too busy gaping open-mouthed and wide eyed at Brass to even move. I had been shaking in anger when Canis had verbally assaulted Brass, but now butterflies beat in my stomach with a heart that beat so fast I thought it would explode in my chest. What had he just done!

Before I could shout out that accusatory statement, he slid his arm around my waist and led me into the portal door behind the platforms. The crowd had faded. I walked in a stupor behind him until the white light engulfed us.

I stammered unable to find the words I wanted to say or ask, or something. Anything. A noisy breath was pushed from my lungs and I imagined the matriarch statues that lined the room rolled their eyes to the sky at my eloquence.

"Save it until we get to the wing," Brass said without the irritation I was expecting.

Was I holding Brass's hand? At one point I looked down at our clasped hands and blinked unable to process what he was doing.

Brass led us into the wing. He bypassed the dusky blue living room with my soft cream couches and into the modest dining room. I stopped short just inside the threshold.

I found my words. "Did you just tell Canis I would have your babies?"

"I did," Brass said, taking a seat at the pedestal table.

I hit the energy plate as I walked in so the cluster of Moroccan lamps above the table lit the room. I pulled out a dusky blue upholstered chair and sat at the white distressed pedestal table I almost never used.

I was close to spluttering. "Brass," I said, feeling out of breath. "You made it sound like..."

"You want a second husband?" he asked, gesturing with his hands.

I did splutter this time. "What has gotten into you?" I scowled at Brass whose lips curled up at me as I crossed my arms. "You're talking crazy. Slate would never agree to it. You guys are just getting back to normal. Please, you should go."

"I have shared you before. I would rather have you than not. I doubt I was on Ash's list, but I am a middle son of a lesser family. I do not have lands of my own or social responsibilities like Coyote. I am free to marry whom I wish. Scarlett, they're going to find out the babies you carry are mine. I want them all to know. You sacrificed your honor to protect our children from Peak. I respected that sacrifice and so I never pushed. I am pushing now. You have to have Slate's children. We'll convince him together that this will work."

I burst out laughing hysterically as my face flushed. "Like, Cherry, Amethyst, and Jett? You'll be like... brother/husbands?" I held my stomach as I started to laugh uncontrollably, the idea was just too ridiculous. I sobered quickly at the flicker of hurt that passed through his eyes. "Brass, I'm not laughing at the idea of marrying you. It's just...

what if Slate gets his memories back? I haven't been taking this list seriously, that's not to say I haven't thought about it."

Brass drew me up short with glittering amber eyes. "Scarlett Tio, you are woman enough. Believe me."

His scent had spiked. I was holding my breath.

"What do we have here?" Slate rumbled from where he leaned in the doorway behind me.

I knocked the seat backwards as I launched up from the table. "He was just leaving," I said in a squeak.

The lights from the lamps glinted in his silver eyes. "Have you two been getting together in my ancestral palace?"

He didn't seem to be addressing either of us and his emotions were walled off from me. "No, I've been alone every day after I leave Ash. Not that anything has happened with him either. It hasn't."

Gods, why was I so nervous?

Slate looked to Brass. Deep amber eyes peered out at me from long lashes under thick masculine brows. His features were strong with square dark honey jaw dusted with a trimmed stubble and symmetrical nose. His lips defined and plump were made for kissing. His eyes shifted to me and I froze like the rabbit I was. They were communicating silently the way they always did.

"Do you want me for your husband, Scarlett?" Brass asked in barely more than a whisper.

A small whimper pushed out with my exhale. "You guys have to leave. I'm tired."

Slate pushed off the entranceway and pulled his shirt over his head with his open waistcoat. I took a step back and shook my head. Slate's scent had spiked. His bronze muscles flexed as he unbuckled the blade belts around his chest. I swallowed.

"What are you doing?" I breathed.

I whipped my head to Brass as he stood from his seat. His waistcoat was on the floor and a lock of his hair had fallen free from the knot at his nape. He tugged his shirt over his head and his eyes flickered to me as he let it drop to the floor. My insides pulsed traitorously, and I gripped my skirts in my fists.

"Testing the waters, girl. I gave my approval for him to court you, not that you take *my* opinion into consideration," Slate purred as he kicked off his boots and started to unbuckle his belt.

Shaking my head, I retreated another step. "What waters? You hate me and he ditched his girlfriend at a wedding to bring me home."

I had spent the night with both men in my bed. I had kissed them both in the same day and they had known it. Both of them had seen me be intimate with the other. This was something else entirely.

Slate's eyes flared as his full lips curled at me. "You are my wife. He wants you to be his wife. We do not know if the three of us can get along, girl. How else will we find out?"

"Talk. Take a picnic some place quiet," I offered.

My palms were sweating where I clutched the thistle taffeta fabric. I watched Slate disrobe to his snug black boxer briefs. When I looked at Brass, he was down to a similar pair in burgundy.

Brass's smile was lopsided. "We know we get along that way, love. We are not foolish. We know alone you will send us away. Together is another matter. We are not making you choose."

"Wait," I breathed, releasing my dress as Slate stalked towards me.

I was circling away from him and Brass caught my elbow as I stumbled over the chair. Slate walked around to where I stood with Brass at my back. I felt lightheaded as my heart raced. Slate stood before me and ran his thumb along my chin to my lower lip. It took an effort not to slide my tongue along the pad of his thumb.

"This does not change things, girl. I will not be moving back in."

My heart lurched painfully. "You just want to use my body," I whispered, searching his eyes.

"It is quite the body. You should be proud. I, *we*, fully intend on putting it to good use."

"No. To both of you. I'm not some toy for you to play with or pass around," I admonished.

"We know you're not a toy, love," Brass said as he began to unzip the side of my dress.

I spun to him slapping his hands away and Slate gripped my hair gently in his fist. "You are my wife. I plan to take you to bed tonight. Do not worry, it is only for tonight. Perhaps I need some persuasion to approve this second husband."

Brass slipped the dress off my shoulders and to the floor when he began to work on my corset. I felt limp and Brass leaned me against his chest as he continued to undress me. His teeth caught my earlobe, and I gasped. Slate still had my hair and lowered his mouth to mine. My eyes slid shut.

"Activate your bonds," Slate said, turning me around.

His rough palms slid over my bared belly and pushed the petticoats down over my hips. Brass tilted my mouth over to his and his tongue found mine as he deeply kissed me. Slate slid his finger over my ring and Brass pressed on my lower lip activating both bonds. Brass moaned against my mouth and Slate's deep inhuman growl reverberated in his chest as he trailed kisses over my breasts.

Slate shifted and Brass lifted me onto the table. Slate walked around and gently pushed me onto my back. His hands ran over my shoulders and cupped my breasts as he kissed me. Brass trailed his tongue up my thighs until his lips pressed between my legs and I gasped against Slate's mouth.

"Oh, *sugarfoot,*" I whispered.

We moved from the table to the floor before we made it into the bedroom. I had been with Chris and Brass once, and it had been horribly hot. Slate and Brass were an entirely different story. I was defiled with veneration. Worshipped with depravity.

In my tired state, we had an enlightening shower, and I fell into a dreamless sleep that doubled as a coma. All of us. I didn't know if either of them would be there in the morning, but I was sleep deprived and delirious.

What happened was impossible. Slate would never have gone along with it, much less instigated it.

Velvet skin slid over my back and my insides coiled as pleasure pooled. A fist gripped my hair and Slate's lips crushed over mine. Our tongues intertwined, and I gasped against his mouth as he teased me, dipping into me, and retreating. I moaned against Slate's lips and he drove into me so I felt his roped hips press with a delicious promise of more to come.

I knit my brows. I brought my hand up to Slate's face as we kissed. The man was uncannily flexible for his size but for him to be facing me....

Slate took my hand from his face and ran it over the crease in his pecs and down his countless bronze muscles ever south until his fingers wrapped over mine between his legs.

Brass.

His stubbled jaw brushed against my throat as his plump lips molded over my skin. It was happening, it wasn't some crazy sex dream. I was my brother's sister.

Brass was inside me. Slate was beside me. I kissed Slate, letting him guide my hand over him and only had a small flare of insane jealousy that he seemed well practiced at sharing a woman. My free hand fisted in the white sheets. I didn't forget that Brass utilized his mind reading abilities while he made love, no movement was insignificant. I felt a delicious pull in my stomach and bit back a moan that would've echoed against Slate.

"Let go, love," Brass breathed against my ear. "He wants to hear you."

Frigga's sweet grass!

I pulsed and cursed aloud a stream of creative profanity, thinking I was not going to last a second longer. They both chuckled breathlessly; cinnamon and cloves, spring and fall and my senses were overloaded by the men I loved.

I felt Slate's teeth elongate against my lips and the sting of his bite as he drew blood. His emotions blossomed in my mind as my blood mingled in his mouth.

"Suck your finger," Slate whispered against my lips.

I shifted my head pulling my left ring finger into my mouth and Brass moaned behind me. He braced his weight on his elbow as I took his hand and sucked his ring finger so his tiwaz tattoo and our bond activated as well. Brass and Slate were in my mind.

I shifted my face to Slate, and he crushed his mouth over mine hard enough so a small cut formed where my rune was. A low moan deep in his chest grew louder with Brass's deep slow thrusts picking up pace. My mind spun with their pleasure and a high moan pulled from my throat.

"*Ah!*" I felt my eyes roll as I clenched around Brass.

"*Scarlett,*" Slate's rumble and Brass's smooth deep voices blended into one as our bonds created a domino effect of mind-numbing pleasure.

Brass rolled from my back and I felt Slate grip my waist flipping me over and pushed my thighs apart with his hips as he kissed along my chest. Tremors shook through me as his palm slid up my thighs.

"Tell us if you cannot handle more," Slate said, tugging a nipple between his lips.

I nodded limply, and he pushed into my sensitive, throbbing parts. Brass cupped my face and drew it to his. His mouth claimed mine as Slate began to move, Brass's hand cupped my breast and Slate guided my hand over his flexing backside. My back bowed on the bed and Brass chuckled.

"The benefit of the bond. Multiple orgasms."

My morning was going to be long and vigorous.

Every time my body felt as if the threads of my existence were being torn apart in another *petite mort;* Slate and Brass felt it. I understood entirely why the French called it *the little death*, forgetting yourself and the world during each climax.

The more comfortable I became with both men, the more limits they pushed with me. I couldn't help, but think they were somehow communicating without my knowledge. Slate and Brass didn't break out into a fist fight as I feared. In fact, I *felt* that they were in sync. There weren't any awkward moments, they anticipated my wants with their own.

I never wanted to leave this bed. I never wanted Brass or Slate to leave. I wanted to be selfish and keep them, to wake up to them both every morning. To have their children, to make love to them until my death.

Frigga's sweet grass, I *was* Jett.

CHAPTER 42
JETT

Scarlett left Ash's wedding early after an altercation with Canis. Jett couldn't find her afterwards, he assumed she'd gone home. He decided to check in on her. Things between her and Slate had been tense, and she'd shut Brass out thinking it was for the best, but she tended not to eat when she was miserable. At least she wasn't training like a lunatic. Likely that was only because Slate and Brass were either at Shadow Breaker headquarters or training rooms.

Sparrow and Hawk were eating lunch out on the covered walkway that wrapped around the cloister when he arrived at the Dagr palace. Jett smiled as he approached.

"Scarlett in?"

Sparrow gestured to the empty seats in front of them. "She wasn't here for breakfast, but her doors are shut, so she must be in. She usually keeps them open. The staff didn't bring her breakfast though. You're free to check in on her. She's been sleeping in and not eating enough. We were glad she has been so busy this week, last week she didn't get out of bed at all."

"See if you can get her out of the palace to get some fresh air," Hawk suggested and Jett nodded.

"I'll give it my all," Jett said. giving them a playful salute and walked to the slatted arches.

Jett opened the door that led into the living room and walked through the wing. He frowned at the scattering of clothes on the dining room floor and the knocked over chairs. There looked like some scuffle had taken place and Jett's stomach turned. He should have come looking for her last night.

Through the hall, the door to the bedroom wasn't shut. Jett heard Scarlett's groans and panicked. He knocked the door open with his shoulder and came up short. Jett balled his hands into fists.

"What the fuck! You fucking bastards!" Jett shouted, and Scarlett screamed.

Tree was curled up on snowy white blankets crumpled on the floor. On his back under the sheer white panels of fabric of the massive bed was Brass. His hand was fisted in her hair as she faced away from him leaning back on his hips. That was not why Jett cursed. Slate had her legs as he kneeled between them. When Jett had shouted, Scarlett had lifted her head from where it had hung back and spotted him *then* started screaming. Slate took a moment to release her legs and move enough so Brass could roll her over and she *called* over a robe.

Jett was too shocked to say anything more or move. He gaped at the trio as Scar covered herself. They were all slick with sweat, they must have been at it for some time. She pushed her hair away from her face and it stuck to her skin everywhere it touched. Slate watched her carefully as one might a criminal deviant, Brass looked like he wanted hold her and offer her comfort.

She was shaking as she raised her head to Jett. "You shouldn't be here," She said in her gravelly voice that had a tremor to it.

"*Me?* Are you fucking kidding me? What the fuck are you doing? Have you lost your mind? Get dressed, you assholes," Jett said, walking into the dining room and grabbing their clothes before tossing them at the men.

"She is a grown woman. Since when is it frowned upon to sleep with one's own wife?" Slate asked smugly.

She rubbed her hands over her face as if she was not believing what was happening. "He's never going to forgive me," she whispered.

"Who?" Jett asked. There was not a third man — of that Jett was sure.

"*My* Slate. When he gets his memories back the new memories won't erase," she was going to cry.

Brass had pulled his pants on and saw what Jett saw in Scarlett as Slate dressed. "Scarlett?" he asked, straightening and pulling his hair back.

"Jett's right, please leave. Both of you. This... was a mistake," she squeaked as she hurried to the bathroom.

Slate caught her gently around the waist. "Easy, Scarlett. Relax. You are only upset because you are not ready for someone to find out," he said in a soothing tone much like the way he used to speak to her.

"It may not look how others think it should, but what you felt last night... this morning — it's real, love," Brass said, trying to placate her.

Her cheeks were already damp. "When you get your memories back, please don't hate me," she said as her eyes scanned Slate's and yanked away from him before running into the bathroom and locking the door.

Jett folded his arms over his chest and watched the men dress. Brass sank down on the bed and rubbed his hands over his face before meeting Jett's eyes.

"We're not taking advantage of her, despite how it looks. I want to be her second husband. I, *we* were showing her, rather than telling her that we worked things through. We did not expect to do it last night, but it happened that way."

Brass looked to Slate who inhaled deeply. "She is my addiction. I cannot get enough of her even when I am furious with her. I do not want her marrying another man. Brass is my brother. I can live with Brass, but some random man the Straumr boy picked cannot be tolerated. Personally, I think it was going rather well. Brass?"

Brass looked to Jett and nodded. "I'm in love with her. I'll take her anyway I can get her."

"I thought you were going to back off?" Jett said, rubbing his palms over his eyes in the hope he could wipe the image of Slate and Brass making love to Scarlett out of his memory.

"I am not moving back," Slate said as the shower turned on in the bathroom.

"Then why are you *here*? You shouldn't be giving her false hope." Jett's jaw clenched. "I don't give a shit who she slept with. You should know better. She's pregnant and fragile and Gods help her, she can't think clearly when it comes to either of you. So you're either with her or you leave her the fuck alone."

"Jett. It's not like that," Brass said, getting to his feet. "Slate, tell him the truth. Go to her and tell *her*."

"There is nothing to tell. I am leaving," Slate said, collecting his beads and fetishes out of the bowl on the nightstand then poured Brass's out in his hand.

"Tell her what?" Jett asked, furrowing his brow.

"Nothing," Slate growled.

Brass shook his head. "You don't lose anything by admitting it. You gain much more. You saw what it could be like, it would be even better."

Slate's eyes flashed. "It was a good time. That was all."

"You're in love with her. You always have been. Stay, brother. Stop trying to pretend like you don't or that that Gods be damned prophecy matters enough to prevent you from being happy. *She* makes you happy." Brass kept going even though Slate's anger mounted.

"She is the best fuck in Tidings, *that* is what keeps me coming back. Lust not love," Slate growled.

If Brass hadn't done it, Jett would have. Brass had leapt to his feet and punched Slate square in the jaw. Jett inhaled sharply as Slate whipped back around and threw punches of his own. It was a long time coming. Jett thought he'd be noble and try to break them apart but ended up getting rolled into it.

"Stop! Stop! Please! I knew this would happen. Slate! Brass!" Scarlett was sobbing and soaking wet with her thin champagne satin robe clinging to her skin.

Wet hair hung in dripping ropes as she tried to pull on the men's shirts. She wasn't thinking and with all the fists flying... She cried out, and all fighting stopped in an instant. Scarlett was on her back, her nose bled over her fingers where she sat on the marble floor.

Slate was the first one to scramble free. For a man who claimed he didn't care about her, his hard features were etched with worry. He placed his hands on her stomach and saw her blood stopped running over her wrists. They'd broken her perfectly straight nose.

"You are okay, Scarlett. The bairn are okay." She raised pink polished fingernails to his cheek and *called*.

Jett healed Brass, and he returned the favor. Brass and Jett scooted up to where Scar sat and glanced away. Brass pulled her robe closed at her legs, but it nothing for the way it clung to her damp skin.

"Please leave," she said in a soft whisper. "This will never work."

Hawk chose that moment to come running into the wing. "Scarlett, dear Gods. Are you alright?" Hawk pushed past them all and scooped her off the floor making the other two men move aside.

"I'm fine, Hawk. Thank you."

She didn't bother fighting him off. Slate and Brass had blood of their own as did Jett on their faces. Hawk glared at them and Jett cringed. He'd been there the week before when he'd put his foot down with Scarlett and saw why Scarlett, Tawny, and Gypsum had come to Tidings so sheltered and well behaved. For all his mild manners, Hawk was a stern parent who didn't care how old they were, if they needed a talking to, he'd do it.

"You boys go get cleaned up. Scar, I'm going to run a bath and send in a tray of food that you're going to finish. Now, I don't know what's going on here, but it ends now. You're family, she's pregnant and has lost her mother and father while finding out this whole other life existed outside of the one she knew. She's strong, not indestructible. You love her? Take care of her. Put her needs before your own. That is how love works. When they're down, you lift them up," Hawk scolded. "Sorry, Scar. I don't mean to talk about you like you aren't here."

"Just get them to leave, please," she whispered.

FORTY-THREE

Hawk had helped me wipe my face and when we left the bathroom, Brass and Slate were gone. Jett had sat on a freshly changed bed with a tray of food leaning against a set of propped up pillows.

"Well, out of all the things I expected to see when I entered your bedroom, a ménage à trois with your husband and lover was not what I would've guessed in a million years. I thought Slate ended things because you slept with Brass? Talk about mixed messages." Jett patted the bed next to him.

I walked into the closet instead and put on my fluffiest pair of socks and fleece pajama pants with a long-sleeved cotton top.

"What do you want, Jett?" I asked coolly.

"Come. Eat," Jett said, holding up the tray.

I did as he bid. When I settled in beside him he transferred the tray into my lap. A simple B.L.T. and cheese and broccoli soup rested on the tray, I could stomach that down even with my lack of appetite.

Jett rested his head on my shoulder as I dipped my sandwich into the creamy cheese. "I didn't mean to interrupt. You left abruptly last night; I came to make sure you were okay."

"Canis confronted me." I told him about the interaction between Canis, Brass, and I the night before and Jett cursed.

"It's good you had company last night in case he sent someone to steal the pieces from you. Did you even think of that? Not that you would have noticed. In all the years I've known Slate and Brass, I've never been able to sneak up on the two of them together."

I gave him a sidelong glance. "I'm not sure to take that as a compliment or an insult."

Jett arched his brow at me. "A compliment, of course. I can hardly judge. My wives would kill me," he said with an arrogant smile.

I sighed and laid back on the mound of pillows. "Jett, I need a favor. I think we can cross off the Minotaurs and Crathode from the tribes who have the last two pieces. I think the Lycans do. It's not on Thrimilci or Mabon which leaves the Jotnar and Bjorn in Elivagar and the Jorogumo and Gorgons in Ostara. We're going to the Lycans next month so..."

Jett pursed his lips. "You want me to go to Ostara to visit the Jorogumo and Gorgons with you?"

"If I go on my own, you'll strangle me," I said, giving him a lopsided smile.

Jett took my tray and placed it on the nightstand pushing the flowers in the vase to the edge. "As will Slate and Brass. They're complete idiots who took advantage of your love for them, but they do care about you."

I rubbed my temples. "Brass wants to be my second husband. They didn't really take advantage of me. I'm my brother's sister." I said ruefully. "I thought I was delirious or drugged last night until this morning. It was completely insane for me to think they could... that I could... I have no idea how you make it work with Cherry and Amethyst, but Slate and Brass are too much for one silly girl. What happened?"

"Slate said something shitty and Brass punched him. It snowballed from there and I got caught up in it. You need a break from them. Who is on this list Ash comprised? Maybe a nice *normal* date would put things into perspective," Jett offered.

"More men? That's your answer?" I chuckled. "It can't make matters worse."

"Take a nap first. You three were at it all night?" Jett probed teasingly, and I scowled.

"None of your business, pervert."

Jett laughed and pulled my head down into his lap.

I kept waiting for Canis to attack or confront me, but it never happened. He hadn't even spread Brass's confession as I thought he would. If he'd told Ash I'd hand-fasted Brass, things could get bad between us earlier on than I could have handled.

Brass had managed to glean from his mind that Canis had two of the stone pieces. It was bad news, but that meant we had two more to get before him. There wasn't any time to think of ways to get the pieces from Canis because I spent my nights reviewing piles of paperwork Ash placed on my desk at the end of each day.

We hadn't spoken about his proposition. Quartz was in Ash's office every night which adjoined mine on the highest floor of Valla U. I had slowly begun redecorating it from how Reed had it with portraits I'd had painted of my mother, father, and family. In the portrait of our family I'd added Quick and Brass. Quick would-be Indigo's husband within the year or next year possibly and Brass was the father of my children. It made sense.

Pearl offered her decorator to help decorate, and I graciously accepted. Leather-bound books Pearl had gifted me lined the shelves as well as a complete collection of Shakespeare published in the early 1900s on vellum from Basal. I asked Pearl what she thought it was worth, and she said I must have a very wealthy admirer because they were worth over fifty-thousand dollars.

Every night I went back to the Dagr palace and collapsed into bed with Tree curled around my belly. I could hardly look at myself in the mirror. I wasn't the first woman to lay with two men, but it was *those* two men. That night I had come between them in the literal sense.

Slate had tried to speak to me at Valla University, but I'd grown used to dodging him. It was harder to do during class, but unless he wanted to talk about it in front of Quick and Tawny, which he didn't, he didn't have a chance. Brass had shown up at the Dagr palace on the weekends, but I locked my slotted doors preemptively and he didn't dare shout from the walkway what he wanted to say.

December came too soon. There were three weeks until the arenas opened and our last challenge, the Ragnarök. Then we would all be tried and true and Gypsum would be inducted into Valla University. Ash and I had our first duties as Prime and his Second that weekend when we led two hundred Guardians into Mabon and repaired Karkinos.

We had done more damage than I had anticipated and while fifty Guardians kept the giant crustacean unconscious with their *calling*, others went inside and repaired the buildings. It took two full days of nonstop work to repair most of the damage so it could be completed through the use of portal doors. All the rogue tribesmen were gone. If it wasn't exactly how I remembered it, I would've thought I'd dreamt the nightmare that was Slate's rescue.

Ash had been especially attentive that weekend. I wished I wasn't feeling so weak and foolish, I would have insisted on my own tent. I was embarrassed to find that his company comforting and familiar. He was proud of me and it showed. Our dinners were private and had a romantic air, but he kept things friendly for the most part, careful not to cross the line. We had agreed on a man to court me.

Brass was competing the first Friday of December. Cory was going up against him and didn't stand a chance. Cory would always be Cocktails to me, my favorite bartender. Slate would be in Cordillera's suite when I finally arrived. Manipulating the patrons with my talents was the least I could do once a month, but it felt like a trap.

I was running late.

Ash kept me so I had to rush getting ready. I chose a cream dress in the Elivagar style, gold metallic lace embroidery swept down the back and over the sleeves of the dress. It had a plunging neckline from its high stiff collar and an empire waist cinched by a gold belt that rested just above my burgeoning belly. My bell skirts kicked as I hurried down the stone steps of headquarters.

I promised Cory I would be there to wish him luck. We'd gone on a few dates in the past week and I found his company refreshingly open and modest. I stopped in front of the metal double doors and evened my breaths as I pulled my loose curls over my shoulder. I had pinned the side of my hair back with a glittering gold comb. Tonight Brass and Slate would find out I was being courted.

I did feel bad about it. He was simple and kind; very low maintenance and he already knew most of my secrets.

No more waiting. I pushed through the doors and listened to my practical gold heeled boots click on the black marble as I walked to the front of the Shadow Breaker prep room. I cringed when I emerged between the aisles and found not only Katydid who was ready to pop, but Rosasite and Mirage. They were competing tonight as well.

The two women were clad in black leather bathing suit concoctions devised by Lera as Cory and Brass stood before Cricket. I smiled at the hairdressers and gave Bronze a quick hug. Brass was following me with his eyes. Cricket had already started oiling Cory.

"I'll give you a hand with that," I said, picking up the glass bottle of citrus smelling oils and trickling some in my palms.

"Thanks," the serious blonde said as she gave me a curious glance.

I rubbed my palms together to heat the oil and ran them up Albacore's back. I peered up at him through my lashes and as he flashed me a bright smile over his shoulder. His scent spiked. I smiled biting down on my lower lip and returned to my work. If rubbing oil over a powerfully muscled back could be called work.

"The Second to the Prime, Delegate to the Grand Mistress, wife of the Dagr patriarch, and Tio greater family daughter massaging oil onto the body of a Shadow Breaker in full view of the public," Brass murmured.

I was sure Cricket and Albacore heard him, but I didn't care. "That's a lot of fancy titles for one woman," I said wryly,. "My favorite is much more modest."

Mother.

I stood as I worked the oil over Cory's abs and along his arms and chest. "You do not have to do that, Delegate." Cory flashed me another bashful smile as his hazel eyes twinkled.

Cocktails was a wonderfully normal and totally uncomplicated man. Our dates were filled with pointless small talk that I found tremendously soothing.

I gave him a smile. "*Scarlett.* I promised I would see you off."

Cricket was oiling Brass who would've made Slate proud with his brooding.

"Will you come to Dark Shadows after?" Cory asked, running his hand over his tousled chestnut hair.

"For a little while, if you like," I told him, rubbing the oils into my hands. "We could go for ice cream instead. I know you have to make an appearance, but one of the few perks about dating a pregnant woman is that I come with every excuse to indulge in a frosty late-night treat at a whim."

I still wore my Dagr ring and the emerald ring. I didn't want it public knowledge that I was looking for a second husband. Ash especially, but he encouraged that I allow myself to be courted. Ash had gone ahead and chosen his favorite, I had a messenger with flowers sent to my wing from the unmarried Sunna heir the next day.

Cory's smile was broad and bright making crinkles at the corners of his hazel eyes. "I would like that."

I stood on my tiptoes and gave him a quick kiss on the cheek. We were taking things extremely slow. Given my history, I thought that was best. While I didn't believe Cocktails wanted to make me a notch on his weapon's belt, I was never one to rush into a physical relationship. I hadn't even kissed Cory yet, and I was perfectly content with that.

With Rosasite in the prep room, I thought I'd be safe from Brass's frustration, or whatever else he might've felt at finding out that I was dipping my toes in the Guardian dating pool. I was wrong.

Brass grabbed the arm of my soft cream dress and yanked me away. He was pulling a Slate and had done it in front of everyone. We walked down one of the black metal aisles of cubbies near the stalls. He gestured to the marble bench for me to sit. I pulled my arm away and fisted my hands on my hips.

"I'm starting to think Jett is right and every man I let close goes a little crazy. Your girlfriend is right there, the man courting me is right there. This is wildly inappropriate," I said in a harsh whisper.

Brass stood in front of me oiled so his dark honey muscles glowed under the lights. His hair was neatly combed into the knot at his nape. His amber eyes were molten.

"Albacore? My subordinate? That is who you've chosen as your second husband?" Brass's voice was not meant for harsh words, but for sweet whispers.

"He's courting me, Brass. I'm not marrying anyone. By the Mother, I swear. I usually take things slow. You wouldn't know because you started kissing me within the first five minutes we spoke. As did your brother-in-arms. I'm not that person," I insisted. "I like taking things slow and —"

"You're running. Not physically, but you might as well. He does not stand a chance against you. I know with Slate and I your usual rules don't apply. They never have. Things *had* moved slowly, love. I saw you months before I kissed you, almost a year before you let me into your bed. We went weeks and then months before you let me back in. I do not want to wait another few months before I'm allowed back. Neither does Slate, no matter what he says. He loves you."

"You are the most genuine, compassionate, and honest man I've ever met and I love you to pieces —"

"But?" he interrupted.

"But, your girlfriend is in *this* very room. I gave you guys a chance. It doesn't work, the three of us don't work. Go back to Rosasite, get married, have babies, Brass. You can have a full life still without having to share."

Brass rushed me and pushed me into the stalls beside us. "You already have my sons. I want to marry *you*."

His hands gripped me to side of my face as he kissed me. He pushed my head back as he kissed down my throat and over the exposed cleavage of my plunging neckline.

... Brass. Stop...

I didn't dare try my voice. I could barely breathe.

"Gods, did you have to wear so many layers?" Brass breathed.

I gripped his roaming hands and gently pushed him away. He rested his cheek on the top of my head as he steadied his breathing. Brass was not one to lose his head. My indecision had broken him.

... I'm sorry...

"Don't," he whispered as I slid from him and walked briskly out of the prep room.

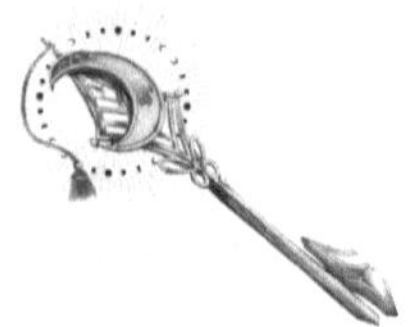

I ended up hiding in the third Vegas room to avoid a similar encounter with Slate. Brass was better at words and emotions than Slate. He would just make that deep growling noise and lift my skirts up against a wall somewhere and then I'd be in real trouble. Brass I could rationalize with, but Slate would take one whiff of my scent and take it as an invitation.

I manipulated the patrons as Lera wanted. Brass won, and I met Cory on the stairs after I passed Gharial. Brass's regular patron, the statuesque blonde, would soothe any wounds I'd caused earlier.

I knew I intimidated Cory. I never had that effect before, but in my new positions, with my abilities, it was easy to see why that would be.

Cory flashed me an easy smile when I met him and we skipped Dark Shadows and got ice cream in the rumpus room. I was nervous Slate would pass us as he left headquarters so I invited Cory back to the Dagr palace.

Cory was a hand holder. It was shaping out much more like the relationship I had with Chris than either Brass or Slate. I got a throw blanket from my wing as he waited on the covered walkway. I wasn't ready to invite him in yet even in an innocent capacity. We held hands and walked to the part of the cloister where I'd planted the morning glory vine.

We laid downside by side on the blanket as Cory traced his fingers along my hand. "What happened in the prep room today?"

I was waiting for the question. I picked at the grass blades beside the blanket as we laid under the stars. I'd changed into a sage colored chiffon halter in the Thrimilci fashion and let my hair loose.

"I don't know when the appropriate time to bring this up would be, but I might as well tell you now. Stop me if I start to scare you at any point." I turned my face towards him and he gave me a lopsided grin.

"I know you are married to Slate and pregnant with his twins, you are Second to the Prime, you are a greater family daughter, the Shadow Breaker delegate, an elemental, and you are opening five arenas in Tidings as the Guardians first organized sport. Scary, Scarlett? You terrify me," Cory said.

I giggled. "I don't think I've ever heard it put that way before. Why did you invite me to dinner then?"

Cory shifted onto his elbow to look down at me. "The Prime has begun to put it out into certain circles that you are looking for a second husband. Not many know about it, but news about Shadow Breakers gets around headquarters fast. I asked you to dinner because I thought you might say yes, whether from pity or interest, it was a chance I was willing to take."

I blushed as I smiled up at him. "There's more. Brass asked to be my second husband. I turned him down because it caused tensions between Slate and him. The twins aren't Slate's, they're Brass's. We were together for a brief time."

He sighed. "But not because you did not want him," Cory said pointedly.

I twirled a grass blade between my fingers like a propeller. "I wanted to warn you. I don't know where this will take us but courting me will come with complications. Slate said he would go along with whomever I choose. Ash, uh, the Prime wants me to have a more...supportive husband. He's also very invested in me and tends to butt into my business a lot. Brass might be another story, that's what happened in the locker room. He isn't backing down."

Cory looked down at me still smiling. "Have you gone to dinner with anyone else?"

"No." I said quickly, "The heir to the Sunna sent me flowers, but aside from social gatherings, I've never had a personal conversation with him. To him, I'm an opportunity, which is fine I guess for second husband in my position." I couldn't help my sigh.

"What do you want out of a second?" he asked in earnest.

I shrugged. "I never thought I would have one. I married Slate for love and that hasn't worked out. Companionship, I suppose. Someone who is relaxed, levelheaded, who doesn't have too much of a career that he can't support me in mine. A man who'll be there when I wake up, who will hold me all night as I sleep. I don't need fireworks, but I do want sparks."

"You and Brass dated? Is there any other serious competition?" he asked, pushing a strand of my hair from my face.

"No. I've only dated four men in Tidings. Ash Straumr, Slate Dagr, Brass Regn, and now Albacore Stone." I bit down on my lower lip; I wouldn't include Balas.

He raised his brows. "The Prime, Patriarch Dagr, a lesser family son who is commissioner of your arenas, and a peasant."

"You're not a peasant," I chastised gently and Cory laughed.

"Yes, I am. I am a bar owner and tender. That is all. I have nothing to offer you," Cory said, letting out a deep breath.

I tentatively reached up to push his hair behind his ears and ran my fingers down his jaw. "That is what I'm looking for. I have everything already. What I want is a man who will stick by me, faithful and caring who wants kids."

Cory's smile brightened to the one that crinkled the corners of his eyes and he leaned lower. "I love kids."

My smile deepened. Cory licked his lips. His scent had slowly been building the more comfortable he was getting on the grass with me. I swallowed hard and Cory lowered his head.

"I very much want to kiss you, Delegate," he whispered.

My giggle was that of a teenage girl. "Scarlett."

Cory's broad smile was as bright as the stars behind him. "Scarlett," he conceded.

His lips slanted softly over mine and my eyes slid closed. It was sweet and innocent. He withdrew and looked down at me searching my eyes. Whatever he saw made him smile and press his lips to mine again, growing bolder. He leaned into the kiss and I slid my hands into his hair.

Cory withdrew again and pressed gentle pecks to my lips. "I have wanted to do that since you walked into my bar. You are the most beautiful woman I have ever seen and incredibly intimidating."

I giggled, and he kissed me again. "I like you, Cory," I said in between kisses.

Cory was testing my limits; he was nervous, and I found it endearing. If I had boyfriends in high school, my make-out session with Cory would have been perfectly in place there. He seemed to sense that he'd found as far as I'd let him go.

"Careful. She will tear your heart out," Slate rumbled from behind us, and Cory shifted from me.

I licked my lips and sat up, self-consciously smoothing my hair and dress. "Slate. What an unexpected surprise."

I turned around and saw that it was not just Slate, but Brass. Cory got to his feet looking uncomfortable and offered me his hand. I stared at his hand and sighed.

"You don't have to go," I told him.

"It is getting late. Will I see you tomorrow?" Cory asked, trying to ignore the two giant menacing jerks five feet away from us.

I fidgeted. "I have plans with my brother, but you can come with. I'll send you a messenger in the morning with the details. Feel free to stay home, I won't be insulted."

"Tomorrow it is. Awarded two Mjolnir, I have a feeling my life will be much more exciting with you in it. Goodnight, Delegate. *Scarlett*," he corrected as he leaned in and pressed his lips to my cheek before he did an admirable job of facing Brass and Slate. "Captains," he said, inclining his head.

Brass and Slate gave slight nods to Cory, to my astonishment, as he walked from the cloister. I collected the blanket from the grass and shook it.

"Leave it, love. You know how much I love the stars," Brass said.

I folded the blanket, ignoring them both until I held in front of me and needed to pass them. "Excuse me, it's late and pregnancy saps my energy."

"Where are you going tomorrow?" Slate asked with glinting eyes.

Sugarfoot. I tried to think fast while not letting Brass into my mind.

"Were you spying on me?" I accused.

"There was not much to see, girl. He was too afraid to touch you," Slate said with a mocking smile and he chuckled. "You are going to get that boy hurt."

"He's older than you," I said coolly.

"Don't change the subject." Brass leveled his eyes at me.

"How was Gharial, Brass?" I asked smugly as I shouldered my way between them.

Slate chuckled. "Do you want me to tuck you in?"

I whipped around. "I will never ask you to my bed ever again." I paused. "Not unless you get your memories back."

"Are you going to keep leading him on? You know he cannot handle you, love. You're hypersexual. I mean that with the utmost respect. You'll only hurt him. There's no point wasting your time and his. Your heart is spoken for, love." Brass said in his smooth deep voice.

I knit my brow and clutched the blanket to my chest. "Hypersexual?"

"A side effect of the rousen. I didn't think you knew that most people are not as amorous as you are, love. You have more...demanding and sudden bouts of desire that can lead to you being reckless or angry. The Gods know neither of us have complaints about it. Slate?" Brass gestured to Slate who chuckled.

"Dear gods, no. I do not have a single complaint about it except that you are not ready and willing at this very moment," Slate said with a curl of those lips.

"I am going to bed now," I grumbled, aggravated that they spoke so casually about bedding me.

"Do not wait long, Scarlett. The longer you wait, the more hostile you shall become," Slate called after me.

"Both of you have other women waiting for you. Go to them," I shouted back.

When I reached the wing and shut the slatted doors, I waited at the main entrance with my palms against the slats. Warm night air wound its way around to tangle with my hair. No cinnamon, no cloves. I left the last door unlocked and showered.

Tree was the only one in my great white canopied bed when I stepped out of the bathroom. I cursed myself for the disappointment I felt and wondered if they went back to those other women as I'd suggested.

CHAPTER

FORTY-FOUR

"This is not the weekend I had in mind," Quick said with an adorable pout that even made me think the Lothario was *extra* attractive today.

Indigo laughed and stood on her tiptoes as she kissed his lips in the Sumar portal room bathed in the blue light. They were so in love it made me want to dance. Indigo knew Ostara better than Jett, but Quick knew it even better than she did having grown up there and run wild as boys without parents are wont to do.

She didn't have classes and where she went, Quick went these days. Jett was leaving the girls behind and would have left me behind if the tribes would've willingly given the piece to anyone other than me.

We were wearing thin waterproof cloaks and traveling clothes that would help us to blend in with the jungles. Cory wasn't as tall as Quick or Jett, but he was a Shadow Breaker which meant he was rippling with muscles I'd had the pleasure of oiling last night.

I couldn't stop thinking about what Brass and Slate said about my hypersexuality. I always outlasted Chris, but I chalked it up to him not

435

being a Guardian. Slate wasn't entirely human and Brass always acted like every time was the last time we would be together. I supposed I wasn't entirely human either. I never stopped to imagine what other side effects the rousen had had on me past my internal inferno of simmering lust. I didn't like to think I was a slave to my impulses as they suggested even if I knew for a fact it was true. I'd proven it time and time again to myself.

Jett handed me a light pack, lighter than the others and I slung it over my head and frowned. "Gods, Jett. I'm not *that* pregnant yet. I can handle a little more weight."

"Your boyfriend can carry the extra weight, Scar. You know you're putting Quick and I in an awkward position," he said, pretending to check his long seaxes as he spoke to me.

Indigo's long corn silk braid fell over her shoulder as she spoke to Cory who was very hard not to get along with since he was so easy going. Quick knew him from the Shadow Breakers and was being friendly enough, but obviously felt the same way Jett did.

"Cory is courting me. If he's going to be a part of my life, it's better he knows what he's getting into now before it goes any further or we'll just waste one another's time," I said, planting a brown booted foot on the reflective floor.

Jett leveled his almond eyes at me. "That is not what I meant. Brass and Spinel have approached Hawk and Pearl about becoming your second husband. Slate has thrown his support behind him."

My blood boiled. "So many times you all joked about the three of us. I always knew if I remotely entertained the idea, they would always gang up against me." My cheeks flushed when I remembered what Jett had walked in on. "If Slate wasn't a complete cache hole, this wouldn't even be an issue. It doesn't look like he's going to get his memories back," I said, changing the subject.

Jett had looked away, his own cheeks reddening. "You were always attracted to Brass. We all knew it. It has always been between the two of them, no one could have suspected they would agree to share you and you would be the one against it. Why are you against it?"

I ran my fingers through my hair letting them slide over the pearls, beads from both men, the peacock feather, and the fetishes. "Because Slate can't share. He's not wired that way. Brass and he were friends before I ever came along, I can't get between them. It breaks my heart to have them fight over me. Slate can hate Cory; it doesn't bother me near as much. Slate doesn't want to be my husband, he... he just doesn't want all the responsibilities. *If* his memories returned, who knows how much worse it'll be if I've married Brass as well. I don't have any answers. I only have questions. Ash wants me to have some arm candy to support me and I admit, I'm lonely. Not for sex, I could have meaningless relations with whoever, but for girly stuff. I *want* dates. Normal dates. Ice cream, picnics, star gazing, and candlelit dinners. Slate isn't very good at that stuff, which never bothered me until I didn't have that *look* anymore."

I gave Jett an apologetic smile.

"Sorry for the vent. I miss him. This new version of him confuses me. He wants me, but he doesn't. He wants me in his bed, but not to support the arenas or my new position. He used to be all or nothing, but now it's this thin trickle. Whatever. Anyway, just be nice to Cory please. He's one of my better choices of boyfriends."

Jett wrapped his arm around my neck and kissed the top of my head. "Chris wasn't bad. Brass would've been good if Slate wasn't one of two of his only friends. Cory is... baby sis, I think you're going to break him. No joke. He's cool. I've met him before, but you're a different woman. Old Scarlett, the one who came here from Chicago would've been perfect for him... but this one." He shook his head and dropped his voice to a whisper. "No judgement. I do it on a daily basis. Two weeks ago, you deftly handled a barghest hybrid and a mind reader all night. Who got into a fight over you because they're both in love with you. You're the Second to the Prime, to the Grand Mistress. You're the wife of the Dagr patriarch. This guy is in way over his head just by hanging out with you much less putting himself in the way of all that by courting you."

I frowned. "He'll be fine. That's why I invited him. To make sure he can handle the good with the bad. He's a trained Shadow Breaker. Brass trained him himself. Quick didn't tell Brass where we were going did he?"

"Where are your other two bodyguards? Those are Brass's Breakers, too. They might tell him," Jett said pointedly.

"I didn't think of that. I never see them; they just appear whenever someone gets too close that they don't recognize. Let's get going. I don't want Brass or Slate to show up at random and demand to come with," I said, giving Jett a nudge.

"Two more men might be a good idea, Scar. No one has checked in on the Jorogumo since dad died and the Gorgons have no official ambassador, though Canis is the last one to have interacted with them if that gives you any idea of what kind of tribe they might be. I've never seen one personally, but —"

"We'll be fine, Jett. I'm Night's child, daughter of spring and summer. This sugarfoot is my destiny. If it's not all a part of some greater scheme, what the fiddlestick am I doing wasting my happiness trying to save this cursed world for?"

None of the other islands were more vivid than Ostara. A sleek white stone bridge started at the portal and spanned the water below it to the shimmering glass like castle that rose straight up from a piece of land that stood narrow and tall high above the water. A second bridge spanned the other side to reach another cliff side. Mirrored spheres nestled in the bridge rails reflected the blue sky.

We stood facing the castle with Ostara's heart down the sloped cliff side. Its wooden homes and shops painted warm pastels and trim carved like white lace was more inviting than the path we would have to take.

"Your castle awaits you, Patriarch Var," I teased.

Jett grunted and Cory blinked. "Gods, I forgot how everyone in your family is so powerful and wealthy. Your cousin... she's Matriarch Vetr, right?"

I nodded. "My other cousin is the heir to the Sumar, my sister-in-law is the future matriarch to the Geol's, my first husband is the Patriarch to the Dagr line. See why I need a little of normalcy now?" I asked, giving him a smile, but he looked daunted.

"We're regular people like everyone else, our problems are just on a more influential scale. For instance, this is the worst idea anyone's ever had in the history of Tidings," Indigo said as we approached the cliff side.

"If we had gone last night, we would have been back by Monday night, but Scar here didn't want to," Jett grumbled.

"I wanted to lend my support to Cory. It'll be fine. We'll just have to do a lot of running when we get there," I defended.

Quick choked on a laugh. "We will be lucky if we make it through the underground river in one piece. We do not even know if the tunnel is high enough or wide enough for the raft."

In the clear water below the castle I could make up forms swimming and slithering in the water. Anguillan moved unnaturally through the water. A hidden cove would lead us to their river that went under Ostara and let out in their lands. It was a bad idea, but if we didn't, it would take a week to go to the Jorogumo and the Gorgons since they were on opposite ends of the island. With the Ragnarök in three weeks and Canis knowing I had the pieces; we couldn't waste time.

"We'll cross that bridge when we get there. Indigo will shift and make sure the water speeds us along, Cory and Jett you guys can *call* the air to push us along. Quick and I will defend in case we're attacked. Get the raft ready so we can blow it up the moment we reach the water. I'll *call,* masking our descent until we reach the bottom."

The mission was my baby, and on my head if we all ended up dying.

We checked our gear and looked down from the dizzying height to our goal. I said a silent prayer and Jett put his hand on my shoulder.

"I go, you go, then Cory, Indi, and Quick comes down last. Cory can help you with the shadows." Jett looked to Cory who gave him a solemn nod.

Jett checked the rope around my waist and then Indigo's even though Quick had just checked it and nodded before giving me a rakish grin and lowering himself over the side of the cliff. My stomach knotted.

"Activate your bond, Indi," I said, hoping that the comfort of her emotions in my mind would help.

Indi nodded and *called* slicing the skin just above her laguz rune that bonded her to me and Jett. It was a little Celtic vertical line with a second slanted line that angled down to the right to look like a barb — water. I did the same, and she gave me a rueful smile.

I stepped to the edge of the cliff side that small plants and clumps of dirt stuck to and got down on my knees slinging them over trying to find purchase. Cory held the rope in front of me and gave me a reassuring smile. I felt awful that who I really wanted there was Slate or Brass. Jett directed me where to stick my feet and I was over the side clinging to the gritty rocks like some ill-fated tree whose seedling had taken a wrong turn in the wind.

Cory was over next and our progress was painfully slow. My fingers were not nearly as calloused as I believed they were which I found out the hard way as they scuffed along the hard stone supporting weight I didn't usually have to bear with my belly rubbing up against the rocks the entire time. My arms shook with my effort to not plummet to my death.

Indigo and Quick were both over and what energy I wasn't dispersing on climbing, I used to mask our bodies from the Anguillan and anyone who might be looking through the castle windows to the five idiots trying to use a tribe's river way to get deeper into the island the fastest route possible.

It wasn't illegal, especially since I was now in the second highest position of power in Tidings and Jett was the heir, but Canis was Canis. Him finding me with five of the pieces trying to confiscate a sixth wouldn't end with me leaving with all six pieces.

Quick cursed and we all flattened ourselves to the cliff side to avoid the stones he'd knocked free. "Are you okay?" Indigo asked in a strained voice.

"Fine, Dove. Keep going," Quick said, and I felt the bond change.

My eyes widened. "Gods, how can you think about sex at a time like this, 'Quick' Silver Regn?" I cursed, and he chuckled.

"I cannot think of a better time than when faced with life-or-death situations. I would much rather be in bed with Dove's legs —"

"Shut your mouth!" Indi said in a harsh whisper. "You activated your bonds, Silver. She can feel what you feel through me. Sorry, Jett."

"I hate having sisters," he grumbled. "I don't mean that, what I should say is I hate having lecherous fiends for friends who have ensnared my once innocent sweet sisters."

Cory and Quick chuckled, and I smiled as we started down again. It might have only been twenty minutes, but it had felt like a week that we clung to that crooked rock wall and when Jett reached the water, things went fast. Jett had gone to Chicago and gotten a river raft; he pulled the cord that rapidly inflated.

"Now!" Jett said in a shouted whisper and he climbed into the raft.

I was down next and then Cory, Indigo, and Quick jumped. Jett focused on masking us while I used my unusually strong *calling* to buffer their falls. We untied the rope that bound us together and I scanned the waters. Anguillan were everywhere and we couldn't hide the ripples the raft made.

"We have to go *now*," I said, kneeling in the raft.

Indigo had already begun undressing and handed Quick her clothes as he put them into her pack. Cory was looking out at the beady eyed scaled monsters with slithering arms and thin mouths that held sharp pointed teeth. Cory was from Valla. Only Leshys lived on Valla, no other infamous tribes as the other islands homed. Indigo dove over the side and Quick sat down saying a prayer to the Mother.

"As soon as I trick her into getting pregnant, we are not going on any more of these outrageous missions. You hear me, Scarlett?" Quick asked, and I gave my belly a pat.

"Doesn't stop me, I doubt it would her."

Quick cursed and the raft jolted as we started to move around the horseshoe bay that led out into the oceans that surrounded Ostara. Cory and Jett *called*, speeding us along with the wind and I *called* shadows to hide us, but the green, bald, scaly heads of the Anguillan bobbed in the waters as they looked for the source of the wake. Couldn't Mother Nature have taken me up on the bunny hybrid tribe?

The air was cooler closer to the water, but the humidity was high and my taupe linen shirt soon stuck to my skin. My cloak was packed around my roll with a few other items I thought might be beneficial to the trip. The rocky sides of the island encased us with the pillar that the Var castle sat upon with the ocean far to our left.

My hand wound around the bungee cord that lined the top of the raft as Indigo pushed us closer into the mass of Anguillan that swam around the pillar's base. The Anguillan, like all the other tribes, were many colors, but bore a general resemblance. Some were striped, some were bright blues and yellows, the ones I took for females had a long fin that crested their scaled heads. Instead of noses, they had two slits for nostrils over a bridge of skin like the Merfolk with gills at the sides of their jaws that flared and flattened as they searched the waters for us.

"They have been given orders to kill all intruders. This may not have been a good idea," Cory said gravely.

He was an omnilinguist, he could speak and understand any language including the tribes. Their allegro tempo beats were meaningless to me. My uncle, Jackal, would be smiling knowingly if he could see me now.

"You think?" Quick asked dryly, and I shot him a look.

"We're going to hit one of them eventually, there isn't enough space to guide between them." Jett said from the front of the raft.

"Do your best, that's all you can do," I said with my blood thundering in my ears. "Canis must want no one looking around. That's kind of reassuring that we might be on the right path."

We neared the pillar the castle sat upon and saw the way the waters smoothed the rocks. Indigo must have seen the entrance to the river, I spotted it right away. We'd have to duck and the sides of the raft would fit, but only just. I was rocked as we collided with the head of an Anguillan looking for us and cursed.

"Go!" Cory shouted.

I let the shadows drop as the nearest Anguillan hissed and dove under the waters to attack us. Cory, Jett, Quick, and I used our *calling* to speed the raft as Anguillan hissed and tried to grab hold of the raft as we passed. Quick pulled an elemental formed Indigo out of the water before Anguillan could pry her from the raft. She dressed as we pushed forward.

Slimy eel fins and limbs knocked the raft about, spiky teeth tried to bite into the raft. We *called* and used the pommels of our blades to knock the Anguillan from the raft.

"There!"

Indigo spun the raft, and we threw ourselves down as the raft pushed through the narrow tunnel. Cory and Jett moved to the front of the raft dunking Anguillan who tried to stop our forward momentum with only enough space to rest their chins on the edge of the raft unless they wanted it to swipe against the top of the tunnel. Quick took up the back while Indi and I used our *calling* to use the air and waters around us to propel us deeper down the river.

It dropped, and the ceiling was higher. We straightened in the pitch-black tunnel but couldn't reduce speed. We couldn't see the Anguillan, but their quick speech let me know they were close and planning another attack. The raft would bump against one every few feet and Cory or Jett would have to knock them off.

"I'm going to shift. Shut your eyes so you don't go night blind," I said as I slowly flared to life.

Cory had stopped to turn to me in awe. "I have never seen you shift so close. You are amazing," he said, dazzled by the flames that ran where my skin should be.

"Yes, yes, she's spectacular. Don't look at her. She'll blind them temporarily, but she'll also blind you. Look for shadows in the waters," Jett said and Cory gave me an easy smile that made his hazel eyes squint and face the front again.

The Anguillan never let up. They followed us along the river so the water was a sea of bobbing heads. Panic edged its way up my spine. We were keeping ahead of them for now, but we were headed into their lands. There would be even more waiting for us.

Hours of being in my elemental form to light our way and *calling* to speed our raft had sapped me. Jett and Cory rotated with Quick beating away the Anguillan attempting to flip the raft, pop it, or pull us out. Indigo sat in the center with her eyes closed focused only on rushing the surrounding waters. The sound of the water changed.

The ceiling narrowed again as light appeared at the end of the tunnel and I winked out and nearly sighed with relief until I caught a clear view of what waited behind us. At least a hundred Anguillan had crammed in the narrow river passage following us waiting for their opportunity to strike.

"They are afraid. They have been threatened." Cory's face was ashen when he looked back at me. "Scarlett, they set a trap at the end of the river. We have to stop the raft as soon as we emerge."

I licked my lips and nodded, the acids in my stomach churned. "You guys hear that? As soon as the tunnel ends, stop. We're going to have to run."

Indigo got to her feet crouching opposite me. "There is one cottage between the Anguillan and the Jorogumo in the jungle. A rainforest. As far as I know, it hasn't been inhabited in decades. No one lives out this way."

I bit my lip. I might have led my siblings, my sister's fiancée and my suitor to their deaths. The light that I thought was our salvation was our death sentence and it approached like a freight train.

"Get out!" Jett shouted.

Pikes were pointed towards the tunnel entrance in the river and the Anguillan were closing in behind us when we slowed. Jett and Cory jumped out and Indigo was pulled out by Jett. Cory grabbed my arms, while Quick pushed me up from behind and leapt up behind me. The forest floor was covered in moss, ferns, and wet dead leaves. Stones, and vines crossed our way, and we all drew blades as we started to hack our way free.

"I'm going to shift. You all follow behind me, this is taking too long."

My voice shook as I spoke. The Anguillan were already climbing out of the river and we weren't even twenty feet through the jungle. If I couldn't burn through the forest, we'd all die there. Jett and Cory were already drenched in sweat at the front of our line and the water that seemed to be in the air all around us. The humidity was thick and made it difficult to pull clean breaths while we panted.

"Scar, you're about to pass out," Jett protested, but his eyes flickered past me.

We all knew it had to be done, otherwise only Indigo and I had a chance of making it out of there. I shifted. My hair writhed around my face as I strode forward so Jett and Cory fell back. I tested my flames against the thick vine and it sizzled before I could tighten my grasp. I smiled and began to strip my clothes off.

Cory was picking up my discarded items and shoving them into his pack. I looked over my shoulder to check on where the Anguillan were and laughed as I shifted in my disembodied voice. Indigo was covering Quick's eyes, given the situation and our imminent deaths, it felt good that there were still certain proprieties.

Unfortunately for my brother, seeing me naked was nothing he hadn't seen several times before. Cory on the other hand was trying very hard to remain grounded by the situation and not stare before I shifted.

I started to run. Moss dried and fried under the soles of my feet. Vines sizzled and parted at my slightest touch. Indigo and Quick shouted directions as I ran. I could hear the whistle of Indigo's bow every now and again as she tried not to draw more attention by using even more *calling* to attack the Anguillan. We didn't want to kill them, they weren't hostile, they'd been threatened.

Very little light beamed through the thick foliage. I hopped over branches and *called* away snakes and other animals that were in our path. I was too winded to speak, so I looked behind me. Anguillan were still on our heels, but we'd gained ground. While clearing a path for us, I'd also cleared it for them.

All the time I spent in my elemental form was wearing on me. No one could help me push through it. We had to make a stand.

"Move past me," I said, stopping, and they skidded to a halt.

I shut my eyes and *called.* The ground shook around us as I used the earth to form a barricade. The Anguillan didn't have weapons, they had no way to break down the wall.

"I should have done this to start with," I breathed, trying to catch my breath as spikes of earth shot up showering us with soil and leaves.

I took a staggering step back as my flames flickered out. Jett caught me under my arms.

"Please put my clothes on," I whispered as spots of black grew in my vision to swallow my sight.

CHAPTER 45
JETT

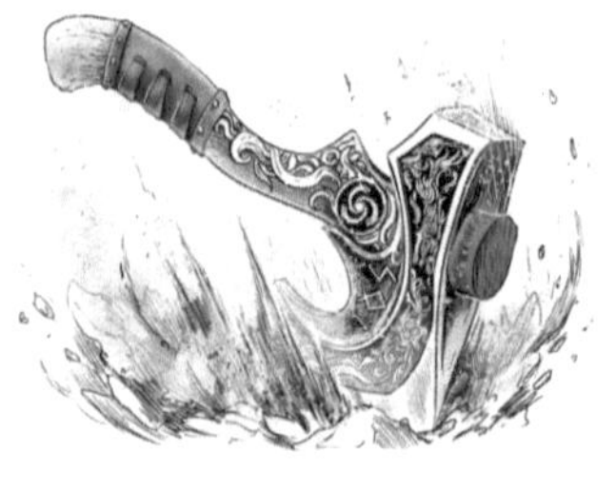

"You're still here," Jett said when they reached the cottage.

Quick *called*, clearing out webs, insects, and dust when they'd chopped through the vines that had encased the door. Jett had thrown a cloak over Scarlett while they ran and took turns with Cory as they escaped from the Anguillan. They could've killed dozens of them. Scarlett and Indigo alone could have, but it was their job to preserve, not to commit genocide. The Anguillan were afraid, not malicious.

If Slate or Brass were there, they would dress Scarlett. From the way Cory's mouth had fallen open when she'd stripped in the jungle, he had never seen her in the nude before. Indigo had passed out as soon as they reached the cottage and Quick had gone in search for a bedroom for her to take a short nap.

Cory wiped his hand over his face after he locked the door behind them and walked to the couch to sit on the coffee table next to Scarlett. "Is this what it is like all the time? I have never been in a fight for my life. I have been in fist fights before, but... I tend bar. I balance budgets and serve drinks. Scarlett recruited me for the Shadow Breakers, but we, my sister and I, only joined because —"

Jett gave him a wry grin with an arch of his brows. "Because it was my sister doing the asking."

Cory blushed. "And networking. My sister and I are young enough to have children. It would open doors to more prominent families and —"

Jett cocked a brow and chuckled. "The Guardian way. I understand, Cory. They beat it into us that we need to breed with the best and have as many children as possible and marry as high as we can. There is no woman higher than Scarlett."

Cory lifted his head furrowing his brow. He was a good-looking guy. He had an easy manner reminiscent of Brass but looked like Chris with a more sincere smile.

"I know, but it is not like that with her." His eyes got far away as he looked at her sleeping face. "I could not believe she agreed to go to dinner with me." He said mostly to himself. "She is your sister, so you do not see her the way other men do. She is not like any other woman I have ever met; it is not just looks. She is sweet and kind, but powerful and determined. Every time she smiles at me I hold my breath and wonder if this is the moment I will wake up." Cory looked up to Jett and chuckled nervously as he sat back. "I can... get her ready. I promise to be a gentleman."

Cory already had her clothes and other than the cloak Jett had tossed around her, she was completely bare. Jett nodded and got to his feet.

"I'll go check on Indi."

Jett walked to the wooden stairs and watched Cory take out her clothes from the pack. He scooted off the table to his knees in front of the couch and took her underwear from the pile and slid them over her feet. Then Jett watched Cory shut his eyes as he pulled them up her legs. Jett shook his head.

Cory treated Scarlett like some kind of priestess or goddess. He worshipped the ground she walked on which wasn't necessarily a bad thing. Scarlett liked to be worshipped, but in one way only. Cory had not ascended to that level yet. The guy was in serious trouble, he was utterly infatuated with her.

CHAPTER

FORTY-SIX

Cory gently shook me awake. We ate a rushed lunch of bread and cheese wrapped in waxed paper with pears and left the locked-up cottage again. Indigo had passed out from exhaustion too, which made me feel better about falling face first naked in the jungle.

The five of us walked and hacked through vines down a rough path that hadn't been traveled in many years.

"Why is Cory looking at me like that?" I asked Jett when it was Cory's turn to lead the group.

Jett chuckled softly making me smile with curiosity. "He offered to dress you and tried to do it with his eyes closed."

I swatted Jett. "You let him touch my unconscious *naked* body? What is wrong with you?"

"I wouldn't have done it. You seemed fine in the cloak, but I was intrigued. I watched him. He didn't cop a feel or anything, but he did ogle. That guy —"

"If you say he's in love with me, I'll punch you so you can't have any more children," I threatened and Jett chuckled wickedly.

"I won't say it then. I have to ask you though, is it some chemical you exude? Or do your lady parts have parts other ladies don't have?"

"You are, without a doubt, the most inappropriate brother ever," I said, shaking my head.

"Very true. I'm glad to be alive and I don't think we killed many Anguillan, if any. Oddly, I feel good about that."

"Me too," I said with a sigh.

The jungle spread further out and came to what looked like giant tree trunks with door size holes in them. They had reminded me of post-apocalyptic apartment buildings, but now I knew they were nests the Jorogumo spider hybrids had built. When Alder had brought us here, the empress She'ik had told us her consort, Drik'er, had taken five hundred Jorogumo rogues and fled.

There wasn't a single Jorogumo skittering along the rainforest floor. The dark gaping holes that the webs had spanned before in the giant trees held none of the multi-limbed tribal members. The feeling that a terrible event had happened ate at me.

I could taste the fear that lingered.

Indigo's powder blue eyes never stopped moving. She started at a run to the large trunk at ground level and Quick shouted after her. We chased them into the spider's den where the empress had lived. There was still an enormous web that spanned the cavernous room with desiccated cocoons hung along the walls.

I sucked in a sharp breath. She'ik had three sets of eyes in her ridged face that had long since been eaten by carrion and insects. Long black pinchers protruded from her jaw, one of which had been broken in half. She had black legs with lime green slashes, her torso was all woman with just a tinge of green. Rows of human like breasts hung from her overly long torso. Her dry black lips were parted, and she'd been dead for months.

"Who would've done this?" Indigo breathed.

Jett and Cory had left us with Quick and came back into the empress's nest. "In the other den, whoever attacked them piled the bodies. There are hundreds of dead Jorogumo in there," Jett said, kneeling in front of She'ik's body.

"So anyone passing by wouldn't see the bodies." Quick ran his hand over Indigo's back.

"Do you think this was why father was killed?" Indigo's tan cheeks were streaked with tears.

"Maybe. There's no way to tell now. They must have took their bodies with them. Only the Jorogumo are here." Jett noted. *"We passed their graves: The dead men there, Winners or losers, Did not care. In the dark They could not see Who had gained The victory."*

Jett sighed.

Quick wrapped Indigo up in his arms and led her back into the daylight. I snaked my arm around Jett's waist and leaned my head against him. He sucked in a deep breath.

"Some must have escaped. We can't stay here," Jett said softly, and I nodded.

"I'm not a fan of the Jorogumo, but they didn't deserve this," I murmured.

"I have never seen a Jorogumo before," Cory said in a whisper.

The three of us left the empress's corpse and met Indigo and Quick in the clearing. I didn't want to inspect the other nests. Jett, Cory, and Quick rushed through them and the surrounding lands as I comforted Indigo. All our father's work establishing a relationship with the tribe, preserving it, guarding it as we were made for... all gone.

Cory came back washing his hands and squatted where we sat on the ground. "How are you both?"

I looked to Indigo who frowned at her boots. "We'll be okay. Our father was the ambassador here, we visited last year. This place is a graveyard," I said somberly.

"Stupid question," he conceded.

On our journey to the Jorogumo lands, the jungle had been a

cacophony of noises. Now there was silence as if whatever had killed the Jorogumo, had managed to deaden all the animals and insects too. The jungle thrived around us reminding me that life went on and if we wanted to, we'd have to get moving. Whoever had scared the Anguillan likely knew by now that we had traveled through their lands.

"No weapons, no bodies. We have to move. It could be that the Jorogumo rogues returned, so that's why there aren't any other bodies or the Anguillan fought with them. The sun is starting to set and we need to make it to the cottages before nightfall. Making a cook fire here would be a very bad idea," Jett said, offering his hand to Indigo.

Cory helped me to my feet beside Indigo and Quick returned. "There are burn marks. Could be a Guardian. You okay, Dove?"

Indigo quirked her lips lifting the beauty mark on her right cheek. "No, who do we see about something like this?" She shook her head. "The Vars are supposed to watch over this island and prevent things like this from happening. With Ash and Sage so close…. I don't know who we can trust."

"You can trust me," I said, flashing her a smile. "I'm Second to the Prime."

The return of the sound of insects and birds calling to one another in the forest sounded like the warm welcomes of peace to my ears. It started to grow dark, and with the trees we couldn't see the sunset. The path led us to the few darkened moss-covered stone cottages we stayed at with Alder. Jett hit an energy plate when he opened the door and the cottage burst with light. It was very quaint and comfortable. More rustic than the country cottages of Valla.

"There are two bedrooms upstairs," Jett said as I *called* cobwebs and dust and incinerated it from the cottage. "I will take the couch, Indigo and Quick can have one room. Scar, you and Cory can have the other."

"Indi, do you want to help me make dinner? You guys go clean up," I said, moving into the small kitchen cleaning as I went.

The guys set about cleaning the upstairs and went to shower and put on fresh clothes. Indigo and I went into the overgrown garden barely visible in the stretching shadows behind the cottage and begun to remove seeds that the animals hadn't eaten and plant them. We used our *calling* to pull weeds and help the seedlings breach the soil. Indigo collected plantains and kiwi while I dug up yams and grew a coconut tree for its sweet milk. Indigo put the fruit in a basket she found at my feet while she walked to the farm pond.

Indigo found fishing poles in the shed and held one in each hand until I filled both baskets and sat down beside her. The comfort of the bugs faded quickly once I was sitting still, and they thought they could make a home out of my clothes. A freshly cleaned Cory came outside and took over our lines so we could bring in the fruit and wash up.

I showered first grateful for my *calling* to have cool refreshing water and took up the jasmine scented soap to scrub myself down. I let my hair air dry and Indigo climbed into the shower after me. The men had left their clothes in the bathroom and I began to wash them in the basin on the floor using a powdered lavender soap I found in the cabinet. Better to have a clean set of spare clothes while we had time to wash them. Indigo wrapped herself in my discarded towel and sighed.

"I feel like I'm in a nightmare. Why wipe out an entire tribe? Is it awful I keep imagining a Jotnar or Risar with a giant can of bug spray?"

I sloshed the shirt I was washing in the sudsy water and smiled. "No. That just means you have a morbid sense of humor."

Indigo changed and helped me finish the wash. Doing simple activities that required little brain power helped me think. As I ran dirty socks over the ridged washboard, my mind cleared. I wouldn't tell Ash. We'd notify Pearl and Tawny so they could send patrols through their lands and see if they had found any Jorogumo. If not, then we'd tell Sterling and Ash because that likely meant the rogues ambushed the Jorogumo. If the rogues were on the other islands... I didn't want to believe the Stygians were organizing another attack.

After we hung the clothes to dry, Indigo and I went down into the kitchen to find Cory gutting and skinning the fish. Jett was cleaning the fruit, while Quick was boiling rice on the cook stove. I set about slicing the plantains and searing them on a cast iron pan. We used dried spices our father had stocked in the cabinets and a melancholy fell over me. The rumors were that my parents had spent time in these cottages. I could almost picture them making dinner together in the tiny kitchen.

"Do you think they had the second piece Canis has? If I had known I was supposed to be collecting pieces, I would've asked before." My boots scraped over the stone floors as I moved the fruit to the island at the center of the kitchen to chop.

"Think positive, Scar. We will try the Gorgons. We may have to find a messenger one our way past town to let the headmaster and mistress know we won't be in classes Monday. We might not be back Tuesday if things do not go well." Jett said helping me chop.

Cory tossed the fish fillets on the pan. I'd given him as little detail as I could about this mission. He probably realized he'd gotten himself into a fine mess by agreeing to come.

"If you want to head back when we pass town since the Gorgons are on the opposite end of the island, that is alright by me, Cory," I said carefully, not wanting to insult him.

He didn't look up from where he laid the other fillets over a second pan. "I am with you. Pewter and Siren are lost if they were trying to keep up with you. We are all you have out here." His hazel eyes crinkled when he smiled at me. "You are sweet for worrying about me."

I blushed and focused on my chopping. Quick stirred the rice and poured it into a large bowl. Indigo set the small dining room table, and I tried to make yam pudding with the coconut milk and spices. I crushed mint leaves into the glasses of water and brought it out to where the others were serving themselves.

"Thanks for cleaning my clothes," Cory said, standing up to pull out my chair.

His chivalrous move perked up my mood. My mother would approve.

"I am used to it when I travel. It's always nice to have clean clothes in a jam. Since no one is after us at this exact moment, it made sense. It was no problem," I said, scooping the wild rice onto my plate. "The fish smells delicious."

Cory beamed.

Cory wound his arm around my waist as he led me upstairs. There were other cottages next to this one, but it didn't make sense to separate. Two bedrooms and the bathroom were the only rooms on the second floor. We took the room Cory had cleaned out while I was gathering food where a queen size bed was against the plain wall. A trunk was by the wrought iron footboard, two stools and a square table were pushed below a shuttered window and a long oval mirror hung across from the bed.

My pack sat on the table next to his and I crossed the room to it and opened the shutters to let in the light. I wouldn't leave the window open; the sounds of the rain forest would keep me awake all night despite my exhaustion. I kicked off my boots and began to change out of my clothes. I wore my white tank top and white boy shorts as I faced Cory with a hand over my pregnant belly.

I padded out of the room grateful for the dark and readied for bed before returning to the room. Cory went in after me and when he returned, I'd already climbed under the thin blankets. The mattress was soft, and I had sunk right into it.

"Are you really okay?" I asked dreamily.

Cory hair flattened over the ivory case of the pillow as he looked at me. "I am. You are an amazing woman, Scarlett. I know you are not telling me everything about what we are doing here, but it means much to me that you would trust me to allow me to accompany you."

"It's not easy being tossed into our constant drama. If you want to leave, don't hesitate to ask. You won't catch any judgement from us," I told him in earnest.

The moonlight cast the shadow of my head over half his face as we laid eye to eye. He had a brilliant smile.

"I am not going anywhere unless you want me to." He shifted closer and his eyes slid lower to peek at me.

I tilted my chin up to meet his lips, and he sighed. The sound of it made me smile. It felt good to be adored and not just lusted after.

"Good morning," I said, walking into the kitchen and washing my hands in the sink.

Indigo, Quick, and Jett were already chopping up the last of the fruit and one of them had found eggs to fry. They all gave me meaningful looks as I took out the plates. I rolled my eyes.

"He's getting ready," I said.

"Did he get any sleep?" Jett asked, curling full pink lips.

I hit the drawer with my hip to shut it as I took out the cutlery. "I do not have casual relations with men. I'm fully capable of spending the night with a man without getting carried away."

"'Morning," Cory said, walking into the kitchen.

He slid his hand over my hips and kissed my cheek as he picked up the plates and silverware before bringing them into the other room. Jett picked up the bowl of fresh cut fruit and Quick grabbed the glasses.

"Someone seems a lot more comfortable with you today," Jett said, dipping his head to my ear.

My cheeks heated as they walked out of the room. I took out a platter for the eggs and Indigo dumped them on.

"So?" she whispered.

I bit my lip. "We didn't have sex."

She giggled. "You fooled around. Admit it. He's... I don't know, lighter today."

I looked towards the dining room and leaned in close she gave me a conspiratorial smile and put her head next to mine. "Don't laugh. I fell asleep."

"While you had sex?" She giggled, and I swatted her arm.

"No!" I hissed. "I told you we didn't. Our making out got a little intense..."

"Like sex with your clothes on?"

I fidgeted and nervously glanced towards the door again. "Yes," I whispered.

Indigo laughed, and I slapped a hand over her mouth. "It's so weird. I forget you went from kissing to sleeping with Brass and no in between. Sterling and I first 'kissed' when we were twelve." She smiled fondly at the memory.

"I've never done that before. Usually, they can't wait to get my clothes off."

"Brass, Slate, and Chris, you mean." She giggled. "I bet."

"Twelve? I thought you didn't..."

She nodded with a sigh. "We didn't until we were fifteen. We thought we would wait until marriage, but that was the year they reopened Valla U again after the massacre and they opened the portals. Sterling and Diamond were betrothed, and we decided to stop waiting."

I picked up the plate of eggs. "I'm sorry, Indi. Do you miss him?"

"Some days more than others." She gave me an apologetic smile. "I love them. Too bad I can't convince them both to marry me."

We spent hours on the narrow path through the heavy vegetation on our way back through Ostara. Purple and white star flowers hung in arches and I recognized them as we emerged from the jungle and came onto the white crushed stone road. The air was cooler Ostara's town heart had was the highest elevation of the island. The floral scent had greeted us the moments the trees thinned. Not much of a breeze made it through the jungle.

Night began to fall as the pastel homes started to pop up. "There is an inn on the far end of town we can stay at," Indigo said as we walked past pastel clad women in light caftan dresses and men in thin jerkins.

I shook my head. "We'll take the town portal to the arena portal and spend the night in the arena. I don't think it's a good idea for us to stay in town."

The rounded arch of the portal was a white marble. Its creator had chiseled to form two tree pillars on either end and a lacework of branches and leaves painted a metallic gold that fanned over the top. We were back to where we started. I held my hand out for Cory and Jett to take who held on to Indi's hand while she clasped Quick's. We walked through the portal together.

Other than Quick, none of the others with me had seen the Ostara arena. Rain was drizzling on the other side of the portal. Indigo gasped once the bright white light faded. Even in the cloudy moonlight, the emerald spire was magnificent.

"Oh, you've outdone yourself," she said wistfully.

The gold scalloped archways that slanted from the top of the emerald spire caught the moonlight. Just below the tip, an iridescent green globe glowed like a beacon like the ones that lined the sleek bridge of the Var castle. The entire arena was shaped like one sharp conical piece of emerald. The portal gate had been installed around a kaleidoscope of green and gold-stained glass in a trefoil arch.

Jett took one look at it and laughed. "Did you come up with this on your own or —"

"Orion and Brass helped," I said, walking over the glass emerald squares that lit at the slightest touch.

"It is a fortress. Are all the arenas fortresses?" Cory asked, and I nodded.

"They are. The portals are also portable and lockable if need be."

We walked under the towering, scalloped archways and up to the solid gold doors. An inconspicuous oval with etching was embossed into the door with three other markings no one but the bearers understood. I fit my wedding ring into the allotted slot, and the mechanisms began to click into place. The doors swung open to reveal the glittering gold hall that wrapped around the arena.

"The club is downstairs, the prep room is just below the arena, which is through that wall, but is only accessible from the prep room.

The stairs lead up to the seats and suites. We're going to sleep in the suites," I told them as Quick shut the doors behind us.

Indigo smiled excitedly taking in the golden chandeliers that hung in intervals from the ceiling. Golden railings lined the sweeping stairways that led to the floor above to access the seats.

We'd open the arenas in a few weeks and hopefully they'd all have the same reaction as Jett and Indigo.

INDIGO

Not all the lights were on in the arena, Scarlett thought it wouldn't be a good idea to draw attention to it in the middle of the night so we only saw the halls and the suites. The little we did see was so opulent and impressive, I couldn't believe my twin sister owned it all and that my fiancée would direct it with his brother.

The French revival style suite was done in creams and sage greens. A wide two-way mirror was gold on the one side and framed by a green and gold trefoil-stained glass arch on the seated side, so spectators couldn't see inside from the stands. Ten ultra-plush jacquard seats were off the platform and faced the window while two more couches were level with the hall. There, tables for the al la carte ran along the wall to a fully stocked wet bar.

A full bathroom was in the hall, there were two for the suites and another two for the cheap seats, though I didn't think there was such a thing here. Silver was already taking out clean clothes from his pack.

"What do you think, Dove?" Silver asked, arching a dark brow.

"I think... once this place opens, we're going to have to restart our six months all over again," I told him flatly and took off my boots.

Silver lifted his handsome olive face to look at me with those deep chocolate eyes. "I love you, Dove, but you do not understand how I feel about you. I do not want another. You have more than enough mood swings to make me feel as though I am dating five different women," he teased, but I sensed the truth in his words.

I smiled ruefully at him and began to take out a fresh change of clothes. "I don't think the others plan to eat together."

Silver's most debauched smile curled his lips. "*Really?* What does our Albacore plan to do with the beloved Second to the Prime?"

"Are you going to run back and tell Brass and Slate? I agree with you guys, I don't think Cory can handle her but maybe she wants a man *she* can handle."

Absorbing other people's powers was an awesome talent until Silver started questioning me and with his lie detecting abilities it made it difficult to withhold information.

"No, no, no. I am all for oat sewing as long as it has nothing to do with you." Silver clasped his arms loosely around my waist and kissed my lips.

"She's an attractive woman, and he's a red-blooded man. Let's shower so we can explore those same attributes ourselves." I sucked Silver's lower lip into my mouth and he moaned.

"Dear gods, let us hurry." He goosed my backside as I walked past him, giggling.

Our footsteps echoed on the green granite floors on our way to the bathroom. Silver held the door open for me and I gave him a mock curtsy as I entered. Gold fixtures and trims framed the creamy wall paper. Silver spun me around to face him and yanked my shirt over my head so my braid fell like a rope against my back.

My hands busied themselves with the removal of his pants as we kissed in between smiles. It was too quiet last night in the small cottage and we'd both been exhausted. Tonight there'd be plenty of space and while still tired, we're more inclined to stay up for a bit enjoying one another's wiles.

Silver stepped on my inseam so I could yank my feet out of my pants. He nearly made me trip over backwards from his forced crab walk into the showers and laughed deliciously when the last article of clothing was shed. I bounced on the balls of my feet and he caught me under my backside as I wrapped my body around him, claiming his mouth. I withheld the temptation to trace his black tattoos with my finger and held on tightly to his powerful shoulders.

"It's not that I don't want to. I do. Very much. More than you could possibly imagine actually now that I think about it. It's just —"

"So say *yes*. Your secrets are mine. I do not want you so I can brag about it, I want you because... by the Mother, Delegate. You must know how you make us feel."

I pulled back from Silver's intoxicating kiss and mouthed *listen*. Scarlett and Cory were in the showers already and she was thwarting Cory's hopes and dreams. Silver rolled his gold-flecked eyes and braced my back against the cool tile wall. I gave him a questioning look which he responded with by pulling his tongue between his teeth and shifted his hips. As he slid into me and started moving, I moaned. The man had no shame... but I wasn't stopping him.

"I don't think you would brag about it. I'm positive you wouldn't, it's one of the reasons I like you, but —"

"I will not leave you. Do not worry. Unless you chase me away, I shall stay with you. I know Slate left you and that is why you are looking for a second. I know Brass and you have been hot and cold. I will not do anything you are not comfortable with."

"What do you mean, Brass and I were hot and cold? I am the one who messed up with Slate, Cory. He's a good man. Just because I'm looking for a second husband doesn't mean I don't love him. I'll always love him even if he's a huge jerk."

I almost cringed at how awkward the conversation had gotten.

"I am sorry. I only meant that I would be there for you. Ro has said you chased after Brass, even when Slate returned. He has not made up his mind on what he wants. She said he was with Gharial the night of our competition. Only rumors. I am sorry I brought it up."

"You didn't say those things, it's fine. I'm not offended. I'm done here."

"Delegate."

Their voices had gotten dangerously close, and the door swung open to the bathroom. I looked over Quick's shoulder and saw Jett. Scarlett was coming out of the shower undressed. Cory was behind her. Jett sucked on his teeth and shut his eyes as he shook his head.

"I don't even want to know." Jett backed out of the room letting the door shut.

I buried my face in the crook of Silver's neck trying to ignore Scarlett and Cory's rampant thoughts. She cleared her throat and grabbed a towel from the shelf then handed one to Cory.

"Don't let us bother you, Quick," she grumbled.

Silver chuckled and carried me into the shower. "That was interesting."

"People will talk. Scarlett is like a celebrity to the Guardians and her drama with Brass and Slate are the biggest things to happen lately, they're bound to gossip. Rosasite is jealous," I said and Silver arched a brow at me.

"I meant that four naked person interlude where your brother saw us... together... like this." He rocked his hips for emphasis and I frowned.

"Gods, you've corrupted me."

"I am trying not to take insult to the fact that you did not even acknowledge that fact that I am, *was*... inside of you."

I put my feet down on the wet shower floor and chewed the inside of my cheek. "Did Brass sleep with Gharial on Friday?"

Silver groaned, but he knew I was not in the mood any longer. "I did not ask. It does not matter. If you have not noticed, your sister has taken up with Albacore."

"Yeah, but if Brass wants her to take his plea seriously to court her, he should be focused on winning her back and not sleeping around," I said, turning on the shower.

"Brass does not sleep around. Gharial and he have been lovers for years. Rosasite is an astral projectionist, she is no doubt spying on Brass. He would never say a word against your sister, Dove."

Silver was right and his words rang true. I quirked a brow at him and he raised his own as I pushed him against the tiled wall. His head fell back against the tile as he sucked in a sharp breath when I bent down to my knees. He made me feel better, now I planned to return the favor.

FORTY-EIGHT

We left at first light. I could tell the others wanted to check out the arena, but time was precious. We couldn't stay on the Gorgon lands so we would have to return by nightfall. It would be another long day of hiking over unfamiliar lands.

Breakfast was made up of the fruit we'd grown at the cottage and bread we had packed before we left. I had to acknowledge that Cory was in a much better mood after we had another very intense make-out session last night and our three traveling companions were back to giving me meaningful glances.

When we broke through the jungle, we reached the Shrouded Bogs. Toads croaked, and the murky duckweed filled waters rippled with slithering snakes and crocodiles. Insects bit at our exposed skin, and we tied the tops of our boots to our calves so the infested waters wouldn't spill into our boots. Mud sucked at our feet and we each used a walking stick to test the watery depths as we walked. We could drown in a swamp as easily as we could a river. Bald cypress trees grew with the tall thick reeds around us giving us slippery roots to walk atop. Knees from the cypress roots broke from the murk like wooden jaws.

Jett led with Cory at my side and Indigo and Quick paired just behind us. Cory kept his hand out for my elbow in case I stumbled, or when my boots stuck too tightly for me to pull out on my own. He gripped the edge of my boot giving it a yank as I leaned on my walking stick and gave me a broad smile when it sucked free.

I told Indigo when we'd run into each other in the bathroom that when I was touching him, he'd caught his seed with his *calling*. She'd laughed and said that's what Guardians usually did. No one had ever done it with me, though not having a mess to clean up after allowed me to fall right to sleep. It hadn't been awkward in the morning as I thought it would be. I had told him I wasn't ready to take it further, and he didn't try. I was thankful he didn't, I might not have been strong enough to turn him down.

The Gorgon lands were veined with tributaries that ran from the river Freya to the ocean coast. The ground never grew more solid, but the waters receded so we could see the mud we traversed with each step as the fog swirled around our ankles.

"This place gives me the heebee geebees," Jett whispered.

"I dream a world where man no other man will scorn. Where love will bless the earth and peace its paths adorn. I dream a world where all will know sweet freedom's way. Where greed no longer saps the soul nor avarice blights our day. A world I dream where black or white. Whatever race you be, will share the bounties of the earth and every man is free. Where wretchedness will hang its head and joy, like a pearl, attends the needs of all mankind. Of such I dream, my world!"

The denseness of the air made you feel as though you had to whisper. The croaking and burping of the swamp creatures were not to be disturbed... until Jett recited an untimely Langston Hughes quote.

"Do you have the smaller raft? We may need it for the return journey. Am I the only one whose legs feel like they're filled with lead?" I asked.

Quick snorted then choked on the thick air. I could taste the earthy scent of compost and dying vegetation. Cory helped yank my foot from the swamp for the umpteenth time and I groaned and looked to the heavens. I sucked in a sharp breath.

"Guys," I whispered.

In the cypresses, eyes watched us. The Gorgons that had been wrapped around the tree's limbs and dropped into the swamps. Indigo yelped as water splashed over her pants and Quick shoved her behind him. Cory did the same to me and I felt Jett's hand on my back.

Aside from the snakes I'd seen in the swamp I was currently in and at the Lincoln Park Zoo in Chicago, I'd never seen a snake up close. The hybrids were six-foot-tall snakes. Beady eyes in flat scaled heads stared back at us. Some had legs with a tail that extended from their spines and others had no legs at all but a thick undulating tail. In their human-like arms, they all held spears.

One of the Gorgons took a step forward, green with a yellow belly and a rattle shaking on the end of its tail. Forked tongues slithered in and out tasting the air. They each wore layers of brightly colored beads around their necks, some crossed them over their chests with fabric wraps around their waists or around their heads.

I stepped out from behind Cory and placed my hand on his arm.

"Do you speak English?" I asked hopefully.

My Gorgon was abysmal. I could ask them where the bathroom was if needed.

They snickered. They were laughing at me. Cory took a step forward — omnilinguist to the rescue. He spoke in a slurred hiss with hard "k"s and "g"s. The rattlesnake hybrid shifted its flat head with preternatural smoothness and answered.

"They are going to take us to their village. He does not know of any pieces," Cory said.

"I don't think we have a choice, baby sis," Jett said in a low tone behind me. "Not unless we want to fight our way out of here. We could do it but we won't be doing any running."

I nodded. "Tell them to lead the way."

A multilevel ancient stone building that looked like a poorly cared for cathedral built in the middle ages was the only building we had seen in hours. It was covered in thick, overgrown vines. Stone pillars laid in pieces over the mossy ground. We had climbed a few broken steps to stand before the entrance of the dilapidated cathedral. The Gorgons made it clear we were not there of our own free will. Cory kept whispering bits of their conversations to us.

A mountain king hybrid with orange and white stripes over a black body had a head full of writhing tails that curled down to its slender waist. It was a woman. There were a few with female figures. The men were built like human men and it was disconcerting. They didn't have hair like humans, just the scaled tails that seemed to have a life of their own as they coiled from their heads.

The mountain king hybrid kept casting looks at me and stuck close to the rattlesnake that appeared to be in lead. We'd walked for hours through the bog. It was the same distance from the portal to the arena as it was from the arena to the Gorgons, but it took twice as long because of the Shrouded Bog.

The mountain king woman passed close enough to me that her cool scaled skin brushed mine. She had red and purple beads layered with white around her throat and over her writhing tail legs. Their bodies were completely covered in their scales and I couldn't see any gender specific parts other than the curve of the female's breasts.

She went into the dark shadows at the entrance of the cathedral and disappeared. More snakes converged around us. Some brightly colored, some earth toned. Few had fangs, but all slithered in their undulating fashion, tongues tasting the air as we waited.

"Activate your bond," I said to Jett and Indigo who nodded.

Cory was the only one not bonded to any of us. I'd have to stick close to him in case we were divided. Three more Gorgons emerged from the shadowed entrance with the mountain king woman. A lime green male with orange eyes, a brick red cobra female, and a king cobra male, hood flared black with yellow bands and black eyes. The hooded cobra was powerfully built and had a presence that commanded obedience. This was whom I needed to speak to.

The king of the Gorgons stepped forward, his skin moving over his muscles as it moved in an undulating motion even though he had legs.

Beads formed a collar around his neck and crossed his chest. He faced me down, tongue flickering, beady eyes cold.

"Zonata says you look for the piece. I am Ophio, king of the Gorgons and keeper of the piece. You are Scarlett Tio. There is a bounty for your capture. You... and your siblings," he slurred.

His beady eyes strayed to take in Jett who was obviously my brother and Indigo. The mountain king snake woman he named Zonata, was looking over us with contempt. My proximity to Cory was drawing more attention to him than I made me comfortable. I stepped closer to Ophio, and he lowered his gaze to me.

"If you have a piece, you know the legend that goes with it. You keep the piece for the one who is sent to retrieve it, it is not yours, but mine." I pulled my chain and collection of five pieces up from where they were nestled against my breasts. "We do not mean you harm. We only mean to fulfill the legend in order save the tribes. *All* the tribes. I need the pieces to do that. Has anyone else approached you about getting the piece?" I asked, bouncing in and out of the Gorgon tongue and English, speaking some kind of new blend I could have called Gorgish.

The snake hybrids snickered making my skin crawl. "You trespass on our lands and make demands?" Ophio hissed.

The lime green garter snake male had a thick tailed torso and kept looking between us and the king. "Where is Grar Dyr?"

He spoke clearer than the king.

"He's not with us."

"You are Night's child? You carry the Grar Dyr's son?"

I placed my hands over my stomach, we wouldn't be able to fight our way free. There were only five of us and hundreds of them. The garter snake's mouth quirked.

"I am the king's aide, Vernal. We know of —"

The red cobra hissed and the rattlesnake male coiled. "They invade. They command. You are outnumbered. If Zonata had not known what you spoke of, we would have collected the bounty by now." The rattle snake hissed in a deep slurring voice.

The king cobra held out a black hand. "Talus." He slid his gaze back to me and looked down at my stomach. "You would not be here if you did not already know we had it."

"We will not just give it to you." The red viper woman hissed.

The king cobra straightened and whipped around. "Naja!"

"Perhaps a game? They win, they get the piece," Vernal offered.

The rattle snake they called Talus shook his tail. There was an animosity between the two snake hybrids. Ophio took a step back and walked to where the red viper stood.

"What does my queen say?"

"Play your game. It is our responsibility to see that the piece is given to the right person." Her eyes narrowed in her brick red scales.

"Your highness." Talus protested and stomped over the moss-covered stones to where Ophio stood with Naja.

Naja and Talus whispered in Gorgon to Ophio. Vernal met the mountain king snake's eyes over the three. Her black tails writhed around her head as she walked over to Vernal. Vernal murmured to her as more Gorgons poured out of low surrounding stone buildings. Zonata looked our way and her lip lifted.

"Indigo, are your mind reading powers working?" Quick asked her.

"I lost them some time last night," she whispered.

"They are not lying, but..." Quick shook his head.

"It's not sitting right with me," Jett agreed.

The three conversing Gorgons broke apart and Talus disappeared into the ruins of the stone cathedral. Ophio's broad head was turned towards me.

"One chance to answer our riddle and you get a chance to ensure your safe return," Ophio said.

"You riddle, we riddle?" Quick asked. "For the piece and our freedom. What happens if we guess wrong?"

The red viper showed her fanged smile. "Then, we keep the piece."

I shut my eyes and sought approval from Jett and Indigo through the bond.

"What choice do we have?" Jett asked.

"Do we have a deal?" Ophio asked.

"I would like to inspect the pieces first," Vernal said, slithering forward.

The garter snake didn't have a spear as the others did. I displayed the pieces on my palm for him, his emotions didn't carry the same tension as the others did.

"They have Ophio's son. Talus will never let you return home,"

Vernal whispered as he feigned interest in the stone pieces around my silver chain. "We will give you the piece and turn you over for the bounty giving the others all your pieces. They will return the prince in exchange. If you have reinforcements nearby, I suggest you call them in once you acquire the piece."

Vernal slithered back to his spot beside Ophio and Zonata. I hoped my face didn't reveal the fear I felt at his warning.

"We have a deal," I told him, and Naja smiled in a way that confirmed my fears.

"While my crest basks in the light, my origin never sees the stars. The heavier my crown, the more shadow shades me," Vernal asked.

Jett smiled jutting out his chin. "I got this."

"Are you sure?" Indigo questioned, and Jett scoffed.

"A tree. Our turn," Jett said smugly.

"What never freezes and never stops eating?" Jett asked.

"Fire," Naja spat before Jett could take a breath.

I shifted uneasily; it was like she knew what he would say before he finished. "Deep is where you shall find the map. My sun never stops shining."

I sighed. *Brass.* "The stars," I answered. "Blood, anger, danger, passion. I am primary."

Vernal's bottom lip twitched but he remained silent. Ophio answered instead.

"Red. No memory of the inside. Your first home."

Cory placed his hand on my belly. "A mother's womb. I have one." He looked to me and I gestured for him to go ahead.

"It comes in many shapes and sizes. Those who have it, know it's worth best when they lose it. Those who never find it, never truly lose themselves."

Jett gave me a side-long glance.

"Love," Naja answered, and Talus returned with a satchel around his broad shoulders.

"Pain when I break through. Then I fall out. I cut and return to gnaw on all that comes my way," Talus said, looking at us past his smooth snout.

With every riddle the tension mounted. Zonata and Vernal were watching us closely, but not participating in the riddling. The

Gorgons gathered all around us could feel the tension and hissed, slithering about. The way we each were guessing between us; we would be there until we passed out from exhaustion. My stomach was roiling, I could feel Jett and Indigo's nerves through the bond. Cory had an outward calm, but he was petrified. The only one who seemed to be as confident as he looked was Quick. I wondered what he knew that I didn't.

"Teeth," Indigo said.

I suddenly felt Quick's excitement. "My turn." He turned to Indigo and gave her a suggestive smile cupping her face.

Now was not a time to be thinking about bedding my sister.

"Open yourself, sweet beauty so I may pluck you," he purred.

I gaped at Quick and Jett grumbled under his breath.

Ophio laughed. It was a breathy rasping sound that he seemed to be surprised he'd done himself.

"A female."

Quick's luscious lips curled. "King Ophio," Quick said in feigned outrage. "A *flower*."

Vernal looked to his king. "Well played, Guardian."

Ophio looked to want to laugh again, but Naja hissed with her forked tongue sliding out from her crack of a mouth. Talus's rattle shook dangerously and Cory was pressing at my side to keep me close.

"I believe that grants us the piece and our safe passage." Jett looked over his shoulder at the sinuous bodies sliding over the stones and deeper into the bog.

"So it does. Come Night's child. Only you, and I will retrieve it. It is a secret."

Ophio slurred the word "secret" exaggeratedly and held out a scaled man like hand for me. I gave the others reassuring smiles and nodded as I walked to him crossing the invisible barrier that had separated our two groups. The smell of them was strange, Talus had a cucumber like scent while Naja and Ophio had a strong drugging odor. Eyes followed me over their round snouts.

Ophio turned, assuming I would follow him, and led me over the moss and vines to the entrance of the building. The air grew thicker when we reached the cathedral that loomed above me. I checked over my shoulder. Cory's brows were knit with worry as were Jett's and Indigo's, but Quick was looking the opposite way running his thumb over the pommel of his short seax. What was going on?

Darkness swallowed me. I felt as though I walked down the gullet of a huge beast until the only light source was behind me and the thin cracks in the walls that speared sunlight into the room. I stopped; I couldn't hear Ophio's steps. I couldn't even hear him breathe.

"Your highness?" I called and heard my voice echo off the walls.

I wondered how big the interior was. My heart was beating rapidly, and I felt the cool smooth scales of Ophio's skin slide against me and disappear.

"You tricked me," he whispered from my right, and I felt him slide his skin across the nape of my neck.

"That's the point of riddles isn't it? To tease and test? Is everything all right here, Ophio? I want to help you. I know the Anguillan were threatened. Who is threatening you? Let me help."

I heard his tongue flicker out and he brushed the fingers of my left hand. "What can one little girl do?"

"This *girl* is the Second to the Prime. I'm assuming you know about the arenas being built between here and town. Those are my arenas. My brother is the heir to Ostara, we *can* help you," I insisted.

Taut arms curled around me until my feet were lifted off the floor and I was run forward. I didn't struggle, he wasn't hurting me. I lost track of the twists and turns he made at his rapid pace but felt his tongue flickering out against my ear every so often in even breaths.

A beam of light illuminated the thick base of a cypress tree and Ophio put me down with a jerk. I turned to face him. His small dark round eyes were intensely fixated on my face.

"My father was Alder Var. I know what it's like to be taken away from my father. Please, Ophio."

"We shall be reunited soon." He hissed, and I realized he'd slowly been driving me backwards.

My back hit the cypress and Ophio braced his arms to either side of me. He was not coming on to me, my words had angered him. He could kill me in there and the only way the others would know would be through the snap of the bond. Jett, Cory, Quick, and Indi could be tied and bound out there as we spoke and I'd have no idea unless they sent me warning... *unless* they were unconscious.

Ophio thrust his hand forward, and I ducked, thinking he was going to strike me, but his hand thunk into something soft. I slid under his arm and stepped back. His arm was thrust to the elbow inside a hollow in the tree that had been grown over by vines. Ophio stopped shifting and withdrew shaking the vine and its fluids from his scaled arm. His thumb ran over a horseshoe shaped stone piece and he held it out to me.

I quickly unclasped my necklace and found a hole in the piece to slide my chain through. All the pieces were made to hang off a chain I belatedly realized. A sticky residue clung to the piece that smeared on my chest when I tucked it back into my shirt.

I looked to Ophio. "You're not going to let us go, are you?"

His slitted nostrils twitched and his forked tongue flickered out. "I guaranteed safe passage. I cannot guarantee it if you fight us."

I furrowed my brow. "You won't let us help you?"

"But you *are* helping me," he slurred.

"I hope you don't mind then that I won't go willingly."

"Then I cannot guarantee that you all will leave here alive," he said with a blank expression.

I sucked in a deep breath. "That's a chance I'll have to take. Wherever you plan to lead us to can endanger my children and I can't allow that."

It was a long-strained walk back out into the light. I was sending warning through the bond so when I broke out into a run and started fighting Gorgons, the others would follow my lead. I didn't want to fight them. Under different circumstances, I would get along with Vernal and Ophio. Maybe even Zonata, I had a feeling she was the prince's wife or lover. If I were her, I'd do whatever it took to get him back. I *had* been her.

Ophio was right behind me when we emerged from the cathedral. Jett's relief through the bond almost made me smile. Cory took a step towards me and Talus sprung. In his satchel were pewter cuffs, nix torques. He snapped one around Cory's wrist before he could react and suddenly the steps were in an uproar.

Indigo shifted into a crystalline woman with ice-blue eyes shooting arrows at those who tried to come near her and Quick. Quick was trying to make his way to Cory who was fighting Talus with his blades, but the snake man was faster. Jett was working his way to me. I felt Ophio lean forward, and I became an inferno.

He hissed taking a step back, and I spun around to face him. I held my hand out. "I don't want you getting hurt," I said in a disembodied voice.

My air blew him deep into the building. I stepped down and used more air to take Vernal and Zonata by ropes and also slung them into safety. Naja and Talus were instigating the fight, shouting orders and striking at Cory and Indigo themselves. I had to get the cuffs off Cory, but I had to reach him first.

I *called* dividing the earth apart and the Gorgons behind the others jumped back. I could hear footsteps running from behind me on the steps made unique by the slithering thick scaled tail that joined it. Quick had yanked up Indigo and started dragging her along the fissure I'd created. Cory's hand was still caught in the cuff and Talus had stuck Cory's side with his spear. I fanned my flames and Naja turned.

"Her! The Knights want her!" she screamed.

The Stygian Knights were threatening tribal folk into capturing me for them. I wondered if every island's tribe had been extorted into nabbing me. I wouldn't be safe alone anywhere, but on Thrimilci and Valla.

Jett lunged toppling over three of the Gorgons who came between us and I leapt from the steps to him. Naja saw that I was approaching, and she spun to Cory.

"Come with or your man dies!"

Time slowed. How did she plan on accomplishing that?

"You can't." Jett cursed as he kept Gorgons at bay at my back.

Quick and Indigo were getting ahead but they were surrounded. We'd have to kill. I sprung my wrist blades and started forward.

"Touch him and I'm going to have to take your threats seriously. You don't want me to do that."

I flexed the flames of my body and the heat was oppressive. Naja sneered, her body coiled. Venom flew from her mouth and into Cory's freely bleeding, open wound. Wind beat at my flames and the Gorgons looked up. I winked out and ran to Cory who had fallen to his knees.

Gorgons were hissing and regrouping to cross the breach I'd created. I yanked the cuff of his wrist retracting my blades and placed my hands over Cory's wound making his eyes rolled back into his head. His blue veins darkened and swelled. The thunk of bodies falling to the ground came as I stole the sunlight. The world darkened; the air evaporated. I slowly pulled the venom from his blood watching the fluid pour from his wound blended with his blood and felt my energy instantly deplete.

I felt the last bits of poison leave his system and fell back on my heels when his wound shut beneath my fingers. Big arms scooped me up clasping a hand over mine so I couldn't spring my blades.

"Open your eyes, Scarlett. I have you," Slate rumbled, and my eyes fluttered open.

His scarred bronze face hovered above mine and his silver eyes glanced sky ward. "Take her, now."

"Cory," I whispered and Slate looked to the ground and growled. "Don't leave him."

I was lifted from Slate's arms into the air and my eyes fluttered shut again.

CHAPTER 49

JETT

"I think I am having a flash back," Quick said, leaning in the doorway of the great hall.

The Aves hall had a long cylindrical bench that lined three of the wooden walls which brightly dyed fabrics swathed. Bark from the massive tree peeks from behind the fabrics. The back wall curved with the tree's shape where the sachem would sit with his family.

Jett felt Scarlett awaken a little while ago and the others had followed him down to where the Aves had placed her in the great hall to lay with Cory. Cory was still unconscious. He laid on blankets and Scarlett had cried over him and then rested her cheek on his chest curling her body around her knees.

Brass grunted. "She didn't cry over you."

Slate gave a derisive snort. "That does not shock me."

Brass arched a thick brow at him. "She stripped you bare and washed you very meticulously."

"If she starts to do that to Albacore, I am going in," Slate growled.

Jett chuckled. "For someone who claims not to care about her, that sounded awfully jealous."

Quick had accidentally activated his bond with Brass on the cliff side when he'd slipped on the rocks. Pewter and Siren had been left behind when they went into the waters below the Var castle and went to report to Brass. Brass and Slate had then started towards the Regn manor in case they were needed. Instead, Brass and Slate had spotted the Aves floating tree on its sky lands and Brass's birdie girlfriends had flown them up.

"Did she fuck him?" Slate growled and looked to Jett.

"No. Little more than kissing," Brass said and sighed.

Birds as tall as a man flew to and fro as they went about their day. Orchards covered every free inch of the land mass that bore thick roots with a few plots of crops. Bright fabrics billowed from the branches and bridges to the stairways. Covered platforms swung from the branches like nests. Lit torches lined the stairs to light the way as they traveled now that dusk had fallen. Branches stretched high into the crimson clouds, the floating island circled the coast and the ocean stretched to the golden horizon. On the other side of the land, jungles and vivid flowers lined the landscape of Ostara.

Jasmine hung in the air reminding Jett of Wren. She'd always smelled of jasmine and roses.

He was wearing loose cobalt drawstring pants that folded at the ankle made for trading with Guardians or stored for visitors. His feet were bare, and he was shirtless. The light fabric of his pants molded to his skin where the breeze blew over the wood paneled platform. The other men wore the same, Quick in a poinsettia red, Slate in a deep purple, and Brass in shamrock green. Slate was perturbed to find that the Aves didn't make black dyes.

Indigo was resting in one of the floating rooms made of wood that hung from the towering tree. A short wood rail ran along the edge of the floor which only held a chamber pot and a stuffed mattress covered with blankets. It was covered with heavy curtains away that enclosed each hanging "nest". Hundreds of nests hung from the tall branches of the tree that reached ten stories into the Ostara sky. Other buildings surrounded the trunk connected by the roped bridges and platforms that held schools and homes that the bird hybrids built.

Wings beat behind them and Jett looked away. He groaned.

A brightly plumed peacock with broad shoulders and a mohawk crest of brilliant blues and greens landed behind the men. Pavo's teal eyes were black-lined, and he was obsessed with Scarlett enough to rival old Slate. His iridescent feathers flattened to his back as he stepped up to the woven doors of the hall. The Aves had human mouths below beaks and were the size of men.

"Is she awake?" he pestered for the third time in the past hour.

Brass was aggravated by Pavo, but Slate had taken an instant dislike to him. Quick didn't seem to care one way or the other but refused to let any of the Aves males around Indigo. Pavo had lifted an unconscious Scarlett from the Gorgons and they had a hell of a time getting him to remove her from his nest. Two more Aves landed and Jett raised his brows at Brass.

A stunning red cardinal woman with a long crest had black skin around her eyes like a mask. Pale red ran down her face, torso, and legs. Lidae's human breasts and hips were covered in a light smattering of shimmering red feathers. She would have been radiant in any race, her looks comparable to a statuesque

The second Aves female was the sachem's daughter, Serinus, a canary hybrid. She was a brilliant yellow with sapphire eyes, though shorter and curvier than the cardinal hybrid.

"Brass, come to the nest," Lidae cooed.

Pavo began to speak in the whistling tweets and trills of his native language. "Take the man already. I have had enough of your boasting."

Serinus's yellow feathers tapered away from her human-like face. "You are only jealous because *your* Guardian would not mate with you."

Quick chuckled. "I am going back to Indigo. I will see you all at dinner."

Quick started to climb the steps roped bridge with an ashen face. He was not a fan of heights. Brass started speaking quietly with the two females and Slate watched with amusement, folding his arms and leaning against hall.

Jett hadn't even noticed Pavo was no longer speaking and hadn't bothered to argue with Serinus. Jett knit his brow. Pavo's teal eyes were locked unblinking inside the hall.

"What are you looking at?" Jett asked, but Pavo didn't so much as breathe.

He stretched his neck to look over Pavo's shoulder. Scarlett *called* water over her naked body a few feet away from Cory. Rinsing the muck of the swamp from her skin and long golden locks as she kneeled with her back to them.

Two homely hermits for sisters, Jett thought for the millionth time.

She paused and looked right at them. Instead of yelling, she *called* over an indigo wrap as a halter and stood. Even though she was four months pregnant, she looked phenomenal. Pavo sucked in a sharp breath. She wrapped a sunshine yellow sarong around her hips.

"Pavo," she said, giving him a wry smile with her too full lips. "You're supposed to look away when a woman is undressed." Her turquoise eyes glittered.

Jett supposed Pavo would be a good-looking guy if he was a human and Scarlett seemed to appreciate that. "*Scarlett*," Pavo whispered like a prayer.

Her smile brightened, and she broke his gaze to give Cory another look. She pressed her lips together into a firm line and raised her head back to Pavo. Her high cheekbones rounded flatteringly when she gave him a smoldering smile.

"Can you help me get him to a nest so I can bathe him? Waking up sticky and worn is never any fun," she said in her gravelly voice.

"Whatever you wish, Scarlett," Pavo said, opening up the woven door and crossing the hall on clawed feet to scoop Scarlett into his arms.

Her wet hair swung out in ropes as he twirled her and she ducked her head when Pavo tried to kiss her. "I'm pregnant and married, Pavo."

Pavo peppered her cheeks with kisses. "Then why are you with this other man? Your other mate does not confront you about it. He must not care. It does not matter."

She gently held onto his hands and pulled them down. "Pavo, he is still my husband. I am Second only to the Prime now. He asked that I take another husband. He... was courting me."

Jett noted her past tense of her and Cory's relationship. The poor guy wasn't even conscious yet.

Pavo bent his powerful body to level his eyes at her. "You are looking for a second husband? What is the Guardian policy on marrying into the tribes?" he asked in complete seriousness.

Scarlett laughed beautifully, taking the edge off the fact she had just laughed at his proposal. Her tan face lost the stress she'd been carrying for the last couple months. She cupped Pavo's face.

"For that, you *may* have a kiss." Pavo's peacock wings engulfed the two of them and they disappeared into the cocoon he'd created.

"Is there a man or tribe that does not propose to her?" Slate rumbled from beside Jett.

Jett started; the big man had an uncanny ability to sneak about unheard. "None that aren't related to her or have been with Indigo."

Scarlett and Pavo hadn't come out of their cocoon. Her feet her visible so they could see her pink painted toes pointed off the ground.

"She is not giving Albacore a bath. Citta can do it."

Citta was their mother's contact within the Aves while she was ambassador. The blue jay woman had stark white human skin with a sky-blue crest that graduated to a lighter color over the rest of her body. She was kind and had sought Slate out. She was one of the two Aves who had looked after Slate when he was rescued. She would bathe Cory and leave it at that. Aves hadn't been around humans in decades aside from those who had rescued Slate and Wren.

Scarlett's toes touched down, and she was blushing from her indigo halter to her caramel hair. "I'm not taking another husband, Pavo. I don't even want the first one anymore. I don't want to be with any man. You see what happens to men who fall in love with me?" she said, running her thumb over his cheekbone.

If she was trying to get him fall out of love, she was failing. "Good thing I am not a man. Stay here. Leave all of it. I can bring you home whenever you wish to visit."

She smiled fondly at him. "I still have to save your world."

Jett pushed the door open the rest of the way and she let her hand fall from Pavo's face. She shrugged her shoulders with a sigh.

"I'm so tired of hurting the men who care the most about me."

Slate shouldered past Jett. "Good thing I do not care about you then," he rumbled and walked next to Scarlett, setting a hand on her shoulder and forcing her a step away from Pavo. "Citta will bathe Albacore. He will be awake soon; his injuries were not bad."

Scarlett pulled away and stepped towards Cory and knelt. She lifted his tattered bloody shirt and ran her fingertips over his smooth flesh.

"He will. Okay," she agreed without looking up. "I'm going with though."

Pavo lent a smooth feathered hand. "I will take you now and bring him after."

She nodded and turned to Slate once she was standing. Scarlett closed the distance between them and twisted her fingers in his long hair at his chest and gave it a tug. Slate growled but bowed his head. She twisted her fingers further and pressed her forehead to his. Jett watched his hands curl as if he wished to hold her.

"Thank you for coming to my rescue and bringing Cory," she said and ran her nose along his.

"I would not have left him. You should have told us you were coming here," Slate rumbled.

"You're right. I'm sorry," she said, her lips hovering an inch from his.

Neither of them would budge that last inch. Instead, she disentangled her fingers and slid her palms down his chest.

"How're Indigo and Quick?" she asked, stepping away from Slate and turning to Jett.

"She's asleep, but good. Quick's with her now. Brass is here too."

Her brow quirked and then she ran her fingers through her hair. "That's good. Lidae and Serinus must be happy."

"Come. I will take you now. You remember how to fly, yes?" Pavo flashed Scarlett a smile that made her lips curl mischievously at him.

"I do. After you," she said. "Then you'll bring up Cory?"

Pavo flashed his smile. "Whatever you wish."

His eyes strayed to her backside as she rolled her hips walking out of the room. Jett grunted as Pavo passed him. Slate was growling deep in his chest but stood stock still. Scarlett froze when she came face to face with Brass and his birdie girls.

Brass turned, and she took a step back into the safety of Pavo's proximity. Brass's amber eyes were molten when he looked at the peacock. Lidae and Serinus stared at Scarlett, but not with any malice just competitive curiosity.

"Scarlett. How is Cory?" Brass asked, and Jett had to give it to him, she would engage him in *that* conversation.

She bit down on her full lower lip and looked at him through her lashes. "He's good. I extracted the poison in time."

"And you?" Brass pressed.

"Good. Your bond with Quick?" she asked, and he nodded.

She pushed her damp hair off her brow and Brass eyes followed the trail of her hand. "Yes."

"Which one of you saw Brass?" she asked, looking between the cardinal woman and the canary.

Lidae's lips curled below her beak. "I recognized him with your mate. He is attractive, your mate," she said, looking at Pavo.

"He's not mine. He's… single. Like Brass. Pavo?"

She faced the peacock and didn't hesitate before wrapping her arms around his neck. He scooped her legs up so she could wrap them around his waist. Pavo gave Brass and his birdie girls a smirk before diving off the platform. Jett's stomach lurched and his head swam with vertigo.

"She's breaking up with Cory," Brass said.

"He almost got killed just for being close to her. Of course she is," Jett said.

The sachem was an old crow whose chest was grey, but head and wings black. He carried a staff with bright colored rings and plumes that dangled from it. Corvus's sons flanked him. Aeetus, the bald eagle with walnut eyes, and Aquila, who had great golden wings. They each had beaks in the style of the birds that they replicated as well as human mouths below their intelligent eyes.

They all stood on the paneled platform in front of the great hall with the sachem formally greeting them.

"Where do you have?" Corvus asked in a croak of English.

"Ostara, sachem," Brass replied, a head taller than the old crow.

"How is your father?"

"With my ancestors."

Brass asked how the crow's father was and he gave the same reply and then Brass stepped back to tie the swath of silk to the railing that ran along the planked walkway. Other sun faded well-worn strips flapped in the breeze with the six bright silk straps, four from their last visit and two more from Indigo and Quick. Brass's red strip was added to the rail.

Jett stepped up and Corvus held out a jungle green colored strip of silk and he took it with both hands with an inclination of his head. It took it in its feathered hands and sniffed his hair.

"Where do you hale?" Corvus asked with a kindly smile.

"Thrimilci, sachem," Jett replied.

"How is your father?"

"With my ancestors," Jett said gustily. "And yours, sachem?"

"With my ancestors." Corvus nodded.

Slate said the same after him and his orange silk joined Jett's. Cory stepped up. He was from Valla and another orphan. He tied his cherry red swath to the railing. When Corvus and Scarlett faced one another his human mouth smiled deeper and he embraced her as a daughter.

"I promise not to make a fool of myself this time," she joked and Jett saw the eagle twins smile for the first time.

"Where do you hale?" the sachem asked.

"Chicago," she said with a smile, and Cory chuckled.

"Your father is with mine and our ancestors," Corvus said and nodded.

He handed her a bright pink silk swath of fabric and she bit her lip. "Why do I feel like this is special for me?"

She bowed her head to the silk and tied it next to the railing. The eagle twins laughed. Aeetus walked to Scarlett and twirled a feather between his fingers. She twisted her hair in her hands and used his feather to secure it. Her narrow braids that held her beads, fetishes, and Pavo's feather hung down over her shoulder.

"Thank you, Aeetus. I'm sorry I lost the other one." Her eyes flitted between his, and Corvus cleared his throat.

"Inside Aeetus, she is spoken for... a few times," he said with amusement in his croaking tone.

Cory, Brass, and Slate were watching keenly with Pavo's teal eyes peeked out from the door. Scarlett smiled and walked at Corvus's side as they entered the hall.

Scarlett sat in the place of honor at Corvus's side as they had eaten. She had smiled and laughed with Aeetus on her other side until they finished dinner.

Aves brought out drums, and some began to whistle an upbeat tune. Male Aves gathered in the cleared space and began a sort of jumping competition that sent the dining crowd to cheering and laughing. Jett and the men joined in much to the Aves amusement.

They were drinking fermented milk called Kumis out of wood carved cups. The music changed, and the men sat down to drink. Quick took Indigo out into the dancing Aves and Pavo appeared just in time to ensnare Scarlett from Aeetus. Pavo spread his brilliant plumes out and Scarlett blushed leaping to her feet. Pavo grabbed her around the waist and spun her around. Her hair pulled free from Aeetus's feather, but she grabbed it and threaded it through one of her braids.

Pavo was light on his feet and Scarlett danced with him until a sheen of sweat covered her and she held up the hem of her skirt, flashing lean thighs as she spun and clapped. Indigo and Quick joined them and Jett leaned forward on the table.

"How are you hanging in there?" Jett asked, furrowing his brow at Cory who didn't seem to be in poor spirits, but he'd seen that look of longing on more than one man's face in Scar's life.

"Only *she* could break things off with a man and make him feel like he failed her. I should have stuck to dinners until we spent more time together." Cory paused. "Gods be damned, she is breathtaking." He sighed. "A few golden moments until my wings melted. I only regret —"

He stopped short and his face reddened. Jett gave him a wry grin. Cory hadn't slept with her. Brass was between Lidae and Serinus, Lidae had also taken an interest in Slate and sat between them. Citta sat on Jett's other side and they spent the night talking about Wren. Hearing the stories Wren had told Citta about them warmed Jett's heart. The blue jay hybrid was easy to talk to and understood the art of listening.

FIFTY

First thing in the morning, I would have to go to classes, but the night was mine.

I'd let down Cory as gently as I could. He took it well. I just couldn't be responsible for another man in my life having a brush with death. Pavo and Aeetus were very good distractions and my guilt was alleviated when I spotted Lidae and Serinus flirting with Brass and Slate. Cory and Jett seemed to be having fun talking to Citta and drinking Kumis.

Indigo and Quick were dancing together, reaffirming my faith in love, while Pavo and I hopped and kicked while we circled around. When he spun me around Aeetus caught me around my chest and stole me away. I gave Pavo a little wave and Aeetus laughed.

"I have never seen a pregnant woman before. Not this close."

"Is that an insult?" I queried.

"Not in the least. You are single now? You came here before with an unconscious man and return with another, yet you are not with either?" Aeetus asked.

"Not single, just not taken. Asexual," I joked.

"I understand. You are a dangerous woman," Aeetus said teasingly and my mood crashed.

Aeetus caught the change and stopped. He led me out of the hall for fresh air and I curled my hands over the railing to face the edge of their sky lands.

"I am sorry if I upset you," he said, running his smooth feathered hand over my back.

"I'm fine. You're right. I am a dangerous woman," I said, taking in the stars over Ostara.

"Is there a problem?" Pavo asked, opening the door so the drumbeats grew louder and faded as the door shut.

"No, Pavo. Do you want to take me for a flight? I'm done dancing tonight," I told him.

Pavo was the most beautiful being I had ever seen. He jumped all over the opportunity to take me out. I looped my arms and Pavo took off before I could even tell Aeetus goodnight. I felt like a shooting star holding on to Pavo's smooth feathers as he flew gracefully through the indigo night sky.

"Come to my nest," he whispered.

"I hurt every male that gets close to me. You've seen for yourself. Brass is the only one I haven't gotten injured, not physically anyway. I'm not willing to chance it. Please take me to the nest." I said burying my face in the soft crook of his neck.

"I can stay with you. No cawing this time," he promised and I could hear the smile in his voice as we landed on the thin ledge outside the hanging platform they called nests.

I stood on my tiptoes and kissed Pavo's mouth. "Have a goodnight, Pavo. I enjoy your company very much, but I need sleep," I said before I pushed the heavy red curtains aside and formed a small flame in my palm.

I unwrapped the bright fabrics from my body and pulled back the thin blankets on the mattress that lay at the center of the room and climbed in. A low railing encased the small room with a chamber pot in the corner and that was all.

I had six of the nine pieces; I should've been celebrating.

No one had died. Cory had come close, and we had managed not to kill any of the Anguillan that I saw, even though Slate had injured Talus and Naja. Injured, but alive.

I tossed and turned until I secured my hair on the top of my head and let the cool night air ripe with the scent of flowers dry the sweat on my neck. Pregnancy made me hot even when there was no heat. I shut my eyes and dozed fitfully.

Kisses were pressed to my lips and cheeks and along my neck. Hands slid over my arm, back, and down my stomach. I tried to rouse but I was exhausted. I didn't need to open my eyes. I could feel the electricity of a certain someone thrumming through my body. There was only one other guess who the man was facing me and kissing my lips.

"Where's Lidae and Serinus?" I asked with a voice thick with sleep.

Slate's body curled around my back and Brass slid his leg between mine. "Do not be rude, girl. We only wish to comfort you while you cannot lock us out."

"Who flew you here?" I asked.

"We walked, love. You ended things with Albacore?" Brass asked in his smooth deep voice.

"Yes. I don't want to be with any of you. You can stay the night, that's it," I whispered and wished I sounded more resolute.

"You don't mean that," Brass said, taking my hand and placing it over his hip.

They were both undressed. Slate *called* against my stomach and I felt him kiss along my throat. I had wanted him to kiss me earlier. I'd almost instigated it myself, but he hadn't even lifted his arms around me when I thanked him for saving me.

"Are you only nice when Brass is here? Feel free to get a nest with just the two of you," I said sleepily, and Slate yanked me away from Brass and onto my back. "Hey!" I said, opening my eyes.

"I am very angry, Scarlett. Do not piss me off worse. I was *nice* to your boyfriend. I do not have much patience left," Slate growled.

I glared up at Slate and his eyes slid down to my bare chest. My skin prickled under his attention. He lifted the chain with the stone pieces and began to count them.

"You should share the burden," Slate rumbled.

I took the pieces from his hand. "It's my burden. I don't care if you guys stay close, but I release you from me. You're free to find your own happiness. Preferably with someone who won't get either of you killed on a weekly basis."

I shifted to look at Brass and slid my left hand up against his stubbled jaw and into his thick dark hair to pull the knot free at his nape. "Find a wife of your own before it's too late. I'm not going to marry you."

"I do not want another," Brass whispered.

"Gharial and Rosasite would beg to differ," I said with a sniff.

Brass had the decency to look away. I'd heard the rumors before Cory had told me but confirming them had hurt. Slate cupped my face.

"You drive a man to fill the void with whomever he can. Do not be hard on Brass," Slate said.

"I'm well aware of your viewpoint on such things. Saying I drive men to sleep around is not only insulting, but wrong. I don't *make* you do anything," I snapped and Slate's big fingers held my jaw.

"You are being very unkind tonight, girl. I know of a way that will change your tune in a hurry," he purred.

Slate didn't make a move to so much as kiss me. I felt Brass whispered breath on my shoulder and I knew he had said something under his breath in a tone so low only Slate would hear him. They did it a lot around me. The night the three of us spent together, they'd done it.

"I want you, girl, but Brass tells me you do not want to sleep with us. He cannot catch your scent as I can." He leaned in close. "You *always* want us."

"Slate," Brass whispered.

Slate looked over my body and bent his head down to my belly and kissed it twice. He gently shifted me back so he could curl his body to mine placing his big hand between my breasts. My heart twisted. It was how we used to sleep together. I missed my Slate.

Brass ran his calloused palm up my thigh and hooked his fingers behind my knee to pull my leg over his. He kept his hand on my thigh and shut his eyes.

"Good night, love."

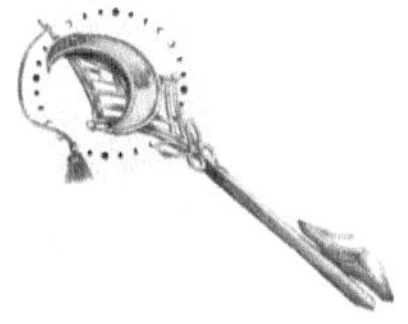

Ash sat on his bed as I bit the blade into my palm.

"I swear I will spend a three-day period during my first ovulation trying to conceive a child or when Slate's memories are returned to him," I said as I slid my short seax into its scabbard.

"*My name is not my own, it is borrowed from my ancestors. I must return it unstained. My honor is not my own, it is on loan from my descendants, I must give it to them unbroken. Our blood is not our own, it is a gift to generations yet unborn, we should carry it with responsibility.*"

I inhaled deeply as my blood oath settled into my skin. Ash looked away, I knew he was trying to hide his triumph, but I could *feel* it.

"Is there a reason we had to do this in my bedroom?" Ash asked, and it was my turn to look away.

He thought I meant to begin our practice now. "I didn't want to do it in our offices because we should keep personal separate from business. We've worked so well together; I don't want to mare it with personal favors," I said, sinking down on his bed next to him.

Ash didn't look at me, he kept his eyes averted. "I have a different proposition for you. Think about it, do not answer now. I know about the or, your *husband's* prophecy. You say you no longer want a second husband and your only one is seeing a khoraz." Ash scooted closer to me on the bed so our thighs were pressed against one another's. "I could broach the topic with Quartz. She believes we are already having an affair, as does most of Tidings. I could make you my second wife, Scarlett. Legitimately, if your husband should meet an untimely death."

"I don't like to talk about it. I won't make plans for *after*," I told him sternly. "If you lift the block on his mind, he'll stop seeing her and we'll be right as rain."

"I meant once his prophecy is fulfilled, Scarlett." Ash took my hand from my lap and held my hand. "As I said, think about it. I have much to make up for with you. This, I know. We have plenty of time to makes amends."

I smiled at our clasped hands. It wasn't overly friendly and his tone was genuine.

"Are you apologizing for slapping me last year, Ash and all the nasty things you've said?" I asked wryly.

Ash went rigid, and I looked to his sharp celadon eyes. "I should never have slapped you." He placed his fingers on my left cheek. "I was hurt you chose him over me."

"I think he could make the same argument," I said ruefully, and his sensual lips parted into a brilliant smile.

"You did not say no."

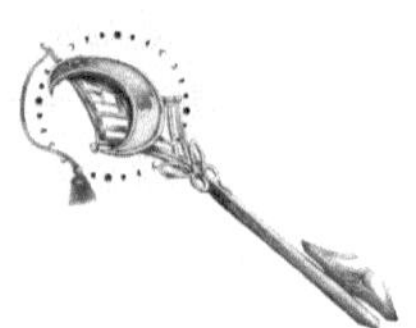

Slate opened his bedroom door and his brows rose. It was late, so he was wearing a pair of black pajama pants that hung low on his corded hips. My resolve faltered; Slate would never agree to this.

Cherry had spent the night in Jett's shared room, Quick was in Indigo's room here at the palace, and Cyan's girlfriend was over. Slate had chosen to give the other two couples privacy, or so I overheard at dinner at Valla U.

I pulled the satin sash on my champagne robe and ran my fingers along the opening. His winter storm eyes flashed silver.

"I'm lonely," I whispered.

Slate's eyes hitched over my tan skin. "You have a cat," he said, his voice dropping in timbre and I laughed surprising myself.

He was funny.

"I want to pet something *bigger*," I said, curling my lips and a growl reverberated deep in his chest.

"Why me and not Brass?" he asked.

I hadn't been to his room since our first night together and just the memory of it made my insides pulse with want. None of the staff were in the hall so I let the robe open to expose my nudity.

"I guess I can go to him instead," I said, turning around.

Slate groaned. "I know what you are doing. Why does this feel like a trap? Are you going to kill me tonight?" he asked in total seriousness.

"Do you think I could manage that?" I purred.

I looked over my shoulder at him batting my lashes. Slate growled clenching his strong jaw.

"Fuck it," he breathed and rushed me.

He caught my wrists in one of his big hands, my robe on the floor forgotten and pushed me up against the wall of the hall. Right there where anyone could have seen us, Slate stretched my arms above my head against the mosaic patterns and shoved his pants over his hips with his free hand. Pinned, he drove deep inside me with his first thrust. I gasped and my head fell back against his chest.

"If you do not plan to kill me tonight, stay in my bed till morning.

"*Without shame the man I like knows and avows the deliciousness of his sex Without shame the woman I like knows and avows hers. Now I will dismiss myself from impassive women, I will go stay with her who waits for me, and with those women that are warm-blooded and sufficient for me; I see that they understand me, and do not deny me; I see that they are worthy of me — I will be the robust husband of those women. They are not one jot less than I am, They are tanned in the face by shining suns and blowing winds, Their flesh has the old divine suppleness and strength, They know how to swim, row, ride, wrestle, shoot, run, strike, retreat, advance, resist, defend themselves, They are ultimate in their own right — they are calm, clear, well-possessed of themselves.*"

"Less talking, more fucking," I said roughly, and he moaned.

I never cursed. It drove him wild when I made an exception.

His hair slid over my shoulders as his hand moved between my legs adding to the delicious sensations that wound through me. His teeth tugged on my ear and my eyes slid shut. I myself had almost forgotten how much I loved it.

My possessive Slate.

I padded barefoot down the hall to the room Ash slept in and roused him. "It took you long enough," he chastened and my cheeks heated.

It was only about ten minutes. I had planned to get him to let me into his room and then *call* so he fell asleep. I wouldn't sleep with this Slate. I shouldn't. Then he took me in the hall. He had spun me around after the first time and lifted me so I wrapped my legs around his waist and we stumbled into the bedroom. I managed to grapple free, and he lunged for me on the couch. That was where he rested. I had straddled his lap and apologized before putting him out.

"Come quick. He never stays asleep for long, even when I *call*. We have to hurry. If he wakes up and finds you in his room he'll go crazy," I said, holding the front of my robe closed.

He would never have sat still and let Ash touch him much less use *calling* on his mind. To be honest, I wasn't sure Ash couldn't do more damage, but I had to assume Ash wanting an elemental in his family line would prevent him from doing something stupid given the chance.

Ash followed me into the black leather room that was Slate's bedroom and sneered. I held my finger to my lips and shook my head. The slightest whisper would wake him up. We had to be ninjas. Ash took in the room. The black tufted couch was turned over with Slate passed out over the back of it. I'd tugged on his pants, but he was bare chested and impossibly handsome. Ash arched an irritated brow at me. I shrugged and made a gesture that said *hurry it up, lecture me later.*

Ash narrowed his eyes at me and then let them slide over my half robe knowing I wasn't wearing a stitch underneath. He sighed and nodded then put his hands on Slate's head where he laid on his back.

Freya's burly boar, it had been intense. Perhaps because we hadn't made love or whatever it was that we'd done, alone since September. The only other time in the last month had been with Brass. This had been animalistic. I'd had to heal Slate from the scratches and bites I'd left on him.

I tried not to squirm thinking about it as Ash worked. A lot of damage could be done in just a few minutes.

"There. It is done," Ash said and I knit my brow.

He looked exhausted, but then, it was in the wee hours in the morning. Slate stirred, and I held my breath. Ash reversed out of the bedroom and I followed.

When the door to Slate's room shut behind me I smiled and let out a held breath. "Thank you so much. I'm sorry it took longer than expected." I couldn't help the beaming smile that lit my face.

Ash curled his lips. "You have a great smile, Scarlett. It will take time for the block to unravel. A few weeks at most. Be patient. I promise I have done all I could."

I reached up on my tiptoes and embraced Ash startling him. It was impulsive, I hadn't planned on it. Ash's arms slowly rose to return my hug. My Slate would be returned to me in a few weeks. I should have done it sooner.

The doorknob behind me turned, and I held my breath as Slate's door opened. I whirled around. Slate's face was a thunderhead. Not my Slate; murderous, feral, and hateful.

"This isn't what it looks like," I said stupidly.

Slate lifted his flexed jaw. "Why would I care, girl? I got what I wanted. She may be a bit worn out for you, but her mouth will more than make up for it," he said, slamming the door in my face.

I flinched back and bounced into Ash's chest, blinking away tears. If you had told me last winter that Ash would be comforting me because Slate said such cruel things, I would have laughed in your face.

"I shall walk you to the portal. It is time to go home, my love," Ash said softly, and I nodded letting him wrap his arm around my shoulders.

There was only one man I'd made love to, who I hadn't hurt, that had taken me out on a real date. When I asked the Dagr messenger if he knew a Balas in Ostara, he looked at me as if I'd lost my mind. I handed him the scroll and waited for a response.

It'd been a week since Slate had stopped speaking to me and I'd retreated into an ice laced abyss where I tried not to let emotion touch me. Everything hurt far too much. I wished every day that he get his memories back and he didn't. I stayed with Ash at night until I knew everyone else was asleep before finally going home so I could avoid any questions.

The light blue and yellow clothed messenger returned, and I stood from the bench as he handed me the scroll.

Young Scarlett,
I am glad you are enjoying the Shakespeare. See you tonight.
Balas

SWEET AND SIMPLE. I hurried to dress in my best Ostara caftan. It was fuchsia with a white underskirt and a thick gold embroidered belt. I pinned the sides of my hair up and styled it into big curls with all my fetishes attached since I wasn't hiding my identity from Balas.

Balas's navy carriage awaited outside the Ostara gate and I hurried inside so I wouldn't be recognized and drew down the shades.

Balas waited in front of the glass double doors of the manor and welcomed me in with a kiss to both cheeks and took my arm to lead me to his quarters.

"This is unexpected. I did not think you would visit me again," Balas said in his seductive voice.

My heels clicked through the empty marble halls until he held open his bedroom doors. I didn't hesitate to enter.

"I wanted to thank you for the Shakespeare. You really didn't have to."

We walked around the sitting room and he led me into the garden. He slowed his pace to a meandering stroll, and we walked over the stone slabs back to the pedestal table I knew was waiting for us with dinner.

"The message was enough thanks. What is really on your mind, young Scarlett? I saw you the night of your competition and you avoided me."

My cheeks flushed as he held the chair out for me. There were red candles lit on the stone slabs around the table. A trolley filled with covered dishes awaited us. His staff had set it all up, but no man planned romantic nights for me like Balas had.

Balas's dark combed hair gleamed from the soft light, the gold buckles on his copper damask satin jerkin shone as he sat across from me. Those dark dreamy eyes were always glittering.

"Balas." I pulled my teeth across my lower lip. "That didn't hurt you, did it?"

He leaned back in the chair and crossed his ankle over his knee as he looked speculatively at me. "No, Scarlett. I believed it was *aventure d'un soir* — for the night only."

Balas took two covered plates and set them before us. He served a garlic soup with baguettes, a salad of tomatoes, tuna, hard-boiled eggs, olives, and anchovies, dressed with a vinaigrette, and duck leg rubbed with thyme as we spoke.

"The Prime wants me to take a second husband. I tend to endanger all the men that care for me. I came here because you don't need anything from me, but my companionship. I doubt you're looking to marry and I'm not asking you to show me any kind of commitment. I'd like you to escort me in public. Keep the younger, thick-headed men away. I don't want love. I want a handsome friend." A nervous laugh bubbled up.

Balas traded my plates as I cleared them and smirked at me. "All that and a body to lay next to?"

I rubbed my lips together and nodded.

"I heard you had a suitor. A promising one. Your commissioner, Regn."

I glanced away as I continued to eat. "He's very close friends with my first husband, his first cousin, and I don't want to get either one hurt by trying to force us together. I'd rather my husband not want anything to do with my escort."

Balas poured me a glass of red wine and ran his fingertips along his lips. "I have not been entirely honest with you. I should not have asked you to join me back in my rooms last time we were together. Our arrangement is more complicated than it seems."

I stared blankly at him. Was I getting dumped? The insane urge to laugh rose up in me. Balas arched his dark brow.

"Please go on. Why should you not have asked me back here? I'm sorry." I got to my feet. "Forget I was here. The books were more than enough of a goodbye, Balas. Thank you for dinner. It was delicious. You have a very talented chef."

"Scarlett, sit down. There is more I need to tell you."

Balas gestured to the chair, and I waved my hand dismissively as I started over the slabs. I felt like a complete idiot. The man *was* a sexual predator. He got what he sought after, and there I was trying to make it into a *thing*. The irony was not lost on me.

The little control I was trying to exert over my life was slipping through my fingers. Balas was a last ditch effort to find companionship in a man who wouldn't be blindsided by me. When I'd thought about it the past week, it seemed smart. Balas was too old for children, he was wealthy, he didn't need my family's wealth. He had probably already been married and since he seemed to have a thing for younger women, I doubted he wanted another one and if Slate got his memories back, Balas wouldn't be upset when I broke things off.

Why couldn't it have just been Slate? After I gave up Brass and threw all my hopes behind Slate, why couldn't he love me?

My throat seemed to be closing. I swallowed convulsively and thought I could feel the sides of my throat touching along the opposite wall. Was I having an allergic reaction to something in the food? I placed my hand on my throat and felt moisture that led up to my eyes. Dear Gods, now I was crying?

Not here. Not now.

I controlled my breaths as I tried to escape the beautiful prison.

Balas had come after me. I hadn't expected that. He spun me around and clasped me tightly to him as his eyes flitted between mine.

"No man tells you no, do they, young Scarlett?" He held my face and kissed the tears that streamed down my cheeks.

"Don't patronize me, Balas," I said roughly.

"Gods, girl. You are *criminally* young. The youngest for me in decades. *Untouchable*," he said in a hushed tone as he brushed his lips over mine and inhaled sharply. "I promised myself I would not touch you again. Not without you knowing all." He brushed his lips over mine again and this time I kissed him back, winding my arms around his neck. "Your lips are even softer when you cry," he breathed.

I ran my hands over his shoulders and began to unbuckle his jerkin. "But you touched," I whispered, and he released me long enough to let the jerkin slide over his shoulders.

His lips curled. "I touched and have wanted to touch since and stopped myself. I have taught my son, and my son's sons that when a woman cries, you do what it takes to please her. I would not want to be a hypocrite."

"No, you wouldn't," I breathed as my belt fell to the ground and he unzipped the side of my dress.

"So, I may forgive myself these actions, yes? They are necessary for your betterment," Balas said roughly as he pulled my dress over my head.

"Forgiven," I agreed.

Balas made a noise in his throat as he removed my under garments and laid me down on white flowers. "So you say. Curse the gods for creating such a body and curse myself for taking it so schemingly. Hush now, Second."

His words meant nothing. I needed his uncomplicated touch not words. He sensed this and began to kiss down my throat heading ever south.

When we finally made it to his bed, he asked me about Slate and Brass and it spilled out of me. I cried, he listened. He was always a good listener. I told him about Cory and how Ash was offering to make me his second wife. I even told him a little about Peak. It was the first time I'd discussed it with anyone and I felt much better after another good cry.

He didn't offer to solve my problems or gave unsolicited advice. He listened and held me. How long had it been since someone just *listened*?

Whatever he needed to tell me must not have been important since he didn't bring it up again. He invited me to stay the night. We made love, and he used his talented mouth until we fell asleep.

Balas had the softest sheets known to man. I woke up with my arm tossed across his chest and his hand holding my forearm gently. He even looked distinguished in his sleep. It shouldn't have been possible. I was feeling amorous after our night together so I *called* water into my mouth before straddling his hips. I ran my fingers through his dark chest hair and over his shoulders as I leaned down to kiss across his unshaved stubbly jaw.

"This is the way to wake up." Balas's voice shouldn't have been able to sound sexier.

"I can do you one better," I said playfully as pressed myself to him and pecked his lips before starting to shimmy down the length of his body.

Balas started to chuckle and stopped, gripping my shoulders firmly. He sat up and shifted me from his lap.

"What's wrong?" I asked as he slid off the bed and started pulling his robe off the chaise.

"Get dressed. *Now*," he insisted.

"My clothes are in the garden," I said, sliding off the bed with the sheet in my hands.

I assumed one of his young lovers had shown up unannounced. It was the reason I'd sent a messenger ahead, to avoid an uncomfortable interlude.

I heard a door crash open in the sitting room and Balas gave me a look so apologetic, for a split second, I thought he was going to murder me.

I wished he had.

Brass used his *calling* to crash the doors open. He was in Shadow Breaker black as if he'd just come from headquarters.

"Brass! Get out!" I shouted.

Brass had taken one look at me and then turned to stare at Balas. "How could you?" he whispered.

"You know each other?" I asked, scooping more of the blanket to cover me but staying on the far side of the bed.

Brass closed the distance between him and Balas and I thought he was going to deck him. I looked at Balas. His face was pained. *Had* Brass hit him and it was so fast I hadn't witnessed it?

"I could not resist," Balas said in a hushed tone.

I looked between the two men and started shaking my head. Impossible.

"You could not resist?" Brass repeated, his voice cracking. "You seduced the mother of my children and you couldn't resist?"

"Your —" Balas's eyes widened.

"*Mine!* My sons! I asked you to come with me to gain her hand from her family. How long has this been going on?"

Brass was shouting. I'd never seen Brass shout. I moved like a wraith past them and to the anteroom before going into the garden for my dress. Neither man noticed me, or if they did, they didn't care that I'd left. I trembled as I pulled on my clothes. I wondered if they were still arguing or Brass had left yet. I wasn't sure what I preferred.

They looked so much alike. Quick looked like him too. I saw Brass and Slate in everyone, I thought it was just me.

Brass and Balas were at a stand-off, I didn't think much had been said in my absence.

"Had I known —"

"You still would've tried! Do not pretend you have not thought the same about Indigo. After all, Silver learned his ways from someone. How long, Spinel?" Brass ground out.

I stood in the doorway behind Brass watching them in a stupor. Spinel, not Balas. Balas was Spinel. Spinel Regn, Brass and Silver's grandfather. My head spun, and I gripped the doorframe to steady myself.

"Two nights," Balas finally answered with a sigh.

"When? Last night and when?" Brass pushed.

"When she returned from Chicago," Balas admitted.

"Her birthday? That was *you*? You took her on her birthday?" Brass staggered back. "I have never been able to find love because no woman could only think of me while she was with me. That may not bother you, but I could never get past it. She is the *only* one who loved me for me. Who didn't compare me while we were together, who never once let her mind stray thinking of being with other men while she was with *me*." He held up a single finger and his voice choked.

"Brass, she is deeply in love with you. She only rejects it because —"

"I know why she does! I do not need you deciphering her ways for me. *I* was her first, *I* take care of her, she carries *my* sons..."

Brass's voice broke, and I started crying. I had no right to cry for what I'd done. Seeing Brass break down, so betrayed, made me wish that the first Jorogumo that attacked me while I peed in the red hills had killed me.

I rushed to Brass, unable to stand it anymore and turned him around to face me. He had tears in his eyes and it broke my heart.

"I'm sorry, Brass. I had no idea. I never ever would have hurt you. Not you. Never you. Gods be good, forgive me. I'll do whatever you want. *Please*. Don't cry, Brass. I love you." I tried to cup his face, but he pushed me away.

"Don't touch me, Scarlett. You want to bed my grandfather? Have at it. He can raise my sons as his own. He did a fine job with us," Brass said, pulling his arm away from me.

"You don't mean that. You just need time," I pleaded, raked with sobs.

"Don't I? I am tired of stepping lightly around you, trying not to push too hard. I was in love with you and I shouldn't have had to apologize for it," Brass said gruffly and used his palms to wipe his eyes.

"I'm sorry, Brass. *Please.* Don't say those things," I begged.

"You and I, *this*, it is done. Do you understand? I will not be rescuing you the next time you get yourself nearly killed." Brass shrugged past me as I clung to him and stormed from the room.

"I ne'er was struck before that hour with love so sudden and so sweet. Her face it bloomed like a sweet flower And stole my heart away complete. My face turned pale as deadly pale. My legs refused to walk away, And when she looked, what could I fail? My life and all seemed turned to clay. And then my blood rushed to my face And took my eyesight quite away, The trees and bushes round the place Seemed midnight at noonday. I could not see a single thing, Words from my eyes did start — they spoke as chords do from the string, and blood burnt round my heart. Are flowers the winter's choice? Is love's bed always snow? She seemed to hear my silent voice, not love's appeals to know. I never saw so sweet a face. As that I stood before. My heart has left its dwelling-place and can return no more."

I could hardly catch my breath as I chased after him. Begging and pleading pathetically for him to forgive me, followed him into the hall, not caring if the staff saw us as I groveled. I pleaded pathetically until he slammed the door in my face. I wasn't sure how long I cried in a puddle on the floor, but Balas, *er,* Spinel was helping me to my feet and apologizing.

"You should have told me. I never would have..."

"I know. I have a bad habit of seducing my son... and grandsons' lovers. Especially when they are as notorious as you are. I have no excuse. I am a covetous man. A collector of rare women and you, young Scarlett, are the rarest. If I had known you carried my great grandsons, I would not have chased you." He walked me to the teal couch and handed me a kerchief. "Scarlett, I am sorry."

"You've said that. Nothing can take back what I've done to him. I didn't know Brass was capable of such vehemence," I said numbly. "You knew who I was all along, didn't you? You really couldn't help yourself and I made it all too easy for you."

Spinel nodded. "I did. I manipulated you. I have decades of experience; you are inexperienced in the chase. I know women and you had not known who I was. Everyone in Ostara recognizes me. We missed one another at the Sumar palace by scarce an hour. Silver had left me moments before after he purchased a proper ring for your sister."

"You should've stopped me from saying those things last night."

He nodded. "I should have, but I had an opportunity to hear your reasons for spurning my grandson."

Grandson. I needed to vomit.

Balas *called* a towel and dampened it with his *calling* before handing it to me. I wiped my face and blew my nose.

"*Balas.*" I shook my head. "That was horribly devious."

Balas was a spinel, a semi-precious stone. I didn't know why I hadn't put it together before combined with his uncanny similarity to Brass and Quick. Indigo had even said the name sounded familiar.

"It is the name my lovers commonly use. A nickname of sorts. Peak used it as a jibe to our relationship." He let out a heavy breath. "I have helped raise six children. None of them have looked at me the way Brass did today," he confided. "He is more sensitive than most. The things he sees in people's minds are the worst sides of them, but when they live a straighter path, it gives him hope. No one has more faith in mankind than a mind reader."

Six children, I groaned. I'd completely forgotten, he was Cordillera's father.

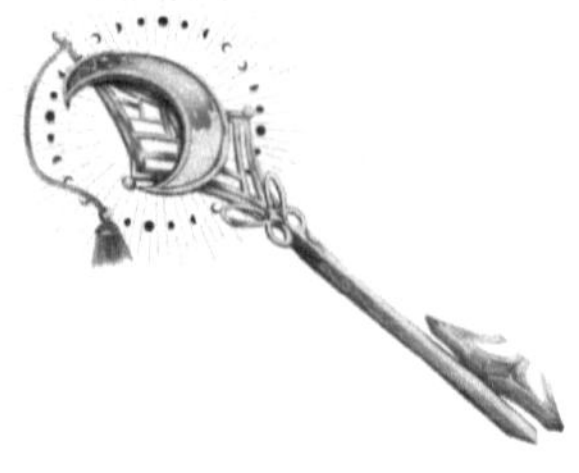

Spinel helped me into a carriage where I bawled until I had no tears left to cry. It drove around and around through the vivid Ostara land-scape until I asked them to bring me to the portal. I took the ebony and copper beads Brass had given me and dropped them on the ground. I didn't deserve them.

AFTERWORD

For more of Tidings's world, family treesquizzes, events, and news from Charli Rahe, please visit www.charlirahe.com and join Charli's Devils on Facebook.

BIBLIOGRAPHY

507

Barrett Browning, Elizabeth. "Change Upon Change." *Blackwood's Edinburgh Magazine LX, no. 372, 1846*

Shakespeare, William. "Cymbeline." *Cymbeline, 1611*

Clare, John. "First Love." *Poems Descriptive of Rural Life, 1820*

Whitman, Walt. "A Woman Waits For Me." *Enfans d'Adam, 1856*

Hughes, Langston. "I Dream A World." *Associated Negro Press, 1941*

Whitman, Walt. "Spontaneous Me." *Leaves of Grass, 1856*

Whitman, Walt. "A Leaf of Faces." *Leaves of Grass, 1856*

Browning, Elizabeth Barrett. "A Woman's Shortcomings." *Blackwood's Magazine, 1846*